Beneath the Texas Sky

Jodi Thomas

ZEBRA BOOKS
KENSINGTON PUBLISHING CORP.
http://www.kensingtonbooks.com

To my mother,
Sally Faye Kirkland Price,
who always believed in dreams for her children

Dear Reader,

I am delighted that Kensington Publishing is reprinting BENEATH THE TEXAS SKY. This book was a joy from the beginning to write. I'll never forget writing eight chapters in seven days while snowed in with my two grade school boys.

Now the boys are in college and this book, hopefully, will again give readers a few hours of pleasure to escape into Texas.

Thank you all for your support,

Jodi Thomas

Jodi Thomas

Part I
Texas, 1865

Chapter One

Bethanie Lane bolted out onto the back porch of her aunt and uncle's hotel in San Antonio. Her breathing outpaced her heart as she rubbed furiously at her arm, feeling as though a serpent had fouled her flesh with its fangs. She rushed down the steps and submerged her arm into the hot washtub water, then began to scrub her skin with harsh lye soap. She would remove the feel of Wilbur's hand or bleed raw from trying.

After a few minutes, Bethanie's breathing slowed and she forced her mind to think of other things . . . of anything except his pawing grip. She brushed back a strand of golden copper hair and watched the spring sun bowing in late-afternoon warmth. The day was almost gone, yet she had another load of laundry to wash. There were never enough hours to complete all the tasks needed to run the dilapidated hotel.

Her torment seemed to grow daily with Uncle Wilbur's increasing attentions. He had begun so carefully at first, Bethanie thought. A hug lasting only a second longer than necessary. A hand placed to brush accidentally against her. A stare that tried to burn through her clothing when he thought no one was watching. Lately, his advances had become more blatant. Her skin crawled at the mere thought of his touching her with those fat fingers.

Bethanie stared blindly across the back lot. People

passing along the walk appeared to blink in and out of sight between missing slats in the rusty fence. Blue and gray uniforms alternated past. The sons of Texas were returning, many with nothing more than a uniform to call their own.

Bethanie frowned slightly as she saw the defeated, slumped shoulders beneath uniforms of both colors. These men were welcomed by such a chaotic homecoming, but at least they had a place to return. In an effort to forget her troubles, she tried to empathize with their plight. Though little fighting had taken place in Texas, the lack of manpower had eroded this young land. Cattlemen, who had been paid handsomely in Confederate bills, were now penniless. Nomadic Indians roamed the upper half of the state, raging war against all white settlers. Longhorn cattle ran wild with markets impractical to reach, and bordering states panicked because of the Texas Fever the cattle carried. Money was scarce, carpetbaggers were pesky, and the past winter severe. Still, these men returned home. They had soil to replant and families who cared about them.

Slinging a sheet onto the washboard, Bethanie attacked her chore with a zest her body no longer felt. Optimism whispered promises in the breeze as she began to rub the wet sheet back and forth over the bumpy metal washboard. Maybe things would get better as winter ended. Maybe business at the hotel would pick up. Maybe her uncle would forget his game of toying with her. "Maybe? Maybe?" The rhythm seemed to echo as she scrubbed.

Bethanie tossed the last sheet into a clean tub of water as voices drifted between the broken slats. "Her parents were Shakers, you know," a woman said as two rather plump figures appeared and disappeared between the fence boards.

"They never married," the other responded. "Just had a baby. Martha told me as much straight out."

"And Martha should know, being the girl's aunt," the first smug voice sounded again. "She said the girl's folks lived in a group marriage. The poor child probably doesn't even know which one of them Holy Rollers fathered her."

"Trash, she is. Nothing but bastard trash."

Bethanie didn't have to wait until they mentioned her name to know the object of their scorn. Whirling, she bolted up the steps and slammed the back door before she could hear more. She furiously wiped away the tears that burned her green eyes as she fought to control her anger. All her life she'd heard the same spiteful conversation. Different places, different times, but always the same. Now here, hundreds of miles from Ohio and with her mother long since buried, still the rumors would not die.

For all her twenty years, Bethanie had been a curiosity, a freak, because of her parents. Shakers by religion, they chose to love each other. In a belief where celibacy was the order, both were forced to leave their communal farm. Bethanie's father abandoned her before she had time for memories of him to form, but Bethanie's mother patiently bore her shame with pride and dignity while assuring that she and her child survived. She always comforted Bethanie by saying all would pass. She'd cradle her child to her and repeat over and over when times were hard, "To everything there is a season. Wait, my little love, for this will pass."

Yet, not even coming to live in Texas seemed far enough away. Bethanie was tired of waiting. She clenched her fists to her sides; patience was a virtue running in short supply. Her mother's teachings of eternal meekness were finding themselves at war with Bethanie's temper. Unable to rid herself of her volatile emotions, she had become an expert at hiding them.

Bethanie climbed up the back staircase unmindful of

the chipped paint and broken bannister. She halfheartedly kicked at a cockroach darting across her path. This place seemed the edge of the world to her, and she had no money to go farther.

Three months after her mother died, Aunt Martha wrote, inviting her to live with them. When she first came to live with her aunt and uncle, Bethanie thought them an answer to her prayers. But soon after arriving in San Antonio, she realized she had traveled across half a country to be an unpaid servant.

Bethanie moved from room to room, stripping linens and watching the sun sink lower over the small adobe buildings that blocked the view of the river. Her mind forced forward happy memories of her childhood. The mornings watching her mother cook breakfast. The afternoons riding bareback through peaceful green fields. The long nights helping her mother prepare ointments for the sick. Shakers were taught, even as children, to care for the pain of others. Neighbors who would not speak to her on the street never hesitated to call Bethanie's mother when someone in their family was ill.

"Girl!" a sharp shout sounded from below. Martha's voice echoed through the hall like the clang of a poorly made bell. "Where are you?"

Bethanie hated being referred to as "girl" almost as much as she hated being yelled at constantly. Hurrying downstairs she tried to compose herself and hide her feelings behind frozen eyes before she faced Aunt Martha. The crafty old woman would spot any anger and misjudge it as defiance. If Martha thought Bethanie unhappy, she would flood her with work as punishment for her ungratefulness. Aunt Martha never set a plate of food before Bethanie without some comment on the cost of feeding one more mouth.

Bethanie had lost several pounds over the past months, yet no one seemed to notice. Her dresses were now old and faded with wear. They hung on her body like rags, yet she dared not ask for even a few yards of material.

Stepping gracefully into the kitchen, Bethanie lowered her eyes in a gesture she had learned caused Martha the least anger. "Yes, Aunt Martha?" she answered in little more than a whisper, forcing her fingers to uncoil at her sides.

"Well," Martha snapped. "You sure took your time in coming." Her aunt was ironing one of her daughter's elaborate dresses. "It irritates me that you can't make time to do this simple chore. Allison needs this dress."

"I was finishing the beds upstairs," Bethanie answered, knowing her comment would be ignored.

Bethanie glanced over and smiled at Allison, who sat sipping a cup of coffee. Allison was a lovely sunny-white blonde with huge pale-blue eyes. She bore no resemblance to her parents. Even though she was eighteen, she stood under five feet tall, her height giving her a pixie quality. At first glance she seemed childlike, but her ample breasts soon dispelled that aura. Allison had shown Bethanie the only kindness she'd known these past months. Thanks to her, Bethanie did not have to sleep in the dingy storage room. When she had first arrived, Uncle Wilbur wanted her to sleep in the little room off the kitchen, which was already crowded with rubble. Allison insisted she share her room on the second floor, and Wilbur always gave in to his daughter. Bethanie was grateful, for she had feared being alone at night since childhood. Allison seemed oblivious to her plight most of the time, but she was never directly unkind.

Martha grumbled. "We're leaving tonight for dinner at the Wagner Ranch. Since they didn't extend the invitation to you, girl, I know you won't mind tending the front desk while we're gone. Not that you will have any business."

"Of course I'll keep the desk," Bethanie answered. She

uld have liked to add, "How could anyone send me n invitation? You've never introduced me to a soul in San Antonio." But, as usual, she bit back her words and held her features stone hard as she'd been taught all her life to do at the unkindness of others.

"Well, we haven't much time. Go upstairs and help Allison dress," ordered Martha. Her cackling voice was a sharp reflection of everything about her. Even Martha's gray hair did not soften her features, but cut into her navy-black mane like lightning bolts. Her figure bore no gentle curves, only angles of cloth. She referred to herself as large boned, never plump. Bethanie never ceased to wonder how such a cold, dark woman had given birth to beautiful Allison. She was surely spring growing out of a frozen winter woman.

Sighing, Bethanie lifted Allison's freshly ironed dress and followed her tiny cousin up the back stairs. Bethanie looked forward to an evening without her aunt constantly shouting for her.

Allison's half-smothered laughter drew Bethanie's attention as they crossed the landing. "Look," she whispered. "Bethanie, come quickly and see the man Daddy is checking in." Allison sighed as if she were a child looking through a candy store window. "I saw him once before when he came to see Daddy. Isn't he something?"

Bethanie moved to the railing beside her cousin. They could see the desk fifteen feet below. Uncle Wilbur stood smiling at his new guest, his fat cheeks rippling as he showed his yellow teeth. Double chins hung around his neck in folds like a huge flesh-colored bandanna. His stomach and the foul odor of cheap cigars preceded him into any room. But it was his hands Bethanie hated most. They were large and fat, with short, porky fingers extending like plump sausages. She detested each time he reached to pinch her cheek or place his palm on her arm. He only laughed when he saw her pull away in disgust, as if she were playing a game and he already knew the outcome.

"He's a dream," Allison whispered between giggles.

Bethanie drew her eyes to the other man below. He was taller than most men Bethanie had seen. Unlike many males out west who were short and dusty with half-civilized expressions tattooed on their weathered faces, this man carried himself like a gentleman. He had the proud, easy stance of someone accustomed to being in control of himself and his surroundings. Something about him seemed vaguely familiar to her.

The stranger's clothes clung to his slender frame as if they had been made for him and not bought for a dollar in some general store. Thick black hair hung to his collar in the back and wedged its way across his forehead as he looked down at the register. His classic features spoke of a blending of Latin and European blood. His strong jawline was framed with a short black beard. He was the most handsome man Bethanie had ever seen.

Bethanie watched his square shoulders angle slightly as he signed in. "Who do you think he is?" she whispered, her voice shaking. She felt a sense of loss at never having known anyone like him.

"Who knows for certain," Allison answered. "He looks dark enough to be Mexican but he's far too tall. Besides, look at the way he wears his gun strapped low and tight. My guess is, he makes his living with it. It's a Colt, too. One of the best made." Both women had learned to size men up by their guns and horses. In this wild country, a man who didn't have the best of both and know how to handle them wouldn't live long.

The stranger turned around, moving in long panther-like strides across the small lobby. As if he sensed being watched, he jerked his head up toward them. Before Bethanie could back away, she found herself caught in his stare. His gaze had brushed across Allison, who normally drew all the attention, and froze on Bethanie. Dark coffee brown eyes delved deep into her soul, embarrassing her with their intimacy. An alert intelligence molded his face as one dark eyebrow raised slightly.

Bethanie's face flushed as though they had just spoken their most private thoughts to each other. The knowledge that this stranger would keep her secrets seemed silently whispered in his stare.

An instant later, the gentleman smiled at her, and she felt blood flame her cheeks as though he had touched her. His vision moved over every inch of her face in a motionless caress.

The warm sensation was new to Bethanie and she looked away in embarrassment. When she dared glance back, he was gone like a predawn dream. No man had ever affected her so dramatically. She felt as if she had shared her entire life story with him in an instant, and he had not only accepted her totally, but also incredibly found her without fault.

"I wish I were staying here this evening." Allison stormed toward her room. She pouted like a small child about to miss a party. "We could open the secret panel and watch him."

Bethanie followed, smiling at Allison's outrageous suggestion. As she entered their room, she glanced at the cheap flowery wallpaper, bubbled and yellowed with age. Someone, years ago, in an effort to quiet a bothersome cricket had poked broom-handle-sized dents in several places. Just beyond the wall was the best room for rent. The room Wilbur always gave guests. Allison had long ago shown Bethanie a secret sliding door in the wall.

Bethanie held up Allison's dress for her as Allison chattered. "Seems a shame to know the panel is there and never use it. I'll bet it was built by some man so his mistress could sneak between these two rooms." Allison giggled as Bethanie buttoned the dress.

Bethanie knew Allison loved the thought of a secret romance having occurred in this very room.

"I know I'm a romantic," Allison laughed as if reading Bethanie's mind. "Not like you, Bethanie. You reason everything out in your own quiet way." Allison sighed slightly. "It's probably for the best."

"You're right about that, dear." Martha startled both girls as she stepped into their room. She had obviously overheard Allison's last comment. "After all, Bethanie won't have much romance in her life. She'll be lucky to find a poor farmer who's willing to marry her. What man wants to spend the rest of his life looking at a skinny wife with tons of long red hair? It reminds me of the dark, muddy water in the Red River." Martha nodded her head sharply. "Yes, it's more mud color than red. How cruel nature's been, Allison, to give your cousin a stick for a body and such awful hair."

As always Bethanie did not reply to her aunt's barbs. She merely stood holding Allison's discarded gown as the other women moved to the door. There was a time to lash back and a time to be silent. Bethanie knew instinctively that anything other than silence would draw Martha's wrath a hundredfold. Yet, each day she felt her tolerance for Martha decaying into open hatred.

Bethanie's dream of a peaceful evening shattered as she watched the family return in less than an hour amid a flurry of excitement. Her uncle stormed into the hotel with Martha and Allison following in his wake. Martha looked fearful as she dragged Allison like a child. Bethanie had no idea what had taken place, but she knew it must have been bad. At first glance, she thought Allison did something wrong. Then she discarded that thought completely. In her parents' eyes, Allison was an angel. Something must have happened at the ranch.

Wilbur walked to the office door and collapsed against the frame like a runner at the finish line. He wiped sweat from his forehead with the handkerchief he always used at meals to clean grease off his fingers. "Is that man who checked in today up in his room?" Wilbur snapped at Bethanie. There was no need for further explanation since they had only one guest.

"Yes," Bethanie answered. "He came back a few minutes ago."

"Well, ask him to come down to my office," Wilbur ordered. "And watch the desk while I talk with him." He grabbed the waistband of his slacks in his eternal struggle to keep his pants up over his spherical body.

Bethanie jumped to do his bidding and to avoid passing the corner of the counter at the same time he did.

The sudden slamming of the office door hastened Bethanie's pace. She ran up the stairs and tapped on the stranger's door. Tension hung in the air as thick as the humidity. An excitement danced in her veins. She believed any change would have to be an improvement.

An instant after she knocked, the door jerked open, startling her. Bethanie swallowed hard trying to remember what to say. The man before her seemed amused at her distress. "Yes?" he asked in a low voice, his dark coffee brown eyes studying her. "May I help you, miss?"

Bethanie found herself staring at a bare, muscular chest framed on either side by a dark blue shirt. She could smell soap and realized he must have been washing up. "My . . ." Bethanie noticed she had to look up at this man, not down as she did most men. "My uncle would like to talk with you."

His expression told her he understood her distress, yet he made no effort to button his shirt. He searched her face as if he were studying something of great value and appreciating each line, each detail. The stranger's thoughtful frown relaxed, blending into a slow, easy smile. "Thank you." He seemed in no hurry to answer the summons but leaned casually against the door frame and folded his arms.

Bethanie watched his mouth and felt a strong yearning to brush her fingers across his lips. When her gaze moved up to his dark eyes, she had the feeling he understood and was daring her to take action. There was a depth of understanding in his eyes that went beyond flirtation. His stare seemed to offer her friendship.

Frantically, she tore her gaze from him and ran toward the stairs, feeling like a tongue-tied child. She had been around men very little during her lifetime and wished she could have said something, anything, to this man. She could think of none of the ideal conversational small talk women say to men. She made a mental note to watch Allison more closely the next time they were out.

Bethanie tried to calm down as she resumed her place at the front desk. In a few minutes she watched the tall stranger descend the stairs. She kept her eyes lowered, trying to appear busy, but watched him closely through her lashes. She gasped in surprise when he winked at her and smiled, before disappearing into her uncle's office.

Thanks to the shabby construction of the hotel, Bethanie had only to lean back against the wall to hear every word spoken. Her uncle allowed no one to enter his office unless he was there, so he had no idea how easily she could eavesdrop.

"I've been expecting you for two days," Wilbur grumbled. "Did you bring news? What are the plans now? They seem to change daily. You wouldn't believe what that fool Wagner told me tonight. Damn well scared my wife to death."

The low voice of the stranger drifted to Bethanie. "All

I've heard lately is that the meeting will be here in three, maybe four days."

"Hell, man!" Wilbur shouted. "I already know that. I thought you'd have fresh news. Wagner and some of the other ranchers with us think the boss may bring in some tough guns to handle any trouble. When I agreed to have the meeting here, I never thought I'd be housing some of the worst outlaws in Texas. Are you sure you know nothing? . . . If you're lying . . ."

The stranger's words were low and deadly calm. Bethanie could hear the steel in his tone. "I said, I have no more news." His tone eased slightly. "I ride out before dawn if you have any word you want me to take back. With Apaches on the warpath, I'm in no mood to hang around. Word is, they are growing braver with each battle. Not even San Antonio may be safe much longer."

"Don't tell me about the Indians. We had problems all during the war, and now they're out for more blood. I can only handle one problem at a time and right now I'm worried about all the men coming here to meet. This could be big trouble for me if I'm caught up in this cattle mess. I . . . ah . . ." Her uncle seemed reluctant to continue. "I have something I want you to take out of San Antonio, and I'm willing to pay you well."

"What do you want me to move?" the stranger asked, only mild interest reflecting in his tone.

Wilbur cleared his throat. "I want my wife and daughter out of town before the meeting. My wife will pack tonight. I have horses. I'll have them ready by the time you leave."

"No," the stranger interrupted. "I don't move people, only information. Besides, if you want them out, why don't you take them?"

"You know I can't leave now, not when I stand to make so much, but I'll pay you two hundred dollars," Wilbur boasted.

"You must want them out badly," the stranger said. "Do you know something you're not sharing?"

"Never mind that. Will you take them somewhere, anywhere, but to safety?"

"No." The answer was as strong as the solid man who spoke.

"You must do this," Wilbur whined. "My daughter must be safely away for a few weeks. There's not another man I'd trust with the Indians gone crazy." He lowered his voice slightly and Bethanie could hear a touch of blackmail as he said, "If you won't take them, I'll blow the lid off all your double-dealings. I've got friends in Mexico and with the Texas Rangers. You'll be a hunted man on both sides of the border when I get through making up all the stories I can about you. I'm sure the boss would like to hear how you're playing both sides of the fence. Why, for all I know, your past may be darker than even I can think up."

The stranger seemed disinterested in Wilbur's threat, but after a pause he asked curiously, "What about your niece? Don't you want her safely away?"

Bethanie's face flushed slightly at his mention of her. "Oh, never mind about the girl. She can stay here and help me. I'm not spending money moving her to safety. She can just stay around here and keep me company till my wife returns," Wilbur snorted.

"I see," the stranger said as he opened the door slightly. "I'll think it over for a few hours and let you know. I have some other contacts to make first."

As the tall man stepped from the office, he glanced toward Bethanie. She saw sadness touch his brown eyes as he looked at her. She lifted her head proudly, not wanting his pity. He lowered his gaze as if he understood her pain, then turned and disappeared up the stairs. Bethanie chewed on her bottom lip. She had to think of something quickly with Aunt Martha and Allison leaving soon. She knew she feared Uncle Wilbur more than any group of outlaws meeting here, or Indians on the trail.

Wilbur filled his office door, patting his barreled belly on each side with fat hands. He knew he had made a bargain the stranger could not afford to refuse, and he was proud of himself for handling things so smoothly. He smiled at Bethanie in a sneer. "Go on up to bed, girl."

As Bethanie moved past him, he let his huge hand rest on her waist. He pulled her close to his chest, his foul breath smothering her. "I've got lots to say to you, but there will be plenty of time later. We need to get to know each other much better, and I predict we'll have an opportunity in the very near future."

To Bethanie's horror, Wilbur pulled her even closer and pressed his fat, fleshy mouth on her cheek. Never before had he been so bold. His lips were hot and sticky against her face and Bethanie felt vomit rise in her throat. She fought to gain control as her tears ran unchecked down her cheeks. In a burst of strength, Bethanie broke free and ran from the lobby. His crude laughter followed her.

Now, more than ever, she must get away before Martha and Allison left. There was only one place to turn. One person who might help. The tall stranger. And there was only one way to get to his room unnoticed.

Chapter Two

Dim moonlight filtered through the curtains of his hotel room as Josh leaned far back in the hard chair and stretched his cramped leg muscles. He glanced over at the bed longingly. I'll wait another hour, he thought. Then that bump under the covers will be my body and not just a decoy. Josh smiled at himself. If there was one thing that had kept him alive, it was the fact that he was always careful, always alert to possible danger.

Josh melted farther into the shadows as he heard a noise beside his bed, the low, swishing sound of boards sliding past one another. He moved his hand soundlessly to his Colt handle as the wall slid to one side. A dark, slender body squeezed through a secret passage and stood beside the bed.

The front legs of his chair almost hit the floor as Josh recognized Wilbur's niece. She hesitated as if afraid. She seemed to be mustering every ounce of courage to force herself slowly forward. She moved gracefully toward the bed and leaned over the mound of covers. Moonlight caught in her hair like a red-gold spark in a dying campfire. He waited, silently memorizing every line of her face, sure the vision before him would be rekindled for many nights to come.

With trained silence, Josh rose and neared the young woman. "Looking for something?" he whispered only an inch from her ear. He could smell the soft fragrance of her hair, like the first hint of honeysuckle on a early spring night.

She tensed, sending an invisible current through the air between them; then she jumped in fright and gulped air into her lungs to scream.

Before any sound could pass her lips, Josh's hand covered her mouth as his other arm pulled her body backward into his chest. The softness of her shoulders felt so marvelous against him, Josh had to force himself not to turn her in his arms and hold her completely in his embrace. He could feel her tremble, and yet he sensed a strength within her, so like another woman he'd known in the past. The memory now caused Josh to lighten his grip. She, too, had possessed a timid courage beneath her tall, slender form. With tenderness, Josh recalled the woman years ago who had been too shy to speak, yet brave enough to save his life.

Josh forced the memory from his mind and whispered into the girl's ear. "Don't scream. I didn't mean to frighten you. If I turn you loose, promise you won't cry out?"

As she nodded slowly, Josh felt her soft mouth move against his hand. Had it been so long since he'd held a woman that he'd forgotten how soft they were? Or was this one even softer than all the others he'd known?

Josh reluctantly moved his fingers away from her lips. Soft or not, he was a gentleman, and it went against his grain to even have to remind himself of the fact. He loosened his hold on her waist just enough so she could turn to face him. As her body carouseled in his light embrace, Josh fought the urge to pull her close once again.

"What are you doing here?" he whispered, acutely aware of the slight rise and fall of her breasts against his chest. "If your uncle sent you to rob me, you're out of luck."

"No!" Bethanie whispered, then swallowed hard.

Mischief twisted a smile from his lips. "Well, if you just came for a visit, why didn't you use the door?"

"I couldn't risk being seen," Bethanie answered hesitantly, ". . . by anyone."

She looked up at him, silently pleading for his assistance in escaping some terrible plight. How could he refuse her anything? Yet she seemed to want more than help. She wanted his trust, his honesty.

Josh released her waist and leaned over the bed. He removed the pillow and spread the cover flat. "Maybe you'd better sit down and explain. I'll light a candle."

Josh pulled up the only chair as she gingerly sat on the edge of the bed. He tried to make his voice lighten the somber mood he'd seen in her eyes. "Are there any more slats in the wall I need to know about?"

Bethanie's face relaxed into a slight smile. "No. Not that I know of, anyway."

Josh twirled the chair backward and straddled it, facing her. He twisted his gun to a comfortable position. Tightly strapped to his leg, the Colt had become part of Josh during the years of war. He checked it as often and as absentmindedly as an old maid might check her bodice buttons. "Now, what's so important?" he asked, rubbing his thumb along his bearded chin.

Bethanie pulled a tiny bag from her pocket. "I want you to take me with you when you leave San Antonio . . . and I'm willing to pay."

Josh studied her as she opened the bag and poured out a handful of seeds. "These are my only valuables. Seeds from my mother's herb garden and my grandparents' wedding bands."

Two matching rings appeared among the seeds as she

continued. "I've kept them hidden, lest my aunt take them. I think they must be worth something."

She held up the rings to Josh. They were unusual gold bands with dark and light carvings on each one. He made no effort to take them as he looked back up into her eyes. She was doing it again, asking for his total loyalty and honesty as if she could endure nothing less. He found he couldn't make light of her request when her eyes pleaded, tearing at his heart. "You must want to leave pretty badly. Before I say yes or no . . . I'd like to know what I'm getting myself into."

Bethanie nodded. "I'm Bethanie Lane. I've lived here with my uncle and aunt for six months. My mother died last year."

Josh offered what he hoped was his most charming smile. "Nice to meet you, Bethanie. I'm Josh Weston." He'd told her his last name as easily as one might at a church social, yet in the months he'd known Wilbur, he'd never used his full name.

Hearing himself say her name jogged his memory like lightning awakens the air in an evening sky. Yet Josh knew his face bore no hint of his thoughts. Deep in his mind came a hazy image of a young girl just beginning to turn the corner into adulthood. It had been the first year of the war. He was running the Union lines with messages. After a month of success, a bullet from no-where grazed his skull. He had awakened to find himself a prisoner of bounty hunters who made their living capturing anyone, white or black, whom they found crossing Union lines. He had been forced to march for days behind their horses, when finally they stopped at a train station in Ohio. By then, Josh was weak from hunger and half mad from the constant pain of his untreated head wound. His captors had made it plain that they got the same money for bodies as for prisoners.

Josh remembered a tall woman and her daughter moving from prisoner to prisoner alongside the railroad tracks. The woman ignored the Union soldiers' warnings and knelt to help Josh. Her daughter gave him water, while the woman cleaned his blood-caked scalp. She rubbed his wound with an awful-smelling salve and wrapped his head as gently as if he had been her brother and not some Rebel deep in Yankee territory. He would never forget the woman's sad eyes or her daughter Bethanie's beautiful red hair.

Now, as he studied the young woman before him, he knew why he'd had the feeling all day that he knew her. Her slight northern accent, her graceful way, her slender beauty, touched a four-year-old memory. She must be the same girl, placed in his path once by fate and now in desperation.

At the point when Josh had given up, a woman's silent courage and strength had pulled him back to sanity. Her daughter's loveliness had reassured him that there was more to life than civil war. Three weeks later he had escaped, but he had sometimes wondered if he would ever see the two caring angels again. Even though he had seen Bethanie's mother only once, Josh felt a sorrow at hearing of her death. He could see her gentleness living on in her daughter. Josh knew whatever Bethanie asked of him, he would grant. He wished she would untie her wonderful red hair so he could see it flowing down her back like the cascade of golden fire he remembered.

Josh realized Bethanie would never recognize him. He must have been only one of hundreds she had seen during the war. Then he had been covered with dirt and blood. Now she was no longer a child, but a woman with wondrously expressive eyes like her mother's.

Josh fought a smile from his lips. "You haven't told me why you want to leave. I'm not in the habit of aiding runaway girls."

"I have my reasons." Bethanie lifted her head slightly.

"I'm not a runaway. I'm almost twenty and old enough to decide for myself where I wish to live."

Josh could sense she would not beg or cry, and his admiration for her grew. She did not have to tell him the truth behind her request. He had seen the lust in the eyes of her uncle.

"Where is it you wish to live?" he asked as he watched her slender fingers move nervously back and forth across the bumpy bedspread. He could tell by her manner that she had no answer to his question.

"That's not your problem," Bethanie answered defensively. "I can take care of myself."

"If I say yes . . ." Josh's eyebrows pushed together in thought. She was about as able to take care of herself as a leaf in a tornado, but he didn't think it would do any good to argue the point. "How much is it worth to you?"

"I'll pay all I have," Bethanie answered honestly, "but we must get out of town before I'm missed."

Josh understood her need for secrecy. If Wilbur suspected she might leave, he would simply lock her in a room until everyone was gone. Josh hated to think about her being left in this place with that disgusting excuse for a man downstairs. Even in the faded dress she was one of the most beautiful young women he'd ever seen. "I don't want your rings, but . . ." he hesitated, a plan forming in his mind. He'd be willing to bet a month's pay she had nowhere to go. Her stiffly held body told him she wasn't looking for a handout, either.

He reached over and lifted the largest ring from her hand. The gold slid easily onto his third finger. Josh examined the fine workmanship as he spoke. "Can you ride?"

"Better than most men," Bethanie answered without emotion.

"Can you use a gun?"

"If need be. During the war there were few men. I had to learn how to shoot."

Josh twisted the ring on his finger. "If I help you get away, will you agree to help me out for a few days? That is, unless you plan to stay with your aunt."

Bethanie chewed at the corner of her full bottom lip. "I'm traveling alone."

"Good," Josh smiled. "Then you may have a few days free. My brother owns a ranch south of Fort Worth. If you'll help out with the cooking for a roundup due to start soon, I'll give you back this ring and consider us square."

Bethanie nodded agreement, but a touch of apprehension colored her eyes a darker shade of green.

Josh added, already thinking of problems they might encounter while traveling, "I'll wear the ring for now. Should anyone ask, we'll explain you as my wife. Proper young women don't usually travel even this wild country without a chaperone, and I plan on dropping your aunt off at the first settlement. You have my word as a gentleman, you'll be safe."

Bethanie was silent for a moment. Josh knew she was considering his last statement. It gnawed at him that she should question his code of honor, but then he had as yet given her no reason to trust him.

She took her grandmother's gold band and slipped it on her finger as if the action sealed a bargain. "All right. I'll do whatever it takes to get out of here. I don't mind helping cook at your brother's ranch. It will give me time to think."

"Fine." Josh relaxed for the first time. He stood and pulled at his bearded chin. "Two things before you go. First, tell no one of our agreement. No one."

Bethanie nodded. "I have no one to say farewell to in this town."

"Get yourself a pair of denim pants and a boy's shirt."

Josh continued. "Second, meet me behind the hotel an hour before dawn. I'll get an extra horse, and you can ride on ahead before your uncle comes out. Later, we can explain to your aunt that I agreed to take three for the price of two."

"Why dress in pants?" Bethanie leaned forward, interested in his plan.

Josh rubbed his forehead with one hand. Weariness rippled his features. "If someone sees us from a distance, I'd rather they think two men and two women are riding than one man and three women."

"I think that sounds wise." Bethanie stood to leave, satisfied with their agreement. As she offered her hand to thank Josh Weston, a sharp rap sounded at the door. She jumped beside him, energy exploding within her.

Josh grabbed her elbow and whirled her toward the opening in the panel. "Get back," he whispered. His body pressed closer to her as he pulled her into the dark corner. "I'll meet you out back before dawn."

Before Bethanie could comment, he shoved her back through the opening. She watched in fear as he pulled the panel almost closed. From her darkened bedroom, she saw Josh's movements through the slit opening. He darted across the dimly lit room. One hand silently pulled the door open as the other rested lightly on his gun.

To Bethanie's surprise a priest stood in the hall. His face was in shadows under his hood, reminding her of the Angel of Death.

"Brother Michael." Josh greeted the priest warmly with a brisk slap on the holy man's back. He grabbed the brown robes of the priest's shoulders and began pulling him in before Brother Michael could speak. Then, Josh quickly secured the door.

"Joshua, my son," the young priest whispered, as he removed his hood to reveal sandy hair and a bearded boyish face. His eyes were light blue with an interesting alloy of kindness and mischief.

Bethanie watched in fascination through the crack as the two men shook hands. They were alike in age and height, but all their features varied. Josh with his dark earth brown eyes and black hair contrasted with Michael's sky blue eyes and sandy curls. Each was good-looking in a strong, independent way.

"Pretty good cover," Mike complimented himself. "Nobody pays any attention to me when I'm dressed like this. My guess is I could stay right here when the outfit has this big meeting next week, and they wouldn't even notice me."

"Now wait a minute, Mike," Josh interrupted. "I know you'd like to stay around, but things are just too hot here for you right now. You're going to be needed at the roundup. Ben says there's bound to be trouble."

"Oh, your brother is a worrier." Mike grunted and moved to the bed. "The roundup doesn't sound near as much fun as being here. I'd give these robes to know who's the boss of this operation." He flopped unceremoniously onto the bedcovers and stretched out with his hands locked behind his head. The bed bounced slowly to a creaky halt beneath his weight.

Josh shook his head in mock irritation as he slapped at Michael's mud-covered boots. "I doubt I'll get any sleep tonight, but should I have the chance, a clean bed would be nice."

Mike crossed his boots, disinterested in Josh's penchant for neatness. "I'd sure think twice before closing my eyes in this place. I wouldn't be surprised if our host, Wilbur Brewer, is the boss himself."

Josh shook his head. "No way—he hasn't got the brains." He looked at the yellowed ceiling. "Speaking of Wilbur, I've got some bad news. He wants me to take his wife, daughter, and niece out of here with me tomorrow. Seems he's heard some stories about a few of his business partners and doesn't want his womenfolk around."

"What?" Mike yelled and sat up. "Hellfire and brimstone, Josh! We can't have three women with us. The riding's hard and fast once we hit open country."

Josh nodded. "I know, I know. But he threatened to blow my cover. I'm not real fond of being shot."

Mike's face brightened. "Let's leave tonight and avoid him. I can be ready in an hour."

"No," Josh answered flatly. "We can take them as far as Ben's ranch. He can see they get a stage from there. I gave my word to his niece and I aim to keep it."

"I don't know. It's dangerous travelin' with women right now. More white people have been murdered by Indians in Texas in the last year than I figure were killed all together before. It's bad enough dying, but what those savages do to the womenfolk ain't fit to talk about in hell."

"I've made up my mind, Mike," Josh stated. "I'll meet you out back at six tomorrow morning."

"All right, ain't no use arguing with you, I can see that. You're probably the stubbornest man in Texas, next to your brother. Must be somethin' in the Weston bloodline." Mike rose from the bed, not bothering to straighten the covers. "I'll go collect my gear and get a few hours' sleep. You brought me a horse, didn't you? It might look funny for a priest to be caught stealing one."

"Sure, I brought one," Josh answered as he unlocked the door. "But I still need to buy another for one of the ladies."

"Well, good luck. I hear there ain't a horse for sale for twenty miles," Mike added as he touched the doorknob. "I'll see you at six, my son." Without another word Mike pulled his hood low and vanished from the room.

Josh waited a few minutes before blowing out the candle and disappearing out the same door.

Though it was not yet ten o'clock, the town already rested sleepily under low, brooding clouds. Spring was an unpredictable, sometimes treacherous time in Texas. Josh walked across the street toward the stables with the casual grace of a powerful animal. Most people had already retired for the evening. Many of the stores were boarded up and abandoned. The war had crippled more than just men; many businesses folded when Confederate money became worthless. Without federal troops, and with most young men gone to war, the wild, nomadic Indians had enjoyed a field day attacking poorly defended settlements. The once wide frontier line retreated east and south, allowing survivors to nurse their wounds and plead for federal troops to reopen forts from the Red River to the Rio Grande.

Josh felt an itchiness deep within himself to leave and avoid not only nature's coming storm but the human one as well. When Wilbur's friends hit town, the small, sleeping settlement would feel it like sandcastles after a wave. If his brother Ben was right, the men meeting here were planning to control the cattle industry in Texas. If so, all the state might feel the ripple if these men weren't stopped somehow.

Josh looked about him, searching each shadowed corner for movement, but the streets were sleeping. San Antonio had suffered many times and always seemed to be able to rebuild. Great men may have died here, like Jim Bowie and Davy Crockett, but the townspeople, like ants after a windstorm, rebuilt their homes with unlimited diligence. These nameless settlers were the ones who would eventually tame this wild land, not with guns, but with hammers and plows.

It seemed as if all his life Josh had been riding into troubled weather. If it weren't Indian raids or Mexican bandits crossing the border, there were always a few men like Wilbur Brewer out to make quick money at others' expense. Josh was bone-tired. The war had knocked all the fight out of him, and now he longed to settle down in peace. He removed his hat and shook his hair in the wind. Peace had never seemed farther away to him than it did at this moment.

Josh stepped cautiously into the darkened stable. Except for a filthy stable boy curled asleep in an empty stall, the barn was deserted. Josh nudged the boy lightly with his boot. "Hey, kid, wake up."

The boy rolled over and rubbed his eyes with dirty fists. "Yeah, whata you want?" He thrashed amid the straw to his feet as if he could, in his small way, defend the stable.

"I need to buy a couple of horses, tonight," Josh answered, wishing he had a washtub handy to throw the boy into. The kid smelled more like a horse than a boy.

"What's wrong with them two you rode in with awhile ago?" the boy asked.

"Nothing, I just need another for a friend. One that's gentle, if you've got one, and another for supplies. About dawn I'll want my extra saddle put on the horse I led in."

The filth-covered child shook his head. "I can saddle your horses, but I ain't got any for sale. Fact is, the only horses I got in this place besides yours and my own nag are three that belong to the hotel keeper. He already told me he'll be usin' two of 'em tomorrow."

Josh thought for a minute. "Saddle all three of his. I'll make arrangements with the hotel owner." If they traveled light, they could make do without a packhorse. He knew Wilbur would plan to keep the third horse here in case he needed it. Well, Wilbur would find himself afoot after tomorrow. He couldn't accuse his own niece of being a horse thief.

The boy straightened to his full five-foot height. "I'll have 'em ready at five, mister, but there be one question," the kid asserted.

"What is it?" Josh asked, fishing in his pocket for a coin to give the lad.

"I'd like to trail along with you." The boy stood tall. "My family's all gone, and I'd just as soon not be in town when trouble blows in. I've been watching the past few days, and something's gettin' ready to happen."

"Sorry, son," Josh answered, feeling regretful about the kid. "You'll be better off here than with me."

"Beggin' your pardon, mister, but my best chances are with you." The kid slung his brown hair out of his eyes. "And that priest," he added with a glint of intelligence in his light brown eyes.

"What makes you think I have anything to do with a priest?" Josh tilted his head in interest. If this boy had put him and Mike together, who else would have?

"Simple, mister." The kid scratched his dirty hair. "I seen him go over to the hotel an hour or so ago, and I know you're the only stranger in town stayin' there. The fat old toad who runs the place has never been the religious sort."

"You're a smart kid. Why do you want to travel with me?" Josh smiled at the dirty suntanned face. Nature had been monotonous in his coloring, for face, eyes, and hair were all a sandy brown. Josh wondered, if clean, the boy's hair might have golden lines as did his eyes when they turned to the light.

"I've been waiting for you." The kid smiled slyly. "My brother was a Ranger. He showed me somethin' once." The kid moved to where Josh had stacked his two saddles. He slipped his first two fingers between the leather of the saddle on the right side. Slowly he drew out a silver badge, the emblem of the Texas Rangers. The metal shone brightly between the boy's muddy fingers. "My brother told me if a Ranger wants to travel unnoticed he slides his badge in here. He said all Rangers do this from time to time, but nobody else knows this hidin' place. He only told me because he knew I would be a Ranger as soon as I got big enough." The boy seemed certain of his ambition.

Josh smiled easily. "What makes you think you have any proof? Maybe I bought the saddle or stole it."

"Maybe you did, mister." The boy seemed to already have thought of that angle. "Or maybe you, or that priest, is really a Ranger. You both got beards, and I ain't seen many Rangers without beards. I figure I'll take my chances. If I don't cotton to riding with you, I can always take out on my own. I know the country as well as any man."

"How old are you?" Josh asked, wondering how many years this child thought it took to make a man.

"Fourteen, almost fifteen." The boy kicked at the straw, obviously trying to distract from his lie.

Josh knew the little fellow could be no more than ten or eleven at the most, but he figured a man had a right to his secrets, even if the man was only half grown. "What's your name, son?" Josh questioned.

"Dustin Barfield, but folks call me Dusty."

Josh remembered Sam Barfield who was killed at an Indian battle along the Pease River in 1860. Colonel Ross had called Sam a fine man and an asset to the Rangers, but Josh made no comment about it to the boy.

"Don't you have any family around here, Dusty?" Josh asked, knowing he must not or he couldn't possibly look so unkempt.

"No." The boy smiled, knowing this stranger was considering taking him along. "But I got a horse, a gun, and even a watch with initials on it."

Josh almost laughed out loud. The child wanted him to know he was no street bum by telling of a treasured watch. "I must be losing my mind, but you can tag along. If we make it across the open country, I know a ranch that could use a good man." Josh put the emphasis on man. "Have the horses saddled early, and I'll be over an hour before dawn.

"Yes, sir." Dusty smiled, spreading white teeth from ear to ear.

"And put that badge back where you found it. You'd better forget you ever saw it," Josh snapped, with as much sternness as he could muster. "You know the Rangers are inactive now."

"Yes, sir." Dusty muttered again. "But not for long."

Josh turned and started back to the hotel shaking his head. The kid was right; a Ranger didn't do the jobs that needed doing just for the pay. If Texas hadn't had the Rangers during the war, there might not be a settler left in the whole state.

Josh decided he must be getting soft in the head. First, he was trapped into taking two women into the wildest country in Texas, then the redhead, and now a boy. This trip might not be the easiest he'd ever tried, but it certainly promised to be the most interesting. And maybe the most dangerous.

Chapter Three

True to her word, Bethanie said nothing about her plans to accompany the other women and Josh Weston out of San Antonio. She packed for Allison, while her cousin rattled incessantly with excitement. The tiny blonde was unaware of any danger in traveling, seeing her adventure only as an outing. Bethanie decided in Allison's case ignorance was probably a blessing and she wouldn't frighten her cousin with reality.

With Allison finally settled in for a few hours' sleep, Bethanie began preparing for her own journey. Tiptoeing down to the kitchen, she rummaged through a load of clean clothes she'd just washed for a man and his three sons. Though the garments were worn, she managed to find two pairs of pants and a shirt that looked close to her size. She crossed the darkened kitchen to a ghostly white jar on the top shelf of a pie cabinet. Martha always stashed household money in the vessel, including all the change Bethanie earned doing laundry. Hoping to pay for the clothes she was taking, Bethanie pulled two bills out and quickly stuffed them deep into the laundry basket.

Bethanie jumped as a noise rumbled from her aunt's room above the kitchen. Hurriedly, she cradled the bundle of clothes to her chest and darted for the front lobby in hope of avoiding any further encounters with her aunt or uncle. The last thing she wanted was for them to discover her plan to leave.

Halfway across the lobby, Bethanie froze in mid-step as the office door creaked open. Her uncle must have come downstairs and, like her, hadn't bothered to turn up the lights. Bethanie watched his face shine in the yellow glow through the windows. Wilbur's fat lips spread across dingy teeth into an ugly greeting. Bethanie could tell by his stance that he'd been drinking.

"Well, Bethanie," Wilbur slurred the words. Alcohol had loosened his bottom lip making the wet pink mass unmanageable. "Did you come down to say good night to your dear old uncle?"

"No," Bethanie answered, slowly easing her way past him. "I had to finish some laundry."

"About that, girl . . ." He staggered toward her as he spoke. "After tomorrow, I don't think you'll have to earn extra money."

Wilbur stood only a few inches from Bethanie in the shadow between windows. "After tomorrow," he repeated in a hoarsely whispered promise. She could feel his foul breath against her cheek. "I think I have another idea about how you can earn your keep." His short, fat finger danced in front of her face almost hitting her nose.

Bethanie leaned back in horror. She didn't want to ignite his temper for fear of awakening the entire household. When he was drunk, he could be as hard to handle as greased liver. She'd even seen Martha back away from a confrontation. "Good night, Uncle," Bethanie managed to say with as much resolution as she could muster.

Wilbur's hand reached and encircled Bethanie's neck, startling her with his swift action. His porky fingers closed around her slender throat like a vise. He pulled her toward him, seemingly unmindful that he was choking her. "How about a little sample of your future work?"

he groaned just before his huge mouth covered half her face.

Bethanie was suddenly suffocating in the fleshiness of his features. As she struggled to free herself, his fingers closed tighter around her neck, bruising their imprints into her skin. Bethanie fought for her very life. Lack of air was rapidly drawing her world closed around her. Her one free fist struck endlessly against his chest with seemingly no effect.

A door opened somewhere upstairs; an instant later Martha's sharp voice sounded. "Wilbur, did you find that letter?"

Wilbur's face moved away from Bethanie with a frustrated growl. He released her throat and let his hand drag down the front of her dress as she gulped for air. "Comin'," he yelled toward the stairs.

Bethanie could hear Martha's steps retreating. She knew if she screamed, Martha would come downstairs. She also knew that Martha would find a way to blame everything on her. There was no telling what her aunt might do to her. Bethanie had to see that nothing came between her and freedom at dawn.

Wilbur leaned closer and whispered, "We're goin' to have fun. I'll have no trouble from you; I'll bet on that. If you want to be walking tomorrow, girl, you'd better not mention this to anyone." His laughter made a hissing sound between his teeth. "Not that anyone would help you."

His fingers pulled at the buttons running down the front of her dress as his sour breath heaved in nauseating waves across her face. "You're lucky. I could just tie you to the storage-room floor and have my fun any time, but I need someone to cook and clean, so I'll let you have the run of the place as long as you behave yourself."

Bethanie stood frozen in disbelief, her fists clenched tightly inside the folds of her bundle of clothes. She tried closing her eyes to make him go away, afraid to speak and provoke him further. Just a few more hours and she would be away, forever free of him.

His lips spread in a predatory smile. "Your time is long past comin', girl." He moved his hand across her chest and pulled at her blouse. One fat arm slid around her waist pinning her to him, as he continued to finger her clothing. The buttons seemed to defy him as Bethanie struggled. She fought to keep from crying out as anger and fear danced frantically atop the adrenalin in her veins.

In drunken frustration, Wilbur cursed Bethanie and her clothing as he pulled her into the spans of his stomach. Bethanie freed one arm as he ripped her blouse open, sending buttons flying in the darkness. He shoved his fingers between her dress and camisole until his hand covered the thin material over her breast. "Slim you may be, but ready to pick." He squeezed her breast painfully until her wild fighting stopped.

"That's better, girl." He whispered as he loosened his grip and began to rub her nipple cruelly with the palm of his hand, forcing her breast first one direction then another. "You may be still now, but I can see the fire in them green eyes of yours. You'll be full of spunk."

Bethanie's breathing was irregular with fright. If she moved an inch to escape, his fingers closed over her soft mound with sadistic force. When she gasped to keep from crying out, she could feel Wilbur chuckle with delight. As she stood suffocating in pain and fear, he once more began his cruel circular movements over her tender flesh. His hot breath brushed her neck as he laughed and lowered his mouth to the soft flesh at her shoulder. His hot, stubbly face was like a slimy creature gnawing at her. Bethanie wanted to scream as he buried his teeth and began to suck her blood to the surface, but no sound would leave her lips.

Slobbering on her skin, he whispered, "We gonna' have some fun in a few hours. You best remember somethin', I could kill you and there ain't no one in this town who'd notice. Besides," he bit at her flesh painfully, "you might even start to enjoy it." His fingers began to pull at her camisole as he explained his long-awaited plans for her in detail.

Wilbur released his grip instantly at the sound of a door opening upstairs. He cursed the interruption as they heard footsteps. His hot palm slid off the thin material covering her breast and pushed her a few inches from him, as if he were discarding trash.

As Martha's form appeared on the landing, Bethanie broke free and ran back into the kitchen. She pulled her dress together and slipped behind the door, gulping each breath. She could hear Wilbur's heavy steps ascending the front stairs and Martha bickering. Bethanie waited until all was quiet before darting silently out back into the cool night air. For several minutes she stood drinking in the calm of the night. Then she began to sob, low, uncontrollable cries of pain.

As her tears subsided, Bethanie crawled beneath the hotel's wooden steps like a frightened animal in hiding. Here in the dirt she felt safe. She had always hated being in darkness, but now the night covered her pain. Fresh tears flowed down her cheeks as she stared into the blackness around her. She had no doubt about what her uncle planned for her if she didn't get away before dawn. His vulgar description echoed in her ears making her flesh crawl. She bit her lip until she tasted blood as she fought for control.

From the rooms above Bethanie, voices drifted out an open window. "Did you bring the letter?" Martha's impatient words sounded.

"Sure," Wilbur answered, "But I don't see why it's so important."

"Simple, you drunken old fool," Martha condemned. "Do you think Bethanie would stay here if she knew her father was alive? The letter must be destroyed tonight. Once I'm gone, you'll stay drunk and Bethanie will have the run of the place. No matter where we put the letter there's a chance she might find it."

"But he ain't no father to her, anyway. Runnin' out on her mother like that," Wilbur slurred self-righteously, as if he were a good example.

Bethanie could hear them moving about their room. "There, the letter's burned along with my link with Bethanie's father. Now she can stay here and help out. She's better off than with some old seaman anyway."

The voices lowered into mumbles as her aunt and uncle retired for a few hours' sleep. Bethanie cradled her knees to her chest, deep in thought. She knew little about her father. The news that he was alive was not surprising, for her mother had never spoken of him as if he were dead. The knowledge that he was looking for her was shocking, but Bethanie saw the news as one more reason to leave. She didn't care about a letter. Any man who would leave her mother wasn't worth finding. She'd seen the pain in her mother's face each time she'd asked questions. Somehow the answers were never important enough to invoke the sadness in her mother's eyes.

Bethanie knew her mother, Mary, had left home at fifteen after her parents' deaths to join a religious group of nearby Shakers. They were a kind, loving people who taught her a great deal about cooking and nursing. The Shakers believed men and women were equal, so when her mother showed an interest in working with animals they encouraged her. Shakers value three virtues: celibacy, industry, and cleanliness. Mary met Mariah, Bethanie's father, when she was twenty. She told Bethanie once that she thought his name was music to say. Mary and Mariah often talked, but even though the Shakers

believed men and women equal, they were not allowed
to work together. He had been an orphan from birth, and
the Shakers had kindly taken him in. They named him
after the ship that brought the original Brothers and Sisters to America. Once, her mother had said that he was
a tall man, three years her senior, with dark red hair.

Mary never blamed Mariah. When Bethanie was born,
they left the Shakers. Before three winters had passed,
Mariah left his wife and child, never to return. Mary
wouldn't rejoin the Shakers, yet she kept their ways all
her life. After several moves, Mary settled in as a cook
on a small horse ranch. Here, with few people around,
she found the only peace she'd ever known.

Tears rolled down Bethanie's cheeks in the darkness.
She wanted so much to curl up in her mother's lap and
let her brush away all the sadness. But her mother was
dead. There was no one but herself to rely on.

Bethanie rubbed her bruised neck, remembering Wilbur's grip. His stubby whiskers had cut her face with
their roughness. In the past six months he and Martha
had chipped away all her faith in mankind. In a cramped
corner under the porch, Bethanie allowed her belief in
people to crumble. Sometime after midnight, she came
to one firm conclusion. If she were to survive, she must
rely only on herself, no one else. There in the darkness
the meek, trusting child died within her. The bruises on
her neck would fade in a few days, but the scars on her
heart would remain. A steel will to survive forged within
her. She was not like her parents. She would not give
up. She vowed to fight and survive. She'd go somewhere,
anywhere, and make it on her own.

An hour before dawn, Josh waited behind the hotel
holding three horses. He watched Bethanie step from the
back door and move toward him as a single lantern splat-

tered pathetic light. She was dressed in pants, as he'd instructed, with a baggy plaid shirt tucked around her small waist. She carried an old, half-filled saddlebag at her side. Her hair was bound into a tight bun at the back of her neck. The harsh clothing did little to hide her gentle womanly grace. Fascinated, Josh studied her as she moved toward him, wondering what her life had been this past year since the war. Judging from what he had seen, her road had not been easy.

"You're on time," Josh stated simply as he handed her the reins to one of the horses. "I brought you a jacket and hat." He didn't bother to tell her they were his own. "We'd best cover up that hair of yours if you want to get out of town unnoticed."

"Thanks." Bethanie pulled the hat on and slipped on the jacket he offered.

As Josh strapped on her saddlebag, he commented, "You sure pack light for a girl."

"I have little," Bethanie stated flatly as she stepped one foot into the stirrup.

Josh moved behind her, his hands encircling her waist to help her into the saddle. With sudden, unexpected violence, Bethanie jerked free. Josh couldn't believe the flash of hatred that reflected in her eyes as she turned to face him.

Her words were low and sharp. "One thing we'd better straighten out now, Mister Weston. We made a deal to get me out of here, but no more. I don't care what your business with my uncle was, but it is vital you understand. You are never to touch me." Her voice was only a whisper, yet Josh could hear the steel in her tone. "If you can't honor that, I'd rather strike out on my own. I won't be handled by any man."

Josh backed off a step, idly twisting the ring which had belonged to Bethanie's grandfather. Any anger he might have felt at her unjustified criticism was overshadowed by curiosity as to the cause of her strong reaction. He held up his hands in surrender. "Bethanie, if that's your wish, I'll respect it. I had no intention of harming you, only to help you up." Even in the dim yellow light, he could see her fiery green eyes challenging him, questioning his word.

"I need no help." Bethanie spoke the words with a newfound bitterness. "Don't ever touch me again."

Josh could see she was nearly at a breaking point. He watched as she pulled herself into the saddle with the easy motion of one accustomed to riding. He wanted to say something, anything, to reassure her, but knew she wouldn't believe him. If he wanted her trust, he must earn it.

Josh turned as he heard Dusty approaching with the other horses. The boy was whistling in high spirits. Josh smiled to himself. Dusty reminded him of his brother. Ben would have loved going on an adventure like this when he was Dusty's age. Josh had a feeling that if he could get Dusty to the ranch, he and Ben would hit it off.

"Dusty, tie the ladies' horses up over there. I want you two to ride on ahead." Josh pointed to Bethanie as he gave the order. "When you reach the edge of town, wait for us there."

"You bet," Dusty answered. He was too young to question the logic of this action. He signaled to Bethanie, and they rode into the shadows.

Josh stood for several minutes staring after them. The girl intrigued him even more this morning than she had last night. He wondered what had happened in the past few hours that had made her so bitter. One thing he knew, the open country would be safer for her than here with that lusting old goat of an uncle. Josh wished there were some way to ease her pain. For the first time in his life, he had the urge to take a woman in his arms and just hold her. Bethanie had made it plain that was the very thing she didn't want.

A muffled step sounded in the alley. Josh's hand rested lightly on his gun handle as he searched the shadows.

Michael, completely covered by his brown robes, walked out of the darkness. "Jumpy this morning, my son." Michael joked, "Where are the ladies?"

"They should be down in a few minutes," Josh answered. "There's only two. I'll explain later." He slapped Mike on the shoulder. "And stop calling me son. I can't believe you'd fool many people with these robes."

"Fine, my son." Mike ignored Josh's command. "Did you bring my rifle?" Mike lifted his robes and checked the Colt strapped to his leg.

"Sure." Josh laughed at the comical sight his friend made.

Mike replaced his robe and folded his hands in an appropriate priestly gesture. "Laugh now, while you've got the chance, for I plan on sheddin' this blanket as soon as I get out of town."

"No, I think you should play along for a few days. Maybe even until we get the ladies dropped off. The wife might drop one of the names we're looking for, if she thinks we're harmless." Josh pitched a rifle to Mike.

Mike caught the weapon with the ease of a trained juggler. "Anything you say. I'd wear this getup for a month to know who's planning Wilbur's meeting. I've watched him for a week and, Josh, you may be right about him. I don't think he's got the brains to ramrod an operation that would control the cattle industry."

Josh nodded. He had talked with Wilbur once too often to believe the man had any intelligence. "We'll talk it over with Ben when we get to the ranch."

The back door to the hotel opened wide and Wilbur stormed out. He seemed irritated by the bundles he carried and quickly pushed them toward Josh. Taking the load, Josh groaned. He should have guessed Bethanie's aunt and cousin couldn't pack as lightly as she had.

Wilbur turned his bloodshot eyes from Josh to Mike. "Who's this?" he blurted out as he waved a porky finger toward Mike.

"Wilbur Brewer, may I introduce Father Michael. He will be riding with us as far as the mission near Fort Worth," Josh answered, noticing Wilbur's sudden smile.

Wilbur pumped Mike's hand as he grinned. He was obviously delighted a priest was accompanying his wife and daughter. "Glad you're goin' along, Father," Wilbur said. "You'll have to excuse me this morning, I'm feelin' poorly, plus the girl who works here is hiding out somewhere. But no great worry, I'll find her."

Josh could see impatient lust in Wilbur's eyes. The old man was probably thinking of what fun he was going to have. Josh smiled to himself, knowing he was spoiling Wilbur's plans.

In a flurry of chatter, the women joined the men outside. Josh made the necessary introductions. Wilbur grunted a good-bye and disappeared back into the hotel, leaving Josh and Mike to help the women mount their horses. Being with these women was like listening to an off-key melody, Josh thought. Martha was sharp and treated everyone like a servant except Allison, whom she treated as a child. Josh gritted his teeth as Allison complained for the second time before they were out of sight of the hotel. He seriously considered making a mad run for it.

As the sun edged over the horizon, Josh and his small band spotted Dusty and Bethanie. Josh rode a length ahead of the others, thankful Mike seemed content to ride with the chattery women. He studied the rolling countryside now green with spring. In a few months the hot sun would bleach the colors into muted hues of brown. Compared to the rich blue-greens of Ohio, where he had met Bethanie and her mother, the pale color of this country seemed thinned by too much water in the paints. To his way of thinking, Bethanie and Allison could be compared in the same way. Bethanie with her vivid coloring made Allison seem washed out, lifeless.

Josh moved up beside Bethanie as they reached the edge of town. In a low voice, not meant to be heard by the other women, Josh asked, "Bethanie, you wanta' ride up ahead with me for a while, until, we're well away?"

Bethanie nodded, understanding his logic. She had no wish to face her aunt yet.

"Dusty, ride back with the women and the priest." Josh smiled at the boy. He seemed to have made an effort to clean up a bit. Josh couldn't help but like the kid and hoped he'd made the right decision to bring him along. This wild country was no place for children, but Dusty seemed strong in spirit, if not yet grown. He reminded Josh of a determined little turtle born with his survival instinct fully developed.

Dusty reined his horse and saluted as he turned and galloped back to the others.

Josh and Bethanie rode in silence for an hour. He studied her out of the corner of one eye. He could not miss the bruises around her neck or the puffiness of her eyes from crying. He watched the way she sat proud and straight in the saddle as she stared ahead, deep in her own thoughts. Even in rags she was the most beautiful woman he'd ever seen.

Toward noon, they stopped to water the horses and eat a few bites of beef jerky. As Martha climbed down from her horse, she spotted Bethanie's face for the first time. "Bethanie!" she shouted in anger. "What in the devil are you doing here?" Her fingers clenched into fists as she stormed at Bethanie like a raging bull. "You have no right to be here."

Josh watched Bethanie stiffen. "I paid my way just as

you did," she answered, keeping her voice under tight control.

"Where'd you get that kind of money?" Martha's face was twisted with surprise and anger. "Well, you just turn around and ride back. Wilbur needs your help, useless as you are at the hotel."

Bethanie dusted the dirt from her pants as she avoided Martha's stare. "I'm sorry, Aunt Martha, but I no longer wish to live with you and Uncle Wilbur. I'll make my own way now, without your help."

"Why, you thankless little tramp," Martha screamed. "You'll be sleeping on the streets within a month." Martha raised her hand to slap her niece.

Josh had had enough of this crow. He stepped between the two women, catching Martha's hand in midair. "That's enough, Mrs. Brewer. Your niece paid me the same amount as you did to come along," Josh lied. He wasn't about to mention his and Bethanie's agreement to this old woman, whose heart must be the size of a raisin.

"You stay out of what's none of your business. This ungrateful girl was holdin' out money while she lived off our good nature for six months," Martha shouted, unwilling to give up her fight. "She's trash, just like her mother. A second-generation whore, probably destined to breed bastard children."

Bethanie's head jerked up, a fiery hatred burning toward Martha. Her fists doubled as she took a step toward her aunt, no longer able to restrain herself.

Josh stepped between them. He couldn't turn this old alley cat loose on a kitten like Bethanie. "Well, that's not exactly the way I see it." Josh fought to keep calm. White lines edged the tiny wrinkles around his mouth. The memory of Bethanie's beautiful mother flashed in his mind. He remembered her sad eyes, which had looked as if they'd taken decades to accumulate so much heartbreak. Now he watched the daughter, strong and silent before him. "Bethanie, hold out your hands, please."

Bethanie looked at Josh, puzzlement brushing away her anger. She opened her hands palm up to him. Her silent action told him, more than words, of her trust in him.

"Now, Mrs. Brewer, your hands." Josh reached for the older woman's hands. Martha's skin was smooth, whereas Bethanie's was raw and calloused from work. "It appears to me you got more than your money back on her keep." He turned toward Martha, anger hardening his every muscle. "I'll hear no more from you. Is that understood? Unless you prefer riding alone the rest of the way?"

Fear avalanched in Martha's eyes. "I'll say no more now." She glared past Josh to Bethanie, her eyes promising to continue her fight later.

Josh turned and walked down to where Mike and Allison stood watering the horses. They were oblivious to the argument behind them. The two had hit it off during the morning ride and now were laughing together as Josh approached.

"Josh, my son," Michael smiled as he pushed his hood further back off his sunny hair. "If you'll take over here, I'll take Miss Allison up to sit in the shade."

"Sure." Josh reached for the loose reins. Mike was playing his role of priest to the hilt. He seemed fascinated with the tiny woman-child.

Allison slipped her small fingers into the crook of Mike's arm. "I'm very glad you're traveling with us," she whispered in a honey-sweet tone. "It's so nice to be able to talk with someone. What better companion than a man of the cloth?" She lowered her blue china-doll eyes in a movement designed to attract attention.

As they moved away, Josh laughed to himself. He wondered how long Mike would be able to keep up his Father Michael act with pretty little Allison around. She was a beauty, but Josh had found himself shying away from that flirty kind of woman. He doubted she was as helpless as she acted.

Bethanie stepped up beside Josh and patted the aging roan she had been riding since dawn. Her voice was soft as she spoke to Josh without looking in his direction. "I'd like to thank you for not telling Aunt Martha about our agreement."

Josh knew it was hard for Bethanie to thank him. He studied the dark purple marks along her neck and felt anger boil in his blood. "Forget it. We have a deal. You'll help me out later when we get to the ranch. Our agreement doesn't concern anyone else." He thought for a moment, then added, "You can ride up front as scout with me if you like." She had been honest when she said she rode better than most men.

"I'd like that," Bethanie answered without smiling. Josh knew her decision was based more on her dislike of her aunt's company than on her enjoyment of his.

"If I'm to help you scout, I'd better tell you I saw an Indian a few miles back along the ridge to the west." Bethanie whispered as if her voice might alarm everyone.

"I know." Josh tightened the girth on one of the horses and tried not to notice the effect her nearness had on him. "I saw him, too. Apache, I'd guess, from his looks. He's following us. What bothers me is the son of the devil doesn't seem to care that we've spotted him. If he were alone, we would never have seen him."

"That's what I was afraid you'd say," Bethanie added as she mounted, no fear in her words.

Josh was proud to see no panic in her manner, only the cautious alertness instinctive to those who managed to stay alive in this open country. She was not like most women who jumped at the first sight of an Indian. This always bothered Josh, because most Indians were as peaceful as the white man. He laughed to himself; that

wasn't saying much in a country where they'd been fighting each other for four years. The only real threat to
Texans were the Plains tribes who had such a heritage
of freedom that they could not accept the reservations.
Should Josh and his group run into them, the Indians
would kill the men and take the women captive.

"Mount up, everyone," Josh shouted over his shoulder.
"We've got a long ride before dark."

Josh made no effort to help Martha or Bethanie, but
he noticed Mike assisted Allison into the saddle with
loving care. As they began to move out, Josh rode alongside Mike for a few minutes. They exchanged plans, then
Josh rode ahead to Bethanie's side.

Josh leaned slightly toward her as he spoke. "If there's
trouble, stay close to me."

Bethanie nodded slightly as she pushed a strand of
shiny red hair from her cheek.

Josh found it difficult to continue his line of thinking
with this beauty so near. "Should we be attacked, you
and I are going to have to ride like the wind. The Indians
will follow us, figuring we are the menfolks. Mike and
Dusty will stay with the women and take off in the other
direction." Josh smiled at her with a twinkle of mischief
in his dark brown eyes. "You think you can keep up if
we have to run for it?"

A tiny smile touched the corner of her lip. "I can keep
up."

Josh knew he was placing her in great danger, but
somehow he didn't want to leave her. With luck his plan
would never have to be implemented, and they would
ride quietly to Ben's ranch. But something told Josh, with
an Indian already following them, that luck wouldn't be
in abundance this trip.

Chapter Four

At dusk the small, mismatched band camped beneath a rambling bluff. All except Martha were too tired even for conversation, but she managed to mumble her irritation over Bethanie's presence long after the sun faded. Though Josh grew short-tempered over her cutting comments, Mike's patience seemed boundless. Josh first thought the robes must have gone to Mike's head, then decided, "Pet the cow to get to the calf" was more Mike's goal.

Josh had tried all day to talk with Bethanie, but, for the most part, his efforts were fruitless. Though her responses weren't as hostile as they were at first, she seemed to prefer silence. By the end of the day, he would have been more than satisfied if Martha had shown the same preference.

Josh paced the fringes of the firelight watching the others sleep. He stopped to adjust Dusty's blanket over the boy's shoulder. The kid had ridden well today and never complained. When they made camp, he'd fallen into an exhausted sleep at once. Josh liked the rugged, half-wild kid. The boy might never have been taught some of the social graces, but he had the intelligent eyes of an animal which had survived many winters of pursuit.

A twig snapped behind Josh, drawing him from his thoughts. He swung in one fluid motion toward the sound, sliding his Colt from its holster in silent readiness. The tiny snap might be only a frightened rabbit, or it might mean death.

Bethanie emerged from the shadows, her green eyes wide with reflected firelight. "I didn't mean to startle you," she apologized.

Josh lowered his gun back into its nest. "It's not a good idea to walk up behind someone in this country," he scolded. His words lost their sting as her beauty registered in his mind. Her hair was loose, drifting in a fiery cloud past her shoulders. Her slender frame moved gracefully, even in the old clothes she wore. She seemed unaware of her loveliness. Josh longed to touch even a curl of her hair, but knew his action would set fire to her emerald eyes. He smiled to himself, thinking that the pleasure of touching her hair as it tumbled so free might be worth her anger. Bethanie's beauty, woven together with her proud, half-frightened behavior, fascinated him. Never had a woman gotten under his skin so completely. Yet, she seemed to pay him only passing notice.

"I want to thank you," Bethanie whispered. "I was harsh to you this morning, and you've done nothing to merit my wrath." She shoved her hands into her pockets, which only served to emphasize the fullness of her breasts.

"You don't have to apologize." Josh slowly moved closer to her. "I'm a man of my word, Bethanie. I wish you could trust me."

He could see skepticism betrayed in the arch of her eyebrow, but her words were only a whisper. "If there's trouble, I want to ride with you." She hesitated. "Don't leave me here with the other women."

"With Martha, you mean?" Josh guessed the truth as he studied her and wondered if even the campfire's reflection could melt their chilling gaze.

"You're observant," Bethanie said. "Only Martha's sleep has quieted her protest of my presence."

Josh wished she would say more, but as always she was conservative with her speech. He must break the silence that was growing between them. "If we split up, Mike will join us at my brother's ranch." He tried to compliment her. "Your skill in handling a horse is amazing for such a young girl."

"I'm a full-grown woman!" Bethanie answered firmly, and turned away. "Good night."

"Bethanie," Josh whispered, wishing she would stay and talk, but knowing they both needed their sleep. "There's an extra blanket by my saddle."

"No thanks, I'm fine," Bethanie answered, her voice defiant again.

Josh frowned. He seemed to cross her even when he meant only kindness. "Now, don't get touchy. I'll use Mike's blanket when I wake him up for watch. These nights get chilly out here."

"Thanks," Bethanie said, "but I don't want any special favors. I'm fine on my own." When she glanced back at Josh, her gaze looked as cold as ice.

"I know." Josh's brows furrowed in thought. How could she think she could make it on her own? He'd been alternating between wanting to spank her and hug her all day. Never had a woman frustrated him so. Everything he tried to do for her was suspect.

Josh watched her walk back to the fire. She curled up, pulling her coat tight around her. She might appear to be a fragile beauty with hair the color of red-gold fire, but Josh decided she had more grit than most men he'd met. All day she rode beside him uncomplaining. Once he'd seen her smile at Dusty so he knew that somewhere beneath her cold, lonely manner lay a tender creature.

Bethanie filled Josh's thoughts during his watch. Just before he finished his shift, he covered the sleeping redhead with his blanket. He noticed she lay only a few feet from where he'd spread his bedroll. Maybe she wasn't as self-assured as he thought. "Wonder if she'd put up much of a fuss if I put my arm around her while she slept? Who am I kidding?" Josh laughed to himself. She'd made it more than plain she wouldn't welcome any advances. Besides, he had plenty of other problems to worry about.

"Indians!" Dusty yelled, scrambling down from the bluff at dawn. "There's Indians coming!"

Bethanie tossed the remainder of her hard breakfast roll in the fire and ran toward the horses and Josh. She had expected this cry all night, yet the fact dwarfed the fear as she felt adrenaline shoot like wildfire through her veins.

"Mount up!" Josh ordered as he slung the last saddle, his own, over his horse. Everyone jumped to his command.

Bethanie flew into her saddle, shoved her hair underneath her hat, and pulled it low over her face. She watched Mike swing Allison up, patting her hand in comfort. Her cousin's face reflected the fright Bethanie felt welling inside her.

Aunt Martha complained loudly as she clawed her way into her saddle and tried to control her mount. The sound of horses' hooves rumbled in the quiet morning air like a far-off thunderstorm.

Josh shouted orders as he mounted. "Dusty! Stay with Mike! Bethanie and I will break and ride south. Mike, stick to the trees and head straight for the ranch!"

"Right." Dusty saluted, laughing with excitement as the thunder of horses grew louder. He was a boy living the wild-wilderness dream all boys have, with no thought of death.

In a cloud of dust, a dozen Indians broke from the ridge line at full gallop.

Bethanie heard them several seconds before her eyes picked out their half-naked bodies from the brown wave. The pounding of her heart harmonized with their ear-shattering rhythm. She leaned forward in her saddle, every muscle ready.

Josh broke from the others and yelled above the drumming, "Ride, Bethanie!"

A heartbeat later, Bethanie joined his frantic pace. They rode south toward open country at breakneck speed. Bethanie molded to her horse and felt only the wind hampering her progress. An unexpected shrill scream blended with the noise around her. The cry was that of a dying animal, vastly different from the wild shouts of Indians. Bethanie glanced back over her shoulder toward the clearing as terror gripped her. She watched Martha slump in her saddle, an arrow deep in her back. Mike grabbed the reins of Martha's horse and vanished into the wooded area to the north. Bethanie saw one warrior break from the band and turn toward the woods. The rest, as Josh had predicted, were riding wildly toward them.

Bethanie pulled her hat down and kicked her horse as the Indians grew nearer. Bullets and arrows whizzed past as she plastered her body low. Her mount was fast and well rested, but she didn't know if she could outrun the half-wild ponies behind them.

A thud sounded beside her, the horrible sound of an arrow hitting its mark. Bethanie glanced toward Josh as he leaned forward slightly in the saddle. He cursed and reined his horse. She had to pull hard to stay beside him. He turned his mount behind a cluster of rocks. It wasn't much protection, but it was better than being out in the open.

"Go!" Josh yelled as he pulled his gun and began to fire at their pursuers. "I'll slow them down."

"No!" Bethanie yelled. "I'm staying with you."

Josh slid from his horse. "I'm hurt, I can't keep up with you, but you can get away. Get out of here! Now!" His face was red with anger and pain.

"No!" Bethanie bounced from her saddle and knelt beside him. "Hand me your rifle," she screamed, leaving no room for discussion.

Josh's handsome features were rigid with anger. He had no time to argue. Cursing under his breath, he turned his wrath upon the Indians. The band slowed their advance as Josh began to aim purposefully, accurately gauging and hitting his targets. The savages stopped just out of range and regrouped. Josh slammed bullets into his Colt as he fumed. Blood trickled in a scarlet stream down his left sleeve where the colorful end of an arrow lodged in his arm.

"You should've left while you had the chance." He spit out the words between gritted teeth as he pulled at the arrow snagged deep within his flesh. "You could be safely away by now."

"Leave for where? I have no idea what direction to ride," Bethanie answered. "You said I could stay with you, and stay with you I will!" She ripped his torn shirt from his arm.

Josh continued firing as she worked. Bethanie had the feeling he was taking his anger at her out on the Indians.

She knelt closer beside him. "The arrow has cut clean through the muscle." Their eyes met, and both knew what must be done.

Josh pulled his knife from his pocket and handed it to her. "Can you pull it through?"

Bethanie swallowed hard and nodded confidently. Tears spilled from her eyes as she cut the arrow off where it entered his arm. As her fist closed around the arrow shaft between his arm and the arrowhead, Josh clenched his teeth and grunted, "Pull it out fast."

Bethanie nodded as she closed her eyes and jerked. The blood-covered half arrow slid from Josh's flesh like a bone pulled away from raw meat. She slung the short, pointed stick away from her as if it were evil itself.

She pulled a handkerchief from her pocket and began wrapping his arm. "Keep firing and I'll bandage your arm. Then we can get out of here." She tried to make her voice sound as calm as her mother's always had when treating the sick.

"Are you insane? They're not going to just let us ride out. You should have kept going." Josh's words were sharp despite her soft touch on his arm.

Anger flashed in Bethanie's eyes. "I suppose you would have kept riding if I had have been hit?"

"Of course not," Josh yelled over the gunfire as the Indians began an unorganized frontal attack. "You're a woman."

"I told you, I want no special consideration!" Bethanie shouted. The attack suddenly stopped, and she found herself screaming in the silent air. Lowering her voice, she added, "I can ride and shoot as well as any man."

Josh leaned against the rock as he reloaded the rifle. "They'll be coming back in a few minutes." As he completed his task he looked up at Bethanie and added, "Don't ask me to forget you're a woman. God knows I'm trying. If you were a man I'd . . ." Josh bit back his last words. His dark brown eyes looked directly into her soul with his sudden honesty. "I've not stopped thinking of you as a woman since I first met you."

Bethanie was too angry to understand the meaning behind his last words. She leaned closer. "You'd do what if I were a man?"

Josh's words were hard. "I'd knock that chip off your shoulder." Anger melted to curiosity in his voice. "And tell me, do you hate all men, or is your venom pointed solely toward me?"

"Chip? What chip?" Bethanie finished bandaging his arm. "Just because I don't want to be handled by you doesn't mean I have a problem. All I ask is to be left alone."

"Fine," Josh answered as the Indians headed toward them with new fury. "If I'm so distasteful, why didn't you leave me?"

"I'm asking myself that very same question," Bethanie shouted as she pulled her hat lower, aware of arrows flying over their heads. "What kind of mess am I going to be in if you bleed to death and I'm left out here alone and lost?"

"Thanks for your heart-rendering concern." A smile touched the corner of Josh's mouth as he handed Bethanie his Colt to reload.

Gunfire sounded another full attack, and there was no time to talk. Bullets hammered into the rocks, sending showers of pebbles exploding in every direction. Josh instinctively drew Bethanie's head down to his chest, then began firing. Her body was stiff with fear, yet she did not pull away. She trembled suddenly in his arms, making Josh realize she was far more frightened than her brave talk had shown.

He cradled her to him as determination set his jawline. "If I make every shot count, we might just have a chance." Josh paused a moment then added, "Like it or not . . . want it or not . . . I'd protect you with my life, Bethanie."

Bethanie wanted to argue that he owed her nothing, but she was too frightened to say anything. She believed his words and found them comforting. No one in her life, except her mother, had ever considered her worth taking the time to know, much less worth dying for.

Finally the attack slackened. Josh whispered excitedly "It's over for a few minutes. They will drag off the dead and return." He brushed her shoulder lightly. "I think I may have killed the leader."

Bethanie raised her head to see the Indians circling around them like ants in the stirred-up dust. They looked unorganized and seemed to be arguing among themselves.

Josh's fingers tightened over her arm, pulling her quickly to her feet. "Now's our chance to run for it." Pitching his rifle to her, Josh grabbed her hand and ran toward the horses. The mounts were wild with fright and dancing in circles. Seconds pounded by in the dust before Bethanie and Josh could mount and break into a full gallop.

An hour raced past in a deafening thunder of hooves as Bethanie and Josh covered the land without stopping. There were no indications that the Indians had followed, but still they dared not slow their pace. They moved across the open land until a faraway patch of green grew into a cluster of trees.

Josh slowed his horse as they reached a stream and the first full cover. "We've got to rest the horses for a few minutes." He maneuvered his animal into a clearing.

"I need to clean your arm if there's time." Bethanie could see his sleeve soaked anew with blood.

"I think we lost them, but we can't spend more than a few minutes here." Josh climbed slowly from the saddle, then staggered slightly from loss of blood.

Bethanie was by his side in an instant. Her arm circled his waist as she directed him toward the shade of a tree. "You're still bleeding." Bethanie's brow wrinkled with concern. She watched him pull his hat off as though it were lead. He ran his fingers through shiny black hair damp with sweat. Tiny white lines of pain rippled out from around his mouth before vanishing into his beard. Bethanie knew he was weakening.

She helped him to a grassy spot under an ancient oak.

"Rest here. I can make a pack to stop the bleeding and prevent infection."

Josh slid down in the grass and rested his back against the tree. The world seemed hazy, and he closed his eyes to clear his brain. He could hear Bethanie rummaging through her saddlebag. In what seemed like seconds she was back at his side. Josh looked up into her face, surprised at the depth of concern he saw in her deep green eyes. She cleaned his wound and wrapped it with a tight dressing made from her extra shirt. He felt her cool palm on his head, but her words seemed far away.

Josh could hear Bethanie taking the horses down the sloping incline to the water. Seconds drifted into minutes as he relaxed against the tree. He heard a rustling of leaves and awaited her return. The morning sun was already hot in the sky, warming his face. He thought of his home and a waterfall with cool depths he often enjoyed after a long day's ride.

Josh bolted wide awake as a strong arm wrapped around his throat and the blade of a knife pressed hard against his stomach. He opened his eyes to see six huge Indians standing in a ring around him. They had approached so silently, Josh had trouble believing the men before him were real. They were Apache, and judging from their paint, all were seasoned warriors. He moved an inch toward his gun, but one buck reached swiftly to remove the Colt from its holster.

Josh's mind raced for a course of action. He'd been in tight spots before, but never one this hopeless. He figured the only reason these savages hadn't killed him immediately was that they planned a slow death for him. If he had killed their leader earlier, they'd let him die inches.

Josh's face filled with pain as he heard Betha

proaching. He hated to think what they'd do to her. A low moan rumbled in his throat as he strained at the iron-tight arms that held him.

"Bethanie," Josh screamed. "Run!" A blow from a rifle butt silenced any further command. Josh's mind splattered with red-and-white lights. Bethanie's face lingered in his last conscious thought.

Chapter Five

Bethanie raised her head when she heard her name. She'd been deep in her own thoughts. As she looked toward where she'd left Josh, the nightmare before her froze her progress. Only yards away stood six bare-chested savages. She'd seen Indians in Wild West shows and peddling wares around the streets of San Antonio, but the men before her were nothing like those she'd seen. The blood-colored paint streaked across their faces frightened her enough without the wild looks in their dark eyes. They stared at her like hungry animals stalking prey. Bethanie took a step backward, then she saw Josh's body suspended between two of them. His arm was covered with fresh blood, and a cut ran across his left cheek. His black hair curtained his forehead and hid his eyes.

"No!" Bethanie screamed as she saw a knife touching Josh's abdomen. "Let him go!" She ran with blind rage toward the men. Slamming her fist into the first painted chest, she fought with all her strength to get nearer to Josh. Another Indian grabbed her from behind and yanked her off his friend, throwing her several feet. Bethanie rolled like a doll, her hat flying off and her hair spilling around her in a frenzy of fire. She ended he roll with a thud at Josh's feet.

Bethanie glanced up to see his bleeding face. He slumped, only half conscious, between two Ind

"Josh!" Her intended scream came out as little more than a whisper. Pulling herself up by his gunbelt, she tried again. "Josh, please answer me."

As she realized he was beyond response, anger mounted within her and exploded like a fire in a leaf-packed chimney. Bethanie twirled toward the men who were holding Josh; the braves jumped away from her in caution. They stared at her as if they'd just seen the dead walk. Their savage eyes now held a touch of curiosity and fear. Bethanie was confused to the point of panic over their bewildering behavior. Were they playing with her, testing her sanity in some wild game that included backing away before they would strike and kill?

"Josh," Bethanie whispered as he crumbled to his knees beside her. "What's happening?"

Josh pulled her to him, holding her head to his chest. His fingers threaded through her hair as he fought his way back to reality. "Bethanie," he mumbled in agony.

After several minutes, Josh spoke. His words were low, forced out between clenched teeth. "I can't pick up many words . . . but it's obvious they are startled you're a woman."

The Indians' voices began to rise. Two of the strange men moved toward Bethanie. She huddled closer to Josh, too frightened to breathe. Before she could react, each brave grabbed one of her arms and began dragging her down the bluff to the wooded area near the water. She screamed in fear, kicking madly at the two men.

Even in her panic, she heard Josh yell. He was fighting wildly as he cursed his captors. As blows rained on him, Bethanie heard Josh beg them with his last words to let her go and kill him. She struggled, but iron grips dragged ·er closer to the stream.

Bethanie screamed as the men pulled her into the ·r. One held her, while the other grabbed her hair lunged her head underwater. He held her facedown a foot into the muddy stream. Bethanie's mind raced in panic as her lungs ached for air. *They're drowning me!* Her brain grew dark from lack of oxygen as her struggling stopped.

As if from far away, she felt the Indians pulling her up. They stood holding her until her breathing grew regular. Then, to her horror they dunked her again. Was this some kind of torture? They repeated the ritual over and over until her arms ached from fighting and her lungs burned for air. Each time they pulled her head up just as she began to pass out.

When Bethanie had swallowed all the water she could endure, the Indians suddenly stopped, and began dragging her back up toward Josh. She raised her head and, through dripping hair, saw Josh tied to a tree trunk. His eyes were closed and he made no movement. The men holding Bethanie loosened their grip, and she knelt beside Josh. The savages back a few feet away.

Pushing her wet, tangled red hair behind her, she asked, "Josh, are you all right?" She knew the question was ridiculous, for he was bleeding in several places, but she prayed he wasn't already dead.

Josh's dark eyes opened in surprise. "Bethanie," he whispered, "what have they done to you?"

She could see the pain and dread in his face as he waited for her answer. "Nothing," Bethanie answered, knowing he feared she'd been molested, "except try to drown me." She pulled her hair back and squeezed water from it. Her clothing was wet and clung to her slender frame, openly revealing her gender.

The savages stormed around her like angry young bulls, arguing among themselves. They seemed to have no leader. She slid closer to Josh and pushed the bloo off his cheek with her wet sleeve. She was trembli hard from cold and fright as she huddled, wishin could place his protective arms around her.

"What are they arguing about?" Bethanie whispered.

Josh shook his head and turned to listen more closely.

After several minutes, a smile touched his bruised lips. He turned to Bethanie with a look of disbelief.

"Are they going to torture us or kill us?" Bethanie whispered, tears of helplessness in her eyes.

"Neither," Josh smiled softly. "They've decided that you're a sign from the gods. None of them have ever seen red hair. They weren't trying to drown you; they were trying to get the color out of your hair."

"Well, why are they arguing?" she asked.

"One wants to scalp you. The others think it would be bad medicine." Josh smiled.

As Bethanie watched in fear, one brave pulled his knife and moved toward her. His face was serious and his savage stare never left her face. Bethanie closed her eyes as he stepped in front of her. He pulled a wet lock free from the mass and cut it.

Bethanie looked up as the Indian moved away, waving her hair like a trophy between his fingers. The others followed him into the woods. Minutes later, Bethanie heard horses thundering off. She sat frozen, trying to control her breathing. She could not believe her luck. All her life she had hated having red hair, and now it had saved her life.

"Untie me, Bethanie." Josh was thrashing, trying to pull free from his bindings.

Bethanie jumped, as if she had forgotten his presence. She quickly untied his arms, then sat back cradling her knees and drawing into herself. Over the past months she'd learned to shut out the world when unhappy. This skill did not fail her now. She was only vaguely aware of Josh moving around her. The fright of moments before passed from her body as her mind went home. Her mother was sitting in their little kitchen, which always smelled of fresh bread. She didn't think of the Indians, or Wilbur, or the future. She wasn't afraid; she was home. She closed her eyes tightly and traveled back to the childhood hidden deep in her mind.

Josh gently laid a blanket around her shoulders. "Bethanie, it's all right now. They won't be back." His voice was soft with concern. He placed his arm around her slowly, testing her reaction. When she didn't resist, he pulled her gently into a warm hug. "Bethanie, they'll not be back. Bethanie, you're safe." He mumbled over and over as he stroked her hair like a parent comforts a frightened child. "I've seen full-grown men after a battle react this way. When life is too frightening the mind needs a little rest. You were strong when you needed to be." He pulled her closer forgetting the cuts and bruises on his body and thinking only of her.

Josh's arms felt warm and safe to Bethanie as she rested her head on his shoulder. His words were a relaxing melody to her. She remembered how angry he'd been at her when she hadn't ridden away. His cry for them to kill him and let her be, still rang in her ears. As Bethanie allowed herself to come back to the present, she curled into Josh's embrace.

Josh finally pushed her gently from him. "You need to change clothes." He ran his hand over her head. "And comb that wonderful hair of yours. We were very lucky. I think once I get cleaned up, I'll be almost as good as new."

Bethanie stood up. She pulled her only other pair of pants from her saddlebag as Josh handed her his extra shirt. She smiled her thank you and looked for somewhere to change. The trees were not yet thick enough with spring foliage to offer much concealment.

Josh lifted his saddlebag over his shoulder. "You dress here where the sun's warm. I'll go down to the stream and clean up. Once I get all this blood off me I think I'll feel a great deal better." He touched the already-drying cut on his cheek. "If it hadn't been for your hair, we'd both be feeding the buzzards tonight."

As Josh moved out of sight, Bethanie slowly removed her damp shirt and camisole. She rubbed his dry shirt over her skin to remove the chill, then quickly slipped it on. She pulled her old comb out of her bag and began fighting the tangles that fell about her shoulders. Her hands were still shaking from fear. She knew it would be a long time before she forgot the sickening panic, or Josh's wild screams of protest when the Indians pulled her down toward the water. He'd fought like a wild long-horn trapped in quicksand when he'd thought the Indians were going to hurt her.

When Josh returned, Bethanie felt a warmth for him unlike anything she'd felt for anyone except her mother. As she watched him coming nearer, Bethanie knew she cared for this man she'd known only a few days. She felt a closeness between them that must only happen between those who share a brush with death. He seemed suddenly shy around her and for once couldn't seem to find anything to say. She motioned for him to sit on a log so she could examine the short gash in his scalp.

Josh's dark eyes studied her movements as she gingerly touched his scalp with a towel. "I think I'll live," he said lightly when he noticed her worried face. "If I died easy I'd have been gone a hundred times before . . ." His words lodged in his throat as he remembered her mother touching him with the same gentleness years ago.

"Josh . . ." Bethanie became aware of his nearness. "I want to thank you . . ."

"For nearly getting you killed?" Josh interrupted her. "You may regret leaving San Antonio."

Bethanie knelt beside him, resting her hand on his knee. "I'll never regret leaving San Antonio, Josh, no matter what happens."

Josh risked touching her damp hair. "You don't have

to say more. I think I can figure it out for myself . . . the problem you had there."

Bethanie looked up and smiled. "Thanks for understanding and for making me feel safe. I believe you'd have given your life for me today. No one's ever cared that much about me before."

"Why not?" Josh answered as he continued to stroke her hair. "I owe it to you twice now."

Bethanie cocked her head sideways. "I don't understand."

"Remember years ago during the first months of the war? You and your mother saved my life. I was half crazy with fever from a head wound and lack of water. Your mother doctored me and you gave me a drink." His voice was low and he could not stop his hand from moving to her face. Tenderly, he ran his fingers along her jawline. To his amazement, Bethanie turned her chin into his palm.

"You were one of the Rebel soldiers?"

"I remember you asked me where I was from and then told me you had an uncle and aunt in San Antonio. Later, after I was free, I wished a hundred times I'd asked their names."

Bethanie raised to her knees and pushed his hair back from his forehead. "We treated many men on both sides."

She leaned closer to examine the thin line high on his forehead that told of a long ago healed head wound. Her breasts brushed lightly against Josh's shoulder as she moved, unaware of the effect her action was having upon him.

Bethanie rocked back on her heels. "I remember many soldiers who were covered with dirt and blood." She smiled. "Much like you were a few minutes ago."

"I remember a beautiful girl." Josh's voice was thick as every sense came alive within him. She was so near.

He could smell her soft fragrance and feel her light, timid touch as her hand rested on his leg. Suddenly, he could bear the closeness of her no longer. "Bethanie," he whispered as he moved toward her. "Bethanie." His lips touched hers as he repeated her name.

Bethanie opened her mouth as if to protest. Her lips trembled beneath his touch as his hand drew her closer to him.

"Never have I wanted to hold anyone as much as I want to hold you," Josh whispered. "Don't pull away from me, Bethanie."

Josh watched her eyes carefully, reading the expressions blended in the beautiful green depths. Her surprise evaporated into curiosity as he tenderly traced the outline of her mouth with his fingertips. Slowly, he slid off the log to kneel beside her, their bodies lightly pressing together as his lips touched hers.

Josh felt his kiss ignite a fire within her. Its flames spread from her satiny lips to each part of her flesh resting so invitingly against him. Shyly, she raised her hand to his chest. He felt her warm fingers brush over his shirt in a halfhearted effort to push him away. His muscular body didn't obey her light pressure and she continued moving her hand as though she found his warmth beneath her fingers thrilling.

"You've driving me mad with your touch, Bethanie," Josh whispered just before his tongue divided her lips and tenderly played with her mouth.

They swayed as dancers to the music of explosive feelings that were coursing within them. Josh's arm encircled her waist to steady her and pull her closer to him. His body pressed against her from his thighs to his shoulders and still he felt the burning desire to be nearer.

When finally Josh was able to pull his mouth away, Bethanie rested her head on his shoulder. He could feel even the slight movement of her breathing. He moved his face into the velvet of her hair and whispered, "I've wanted to hold you since I first saw you in the hotel."

For a long moment they clung to each other, the brush with death lingering in their thoughts. Josh realized he'd never felt more alive than at this moment. His senses engulfed him into endless folds of new sensations. The air smelled fresh and seasoned with spring. He could feel the warm sun against his back and Bethanie against his chest. Her heart pounded next to his own, and her soft breath against his neck warmed like a southern breeze.

"Bethanie," Josh whispered. "Don't be afraid of me. You must believe I'd never hurt you."

The dam that had been bottled up for months in Bethanie suddenly broke. Gulping for air, she cried her pain, "Josh, hold me. Hold me."

Josh touched her hair and urged, "What is it, Bethanie?"

Bethanie nodded as if silently agreeing to confide in him. "These past few days seem like one long nightmare. First Uncle Wilbur's assault, then the endless ride yesterday, and now almost being killed by Indians." She clung to him tightly as tears rolled freely down her cheeks. Josh smiled as he kissed her wet face and pulled her to him. "Trust me, Bethanie. Let me into that quiet world you've built."

"I must," she whispered, her fingers clutching his shirt as if she were suddenly afraid of being alone. "Or I'll go mad." Her sob tore at Josh's heart. "I need someone. I can't be alone any longer. Just for a few minutes let me need you."

Josh had never been asked such a question. "I'll be here and my shoulder can withstand a flood of tears, so go ahead and cry." Josh gently lowered himself into a sitting position, pulling Bethanie with him. He sat facing her with his leg bent to support her back.

As Bethanie cried out her pain and fear, Josh felt a

depth of tenderness for her he'd never felt for a woman. He loved the way she'd been brave in the face of danger. He loved the strength he'd seen in her when she'd faced Martha's wrath, and the silent courage she'd shown at leaving the hotel. But most of all, he loved the touching way she needed him. He kissed her cheek as she cried and realized his need for her was no less than hers was for him.

When Bethanie finally stopped crying, she wiped her eyes and mumbled an apology for her display of emotions.

"Wait," Josh held both her shoulders. "I . . ." he tried to put his thoughts into words. "I feel like a young pup." He laughed. As he looked at her beauty, a smoldering fire from within warmed his face. "This is what I want to say." He drew her to him, pulling her body hard into the wall of his chest. The honesty of his action spoke more than words ever could.

As his lips found hers, this time there was passion burning in his kiss. Bethanie did not withdraw. His body wouldn't have allowed it, even if she'd wanted to retreat. She wrapped her arms about his neck and moved even closer to him. He could feel her need for him rushing to meet his own longing. She was no longer holding back, but accepting all he offered and asking for more.

Josh's kiss grew bolder as his hands moved over her. He smothered Bethanie's gasp as his fingers slid up under her shirt. He spread his hand over her flesh and felt her tremble in his arms. Yet, she didn't fight, but met his kisses with a hunger of her own.

Josh's fingers moved in waves along her slender back as he showered her forehead with warm kisses. His mouth returned to her hungry lips. Her zeal surprised him as Bethanie pulled his mouth once more to her lips.

The knowledge that she was enjoying his embrace as much as he boiled in his blood. While his tongue traced her lips, Josh moved his hand up to cup one of her breasts. This time it was Bethanie who smothered Josh's gasp as he felt the fullness of her.

Bethanie laughed at his shock. He hadn't guessed she would be so well developed. His warm hands explored her flesh with tenderness and awe. Bethanie leaned back against his leg, enjoying with sheer pleasure as a new ecstasy filled her body and soul. She wanted Josh to see the joy in her face as he touched her beneath the loose shirt she wore.

Josh began at her neck and moved his mouth slowly down. His kisses heated her skin, already warmed by the hot sun overhead. Josh moved to her ear and whispered, "God, you taste wonderful."

Reaching the buttons of her shirt, he paused before returning to her ear. Circling his open palm lazily over her nipple he urged, "Unbutton your shirt, Bethanie. Let me see what I hold." His mouth branded ownership across her hot cheek.

Bethanie suddenly pushed Josh from her and leaned away from him. His hand cupped her breast as pain touched his warm brown eyes. "I can't let you go," he answered, fearing her withdrawal. His words were half cry, half command.

She smiled at his contracted face. They were facing each other as they sat on the ground only inches apart, and she had to fight the instinct to return to his arms. His hand slid from her breast, and his face saddened in thinking he had gone too far. Slowly, deliberately, she raised her fingers to the top button of her shirt. She watched his face change seasons with each button's undoing. Bethanie leaned against his leg and threw her head back, her red hair cascading over his knee. The warm sun touched her face as his hand slowly spread her shirt apart. She heard his sharp intake of breath as one mound was exposed. Smiling to herself, Bethanie wondered if his view gave him nearly the pleasure his hands gave her. She opened her eyes as his head lowered between her breasts. The whiskers of his beard brushed her pink tips. Bethanie gasped in surprise as Josh's mouth covered one nipple.

Bethanie let her arms fall to her sides as she sat powerless to do more than gently sway to the magic of his mouth and hands on her body. He returned again and again to part her lips with his fire. She answered his kiss and tried to press close to him, but repeatedly he pushed her away so his hands could roam freely over her as he whispered wonder in her ear.

Josh finally wrapped his arms tightly around her and held her to him. "Bethanie, Bethanie," he whispered in a low voice thick with need. "I want you more than life itself. I never thought it possible to hunger for a woman so. I don't want to frighten you, but I cannot let you go."

"I know," Bethanie answered. "I love the way you touch me. I've never been touched before."

"You're a virgin?" Josh stated more to himself than Bethanie. "I should've realized. How could I have thought otherwise?" He hadn't believed the names Martha called Bethanie, yet it never occurred to him that a woman so beautiful who had reached twenty would be untouched. "No man has been with you?" he whispered.

"Of course not," Bethanie answered with a touch of anger mixed with her confusion over his reaction. "Except for Wilbur's pawing the night before we left, I've never been touched by a man." She ran her hand slowly over his chest.

Josh tried to ignore her touch. Could it be true she had no idea how her fingers stirred his blood? He kissed her palm. "Bethanie, I never thought I'd be saying this to a woman, but we've got to slow down." He stroked her hair lovingly. "What I feel for you is stronger than just passion. I've never taken a virgin, and I will not take you now."

Anger flooded Bethanie's brain as fire flushed her cheeks. "What makes you think it's all your decision? I've got a mind of my own. Besides, my virginity is mine to give, not yours to take." She pulled her shirt together. "But don't let me challenge your warped code of what's right."

Bethanie stood and stormed toward her horse. Josh followed. He raked his fingers through the dark thickness of his hair. "Bethanie, I don't understand your anger. You're mad because I won't take you here in the grass?"

Bethanie's hair swung around her in a whirlwind as she turned from him. "I'm angry because you think you could ever take me, period! I have something to say about it. I've lived all my life without a man around. I think I can continue the pattern without any problem."

Josh followed her to her horse. "Bethanie, listen to me." He grabbed her arm and swung her to face him. "I live by a set of rules. One just happens to be leaving innocent girls untouched."

"Fine." Bethanie jerked her arm free. "Then, don't touch me."

Josh slapped his hat against his leg in frustration. Why couldn't she understand that sometimes a man's code is all he has to live by in this wild country? He bit his tongue deciding not to say more now. The fire within her seemed to blend as mightily with anger as with passion, and he didn't want to fight with her. He took a long breath and managed to keep his voice calm as he said, "We'll talk later. Right now we'd better double back and find the others."

They mounted their horses in strained silence and retraced their path. Though Josh seemed occupied with watching for Indians, Bethanie's thoughts set judgment on her recent actions. Being in Josh's arms had felt more wonderful than she'd ever dreamed, but had she given herself too quickly over to her feelings. All her life she'd been careful to hide emotions of pain; now she seemed to have no bars on her feelings of love. Her lack of experience with men left her confused and frustrated, but she finally came to the conclusion Josh would be worth the effort to understand. She was angry at him for setting the law down for them both, but she respected him for his action. She knew very little about him really, but he was a man worth knowing. And worth loving.

Chapter Six

The dying March sun blinked between an aging line of elms as Bethanie and Josh discovered their hastily abandoned campsite. It seemed years to Bethanie since she'd mounted at dawn to Josh's shouting and heard the thunder of horses coming up the ridge. Had it only been this morning when she'd heard Martha's scream of death? All lay quiet now; nature in its kindness had brushed over the frantic scene with a tranquil breeze. She felt as if she were much older than she'd been when she left this camp. Having lived through the fear of attack somehow lessened the nightmare. Life seemed a series of unforgettable minutes strung together with the thread of time. Bethanie knew she'd lived a few hours today which would endure forever in her mind.

She watched Josh follow a set of tracks which led in the direction of the woods. His head was down, his hat low, shading his eyes. She wanted to catch his glance, but Josh was concentrating on his task. Bethanie could still feel his touch on her body . . . his lips on her mouth. He'd awakened a feeling in her she hadn't even known existed. She studied his profile with alternating waves of anger and longing. He was a handsome man, with his dark hair and brown eyes. The beard that framed his strong jawline was thick and trimmed short. She wondered how many other women he'd held so tenderly. This

new way of touching which he'd taught her was both
thrilling and frightening.

They rode a mile in silence before Josh reined up,
swung from his saddle, and knelt to study the ground
more closely. As he stood and paced slowly, leaves crackled noisily, crying a crumbling death in the silent spring
air. He read signs Bethanie failed to see or understand.
"They stopped here," he stated, his voice sounded tired
and worried.

"Why?" Bethanie asked. She saw only new green life
shooting out from underneath the golden foliage of winter.

Josh walked in a circle ignoring her question. He
kicked at the ground, then headed toward a cluster of
trees hovering around a large, fallen tree trunk. Slowly,
he moved to the old log bordered by a white skirt of
rocks. He removed several of the stones and dug a few
handfuls of dirt out from under the log. As Bethanie
watched with interest, he replaced the rocks and stood
to face her. His voice was sober as he spoke, but his
eyes were filled with kindness. "They stopped here to
bury your aunt."

Bethanie scrambled off her horse and ran toward Josh
as he continued. "I was afraid she was dead when I heard
her scream. It's a wonder she made it this far from camp.
Mike knew leading a horse would slow him down. He
buried her under this log to keep animals from getting
to her. We can bring some men back to get the body
later, if your uncle wishes."

Bethanie knelt beside the rotting log. She pulled wild
honeysuckle vines over the decaying wood, freshening
the air with their sweet smell and blanketing her aunt's
grave. "Are you sure it's Martha's grave?" Bethanie
asked in disbelief, not hearing all Josh was saying.

"Yes," he answered the question that needed no answer. She'd heard Martha's cry and seen the arrow lodged

deep within her aunt's back, yet still her mind needed to question.

Bethanie pulled off her hat and shook her head, allowing her still-damp hair to blow freely for a moment. Aunt Martha was a cruel woman, but this seemed a harsh way to die. Even with her cold heart, Martha warranted more than an unmarked grave in the middle of the wild country. She'd never shown Bethanie anything but contempt, yet Bethanie was saddened by her death. Now, Bethanie realized, Allison was her only blood kin. Her only family. She reached across the log and touched the tiny flowers of the wild honeysuckle vine as gently as one might brush the covers over a sleeping child. Death had claimed another as it had claimed so many of those in Bethanie's life.

Josh moved behind her and placed a hand on her slender shoulder. "It had to be done, Bethanie. If they'd stopped longer, they'd all have died."

"I know," Bethanie answered, yet his reasoning did little to lift her spirits. She stood and dusted her denims.

As Josh moved nearer, Bethanie turned and walked back to her horse, impatient to be gone from this place. He nodded, not resenting her action, but accepting it. "I know you well enough by now to know that you don't plan on talking about it." He took a long breath. "I don't think I've ever seen a woman with less to say." He was talking more to himself than to her. "I'd like to hold you until the woman I saw this afternoon returns, but you'd pull a mask over yourself as thick as night."

Bethanie didn't want to hear any more. She wanted to change the subject away from both her aunt and this afternoon. "Where do we go from here?" She stepped gracefully into the stirrup.

Josh seemed to understand her question, yet his eyes studied the slim curve of her back as he spoke. "This is as far as we can track the others. From this point on,

Mike is making sure to cover his trail. See the brush marks?" He pointed to the tiny crisscross marks on the ground. "My guess is, they led the horses down to the stream and rode northwest. We'll never be able to follow them, but we can travel faster. If we go north, we'll be harder for any Indians to follow. We'll reach the ranch no more than a day after Mike."

"I wish I knew if Allison was all right," Bethanie wondered aloud, searching the trees to the north, half hoping her tiny blond cousin would appear. She felt a sudden closeness to Allison in knowing she was the last of her blood kin.

"She must be all right. Three horses left this clearing. Dusty will help Mike with Allison. She's no horsewoman, but the boy's a survivor. I knew it the minute I saw him. He reminds me of my brother years ago before the accident. Ben was as wild as the Texas wind and I, being five years younger, could never keep up." Josh laughed to himself, remembering some long-ago day. "We've got some hard riding before sundown, so let's go."

Bethanie urged her tired mount into action. She wondered what Josh meant about an accident, but there was no time to talk as they rode away from the unmarked grave of her aunt.

Josh rode hard, and by nightfall every bone in Bethanie's body ached in fatigue. The country was growing flatter with longer patches of land between clusters of trees. She rubbed her neck, tired of searching the ground for rabbit holes that might cripple her mount. They silently watered the horses before Bethanie curled up on the ground, too exhausted to eat the piece of dried jerky Josh handed her. She was only vaguely aware of Josh building a small fire. For once she slept until dawn without disturbing dreams.

As the sun brushed the morning, Bethanie rolled to her side. The air chilled her cheek as a warm arm moved across her waist. She came fully awake, the knowledge that Josh lay beside her registering in her sleep-numbed brain.

She shoved away and scrambled to her feet, waking Josh with her haste. He opened sleepy brown eyes and smiled up at her. He looked younger with his hair out of order and worry lines gone from his forehead.

"Mornin', beautiful." Josh raised to one elbow, his alert eyes growing awake to danger as he watched Bethanie pacing before him.

She stormed suddenly at her unsuspecting companion. "Is there not enough room in this vast land? Must you sleep on top of me?"

Josh rose and began pulling his boots on. "Do you always wake in such a grand mood?" he questioned, raising an eyebrow in half laughter, half curiosity.

Bethanie clenched her fists. "Only when I find myself pawed in my sleep." Her voice rose with each word, sending nearby birds fluttering from their nesting places.

Josh was completely awake now and angry at her accusation. "I wasn't pawing you. I was trying to keep you warm." He rolled his blanket hastily into a lopsided tube.

Bethanie's green eyes flashed fire at him before she turned her back. She kicked at the pile of ashes sending the remains of last night's campfire flying. When she turned back, Josh was busy saddling the horses. She knew he was right, and she regretted her outburst. Bethanie frowned, deciding she must be losing her mind. Where was the calm girl who only a few nights ago had said she needed no one? Where was her mother's endless strength that Bethanie always modeled her behavior after?

Bethanie neared Josh as he placed the saddle on her horse. "I'm sorry," she said to his back.

"What?" Still angry, Josh turned to face her.

"I'm sorry," Bethanie repeated. "If I had a bed, I'd climb back in and get up on the other side."

Josh couldn't keep a smile from tugging at the corners of his mouth. "Maybe we're both a little touchy. I'm not worth much without coffee and Mike has the pot in his supplies." Without hesitation he opened his arms, welcoming her. Bethanie stepped into his embrace as an act of truce. He held her tightly for a moment, then smiled down at her. "We'd better ride. With luck, we'll reach the ranch late tonight." Brushing back a strand of hair, he kissed her lightly on the forehead.

They mounted the horses in silence. Josh rode hard and fast as the sun moved across the endless sky. He only stopped to water the horses and hand Bethanie a few bites of food. By midafternoon, gloomy clouds bubbled over the sky, promising rain and cooling the air.

As the day passed, Bethanie's mood blended with the cloudy sky above. Though she rode beside Josh without comment, questions rumbled in her mind as the sound of faraway thunder rumbled in her ears. Soon they would be at his brother's ranch. Would he leave her there? Would she ever see him again? If she did see him, eventually she'd have to tell him about her parents, about how her mother and father never married. How Aunt Martha's names for her were true, she was a child without a father. Josh didn't seem the type who would judge her for her parents, but neither had others over the years. She knew firsthand how strong he was on principles. He said he had a set of rules he lived by. Maybe one of those rules was not getting involved with illegitimate offspring. Bethanie didn't even have a last name. Her mother had told her once that when the Shakers took her father in as a baby they gave him only one name, Mariah. So he wouldn't have had a last name to give Bethanie even if he had seen fit to marry her mother. She used Lane simply because her mother had worked on a small ranch called Willow Lane.

As Bethanie rode, she remembered her first year of school when friends pulled away, one by one, because their parents didn't want them around a child without a father. She'd been so withdrawn and lonely, her mother had finally taken her out of school. She completed her education at home with a mail-order tutor. No matter where her mother worked as a cook, part of her agreement always included the money for the tutor and books. Bethanie didn't mind not going to school, for she loved doing her lessons in the kitchen while her mother worked. The thought of Josh staring at her with contempt as so many others had chilled Bethanie even more than the northern wind sweeping over the land.

Rain began splattering on them in huge droplets by late afternoon. Josh pulled his horse up a rocky area that seemed to lead in no direction. The low, rocky hills spread over a small area like hastily abandoned toys of a giant child. The rocks were dark with rain and looked cold and unwelcoming.

"This storm's about to break," Josh shouted above the violent thunder. "I remember a cave around here somewhere. We're only a few hours' ride from the ranch, but we'll never make it in the downpour that's fixing to hit." He dismounted and led his horse into a maze of stone canals.

They walked to a small boxed-in area which would offer the horses some shelter from the storm. Josh pulled the saddle off his horse and staked the tired animal. "This rock is high enough to keep the horse out of danger from flash floods. I've seen these sudden spring storms build a six-foot river in an hour that'd be swift enough to sweep a horse down."

Bethanie followed Josh's actions with less ease. The shadows from the rocks around covered them, giving the area a dark, brooding atmosphere. Her horse was skittish, seemingly afraid of the shadows.

"The cave's just a few yards this way," Josh yelled as he slung his saddle over his shoulder. "Leave your saddle and I'll come back for it."

"I can carry it," Bethanie stated with more energy than she felt. She noticed his eyebrow raised in frustration, but he made no comment. She would do her part whether he approved or not. Bethanie didn't want anyone to think of her as helpless ever again.

They climbed slippery rocks for several feet until Josh suddenly disappeared into a black hole between two boulders. Bethanie followed only a step, then froze, afraid to move farther into the blackness that surrounded her like a thin, musty soup. She could hear Josh rummaging in his gear a few feet away. A match struck and an instant later a candle's golden glow lit the tiny cave.

"I only have this stub of a candle, but it'll last till we get bedded down." Josh placed the candle on a jagged rock table. "There's not much room in here, but you can spread the blanket there." He pointed to the back side of the cave. "I'll spread out here by the entrance."

"All right." Bethanie shivered; she'd rather not be by the front, anyway. No telling what might crawl in out of the storm. The width of the cave was little more than that of a double bed, but at least it was dry.

As she laid down the blanket, Bethanie heard the clouds release their promised wrath. The thunder seemed to echo off the walls of the cavern, giving her an eerie feeling. Their small haven between these rocks had been made by some ancient tumbling of the earth, and its timeless darkness seemed to resent the guests. Bethanie was too tired to let the place spook her. She crumbled slowly down under the blanket and pulled it tightly around her.

She relaxed, watching Josh's shadowy form in the candlelight. He stripped off his coat and gun. As he bent to place them beside the candle, Bethanie studied the trim, muscular line of his body. His raindrop-spotted clothes molded to him like a second skin. She felt an ache within her to hold him, a longing to feel his arms warming her. Frustrated, she turned her back to him. Yet, as she listened to his movements, she couldn't turn him from her mind.

After several minutes, Josh blew out the candle and lay down only a few inches away from her. "Bethanie," he whispered, "are you awake?"

Bethanie didn't move or speak. She was afraid of what he was going to say. She wanted to sleep and not think about all that had happened between them. Or of how it might end.

"I need to say this, whether you listen or not," Josh stated with determination. "Since I first saw you at the hotel, I've been attracted to you. I can see your movements in my mind's eye as clearly as if they were before me in bright daylight. But it's not just your body I'm mesmerized by." His unexpected laughter filled the tiny space. "Though I must admit it holds a few beautiful surprises. But, I'm attracted to you . . . your high, strong spirit, and the fight I see in your eyes. I've watched you face danger with bravery, and hardship with uncomplaining strength. Yet I've seen you be kind and patient with Dusty and defiant with Martha." He was silent for a long moment, then added, "You're a fascinating woman."

Josh paused and Bethanie felt tears flood her eyes. He continued complimenting her in his warm voice, caressing her with his words. She turned silently toward him in the total darkness.

Josh's tone was low as he hesitated slightly. "Bethanie . . . I guess what I'm trying to say is, I'm in love with you." He laughed nervously. "I can't explain it; but one thing I swear, I've never loved anyone in my life before. I always thought when it happened there'd be a time when I wasn't sure, when I'd have to think about how I felt. But, Bethanie, what I feel for you is fact, and time eternal will never alter it."

Bethanie reached toward him in the darkness. An instant after she touched his shoulder, he was pulling her to him. He encircled her in his strong arms as if fearing he might lose her. His hold was so tight, Bethanie could barely breathe. She ran her fingers into his thick hair and drew his face close to her.

"Josh," she whispered as his lips covered her mouth. There was no need to talk, for they both felt the other's tender emotions as they molded together. "Josh, I feel the same as you, but I'm afraid."

"Afraid of me?" Josh whispered.

"No, afraid you will turn away from me." Bethanie's voice was soft, her words blending with the splattering outside.

"Never," he laughed. "Never . . ." His words trailed away as his mouth once again found her lips. As his kiss deepened, Josh gently began to move his hands over her damp clothes. He trembled slightly as his fingers slid into her shirt, touching the warm softness of her flesh. He pulled an inch away and whispered into her hair. "I've tried all day to push the feel of you from my mind. To forget the sweet taste of your lips and body. I've raged war with my feelings and almost lost my sanity. I think I'm addicted to you."

Bethanie tingled with a warmth flushing her skin and burning her cheeks. Josh was so sure he'd never turn away from her, how could she doubt his word? The fire from her cheeks spread through her limbs and centered on each spot Josh touched. She found him even more exciting under cover of night. Without sight, her other senses sharpened to aid her. Timidly, she placed her hands on his chest and struggled with his shirt buttons. As his shirt opened to her efforts, she pressed her fingers over his muscular chest. Her hands drifted over his shoulders and touched his injured arm.

Josh tightened in pain and Bethanie stopped. "Did I hurt you?" she whispered.

"No," Josh laughed. "Your touch could never bring me anything but pleasure."

Timidly she began to move her fingers over his flesh, carefully avoiding his bandaged arm. Bethanie was so fascinated with her exploration, she hardly noticed Josh was skillfully unbuttoning her shirt and pants. His palm slid unhampered from her shoulder to her flat stomach. He laughed with joy as his hands moved up and down her body. Each stroke of his fingers descended deeper into her denims, until he reached the curly hair covering her womanhood.

As Josh moved his fingers over her abdomen and lower, Bethanie let out a low moan and rolled to her back, allowing him more freedom to explore. He moved above her, pulling her clothes free from her hips. Slowly, lovingly, he began to show her of his love, touching her as softly as snow one moment, then pulling her so near the next second that she could hardly breathe. He'd move above her as his fingers caressed each curve of her flesh and his mouth lovingly tasted each hollow and mound. She moved her head from side to side in sheer pleasure as rapture flooded her brain. He stroked and tugged at her nipples until they were pointed and begging for more attention. Bethanie couldn't have directed him, but she responded with new joy to each touch. His breathing grew more rapid, yet his touch was unhurried, almost lazy as he explored. His fingers would slide over her most private parts, then brush away, only to return with slightly more pressure the next time.

Josh shifted to his side and lay close to her as his hand played with the inside of her thigh. "You don't talk much for a woman," he whispered, playfully kissing her ear.

"But your body tells me a great deal." As he spoke he moved his fingers between her legs to the warm mound covered with hair.

Bethanie moved to his rhythm. She wasn't afraid or ashamed. To her surprise, she knew all that was happening was right for her. In a few hours they would be at his brother's ranch, and she had no idea which way her life would turn, but she'd have tonight. Her first taste of love would not be rape from a drunken uncle, but the gentle paradise of Josh's arms.

Josh moved his hand up suddenly to cup her breast. His words reflected his pain, as if he were being tortured. "Why don't you stop me, Bethanie?"

"Do you want me to stop you?" Bethanie whispered in confusion. How could he touch her so lovingly and want her to stop him?

His voice was low, the words tearing from him. "I'll not take a virgin. I must not. You don't belong to me." He removed his hand. "I love you, and the feel of you is opium to my brain, but I will not."

Bethanie heard the sadness in his words and the cold pain of his withdrawal from her side. He was an honorable man and wouldn't go against the set of rules that forged his behavior. The air seemed suffocatingly thick as they lay in total darkness, listening to each other breathe.

Bethanie raised to one elbow. "Do you want me, Joshua?" she asked in her brief, frank way.

"More than anything," Josh answered. "But . . ."

Before he could finish, Bethanie rolled the inches between them. Her breasts pressed against his bare chest. "There is no more to be said. I am yours," she whispered, knowing she meant for a lifetime, and not just for a night.

Josh groaned in a blending of pain and pleasure as he pulled her closer. "I can't fight myself and you, too. Be mine, then, Bethanie, for tonight and forever."

Bethanie pushed her fears of the future aside and gave herself totally to this man. He had spoken her very thoughts, and she knew they were meant for each other. Tomorrow would be time enough to talk of her past. Tomorrow.

Chapter Seven

Gray dawn filtered into the cave in varying hues of smoky light. Tiny specks of dust danced in the humid sunbeams, forming a lacy, transparent curtain across the opening. Bethanie stretched, allowing her mind to drift back to the night hours. Josh had made love to her with a passion and caring unlike anything she imagined could exist on this earth. In the vibrating peaks and quiet, holding valleys, she found a world of fathomless wonder, a place of belonging she'd never known before. When he had finally moved inside her, Bethanie knew she'd love this man all her life. They became one in spirit as well as in flesh. Afterward, in the lethargic motions of returning to earth, he'd held her close and they'd listened to the music of the rain outside.

As Bethanie pulled the blanket from around her face, she realized Josh's warmth was no longer beside her. Panic filled her, disturbing her tranquility with lightning force. Could he have left and encountered trouble? She scrambled into her scattered clothes. The borrowed cotton shirt fought briefly with her frantic fingers. Thoughts of Josh being attacked by stalking Indians or wild animals filled her mind as she pulled her pants over her hips. What if he'd heard some noise and left to investigate without waking her? Worse, Bethanie thought with fearful pride, what if he'd just left her as her father had, without any good-bye? With no thought of caution, Bethanie darted from the cave.

The rocks formed wet, slippery walls on either side of her as she maneuvered down the stone trail in the direction where they'd tied the horses. The morning was blindingly white. A lone vulture circled a quarter mile to her left, crossing the sun with each trip. As she rounded the curve where the animals had been tethered, she slipped and tumbled into the opening.

Pulling her tangled hair from her eyes, Bethanie saw Josh standing between the horses. His laughter rattled the crystal-clear morning and danced across the stony earth, newly washed with rain. He hurried toward her, smiling. His hat was propped back, allowing the sun to touch his face.

"Morning." Josh's eyes warmed to a hickory brown as his gaze traveled over her possessively. "A man could get drunk with one look at you, woman. But we need to work on your entrances." He dropped the reins, forgetting his task completely. "Come here," he whispered, pulling her to her feet. "Let me see if you broke any bones in that tumble."

Bethanie laughed with excitement and relief. "I'm fine, really." She was foolish to think Josh would leave her. Last night they had shared dreams and plans enough to last a lifetime.

Josh kissed her nose as his hand moved tenderly down her back. "You look great in the morning." His eyes turned a smoky brown. "But you felt magnificent in the darkness of the cave." His voice grew husky with remembrance. "I was blinded more from the want of you than the night. I only regret I couldn't see you." He pushed her hair back from her eyes. "What about you? Any regrets?"

Bethanie shook her head. She was unable to express how last night had been the most wonderful night of her life. Even now, as she stood looking up into his laughing dark eyes, she warmed to the memory of his touch.

Josh broke into her thoughts. "I'll have to get used to a quiet woman." He kissed her once more, then pulled her toward the horses. "I can't wait for you to see the ranch. My brother Ben and I started it before the war and he ran it while I was away. I've never thought of settling down . . . until lately." He winked as he said the last words.

Josh continued to talk about the ranch and his brother while they ate the last few strips of jerky. "Ben couldn't fight." His tone grew sad. "I guess I'd better tell you before we reach the ranch. He had an accident when he was seventeen, the spring before Dad died. Ben walked in on a bank robbery. He jumped on his horse to go after one of the robbers. A stray shot hit his horse and Ben took a bad fall. Dad never allowed Ben to feel sorry for himself or any of us to pamper him. He made Ben do everything alone from the first." Josh swung into the saddle and pulled his hat tight. "You'll understand when you meet him later today. We'd better ride. We're getting a late start."

Bethanie climbed into the saddle. "I'm sorry, I overslept."

"You didn't get much rest last night," Josh laughed. He looked younger and happier than he had yesterday. The bruise over his cheek showed as a reminder of the Indian fight, but the light of his eyes spoke of last night's loving.

Josh turned to glance in the direction of the cave. "I hate to leave this place. I'll never forget it." He reached to touch Bethanie's hand. "I don't want to hurry you, but I love you and plan on spending years telling you so."

Bethanie's cheeks reddened. In a few hours her life had taken a wide turn. As she rode beside Josh, she thought how bright her future looked. It was like a fairy tale almost too wonderful to be true.

Josh led Bethanie across open country at a pace meant only for the sturdy. They saw no other humans, only occasional burned dugouts which loomed as ghostly reminders of battles fought and lost. "We're riding the border of the frontier now, the edge of civilization," Josh said more to himself than to her. He seemed to need the reassurance of conversation as they neared the charred hulls of homes.

"Before the war, my uncle's family settled here. He had been with Sam Houston at San Jacinto when Santa Anna was captured. After Texas gained independence, my aunt and uncle were one of the many families who pushed ranching into this Indian country." He seemed unable to tear his eyes from one skeleton of a home. Bethanie didn't have to ask what had happened in this spot years ago.

"Did anyone survive?" She moved closer to him, wishing she could reach out and hold him.

Josh shook his head. "They were the last of my kin, except for Ben. In the early days a scant line of Federal forts offered them some protection. But with Texas's secession the Federal troops were pulled out, and the ranches shrank back like withered hands of an old man. We tried to combat the Indians on our own, as Governor Lubbock helped organize the Texas Rangers. We had some success, but the land was too vast for a tiny army of volunteers to cover."

Josh found talking as comfortable as Bethanie found silence. "Economically, Texas suffered less than any other Confederate state due to the war. Yet, last year when it ended, folks estimated cattle outnumbered people six to one. Our ranch lies northeast of San Antonio along this frontier edge. But we've taken care not to be caught off guard. Ben swears what happened to my uncle's family will never happen to the Weston Ranch. You should be safe once we reach there."

Bethanie smiled. "I'll be with you."

Josh winked, the sadness leaving his face. "You bet. Between the two of us, we're an unbeatable team." He kicked his horse into a swift pace, and Bethanie joined him.

The sun marked late afternoon as the two weary travelers climbed a ridge and caught sight of the Weston Ranch. Bethanie was shocked at the size of the main house. In a country where most ranches were little more than two room dugouts, this large one-story home looked enormous. The main buildings were nestled beneath a jagged rock formation protecting them from the north wind. Nature's high stone wall also provided a natural defense on three sides from Indian attack. This was why Josh was so sure the Weston Ranch was safe. About fifty feet from the main house stood the bunkhouse designed with a long porch running its length. A corral and large barn lay just to the left of the bunkhouse. Ancient cottonwood trees backed the buildings as if hugging them close in the protective nest of the cliffs above.

"There she is." Josh pointed proudly toward the ranch. "Look over behind the house. See those trees? Wait'll you see the hidden falls over by the cliff's edge. The only way to get there is a winding path from the back of the main house." As he spoke, they heard the faraway clang of a dinner bell. "Come on!" he shouted. "They've spotted us. I'll race you in."

They both laughed like children racing the tardy bell and kicked their horses into action. Bethanie loved the feel of the wind as she rode. She had dearly missed riding during these past six months while in San Antonio. She jerked her hat off and let her hair fly free behind her. The wind in her face warmed her as she raced to equal Josh's skill.

As they grew closer Bethanie watched people pouring out from both buildings to welcome their arrival. She felt a strong sense of coming home as she neared the ranch. This was the house she had pictured as a child. Its open porch and cool shade seemed to invite Bethanie into its folds like a mother hen opens her wings to cover her chicks. The men were waving and shouting Josh's name amid hoots and yells. Josh was ahead of her by three lengths as they reached the main house.

Breathless, Bethanie pulled her horse up beside Josh. He was already tying his mount to one of the porch supports. The long white-painted porch skirted out from the house, reminding her of the southern homes she'd passed when coming to Texas. The windows were long and slender and two huge elms shaded half the front, while the other side sported a long wooden incline painted the same white as the porch.

Bethanie slung her leg over the saddle horn and froze as she caught sight of the man in the ranch house doorway. His features were almost identical to Josh's. His black hair was brushed lightly with gray at the temples and his dark eyes watched with a mixture of joy and sadness as Josh neared. His beard was trimmed short along his strong jawline, and his dark shirt made his skin seem pale. Bethanie couldn't take her eyes from this man, for unlike his brother, he was sitting in a wheelchair. His powerful shoulders seemed mismatched with his thin, lifeless legs. He smiled with only his lips as he rolled his chair wheels over the threshold.

"Ben!" Josh shouted as he grabbed his brother's hand. The two men looked at each other with the love and respect only brothers share. There was a closeness between them born of blood and years of understanding.

Josh turned to Bethanie. "Bethanie, I'd like you to meet my older brother, Ben Weston." There was a pride in his tone as he introduced his only kin.

Bethanie smiled and stepped forward, trying to pull her hair into some semblance of order. She suddenly wished she had combed it before meeting Ben. He was Josh's family, and she wanted to make a good first impression.

The effect she feared materialized in Ben's stern look. "Welcome to the Weston Ranch. Can't say I think much of women dressin' as men, but you ride better than most of the hands on this place." There was an unmistakable coldness in his voice that frosted the air between them. Bethanie's shyness turned to glacial proportions.

"I asked her to dress like that to get through the open country." Josh dismissed Ben's gruff tone lightly as his vision caught sight of a woman stepping from the house to join them.

Bethanie reddened under Ben's stern gaze. She watched his right eyebrow lift as he studied her like a king watching a peasant from his throne. Any pity she might have initially felt for him dried up under his critical eye.

"Bethanie," Josh said. "This is Ruth. She's been taking care of Ben and me for half my life."

Bethanie smiled at the tall, willowy woman before her. Ruth nodded with respect before lowering her head. Her long brown hair was braided in a single plait down her back, and her dark brown skin hinted of Indian blood. Her face was wrinkled by a blend of weather and age. Bethanie tried to sound friendly, but with little success. "I'm happy to meet you."

Ruth rubbed her hands on a spotlessly clean apron. "I'll set two more places." She looked at Ben for affirmation. The nod was so slight Bethanie wasn't even sure she saw it.

As Ruth took a step backward into the house, everyone on the porch suddenly heard Allison's shrill scream. "Bethanie!" The blond girl yelled as she ran through the crowd on the porch and threw her arms around Bethanie. "I was so worried about you," her tiny cousin whimpered. "We were so afraid you might be dead."

Allison burst into uncontrollable tears. Her usually perfect dress was in disorder. She reminded Bethanie of a flowery houseplant left out in the weather. "Mama's dead," she cried over and over between sobs.

Bethanie patted her cousin's shoulder and looked over to Josh. "I'll take her inside," she said. Ben motioned with a frustrated wave of his hand for Ruth to assist.

The women moved into the house leaving the men talking. Ruth walked briskly through a huge main room to the hall, which opened into what looked like three bedrooms. The housekeeper's voice was cold and formal. "I put Miss Allison in Josh's bedroom. He can sleep in the bunkhouse." Ruth's face was emotionless, resembling brown paper wadded up, then spread smooth a hundred times. Bethanie wasn't so sure about her age, for her walk and voice told of a woman under forty.

"I'd like some tea, please," Allison whimpered through her sniffles as she collapsed onto the bed.

Bethanie moaned slightly. The angels must have blessed Allison with being eternally oblivious to anyone's needs except her own. The fact that Ruth must have a hundred things to attend to with houseguests, or with Bethanie just having ridden in, never crossed the fair-haired girl's mind.

"I'll make the tea," Bethanie answered, moving to the door and trying to brush some of the trail dust off her clothes.

"No, I'll get it," Ruth answered curtly. "You stay with her. She's been crying ever since she arrived last night."

"Thank you." Bethanie accepted Ruth's offer and moved to the basin. She couldn't really blame Ruth for her coldness toward them. After all, who would want a house full of strangers to cook for, but then Allison had just lost her mother and needed kindness, not impatience.

"Oh, Bethanie." Allison pouted from her bed. "This is the most dreadful place, and Mike isn't even here to comfort me. That man in the wheelchair sent him off within an hour of our arrival."

"I'll be here with you," Bethanie said as she looked around the rather drab room. This house was large with wide halls and doors. Bethanie noticed the floors were hardwood and tile with no rugs. A house built for a wheelchair, she thought. If this were Josh's room, it certainly didn't reflect his personality. She had seen more decorating put into hotel rooms. The walls were white with only one small bookshelf mounted on one. The bed was full size, but the covers looked like they were blue army issue. The bedroom windows were high, and Bethanie could see the shadow of bars outside them. More protection from the Indians, no doubt. Josh must spend very little time here, for she couldn't see one thing marking this room as his.

An hour later, Bethanie comforted Allison and tucked her in for a nap. She stepped silently out into the main living area. She could never remember seeing a room so large in a home. It reminded her of a small hotel lobby she'd seen once. Ben sat at a huge oak desk in one corner. Books lined the walls on either side of him. A large couch and several chairs were grouped around a fireplace, with one space left for a wheelchair. The walls were a colorful blend of Mexican and Indian art designed to please masculine taste.

"Is that woman finally quiet?" Ben asked without any

other greeting. His whole face seemed to wrinkle into a frown.

"Yes," Bethanie answered, and stepped closer. This man wasn't going to make it easy on her. "Where are Father Mike and Dusty?" She had to think of something to say; they couldn't just stare at each other until someone else came into the room.

"Father Mike?" Ben raised an eyebrow. "Oh, they left with most of the men to help with the roundup. On top of the Indians, we've been having trouble with cattle rustlers and northern carpetbaggers trying to swindle us 'dumb southerners' out of every inch of land." He laughed a short, deep laugh that sounded more like a cough. "We have more plagues than Moses."

When Ben looked up at Bethanie, she had the distinct feeling he regarded her as just another problem. He looked her straight in the eye as if sizing her up. "Mike said he'd stop by and wire Allison's father about his wife's death." He watched her closely. "You're not the whiney type, are you." His last sentence was a statement, not a question.

Bethanie thought she heard a note of respect in his voice. He was a man who must have had a great deal of pain in his life. She wanted to tell him she understood how lonely it must be for him, but instinct told her he wanted no pity.

Josh appeared at the open front door, relieving Bethanie of any need to respond. "I see you're getting to know Ben." He smiled. "We've got some big problems with the roundup. I'm riding over to help. Those longhorns are plum wild after running free for the past few years." His eyes met Bethanie's, and she saw them darken slightly. "Wanta come along? We can reach the camp before dark."

"Yes," Bethanie answered, thankful not to be left with Ben and Allison.

"Now, hold on, Josh." Ben shouted as if all in the room were slightly hard of hearing. "You're not taking a woman out there, even one that looks like a boy." He pointed one long finger at his younger brother.

"But Bethanie can ride," Josh argued, touching her shoulder lightly.

Ben shook his head, "What about Indians? Out in the open you'll have all you can handle watching cattle. You can't keep an eye on her, too. If she's here, you know I'd fight to the death before I'd let Indians take this place."

"Bethanie's a good shot." Josh's voice sounded less sure of his logic. Bethanie knew he was thinking of the Indians they had encountered only two days ago.

Ben slammed his pen down on the desk as if to end the discussion. "Yes, but she's not a man. Women don't belong some places, not with thieving rustlers around. Besides, you're not leaving me alone with that whimpering girl in yonder." He nodded in the direction of Allison's door.

Josh laughed. "He's right, Bethanie. You'd better stay. Besides, you haven't had a good night's sleep in days. I know you could use the rest."

"But . . ." Bethanie began. She felt like Daniel left with the lions.

Josh smiled lovingly at her as he pulled her out the door and onto the porch. "I'll be back in a few days, a week at the most. You and Ben will get along great—neither of you ever wasted a word." He kissed her forehead.

Bethanie folded into his embrace as he pulled her out of sight of Ben's window. His kiss was warm and loving, reminding her of a few hours ago in the cave. "I'll be back soon, I swear," he whispered with a promise in his smoky brown eyes.

Ten minutes later, Bethanie blinked away a tear as she

watched Josh from the dining-room window. He swung into his saddle and smiled back at her. Touching his hat in a silent salute, he rode away. The urge to bolt from the house and run after him boiled within her. She wanted to touch his face, to hold him tight, just once more. A few days would be an eternity without his smile, a lifetime without his touch. But Bethanie held herself fast. She'd waited a long time for the joy of loving him; she could wait a few more days.

Bethanie straightened slightly, aware that Ben could easily see into the dining area from where his desk sat. There was much to do. She had to take care of Allison in her time of grief. Part of her wanted to tell the world about her love for Josh, but she knew now was not the right time. She turned to face Ben and found him staring at her with cold, dark eyes.

Ben rubbed his forehead with his first finger and thumb. "Have you nothing else to wear?" he frowned.

"No," Bethanie answered simply.

"Ruth," Ben bellowed in the direction of the kitchen. The housekeeper appeared at the door before Ben's voice quit echoing around the room. "Put Beth in Mother's room," he ordered. Then to Bethanie, he added, "My mother died several years ago, but we left her room pretty much the same as it was."

Ruth eyed Bethanie with open hostility. "She can sleep in with Miss Allison. No use opening up that room."

"No," Ben stated, not bothering to explain his logic to Ruth.

Bethanie tried to ease the tension. "I don't mind sharing a . . ."

Ben's voice made both women jump. "No!" he repeated.

Bethanie knew the subject was closed. How she hated men who thought their word law. But she had to get through the next few days. Maybe she could at least make friends with Ruth, and pride would never allow Bethanie to be waited on. "I want to help out while I'm here." She tried to smile at the cold woman.

"That's more than Miss Allison offered," Ruth snapped, an ounce of harshness leaving her voice. "I've been waiting on her all day."

"I'll do that, plus I can cook fairly well." Bethanie added, "If you'll allow me?"

"Good," Ben stated. "Ruth can use some help around here. I never could abide helpless women like that brat in there."

As if on cue, Allison yelled for Bethanie.

The next few days passed in a pleasant routine of housework. Ruth never talked to Bethanie, except to give orders, but Bethanie enjoyed the work, thankful to have her hands busy while her mind was filled with thoughts of Josh. Ruth liked to cook breakfast alone, but accepted help with all the other chores. She explained that she couldn't face anyone until she was wide awake, not even a helper. Allison spent her time sleeping, moping around the house, and taking all her meals in bed. She avoided Ben after a few encounters, referring to him as a dragon on wheels.

Ben ate in the dining room, and to everyone's surprise, insisted Bethanie join him. They talked very little during the meals, but slowly Bethanie lost most of her fear of him. He constantly referred to her as Beth, which bothered her, but she felt it would have been rude to comment. Though he never complimented her, neither did he criticize her as he did Allison. The only subject she and Ben both seemed to enjoy was horses. Bethanie would have thought, since a horse put him in a wheelchair, he'd hate the animal. Yet he bore no resentment to the creatures and seemed to enjoy Bethanie's stories of growing up on a farm where horses were bred.

On the fourth evening of Bethanie's stay, a storm darkened the spring sky. Thunder rattled the house as she sat mending one piece of clothing after another from a large pile Ruth had given her to finish. Ben worked at his desk as usual. A comfortable silence rested between them. Allison was in bed and Ruth had retired to her small room off the kitchen.

Ben broke the hour's silence. "I got a telegram from your uncle today." His voice was completely void of emotion or interest.

Bethanie glanced up, trying to hide the fear she felt growing inside her. "Is he coming?" she asked quietly.

"Yes," Ben answered, his mahogany eyes now watching her closely. He pulled at the short hair of his beard as he studied her.

"When?" Bethanie asked, dropping her sewing in her lap. She hated having to pry information out of Ben, but he seemed unwilling to volunteer any.

"Three, maybe four days." Ben returned to his papers, ending the discussion.

Bethanie tried to steady her fingers and continue sewing. She had nothing to fear from Uncle Wilbur now. Josh was near. Yet even the thought of seeing Wilbur again sent icy chills up her spine. She'd never forget his pawing fat fingers pulling at her clothes. The simple sewing task now seemed impossible as the memory of his assault invaded her thoughts.

Bethanie excused herself quickly and disappeared into her room. She was thankful to Ben for giving her a room alone. The fearful nightmares she always dreamed hadn't plagued her here. The room was warm and inviting, with a beautiful patchwork quilt on the bed and a hand-carved rocking chair beside a tiny fireplace. The only rug in the house circled in front of the fireplace and a lovely full-length mirror, also hand-carved, stood in one corner. Everything in the room had been left untouched as if the woman who decorated it might return any day.

Bethanie felt more at home in this room than she had anywhere since she had left Ohio. Tonight, as always, she left the door open slightly. It was comforting to know Ben was just across the hallway. Though he barked a great deal, he was no threat as a man to her. Yet his nearness seemed to keep her haunting dream at bay.

As Bethanie turned up the lantern, she noticed something dark lying over the bedspread. She lifted the material to discover a dress of chocolate brown.

Ben's harsh voice sounded from the doorway. "I had Ruth wash it for you. It was one of my mother's."

Bethanie turned to face him, holding the dress like a treasure. "It's wonderful, but I can't accept it."

"Nonsense, Beth, you're earned it ten times over these past few days. It's nothing fancy, just warm and serviceable. I hope it fits. My mother was tall, but not as tall as you are. I asked Ruth to let the hem down."

Bethanie was moved by his unexpected kindness. Not one man in a hundred would think of the details, but Ben's sharp dark eyes apparently missed little.

She knelt beside his chair. "Thank you, Ben." She would have touched his hand, but he wheeled backward, out of reach.

"I just hate seein' a woman dressed like a man. You'll find undergarments in the chest. Help yourself to them and if you need anything else, you've only to ask." He seemed embarrassed at the whole conversation. "Say no more about it. Good night, Beth." He wheeled across the hall and went into his bedroom.

The next morning Bethanie bathed and put on her new dress. Ben had been right; it was nothing fancy, only a plain wool, but it was far nicer than anything she'd worn in months. The bust was snug and the waist a few inches too big, but Bethanie thought it was grand. She brushed her hair to a shiny gold, then hurried to join Ben at breakfast.

"Good morning." Bethanie smiled as she neared the table.

Ben's only reaction was to lift his maverick eyebrow. "Not much good about it, or hadn't you noticed? Rain still coming down in buckets."

Bethanie slipped into her chair. She'd slept wonderfully last night during the rain, dreaming of the stormy night in the cave. She awoke once and could almost feel Josh's arms around her. A memory now flashed through her mind as she thought of something she'd seen in the darkness. She remembered rolling over and seeing the shadow of Ben in his wheelchair at her door. Bethanie cleared her mind. She must have dreamed it. She helped herself to some eggs and began to eat in silence.

Ben bumped the table leg as he moved to refill his coffee cup. Bethanie glanced up from her plate. "I'll refill that for you," she offered.

"I don't need any help," Ben snapped, "and I never ask for anything."

"I'm sorry," Bethanie answered, embarrassed and surprised at his outburst.

"Don't ever be sorry for me. Understand, Beth?" Ben yelled as he slammed his fist hard on the table.

Bethanie's green eyes flashed fire as she forced herself to remain silent. She stared at Ben's angry face and wondered how she could ever have thought he looked like Josh. He was a cold, bitter man, crippled more in his mind than in his body. His dark eyes never left her as she stood and moved toward the kitchen, her food barely touched.

"You didn't finish your breakfast!" Ben shouted after her.

"I've work to do," Bethanie managed to retort before she reached the comfort of the kitchen. Nothing would have made her return to her place. He seemed to be watching, waiting for her to make a mistake. He looked for bad in everyone, she decided, even her. Well, she wasn't giving him the satisfaction of seeing her angry.

Ruth greeted Bethanie with her usual nod and handed her a clean apron. Bethanie rolled up her sleeves and began the baking. All day the rain pounded as Bethanie baked loaf after loaf of bread. She did her best, knowing some of the bread would go to the men at the roundup. She ate a quick bite in the kitchen with Ruth at lunch. The housekeeper asked no questions, but Bethanie guessed she'd heard Ben's outburst even in the kitchen. Allison wandered in to watch several times but offered no assistance.

As evening came and the rain continued, Bethanie grew restless. Every afternoon she'd walked the few hundred yards to the small, hidden falls nestled along the same ledge that protected the house. The area was overgrown and a small waterfall splashed loudly among the rocks. Bethanie remembered Josh telling her of the falls. He was right when he'd said it was separate from the world. She frowned as she worked, for today the path would be knee-deep in mud, so she must keep busy in the house.

Allison retired early, as usual, and Bethanie set the evening meal before Ben. She'd thought of eating in the kitchen with Ruth, but decided she might anger Ben more. How would it look when Josh returned if she and Ben were at each other's throats?

As Ben rolled his high-backed wheelchair into his place at the table, he nodded his usual greeting. He looked tired, and Bethanie wondered if he felt as cooped up as she did tonight. Even if his outings were only to the bunkhouse and barns, they'd been canceled today. He seemed on edge, as if the storm had wound his nerves tightly.

They ate in silence with only the rain clamoring above them. Ben pushed away his plate just as a pounding sounded at the door. Before either could move, the door flew open and Dusty entered along with the storm. He fought briefly to close the door, then stood dripping wet, staring at Ben. He was such a little boy, trying to stand tall like a man, Bethanie thought. His fight with the weather left him looking battered and defeated.

"Get him a towel and blanket," Ben ordered Bethanie. "Boy, come over by the fire. You look half drowned." He rolled toward the fireplace, and she ran to get towels.

When Bethanie returned, she helped Dusty dry his hair until he pushed her away reluctant to accept more mothering. His chin was held high and strong though his eyes were puffy from crying.

"I come here to tell Mr. Ben somethin'," he said, pulling the blanket tight around his shoulders. "I wanted to stay out, but they wouldn't let me."

"It's all right, son," Ben said with more kindness than he'd ever shown Bethanie. "Tell me, how's the roundup?"

"It was fine, sir, till yesterday. We brought several hundred head around to brand. Then the storm must've stampeded them. The thunder sounded like gunshots to me. Those longhorns went crazy. We was tryin' to stop them, but could hardly see, 'cause it was rainin' so hard." His speech was coming in gulps now. "They headed into the river. It was overflowin' the banks and mighty swift. Mike yelled for me to stay out of the water, but him and Josh went in."

Dusty buried his head in his folded arms as he curled into a ball. Bethanie sat beside him and put her arm around his shoulders. Such small shoulders to bear the load of one who thought he was a man.

Ben moved closer. "What happened, son?" he asked, just above a whisper.

Dusty raised his head. "The cows went crazy. We was all so tired, 'cause we slept in our saddles the night before." Tears rolled down his eyes as he bit his lip and sniffed loudly. His voice faded. "An hour later, maybe more, only Mike came out of the water."

Ben's voice was low, barely above the crackling fire. "What about Josh? What happened to my brother?"

Bethanie's hands knotted into fists, and her eyes closed tightly as Dusty said painfully, "He must've drowned. We found his horse downriver, badly cut up by horns. They looked ever'where, but his body must've been carried off in the river." Dusty crumbled, and Bethanie covered him with the blanket. He was only a boy, and he'd used every ounce of energy to tell his heartbreaking story.

Bethanie hugged the boy to her and fought an internal battle to break and run screaming from the room. From this place where all she saw was Josh. From the shattered remains of her future without him. From life and all its pain. But her mother hadn't run. Her mother had fought life's long battle without support, without tears, and without a man. Bethanie silently reminded herself she was her mother's daughter.

The three sat in silence for a long time. Ben, hands folded, stared at the fire, deep in his own private grief. Dusty lay curled half asleep on the couch. Bethanie sat erect, listening to the rain. She twisted her ring that had once belonged to her grandmother. The matching ring was on Josh's finger somewhere in the river. And there in the river also was her heart. She didn't cry, but closed her eyes and returned in her mind to her mother's kitchen. She pictured each detail of the room, down to the smell of the bread that her mother always made. Josh had lied. He had said he'd come back and he didn't, just like her father. Bethanie mourned his lie silently and closed her heart to all men. She would survive. She would make it, but alone.

Chapter Eight

Two days passed like a slow-moving fog over Bethanie's mind. She worked continuously, trying to tire herself, hoping she'd no longer think, wanting to wear her body numb so she could sleep. The sun returned, drying the land, but the wound across her heart seeped in slow pain. She bore her heartache inside. Even Allison was unaware of her suffering as the tiny blonde wandered about the house, waiting for Mike's return.

Most of the ranch hands drifted in after the storm, disheartened at watching their hard work scattered. Large meals had to be prepared and constant chores attended to. When the stampede ended, two bodies were found, but neither one was Josh. The men went about their work with Mike serving as foreman and Ben making all decisions from his desk. A preacher was summoned to perform the burial service, while the household passed the hours in silence. Ben grew moody and remote from the others, withdrawing into his thick shell. He turned to his work, allowing all other parts of his life to die with his brother.

On the second morning after Dusty had brought his news, Bethanie watched from the dining-room window as Mike finally returned with the dead men's bodies. He rode slumped in the saddle with fatigue as he pulled two horses along behind him. A corpse was slung over each horse, with only threadbare bedroll blankets to cover them. Bethanie's breath caught in her throat at the sight even though she'd been expecting the bodies since dawn. She rubbed her forehead against the glass as if to draw the cool feeling into her brain. For a moment she was glad they hadn't found Josh's body. She couldn't have weathered seeing him tied across his horse as these men were.

Mike spoke with Ben for a few minutes on the porch and gave Allison a more-than-brotherly hug. Bethanie turned back to her work in the kitchen. She could think of nothing to say to Mike. He'd always given Allison his undivided attention, and the frightened woman-child needed him now more than ever. Ruth offered to prepare the bodies, leaving Bethanie alone with her thoughts. She could dream that the stampede never happened, or relive the night in the cave one more time in her mind.

As Bethanie worked, she thought of her mother and wondered if Mary had dreamed of Mariah long after he left them. Could that explain why she never talked about him? By answering her daughter's questions, she would have had to face the fact that he was gone forever. Bethanie remembered many times watching her mother smile as she worked, unaware that she was being observed. Were her daydreams of Mariah as Bethanie's now would be of Josh?

Bethanie was busy making pie crusts when Mike came through the kitchen door. He looked thinner, and his sky-blue eyes bore a sadness about them. Without his billowing brown robes to disguise his lean form, he seemed stronger, more in charge.

Mike began with small talk, not knowing how to say what was obviously on his mind. "The preacher arrived a few minutes ago."

"I know." Bethanie nodded and pushed back a curl

from her forehead with a floury finger. "We'll have the service in the morning."

"Yeah, the two fellows never mentioned any family, so we'll bury them here." He paused playing with a metal piece in his hand. "Bethanie, I wanta tell you something."

"All right," Bethanie answered, not stopping her work.

"Josh and I talked the night before he drowned. He said he wished he'd been straight with you about somethin', so guess I'll tell you now."

"There's no need to say anything." Bethanie wasn't sure she wanted to know something Josh had left out about himself. Nothing really mattered now, anyway.

Mike leaned against the table. "I know, but he'd want you to understand. You probably figured out I ain't a priest."

Bethanie knew her smile never touched her eyes. "I never really thought you were."

Mike's boyish dimples dented his cheeks. "Well, Josh and I were trying to stop a gang of cattle thieves." He laid a metal star on the table. "He was a Texas Ranger. He rode with Colonel Ross before the war. When Ross was made a general in the Confederate Army, Josh served under him once more. Ross used to say Josh was the most honorable man he ever met. Don't know if it would matter any, but he wasn't a no-account like your uncle believed."

Bethanie turned the badge of the Texas Rangers in her fingers. The pointed star was worn, but still glinted in the morning light. "There was no need to tell me. I knew all I needed to know, but thanks for clearing up a few mysteries."

"He said he never meant to deceive you, but at first he had to know you weren't in league with your uncle." Sadness filled Mike's blue eyes. "He told me he loved you, Bethanie. I ain't never heard him say that about any woman, and I've known him for years."

A tear rolled down Bethanie's cheek. She rubbed her hands on her apron harshly, as if the cleaning could rub away the pain in her heart.

Mike stood and touched her cheek. "He told me he knew you loved him even though you never said the words." Mike patted Bethanie's shoulder gently. She rested her forehead on his chest, as she fought for control. Mike smelled of leather and horses, as Josh had. She forced back the tears as her mind hid away the one tiny joy Mike had given her to cherish amid the sorrow. Josh had been so sure of his love, he'd told someone. Bethanie knew she would never love again, but the knowledge that Josh was so sure was comforting.

"Thank you, Mike," she whispered as his arms encircled her in warmth.

Bethanie hardly noticed the door from the dining room open as Allison slipped in. "I can't believe it," she shouted, startling them. "First you tell me you're not a priest, and next I find you in the arms of my cousin. Color spotted her normally pale face as she dug her fists into the sides of her tiny waist. For an instant, a slight resemblance to her mother showed in Allison's manner.

Bethanie stepped back, aware that Mike covered Josh's badge with one hand and slipped it into her apron pocket.

"Allison," he shrugged. "I was comforting Bethanie, that's all. You know where my affections lie." His distraught face revealed much of his feelings for Allison.

"Mike, really. Bethanie is no sadder at our leaving than I am." Allison's rosebud lips pouted. She was enjoying Mike's distress.

Bethanie and Mike exchanged glances, both realizing Allison knew nothing about Bethanie and Josh. With a slight nod, they agreed to let it remain so. Bethanie couldn't have faced Allison's questions about Josh and their relationship.

Mike's blue eyes danced with mischief as he looked at Allison. "Isn't she lovely when she blushes, Bethanie? Like a little china doll."

Bethanie moved to the stove as Allison lovingly scolded Mike. They sat at the table, lost in each other. Mike gripped her tiny hands in his as they talked. He was as fascinated by her as any man Bethanie had ever seen. He studied her every pose as a painter might examine a model.

Bethanie slipped unnoticed from the room. She would give them time alone, for, as she knew, shared moments were too precious to lose. Her heart felt like a ton weight as she longed for Josh by her side. To feel his arms around her once more would be worth any price. But Josh was gone and she must make her own way with only the memory to comfort her.

Bethanie moved through the dining area to the main room. To her surprise she heard several male voices. As she entered the room, Ben caught her eye. "We have guests, Beth. Will you bring coffee?"

Bethanie nodded as she glanced over the men who were warming themselves by the fire. One was a tall, slender man carrying a tattered Bible. Two others were strangers, but as they shed their coats, Bethanie noticed their guns were strapped low like gunfighters. Another large man, with his back to her, was wrestling with his coat. As he turned slightly, Bethanie's breath caught in her throat. There was no mistaking Wilbur's frame or stance. She darted unnoticed back into the dining area. She was out of sight to all but Ben, and he seemed to pay no notice to her. Bethanie's heart pounded wildly in fear as she listened to the men.

Wilbur's voice filled the air. "I came as fast as I could. I'm so thankful my daughter and niece survived. I thank you, Mr. Weston, for housing them, but I'll be takin' them home in the morning. I've got a business to get back to."

Ben raised one eyebrow. "You're welcome to sleep in the bunkhouse tonight, along with Preacher Wilson here and your two hired guns." There was a note of distaste in Ben's voice as he mentioned the two men.

"Oh, they ain't hired guns," Wilbur babbled. Ben seemed to make him uncomfortable. He always talked faster when he was around someone he disliked. "They're just friends I thought I might need if we ran into any Indian trouble."

Bethanie could listen to no more. She hurried back to the kitchen. Allison and Mike were too engrossed in each other to notice her. "Allison," Bethanie cleared her throat. "Your father's here."

Allison jumped up in a flurry of ruffles and ran from the kitchen, discarding Mike like a forgotten toy. Bethanie went about making coffee as Mike sulked like a hunting dog in winter. She felt sorry for Mike. He was falling so hard for Allison.

"She's going back," Mike said more to himself than Bethanie.

"I guess so," Bethanie answered. "Unless you ask her to stay."

"I can't," Mike said thoughtfully. "Maybe next spring, but not now. Guess I'm just not as sure of her as Josh was of you."

Bethanie nodded, trying to understand. If Mike loved Allison, what did it matter if it were this spring or next? "Did you tell her you're a Ranger?"

Mike leaned forward threading his fingers deep into his blond hair. "No," he mumbled. "I can't jeopardize everyone. Allison likes me, but her loyalty to her father is great. Josh believed Wilbur is in league with some Mexicans who are trying to monopolize the cattle sales, but Ben thinks he's working with one of the ranchers between here and San Antonio. Either way, Allison may end up in the middle of one big mess."

Bethanie laid her hand on Mike's shoulder. "You're right about one thing. It's better if she doesn't know." She knew Allison well enough to know her sweet cousin couldn't be entrusted with a secret. She would probably never willingly hurt anyone, but sometimes her mouth rambled more than an apple in an empty wagon bed.

"As soon as this mess is cleared up, I'm going to resign from the Rangers." Mike smiled lopsidedly. "Do you think Allison will wait for me? I'd like to marry her someday."

Bethanie tried to sound hopeful. "She would be a fool if she didn't."

The answer seemed to satisfy Mike. He stood and gave Bethanie a brotherly kiss on the cheek. "I can see why Josh was so crazy about you." He pulled on his hat. "Tell Allison I'll see her tomorrow night. I've got to check the herd. If I don't leave out the back door now, I'll never go."

The coffee boiled ready, splashing onto the stove, as Mike closed the back door. Bethanie braced herself and picked up the tray of cups and coffee for the men out front. She dreaded being in the same room with Wilbur, but knew she would be safe with Ben present. Cold as he might be, she knew he would allow no one to harm her in his house.

To her relief, Ruth met her at the dining-room door and offered to take the tray from her. Bethanie was able to slip back into the kitchen to her quiet peace. The kitchen was large and always seemed cold when they weren't cooking. In summer it would probably be the coolest room in the house, thanks to the cliff's shading. She hugged herself and sat by the low coals trying to stop shaking. Her mind hadn't dealt completely with Josh's death and now she must deal with Wilbur.

Bethanie managed to avoid Wilbur all evening as she tried to think of a way to keep from returning to San Antonio with him. She was thankful Ben didn't invite Wilbur to the house for dinner. Allison ate in her room as usual. She was sulking over Mike not saying goodbye, and crying because her father insisted on leaving in the morning.

Bethanie ate silently across from Ben, lost in her own thoughts. She knew one thing for certain, she would not go back. Maybe Ben would loan her money to go East. She could look for work somewhere. She had enough education to teach school or perhaps work as a cook on some farm as her mother had done. She doubted if Ben would give her work here, for after the roundup Ruth could easily handle everything.

Everyone in the house retired, yet Bethanie spent late hours in the kitchen, hoping to find some solution to her problem as she cleaned. There must be a way to avoid returning with Wilbur. As she stepped onto the back porch to throw out the dishwater, a fat shadow jumped toward her. Strong porky fingers grabbed her arms as soapy water spilled over Bethanie's skirt. She jerked back, but Wilbur was too strong for her. He pinned her against the rough wall of the house with his bloated body.

"Well, well," Wilbur said without parting his teeth. "Now, Bethanie, you haven't greeted your dear old uncle yet."

"Let me go or I'll scream," Bethanie answered, twisting her arms in panic.

"Why cause a ruckus?" Wilbur shrugged and let her go. "I can wait. Come dawn, you'll be on your way back to the hotel with me, and then we can have our fun. With Martha gone, I'll be needing you more than I thought. I was too easy on you before. You got high and mighty, but I'll bring you down real fast, girlie. You ain't nothing but trash, and don't you forget it just because we treat you good."

"I'm not going back with you!" Bethanie cried, rubbing her bruised arms.

Wilbur raised his hand to strike her, then thought better of it. "Who's gonna stop me from taking you? These people ain't gonna interfere with a family squabble. That cripple, Ben, is the only one who's got any spirit and he's worthless." Wilbur grinned, showing his yellow, decaying teeth. "No, I'm telling you, come mornin' you're going back. I already promised the two men with me they could have a turn with you tomorrow night as long as they take you out of Allison's hearing."

He laughed his cruel laugh. "I'm posting a guard, so don't think of running away. You might as well set your mind to the fact that your bed is made and ain't nothing gonna change."

Bethanie twisted against the house, pawing her way to the back door. She bolted and jumped inside with Wilbur's words in her ears. He had her life all planned. Bethanie locked the door and leaned against it. Thank God he had to sleep in the bunkhouse. She couldn't have stayed under the same roof with him overnight. Just the thought that he was on the ranch sickened her.

Taking a deep breath, Bethanie slowly walked through the dark house to her room. She had to control her fear and think of something.

Welcoming the quiet solitude of her bedroom, Bethanie knelt beside the tiny fire and held her skirt out to dry. The dress was the only thing of value she owned and it had been given to her by a stranger. She looked around the room, watching the shadows of the fire dance across the walls. This might be her last night in this comforting room. The colors had seemed to welcome her before, but now they gave no answer to her problem.

Why couldn't their warm glow heat the icy cold feeling in her chest. Bethanie wished she could talk to the ghosts who must haunt this room and beg for help.

A light tapping at her door startled Bethanie. She hastily wiped the tears from her cheeks, "Come in," she whispered, wondering what Allison wanted at this hour.

To her shock, Ben opened the door and slowly rolled his wheelchair through the entrance. His dark hair was tousled, and his shirt was unbuttoned halfway down his chest. Though his appearance told of his hurried rising from sleep, there was no hint of slumber in his eyes. He moved to the edge of the rug she was sitting on and folded his hands, staring at her for a long moment.

"Beth," he began as he lowered his eyes to examine the arm of his wheelchair. "I'll not waste words. Ruth came to me tonight. She told me of a very disturbing conversation she overheard outside her window between you and your uncle." There was no emotion in his voice. Bethanie heard no sign of caring in his tone and, thankfully, no sign of scorn.

Bethanie's face reddened, and she turned away to stare into the fire, not knowing what to say. How could she tell this cold man anything? Yet he was her only avenue of help.

Ben continued. "Wilbur told me you were orphaned, and he took you in. He also said you were worthless and of little help, so I know he's a poor judge of women."

Bethanie smiled at Ben's offhanded compliment. She could just see Wilbur trying to tell Ben anything. Ben's honest statement about her told her why his men must respect him so. He might be cold, but he spoke his mind when needed, without lies or flattery.

"Do you want to go back to San Antonio?" Ben asked bluntly as he rolled a few feet closer to her.

"No!" Bethanie answered emphatically, "I'd rather die." She looked up at him, allowing him to see the tears bubble over and run down her cheeks. She had to be truthful with him.

Ben's face wrinkled with her sudden declaration. He rubbed the short hairs along his jawline with his thumb. "I've been thinking about another way out, but it may not be much more to your liking than death."

"What?" Bethanie was intrigued, willing to hear anything. She'd heard Ruth say that Ben was a very smart man. He had to be intelligent to run a ranch this large from his desk. Maybe he'd thought of a plan she had overlooked.

"I first thought about loaning you money for a ticket out of Texas, but he just might find you while you waited for the stage, and I can't spare enough men to fight his two hired guns."

"Oh." Bethanie let her shoulders drop along with her hopes of escape. This had been her only plan, too, and Ben was right about it. Even if she could get to town, she might have to wait days for the stage.

Ben cleared his throat. "From the first time you walked into my house, I've cared about your welfare. Cared more than I've ever allowed myself to for a woman."

Bethanie looked up in surprise, but Ben was staring at his lifeless legs as he continued. "If we were married, he couldn't take you."

"What?" Bethanie asked in disbelief. Ben seemed nervous for the first time.

"I said, if we were married you'd be my responsibility and he would have no rights. I can wake up the preacher and we can get it done tonight."

Bethanie put her hands to her chin and thought about his wild suggestion. She wasn't sure she would be a great deal better off with this cold man. Ben had been none too friendly these past few days. What would he be like if they married? But he was an honest man who was definitely respected by those around him.

"Do you plan to marry another?" Ben asked, as if the thought had just occurred to him.

"No," Bethanie answered, "I never planned to marry at all. I think you wouldn't make such an offer if you knew about me." She closed her eyes as she forced the words from her. "My parents were Shakers. They never married. I've been told that no decent man would ever marry me."

A long moment of silence passed between them. Finally Ben asked, "I've read about the Shakers. They are a kind people, dedicated to cleanliness, industry, and celibacy." His voice slowed slightly at the last word.

Bethanie nodded, surprised at his knowledge. "My parents broke one Shaker law, obviously." She studied his intelligent face more closely. She had met very few people over the years who understood Shakers. Most folks were afraid of them, thinking they were possessed because they danced and spoke in tongues. Some even thought them witches because of the ointments they made from the marrow of hog jaw, the repulsive substance believed to have great healing powers.

"Do you hold with Shaker beliefs?" Ben asked.

"Most. I was taught nursing and the use of herbs from my mother. She was a kind woman, who did her best to live by the faith." Bethanie looked back toward the fireplace. What else could she say? Martha's words kept pounding in her head, "No decent man will marry you."

Ben seemed consumed with his own thoughts. He was probably wishing he had never asked her to marry him, Bethanie thought. Josh might have overlooked everything because of his love, but Ben did not hold such feelings. How could he ever withstand the future gossip?

Ben's voice was as firm as his grip on the arm of his wheelchair. "Well, Beth, make up your mind. We haven't got much time. I'm a respectable man and I'm offering marriage."

"But people would talk." Bethanie shook her head. "They've always talked."

"They probably would. More about why you married me, than why I married you. But as Mrs. Ben Weston, I promise you they would never say a word in front of me. Half the people in Texas have something in their past they don't want brought up. Your parents' sin seems no greater than what most people have to hide."

Ben studied her with his dark, coffee brown eyes. "I can see how you fit being from Shaker background. You're definitely industrious and believe in cleanliness. As for celibacy . . ." He stopped, at a sudden loss of words. He raked his fingers through his black hair. "I say this in order to be truthful right from the start. I can do my duty as a husband, but I will not demand it. You can have this room as yours and continue to help out on the ranch as you have this week. I know I'm no bargain for a husband, but when I'm dead this ranch will be yours. Josh was my only kin. You'll always have a home, and I'm not a poor man. But understand this, Beth. Once you're my wife, it will be for life. What I have, I hold. There will be no leaving once Wilbur is gone."

The idea of a home appealed to Bethanie. She had spent her life living in the back quarters of ranches where her mother worked as the cook. She could never remember having her own room. "You'll not force yourself on me?" she questioned. She didn't want a repetition of her problem with Uncle Wilbur.

Ben laughed dryly. "I can hardly do that, but if you choose to come to my bed, you come to stay. I'll not play games with the marriage act. Whether or not you cross that hallway is up to you. I'll respect you as my wife either way."

Bethanie studied Ben. The gray hair at his temples

flashed silver in the firelight. There was no emotion in his face. He was making a business deal, she thought. She was getting away from Wilbur, and he was getting a housekeeper. It was a fair trade.

Bethanie lifted her chin. "Tell Ruth to wake the preacher," she said as she stood and began straightening her dress. Her only dress. Her wedding dress.

At dawn Wilbur cheerfully loaded his packhorse. He shook Ben's hand and said his thanks in a hurried tone. His smile widened as Allison and Bethanie stepped onto the porch. "Mount up," he ordered, showing his yellowed smile as he stared at Bethanie. He seemed relieved that he didn't have to go searching for her this morning.

Allison moved to her horse and allowed one of Ben's men to help her up. She smiled sweetly at the cowhands who wandered out of the bunkhouse to wave goodbye. Bethanie stepped behind Ben's chair as he had instructed her to do.

"Bethanie!" Wilbur shouted in frustration. "Get on your horse."

"She's not going." Ben smiled at Wilbur's reaction. The fat old man puffed up like a toad. Ben's gaze left no doubt about how little he thought of the man before him. With a nod he signaled his men to move closer to the porch.

Wilbur slung his reins to one of the men and stormed to the foot of the porch. He shoved at the cowboys who stood planted in front of the steps. "Now look here, mister, you have no right interfering with family matters." Wilbur took one step up the porch, pulling up his belt as he walked. His fat cheeks reddened with anger at the needless delay.

"You're right," Ben stated as he lifted a gun from under the blanket that covered his legs and laid it carefully in his lap. "My wife stays with me." His words could have been said in mild conversation, but their force was disquieting upon Wilbur.

"What?" the fat man screamed, his face a red beet of anger. "Your wife?"

"That's right," the preacher said as he stepped onto the porch, unaware of the drama before him. "I married these two last night. Quite a hurry to tie the knot, I must say."

"Bethanie!" Allison cried. "You didn't marry him!" Her emphasis on "him" left no doubt what a poor choice she thought Ben to be.

"Yes." Bethanie held up her head proudly, though her fingers were white from gripping Ben's chair. "He's a fine man, and I'm honored to be his wife." She would not allow anyone to see the sorrow in her heart or the relief that blended with her blood and flowed in a calming wave through her body.

Allison shook her curls in disbelief. Her pouting bottom lip stuck out, telling all of her unhappiness. Bethanie knew Allison was already thinking of how this marriage would affect her.

Wilbur snorted a laugh. "He's a cripple and not . . ." He stopped and thought better of any further comment as Ben's gun pointed toward his enormous gut.

"I'm man enough to kill anyone who touches my wife." Ben's voice was slow and deadly earnest. "Try me," he dared. Even the two hired guns could tell he was serious, and they knew better than to mess with a man and his wife. They both looked away, wanting no part of this fight.

Wilbur backed off the steps, beaten. "Well then, she's yours. I'd never get a girl as plain as her married off anyway. She'll be a cold, hateful wife, and you're welcome to her." He clumsily mounted his horse. "Don't come crying back to me, girlie," he added to Bethanie.

"I never will," Bethanie answered as she relaxed her hands on the back of Ben's chair. No matter how cold Ben was to her or how hard the work was, Bethanie knew she would never leave. Ben had kept his word and saved her from Wilbur and a living hell. She would be a good companion to him.

Wilbur jerked his horse around and rode off without another word. His two hired guns followed, along with his complaining daughter.

Ben turned in his chair, and Bethanie thought she saw a touch of victory curl his lip into a tiny smile. The same smug grin threatened to wrinkle her lips. They had beaten Wilbur.

Ben's eyes were unreadable as he looked at her. "I'm ready for breakfast," he said as if nothing had just occurred. "Preacher, will you join my wife and me?" He rolled his chair past Bethanie, "We've got much to do today, Beth."

Bethanie followed Ben into the house. He handed the old gun to Ruth, but addressed the preacher. "Sam Walker gave me that old Walker-Colt himself. He helped Samuel Colt invent it for the Rangers during the Republic of Texas days. I got hurt during a bank robbery when I was a kid and Walker came to see me. He said anyone foolhardy enough to take on three bank robbers deserved a real gun."

The preacher knew nothing of guns and had no desire to increase his knowledge. "I'm sure it is a very nice gun," he commented as he eyed the food on the breakfast table with true interest.

"I keep it in my desk. Haven't had any use for it in years. It felt good to have it in my hand once more." Ben looked up and smiled a half grin at Bethanie. "But I guess I'd kill a man if he tried to take my wife."

She knew this was the start of her new life. She smiled to herself. She felt valued by this cold man. She had a room of her own, a house to run, and a husband who made no demands on her body. Life might not be full of joy, but Bethanie was satisfied with her bargain.

Chapter Nine

Josh clung to exposed tree roots along the muddy riverbank, trying to regain some of his strength and bring his breathing back to normal. Though he was a strong swimmer, the current had fought him for every inch. While rain poured down violently, Josh could barely tell when his head was above water. He rolled over in the sticky mud and grabbed a low tree branch. He knew he was far downstream from the herd; but, at least he was alive.

As dawn changed the sky from black to gray, Josh crawled farther up the bank and collapsed under the protection of an ancient cottonwood tree. Soon, he would have to start the long walk back to camp. Hopefully, Mike would find his horse and send a rider to search for him. Josh only hoped the man would travel this far downriver.

Josh heard voices from the other side of the tree and almost shouted with relief. Then, his years of training during the war slowed his curiosity to caution. Crawling on his stomach, he moved until he could see three men squatting by a half-drowned fire. The slow drizzle made the men seem more like ghosts than humans. Josh flattened himself in the grass and listened to their talk.

"Well, Ran, we scattered the herd pretty good," one man in a tan parka and black hat mumbled. He sloshed the last ounce of coffee around in his cup before slinging it behind him, almost hitting Josh.

Thanks to all the mud caked to his clothing, Josh more closely resembled a tree root than a man. He burrowed an inch deeper into the soft earth.

"Yeah," the man called Ran answered. "With the help of this storm, I doubt if anyone will ever know we started that stampede."

The man in the tan parka nodded. "We slowed the roundup just like Mr. Mayson told us to. It'll take them a week or more to find those wild cows."

The third man interrupted, his voice peppered with age. "We'd best report in. Smother the fire and let's mount up." He nodded toward the one in the tan parka as he and Ran stood. They moved toward their horses, blurred by rain from Josh's view.

The man in the tan parka stood and began kicking at the fire. His halfhearted efforts were met by sputtering flames. Josh rose from the mud and moved behind him as silently as a cloud's shadow drifts across the ground.

Josh lifted his wet gun from its holster as the man leaned to pick up the coffeepot. The butt of Josh's Colt slammed into the stranger's skull with a dull thud, and the stranger crumbled to the ground.

Josh dragged the limp cowboy behind the tree and stripped the parka, hat, and gun from him. Seconds later, Josh joined the other two men with the black hair pulled low and the tan parka covering his identity. As the trio mounted, rain made conversation and sight difficult, so Josh had no trouble riding with the other two cowboys. He had no idea where they were headed, but he intended to find out.

They rode until mid-afternoon. Rain turned to fog as Josh fought to stay awake. Finally his efforts were rewarded as he saw a ranch materialize in the gray soupy mist before him. The markings over the gate indicated it was the Pair of Spades spread. Josh had never been on this property, but he'd heard a great deal about it. All bad. The owner, a Mr. Mayson, had been a gambler until the end of the war, when he lucked into this ranch. Josh had heard he was offering every rancher within a hundred miles three dollars a head for their cattle. The offer was absurd when northern buyers would pay ten times that if the ranchers could get their beef to the railroad. But other states had enacted a yet-unchallenged law to stop herding across their land. Texas fever killed their livestock when these longhorns were allowed to cross the states. There were rumors of Texans being arrested and even killed when they tried to travel across other ranches to get to market. So a few of Josh's neighbors were tempted by Mayson's offer.

Josh slowly pulled up his horse. It was clear to him now. Mayson had found a way through the blockade and wanted to make sure no other rancher got there ahead of him. Without either of the other riders noticing, Josh turned around and vanished within seconds. He headed toward the nearest town, tired but excited.

The next morning Josh placed a telegram to Austin requesting information on Mayson and cattle laws. By late afternoon he had his answer.

Josh smiled as he read the telegram from Austin. What a lucky turn of fate. If he hadn't been swept downstream, he'd never have discovered Mayson's scheme. The Rangers had been waiting for weeks for some clue, and now Josh could see the pieces all falling into place. He and Mike had been mistaken to think Bethanie's uncle might be masterminding this plan. Mayson was the one they were after. He must have been the man who set up the San Antonio meeting involving every outlaw in these parts. A man who could control the cattle money in Texas would win the state.

Josh decided to get a good night's rest before heading

back to Ben with his news. He considered sending a telegram to his brother, but decided he'd rather bring his good news in person. The fear that they might think he was dead crossed his mind, but surely Ben would know he could take care of himself. He decided to ride by a few of the other ranches and see if they were also having trouble with the roundup. After all, what could a few days matter? Bethanie would be waiting for him.

The memory of her beside him in the dark cave stirred his blood as it had the nights during the roundup. There was so much he wanted to tell her, so many parts of his life he'd never shared with anyone. Josh ran his fingers through his thick black hair. He could almost see her before him, her green eyes changing from ice to fire, her soft, quiet manner exploding with anger when she was pushed too far. She had her mother's nature but somewhere she'd inherited a fire that could warm quickly in both anger and passion. Never had a woman so woven her way around his heart.

Bethanie spent her first day as Ben Weston's wife cleaning house. The sun was warm and bright, so she pulled drapes and bedspreads out for airing. She beat the house's only rug several minutes before replacing it in her bedroom. Ruth was quiet, as always, but asked Bethanie's opinion on several matters.

Bethanie had feared Ruth might show anger at losing her position as woman of the house. To her surprise, Ruth seemed relieved. Bethanie wondered at the strange bond that held Ruth to Ben. It didn't seem to be love, or mothering, but simple devotion. It was as though there was some unalterable script already written for her life and Ruth must play it out without emotion. She didn't enjoy her lot or begrudge it, only waited out each day until the role ended.

By evening, the large ranch house glowed with rare beauty. The rooms smelled of lemon oil and fresh air. Ben made no comment, only ate his dinner and returned to his desk. For him the day was no different than any other working day.

Bethanie watched him as she altered an old dress to fit her. After an hour she realized he didn't plan to comment about the day, and she decided to retire. She stood and walked to his desk. "Good night, Ben."

Ben raised his eyes from a book. "Good night, Beth." He lowered his gaze, dismissing her. His long slender fingers lightly tapped the arm of his wheelchair, as if he were impatient for her to leave so he could get back to reading.

Bethanie went to her room. Ben had been honest, she thought. He'd said everything would be the same, and it was. Why had she thought they might at least talk, perhaps become friends. She scolded herself. What had she expected? Ben had given her the protection of his name and in return she would be mistress of his house. That was it, no more, no less. She would sleep in her room, and he would be across the hallway. Even though he'd said he could do his duty as a husband in bed, he had also said he would never force his attentions on her. As Bethanie crawled beneath the beautiful patchwork quilt, she decided there were worse places she could be. She had a home to call her own and plenty to keep her busy. As in the nights before, she left her door ajar. Her dreams were not so bad when she could believe someone else was near.

Yet in the darkness before dawn, her nightmare returned as it had since she was three.

"Run, Bethanie, run!" her mother shouted.

"Run out back to the trees."

She was so frightened. As she jumped out of bed, Bethanie could see lights all over the front of her house. She stood on her toes to peer out the window. She didn't understand. She ran and ran until she heard her mother scream. Bethanie slipped in the wet grass and fell. She was falling . . . falling.

Bethanie jerked awake. She pushed her damp hair from her eyes and sat up in bed, trying to convince herself of reality and slow down her breathing.

"Beth," Ben's silhouette in the doorway cast a shadow across her room. "Are you all right? I thought I heard you cry out."

"I'm fine," Bethanie lied. "It was just a dream." She could see Ben was bare-chested. Powerful muscles spread across his upper frame, covered only by a patch of black hair in the center of his chest.

Ben reached for the door handle. "Good. Get some sleep." He began to roll back out of the room, his hand pulling the door with him.

"Ben."

"Yes, Beth." His voice was low.

"Will you leave the doors between our rooms open?" She didn't want to admit being afraid, but the thought of the door closing unsettled her.

"If you wish." Ben's tone wasn't as harsh as usual. He backed away out of her sight.

"Thank you," Bethanie whispered, knowing he probably couldn't hear her. "Thank you for everything," she mumbled as she rolled over and fell into a peaceful sleep.

When dawn lightened her room, Bethanie tied back her red hair and made mental notes of her day's plan. For months she had carried a tiny pouch of seeds from her mother's herb garden. This afternoon she would pick a place to plant the seeds, maybe down by the waterfall Josh had loved so dearly. This was her home, and this was where her garden would be. Bethanie smiled wistfully. In the years to come she would work among the herb plants and think of Josh and their brief moments together.

Bethanie spent the morning baking, while Ruth worked silently by her side. As the sun grew warm so did the kitchen. Just after lunch, Ruth retired for her nap, and Bethanie decided to walk over to the hidden falls. She could pick a place for her garden while she enjoyed the cool shade surrounding the enchanted spot. She'd never noticed anyone else going up the rocky path and knew she could find privacy there. Bethanie smiled to herself as she pulled her bandanna from her hair and stepped out the back door.

Josh cleared the ridge just in time to see a glimpse of a redheaded woman disappear down the path leading toward the falls. He felt his pulse increase as he edged his horse down a little-used back trail toward where Bethanie had disappeared. He could hardly wait to hold her. She'd been in his thoughts every hour. He rode slowly, allowing himself to savor the exciting anticipation of her. Never in his life had a woman so haunted his waking and sleeping hours.

As Josh stepped into the clearing at the base of the falls, he couldn't believe his eyes. Bethanie was facing the water with her back to him. She was slowly removing her clothing. Josh thought of stopping her; this was too cool a time of year to bathe outdoors, but he could not bring himself to halt the lovely unveiling. She was the most beautiful woman he'd ever seen, with her long arms and legs shining white in the sun and her full hair tumbling past her waist. He watched silently, reverently studying the masterpiece that was his alone to possess. His eyes never left her form as he unbuttoned his own shirt.

Bethanie hesitated only a moment before plunging into

the cold pool. An instant after she jumped, Josh's nude body hit the water beside her.

When Bethanie's head came up, she slung her wet hair high out of her face. She opened her eyes and saw Josh standing chest deep in water only a few feet away. Her senses told her he was beside her, yet her mind revolted violently in disbelief.

"Hello, my beautiful love." He laughed at the surprise in her eyes. How could a woman be so lovely? He ran a finger lightly over her shoulder to feel the silkiness of her skin.

"J-Josh!" Bethanie couldn't seem to control her voice. "I thought you were dead. Everyone thought you had drowned." She shook her head. "This can't be real." He couldn't be here. Her longing for him must have driven her mind beyond reason, yet her fantasy was complete even to the healing wound on his left arm.

Josh moved toward her, his touch denying her words. He could see the shock in her green eyes. She truly must have believed him dead. He could see it in the shadows of her eyes. A pain within him echoed her feelings. How she must have suffered if she thought they'd lost each other? He never wanted to see her hurt again, for the pain burned through him also.

Determination set his face. He would make her forget all the worry she'd suffered, all the pain. "Well, if I'm a dream, I'm the best one you're ever going to have." He pulled her into his arms, their flesh touching the full length of their bodies. Her full breasts flattened into his hard chest. Josh thought he would surely go mad at the softness of her.

"But, Josh . . ." Bethanie began, still not believing he was alive and with her. Josh's mouth silenced her protest with his hunger. Bethanie pushed at him briefly, before giving over to her wonderful dream. How could one fight a fantasy?

Their fire for each other was so great, neither noticed the cold water splashing around them. His kiss was tender, yet demanding. She felt a wild fire start deep inside her and spread rampant through her limbs. Every part of her begged for his touch, his embrace, his kiss.

Josh lifted Bethanie in his arms and carried her to the grassy bank. This had always been his favorite spot on earth, but today it was heaven. He pulled the bedroll from his saddle and encircled them both with its wool. "I love you," Josh whispered. "Do you have any idea how much I love you?" He buried his face between her cheek and shoulder. "God, you feel wonderful, more so than I ever remembered."

"Josh," Bethanie pushed him slightly away. "We must talk. We can't do this." The realization that he was truly alive and with her was beginning to sink into her brain.

"Oh, you want to talk." Josh laughed as he boldly slid his hand up and down her body. "Well, as I remember, you have much to say, but not with words."

Bethanie opened her lips to speak, but Josh's mouth closed over hers. His kiss was strong and deep as his hands ran possessively over her breasts. He gently pulled her down on top of him in the grass. Red hair fell around them like a damp curtain, as their bodies sparkled in the sun.

"We'll talk, Bethanie . . . later," he whispered.

"But . . ."

Josh silenced her once more with his kiss.

Bethanie raised in an effort to move away, but she only succeeded in holding her breasts a few inches above him. Josh laughed as he pulled her back down and buried his face between her velvet mounds. He moved his mouth back and forth between her soft flesh, nuzzling, tasting, exploring. Bethanie cried out and struggled slightly as he gently savored her flesh. Josh pulled her closer in reassurance as his hands roamed her back, plunging deeper with each stroke until they covered her hips. His fingers lovingly brushed fire over the curve of her back as his mouth branded ownership over her breasts.

They were lost in a world of each other, as his demands reached her very core. Bethanie could no longer think with her every sense exploding. His fire for her warmed her skin like an eternal sun. His brown eyes bore a dark, flaming passion that excited her. His short beard tickled her face as he showered her with kisses. He was the raging waterfall plunging into the quiet pool of her being.

Josh groaned and rolled over, pinning her underneath him. His muscular thigh separated her legs as his chest pressed her down. Bethanie raised her hand to block the sun from her eyes. Josh rose to his knees above her, smiling tenderly as his long, strong fingers swept from her shoulders to her thighs. Bethanie moaned and swayed to the caressing fingers washing over her. The wind brushed a cooling breath across her body, only to have the heat return again as Josh's hands stroked fire to her flesh once more.

She watched him above her. His powerful muscles tightened as he brushed her flesh with his fingertips. The sun splashed diamonds across his damp shoulders and the breeze moved a black curl over his forehead. The hair covering his chest was already dry and swaying slightly across his lean form in the breeze. Bethanie spread her arms wide above her head and gripped the ground, lest her dream take her skyward. She studied his wonderful body in detail. He seemed fascinated as her bright nipples peaked beneath his thumb's circular motion. Then, his attention wandered suddenly, and his hands followed in intricate pursuit.

The cool wind on one side and Josh on the other competed for her warmth until Bethanie could endure no more. She lifted her hands and pulled him closer to her.

Running her fingers into the softness of his damp hair she gloried in his smothering kisses. When his lips found her yielding mouth, his weight flattened her against the grassy earth. She was lost somewhere beyond her wildest fantasy. Josh's kiss was demanding, pleading, begging. She could no more deny him than stop the beating of her heart.

He held her shoulders tenderly as he entered her, laying claim to what would always be his. Bethanie cried out in joy as he moved within her. There was nowhere else at this moment other than in his arms. As she felt his release deep inside her, an explosion shook her entire body. They were one in a timeless ritual of love. She clung to him, reluctant for even the tiniest moment to pass.

Josh lay for several minutes holding Bethanie, wondering how this time could have been even more wonderful than the first. He knew she was made for him, a perfect match. "I heard an old legend somewhere," he whispered into the dampness of her hair, "about how man once was double in height. When God decided to have two sexes He cut man in half. When a man finds his other half on this earth, he walks twice as tall." Josh kissed her forehead. "I've met my mate."

"I love you," he whispered. His hands could not resist returning once more to cup her breasts. Even though his passion was spent, Josh couldn't believe the softness which filled his palm. "I've thought of you constantly these past days."

He pulled the bedroll blanket over her as she lay resting in his arms. "You're so perfect. The very touch of you may someday drive me mad." Josh moved his hand lazily down her side to her hips.

Josh studied Bethanie's face, but her eyes were closed as if in sleep. "Dream, Bethanie, if you wish, but it is the reality I prefer." He pulled her closer, allowing her to feel his need for her. "We'd better get married fast. I don't plan on spending a night without you in my bed."

Though Bethanie lay perfectly still, Josh began kissing her throat, pushing her hair from her silky skin as he moved toward her mouth. As he reached her lips, Josh pulled back to study her face.

He saw an eruption of pain in Bethanie's eyes as she looked at him. She twisted violently away from him. A sudden chill pierced Josh. He reached for her, but she rolled away.

Bethanie stood quickly, avoiding his touch, and silently began to dress. He could hear her short intake of breath, telling him her sorrow was too great for tears. Her slight cries tore at his heart with more pain than a blade could inflict.

"What is it?" Josh knew something must be terribly wrong. Could it be possible she didn't love him? No, Josh's mind rejected that thought. No woman could respond so willing with her entire body and not be in love.

"I tried to tell you before," she began, fighting to control her breathing. "Didn't you stop by the house?"

"No, I saw you when I rode in." Josh stood and pulled on his pants. He knew by her tone that something must have happened. "What's wrong? Is it Ben? Is he hurt?"

Bethanie bit her lip until she tasted blood. "Ben's married." She could see disbelief and anger blend in Josh's handsome face. Her hands were shaking so badly she could barely button her dress. Her own pain was multiplied by the hurt she must deal Josh after loving him so completely.

"Married?" Josh yelled. "Are you crazy? Ben married? To who?" Josh stepped toward her. "Is this some cruel joke? Ben would never marry; he's tied until death to that wheelchair."

"He's married to me," Bethanie whispered as she

turned to face Josh. There was no hiding. She must hold her head high. What was done was done.

Josh's face drained of blood. "You're serious, aren't you?" he said, unable to even pull on his shirt.

"Yes. We were married two days ago by a preacher." Tears rolled unchecked down Bethanie's face. "I tried to tell you, but you wouldn't let me."

Shock turned to anger in Josh. "Hell, Bethanie, I was only gone a week. Didn't you believe I loved you and would come back?" He grabbed her shoulders and shook her violently. "I'd fight any man for you, but not Ben, not my own brother." The full force of her words registered on him like an avalanche of iron, and he jerked away from her. She was his brother's wife.

"We thought you were dead!" Bethanie gulped in fright and heartbreak. The memory of Ben's words returned to her mind. He'd said he'd kill anyone who touched his wife. "Wilbur came to take me back to San Antonio and Ben offered to marry me to stop him. It was the only way we could think of to stop Wilbur."

Josh slammed his fist into the bark of a nearby tree, not noticing the bloody splits in his flesh, so deep was his hurt inside. "Dear God, Bethanie, what have you done?" He raked his unharmed hand through his wet black hair. "What have you done?"

Anger flashed in Bethanie's eyes. "What have I done?" she cried. "I've married your brother because I thought you were dead." She stepped closer, her face hot with anger. "Where were you? Why didn't you come back or let us know you were alive?"

Josh frowned. He felt the depth of his loss in every cell of his being. "I had work to do." His discovery of Mayson's plan seemed feeble now. What did it matter if Mayson swindled every rancher in Texas? Josh had lost Bethanie. He had lost the only woman he'd ever loved.

Bethanie closed the distance between them. In anger

she began pounding in his chest with a fiery rage aimed at the world. Josh gave no defense. Finally her anger turned to sorrow, and she collapsed in his arms. "Hold me," she whispered beneath her tears. "Hold me once before you let me go forever."

"No," Josh cried as he crushed her to him. "No, Bethanie." How could he live without her? How could he see her and not touch her? How could he fall asleep without her softness beside him? Anger pulsed through his every cell and solidified into grief.

"We have no other choice, Josh," Bethanie answered. "Hold me now, for when we leave this place, I'll be Ben's wife."

Tears rolled down Josh's cheeks as he buried his face in her damp hair. He felt her soft body beneath his touch and moaned. "If I live forever and reach all my dreams, my only memory will be of you. God, how I love you, Bethanie!" But he knew she was right, there was no other way. If they spoke of their love again, it would destroy Ben and the moral code all three set their lives by.

"In time you'll forget me." Bethanie tried to console him even in her own grief.

"The moment I draw my last breath," Josh answered.

Bethanie silently pulled away from Josh and moved up the path toward the house. Her heart was pounding so fiercely she thought she might die from its rumbling. To lose him once had caused withdrawal into her own world, yet to lose him twice pushed the realms of her sanity.

Without being conscious of her reasons, Bethanie did what her mother had always done when she was sad. She turned to work. Somewhere the logic lay embedded inside her that if she worked hard enough and long enough, there would be no time to think of unhappiness.

* * *

Long after Bethanie left him, Josh sat beside the waterfall. She was gone from him. As dead to him as she had thought he was to her. How could he live with the pain he now felt? How could he ever see beauty again without her by his side? Would he ever watch a sunset and not see the warm gold of her hair? Would any woman ever feel so right in his arms? She was as vital to him as the air and now he must leave her.

Before he left the hidden falls, Josh knew what he must do. He would congratulate Ben, then announce he was leaving with Williams, another rancher, to drive a herd northwest. The mining camps in Colorado were in need of beef, and rumors were you could get as much as forty dollars a head. He would explain to Ben that he must get back to roundup. Ben would understand his hurry, and Bethanie would know the true reason.

The next morning Ben was in a wonderful mood and had even invited neighbors over to celebrate his brother's return and the first Weston marriage.

Bethanie tried to keep from watching Josh as the company arrived. She'd taken great care to look her best in her one good dress. She didn't want anyone feeling sorry for her or Ben.

As Josh and Ben talked with the men on the porch, Bethanie tried to concentrate on the women sitting around the dining table. They were sisters and obviously "cut from the same cloth," as Bethanie's mother would have said. She guessed they could be no more than forty, yet the Texas sun had already tanned their skin to a wrinkled brown. One was married and the other two were widows of the war. Most folks around these parts just referred to them by the collective name of "the sisters."

Bethanie tried to look cool and calm as the three women watched her every move. They talked about the weather and canning for about half an hour before the conversation turned to Bethanie's wedding. They had several questions about how she and Ben had met and why they had married so soon. Bethanie patiently answered with only the bare facts as she saw Josh move to the large elm outside the window. He was talking with one of the men, but she could feel his eyes watching her. The need to go to him was a physical pain within her, but she forced herself to remain motionless.

Finally one, the oldest of the three duplications, interrupted her thoughts by asking how different it must be being married to a cripple. Bethanie smiled and replied she had no idea, for she'd never been married to anyone else. Bethanie was saved from any further questions by the door opening and the last remaining husband of the sisters motioning time for departure. From his manner it would have been impossible to tell which of the three women was his wife.

When Bethanie moved to the doorway to say her goodbyes to the visitors, she saw Josh leading his horse from the barn.

"I better be leaving." His words were friendly, but Bethanie could see the pain in his eyes.

Ben waved to the neighbors and turned his attention to Josh. "Before you go, I want to ask you one more thing. Beth has taken a liking to that falls you've always considered yours. I wonder if you'd mind if she planted a garden down by the water. I've already told all the men it's off limits."

Josh's gaze raised behind Ben to Bethanie as she stood at the doorway. "It's hers . . . and Dusty's." He added the boy's name. "She'll need some help to plant."

Bethanie was surprised Ben even knew she wanted the space for a garden. Ruth must have told him. "Thank you," she said to both Ben and Josh. "I'll plant herbs that can heal any wound." When she looked into Josh's eyes she wanted to add, "Except a broken heart," but Ben was too near.

"Well," Ben sighed. "Take care of yourself, little brother, and we'll see you in the fall."

Josh pulled his hat low. "I might just stay up in those mountains and try my luck at mining."

Ben laughed at what he thought was his brother's kidding. "You do that, but if you ever need me you know where to find me."

"Take care of Bethanie and Dusty." Josh's words were losing the battle to stay lighthearted.

"With my life," Ben answered.

Bethanie could not speak as Josh turned and rode away. She wanted to run behind him and beg him to take her, but could not. She was another man's wife and Josh's code would never allow any answer except the one at hand.

The days that followed melted together for Bethanie. Ben talked with Mike, trying to think of a way to incriminate Mayson, but the man was as slippery as a water moccasin in knee-deep mud. Nothing but the few words Josh overheard the morning after the stampede pointed to Mayson's involvement. Bethanie had lived in Texas long enough to know that a man didn't accuse his neighbor of anything unless he had proof or an itchy gun hand.

Bethanie's pain over Josh lessened into a dull ache as the days grew longer into summer. She forced herself to plant her garden, as planned, beside the waterfall. Here the young plants were protected from wind by the cliffs and sun by the trees. The area was beautiful, with fifty yards or more of forest growth sprawling out in both directions from the pool at the base of the falls.

Somehow the fire she had discovered with Josh forged her determination to be a better wife to Ben. She was patient and kind and, above all, industrious. Ben's attitude was as constant toward her as the orbit of the earth, yet

Ruth grew gradually more kind. The women worked side by side without talking most of the time, but a warm acceptance grew between them. Ruth readied the kitchen each morning, and Bethanie cleaned up late each night. Ruth even provided her with a few old dresses to clean in so Bethanie could save her brown dress for Sundays and evenings. She found enough blue wool material and began sewing another dress. Each night. she dedicated an hour by the fireplace to tatting. The thin white string in her fingers slowly wove into tiny lace circles she would eventually put on her collar and cuffs.

Bethanie and Dusty's presence brought a great change in Ben, thanks to Dusty. For the first time in years, Ben left the area around the ranch house. The boy had taken a great liking to Ben and offered to drive him anywhere. Dusty even oiled an old buggy that had been left abandoned in the barn for years.

Ben would never have left on his own, for just the dropping of a rein would have rendered him helpless. He would also never have asked a hired hand to waste his day traveling around with him. But the boy was a different story. Dusty would pull the buggy around back, for Ben didn't want anyone to see him drag his legs. He had a rail built, so that he could pull himself up beside the buggy. With Dusty to drive the buggy, Ben could cover his ranch land. The boy loved going everywhere with Ben, and Ben loved his new freedom.

Ben loved to talk about politics, and Dusty was a willing listener. With Texas recovering from the war, governors were passing quickly. When the South had been defeated in 1865, Governor Murrah had fled to Mexico. The men would sit around after supper and talk about who would be the next man to lead Texas. Dusty would never leave until the last man said good night.

Dusty was often the topic of conversation at dinner between Bethanie and Ben. She suggested he move into

Josh's room. Ben liked the idea, but Dusty refused, saying he would sleep in the bunkhouse with the rest of the men. He could be no more than twelve, Bethanie thought, but he never let anyone forget that he thought himself a man. Maybe that was why he loved Ben so. Ben never talked down to him. He ordered Dusty around sometimes, but then, Ben ordered everyone around.

Ben and Bethanie's first argument came one evening, close to the end of their first month of marriage, and it, too, was thanks to Dusty. Bethanie ate half her dinner before she mustered the nerve to ask, "Ben, I think we should do something about Dusty's education."

Ben wiped his beard with his napkin. "I think the boy will learn all he needs to know working here on the ranch." He returned to the meal, as if his statement had concluded the discussion.

Bethanie wouldn't be put off so easily on something she believed in. "I could teach him a few mornings a week, and I know a man back East who would send a new supply of books every three months." Her food was completely forgotten now, and what she'd already eaten lay like lead in her stomach. She'd never opposed Ben.

Ben didn't realize he was in a battle. "He'll have enough trouble learning how to stay alive."

Bethanie leaned closer to Ben. "Texas will not always be wild and eventually his education will pay off."

Ben was growing tired of the discussion. "I think not, Beth." He wheeled his chair backward and headed for his desk.

Bethanie wouldn't abandon her cause. She didn't want Dusty to grow up to be like so many men in this wild country, ignorant of the world outside the range. "We'll talk about it more tomorrow," she stated firmly to herself as she began stacking the dinner dishes.

Much to Ben's displeasure, they talked about it for three days running. Bethanie never yelled or pouted, but

Chapter Ten

The hot Texas sun burned spring away as the nights fought relentlessly to remain cool. Spring's early promise of lush green now lay dried and parched under the daily baking. Old-timers predicted a harsh winter to come as they stared day after day at cloudless skies.

The floor in the main room of the Weston Ranch looked the same dusty brown as the weeds outside. Bethanie decided this was as good a day as any to scrub the neglected tiles. In her month as Ben's wife, this was her first opportunity to tackle the huge floor. She watched Ben leave with Dusty, knowing she had the entire morning. With determination, she tied her hair into a braid and put on her oldest dress. Rolling her sleeves high, Bethanie knelt and attacked her task with vigor.

The strong soap stripped layers of dirt off the tiles. She rubbed each square dry with rags until her reflection shone in the polished floor. The brightly colored rugs hanging along the walls seemed to cheer her on as they were reflected in each clean tile. Bethanie hummed as she worked, proud of her labor. The old Shaker songs her mother once sang ran through her mind now as wordless melodies.

Halfway through her chores, Bethanie jumped at the familiar bang of Ben's chair against the door. She'd been stubbornly, unrelentingly presented her side. On the fourth morning Bethanie won and ordered Dusty's first schoolbooks. Ben spent the morning mumbling about being warned once never to marry a redhead. Dusty fought the idea of book-learning as violently as Ben had, and lost in half the time.

As Bethanie began her second month of marriage, a fleeting thought turned into a nagging worry. The days passed and she waited for her time of month to come, slowly realizing the possibility to be fact. She was pregnant.

The sickness in the morning was slight, but she only took warm tea until noon. Ben paid no notice of her change in eating habits. Her new problem monopolized her thoughts as she went about her daily duties. She was going to have a baby, and she had not yet spent a night in her husband's bed.

so absorbed in her work, she hadn't heard horses approaching.

With a gust of hot air, Ben clambered in. He was followed closely by two strangers. Bethanie rocked back on her heels and watched as they tracked dirt across her newly polished floor. Though housework was a never-ending job, a disheartened sigh escaped her lips as she saw her work laid to waste before the task could even be completed. She had the nonsensical urge to stand and yell, "Wait until I've finished before you track this floor up again."

One stranger was tall and wiry with a black mustache that stretched from ear to ear like a tightrope. The other was a short, nervous man, who patted his gun like one might pat a faithful pet. Bethanie couldn't help but stare at their dirt-covered boots as they crossed the room, following Ben to his desk.

"Beth!" Ben yelled, then turning, saw her on her knees. "Get up, Beth," he scolded. "We have company."

Bethanie rose and came to his side. "I'm sorry, gentlemen. I wasn't expecting guests."

"This is Wes Mayson." Ben waved toward the tall, bony man dressed in black. The stranger was a few years older than Ben. "And his foreman, Sam Burns." From Ben's offhanded introduction, Bethanie knew these men were unwelcome visitors. Ben might not be cordial, but among friends he was always proper. His lack of social grace was an unspoken insult.

"Nice to meet you." Bethanie tried to push her unruly strands of hair out of her face. "May I offer you some coffee?"

"Well, that would be right nice of you, Mrs. Weston." Mayson smiled, spreading his mustache into a thin line above his ample teeth. "May I say that I've heard what a beautiful wife Ben Weston had, but you outshine even the gossip's description." He winked at her as he smiled.

"Thank you." Bethanie kept her voice formal and moved a step closer to Ben. She couldn't put her finger on why, but she didn't like Mayson. Just as one glance at sour milk is enough to tell you all you need to know, something about Mayson was bent out of balance. Maybe it was the too friendly smile or the wink promising future closeness. Bethanie felt her flesh grow cold, and she quickly turned to the other man.

The runt of a foreman gave her a quick nod that looked more like a hiccup than a greeting. He hurriedly moved to the window and began pacing like a trapped weasel in an empty henhouse.

Mayson spoke in a loud voice designed to draw everyone's attention. "If I had such a lovely wife, I'd not work her so hard." His voice bore a joking tone, but his eyes held a touch of lust as he studied Bethanie with frightening intensity. "Unfortunately, my wife died last year in childbirth. She left me a screaming boy to raise."

Mayson's words were sad, but his tone left Bethanie wondering if he were saddened by his wife's death or merely annoyed.

Ben looked down at his desk and showed no sign of having heard Mayson's comment. After a few minutes of shuffling papers, he asked, "What are you here for, Mayson? It's a long ride from your ranch. I know this isn't a social call."

Bethanie seized her opportunity to vanish and fetch the coffee. She didn't bother to wait for Mayson's answer to Ben. Both of the newcomers made her uncomfortable. She had a feeling she would be happy to wash away the dirt they left behind from her floors.

Ruth was already preparing the tray when Bethanie stepped into the kitchen. Bethanie wondered if the woman heard everything that was said in this house. She even seemed to second-guess Ben's requests. Bethanie

thanked her for the tray and reluctantly returned to the men.

Ben sat with his fingers pressed flat on top of his desk as if holding the huge oak piece on the floor. Mayson leaned across the desk toward Ben, his voice rising with each word. "Look, Weston, you've got to sell. With winter coming on, half the stock will die off if we have another cold spell like we did last year."

Ben knotted his hands into fists. "I'm not about to sell my herd for your prices, Mayson. I'll not be part of your scheme. I'd rather see them freeze first." Ben's voice seemed calm, yet the look in his dark eyes left no doubt that he meant every word. In a cold tone he added, "You'll go too far someday, Mayson."

Mayson's cheeks puffed in hot anger. He seemed to be struggling to control his boiling blood. He stared at Ben's wheelchair as if debating an answer. Finally, in frustration, he whirled and stormed toward the door. "You'll be sorry, Ben Weston. Come spring you'll be lucky to have enough cattle alive to feed your ranch hands."

Sam Burns, Mayson's foreman, danced behind his boss like a man closely trailing a rattlesnake. They were out of the house before Bethanie realized what was happening.

She could hear Mayson giving orders to Burns, then the sound of horses being kicked hard. Bethanie quickly retraced her steps to the kitchen. She stayed there until she heard the door close and knew it was safe to return to her work. As she knelt beside her bucket, Ben moved in from the porch and crossed the room toward her. Bethanie noticed the six-gun he usually kept in his desk lay wedged between his leg and chair arm.

Ben stopped in front of her. "Let me see your hands," he ordered with more anger than she had ever heard in his voice.

Bethanie raised her red hands to him. She was shocked at his outburst. His attention seemed centered on her, completely removed from the men who just left.

Ben cupped her hands in his hard fingers. "It's embarrassing to find my wife scrubbing floors. I'll not have it," he commanded as he pushed her hands back toward her.

"But . . ." Bethanie began, her anger flaring. The tension from the visitors had set her nerves on edge, and now Ben was attacking her for no apparent reason. "I'm keeping my part of the bargain." She lifted her chin. "You wanted a housekeeper, and I try hard." She couldn't believe he was criticizing her work.

Ben's anger surprised her. "I wanted a wife!" He cut her off sharply, frustration at both her and himself showing in his actions as he turned around and moved away.

"I am your wife," Bethanie answered in a whisper to the back of his chair. She watched him moving back to his desk. She knew what he meant by a wife, but he'd said it would be her decision, and he would keep his word. He was as honor-bound by his word as she was to their marriage.

They talked little all evening, for Bethanie was lost in her own thoughts. He tried to tell her about the runnings of the ranch, but she only half listened. She knew she must do something quickly. Her problem was one that would not wait. She could run away, but where? She couldn't ask Ben for money to leave him. She could tell Ben the truth, but she feared what he might do if he knew his wife were carrying Josh's child. No, she wouldn't come between brothers.

As Bethanie said good night and went to her room, she knew only one plan would work. She wouldn't raise a child without a father as her mother had raised her. No one would ever laugh and make fun of the baby she carried. She must make her marriage more than in name only. Not for her sake, nor for Josh's, but for the baby growing inside her. Her baby must have a birthright. The child would not suffer for her folly even if she must lie.

Bethanie bathed and slipped on a freshly washed nightgown. In her mind she talked with her reflection in the mirror. "This is the only answer," she told herself firmly. She had to make Ben believe he was the one who fathered her child. After all, he said he could. Well, now he would think he had. Babies come early all the time. It wasn't as if this were some stranger's child.

A tear drifted down Bethanie's cheek. She hadn't heard a word from Josh since he'd left over a month ago. She knew he wouldn't return until the pain she had seen in his eyes healed. If it were even a fraction as great as her own pain, Bethanie feared she might never see him again. She must make her own way. She'd been taught all her life to be honest and now she must tell the greatest lie of all in order to protect her child who had no voice in the matter. Bethanie combed her long hair as determination set her sad face.

An hour later, Bethanie's bare feet made no sound as she walked across the hall to Ben's bedroom. The room had always seemed somehow off limits to her, even though no one had ever said anything. Ruth cleaned it daily, offering Bethanie no reason to enter, before tonight.

Her hand shook as she pushed the door wide open. A warm glowing fire greeted her from the fireplace. The room seemed warmer than any other in the house. Probably Ruth's doing, Bethanie thought. The woman always ensured Ben's comfort without seeming to fuss over him. Bethanie saw the darkened frame of a bed with Ben's wheelchair beside it, as if the chair stood at attention beside its master.

She watched in frozen silence as Ben rolled over in bed and squinted at the light from her candle. For an instant, Bethanie could see a resemblance to Josh. His dark hair was out of place, and the gray didn't show in the dim light. His short beard framed his jaw, giving the same strong effect as Josh's beard. His eyes were dark coals of mirrored firelight.

The likeness vanished as Ben spoke. "What is it?"

"It's me." Bethanie straightened her shoulders and her determination. She stepped to the bed and set her candle on the nightstand. His furnishings were heavy oak and seemed as immovable as the man before her.

Ben was wide awake now. His strong bare arms pulled his body up into a sitting position. "What do you want, Beth? It's late and I've got a full day tomorrow."

There was no softness in his voice, but Bethanie did not let that deter her. All other doors were closed to her now. "I . . . I've come to sleep with my husband."

Bethanie gripped the flannel of her gown as she tried to stop the violent shaking of her body. What if he refused her? What if he didn't?

"And do your wifely duty?" Ben's tone seemed skeptical.

"And do my duty," Bethanie echoed. He was not making this easy for her.

Ben's voice was hard between a bitter smile. "Pardon me if I doubt your word." Bethanie knew he didn't believe her. He had given her so much—his name, his protection, a home—but they had been married a month and she'd never crossed the hallway between their rooms. He'd told her once, he had been hurt too many times by people trying to be nice to him. She watched his eyebrows knit together as he studied her.

"Do you want me in your bed?" Bethanie asked, fearing he would refuse.

"Not yet." Ben folded his arms over his hard chest. "First, I need you to prove to me who is man and who is wife in this room . . . Remove your gown." His words were low, but Bethanie knew he was deadly earnest.

"Now?" Bethanie questioned. "As I stand here?"

"Remove your gown, or leave. I'll not be questioned in my own bedroom." His eyes were cold and dark brown as he watched her without any hint of emotion, without the slightest sign to indicate he cared one way or the other.

Bethanie knew he was testing her, but she couldn't turn and run. He wanted her, but not as an equal. She took a deep breath and began unbuttoning her gown. She saw shock register briefly on his face and knew he'd thought his demand would force her to leave.

As her cotton gown fell to the floor, Bethanie could not meet Ben's gaze. She forced her vision to the charcoal drawing behind his bed. The sketch of horses running wild reflected her desire to flee.

"Step closer," Ben ordered, his words low now. "You're my wife, Beth Weston, and you are a beauty."

This was the first compliment Ben had ever paid her. Bethanie looked at him and wondered if he was complimenting her or himself. The look on his face revealed nothing of his thoughts. His dark eyes studied her as his thumb ran up and down the short whiskers of his jawline. Bethanie was surprised to see a touch of indecision cross his face. Could this hard man be unsure of himself?

Ben slowly lifted his hand and closed his warm palm over Bethanie's full breast. She forced her body to remain frozen and not withdraw. His powerful fingers began kneading her flesh roughly as though he didn't know how sensitive a woman's breasts were. Her pink nipples peaked to his rubbing.

"Say it again, Beth," Ben insisted as he cupped her breasts in his hand.

"Say what again?" Bethanie's voice was shaking.

"Say you are my wife and will lie beneath me. I won't

try to break you. I'll not demand too much of you, but in this bedroom you must agree I am master, or I'll not have you in my bed." His words were as cold as his stone dark eyes.

Every ounce of Bethanie wanted to run, but she thought of the baby deep within her and knew she must do this thing. "I am your wife, and I will lie beneath you and do my duty."

Ben lessened his grip on her breast. "I know that took a great deal for you to say. I never thought I'd have such a fine wife. You're strong and spirited in mind and body. From this night, you're mine. Do you understand? Beth, from this night I will not sleep alone again."

Bethanie knew exactly what he was saying. This was not going to be a one-night stay as she had hoped. She was crossing a bridge that could not be retraced. "I understand," she whispered.

"Put on your gown and go around to the other side of the bed," Ben said with more gentleness than his usual tone.

Bethanie quickly pulled up her gown and slid into bed beside her husband. She lay on her back waiting. Staring at the ceiling, she wished she were home with her mother. But her mother was dead, and this was her home.

Ben scooted down beside her and placed his hand on the flat of her abdomen. He spread his fingers wide and moved up and down across her body, lightly pulling at her flesh through the material of her gown.

Bethanie closed her eyes tightly and felt tears spill down both sides of her face. She lay frozen as Ben's hand pulled her gown open and touched her flesh. He moved his palms up from her thigh to her breast and down again. His action was not loving, only exploring, as if he were trying to learn every inch of her body. He seemed to want to prove something to her or to himself. He twisted her nipple between his fingers and thumb until her traitorous mound pointed once more to his satisfaction. "I've watched you move many times and wondered what softness lay beneath the bindings of your bodice. You're full and ripe."

Bethanie pulled an inch away. She resented being talked about like a cow. At this moment she hated Ben Weston. She hated his coldness and high-handed manner. She even hated being called Beth.

Ben's hand closed like a vise on her shoulder and drew her back. "Don't pull away from me, Beth."

Bethanie nodded slightly as he released her shoulder and slid his hand back to her breasts. His fingers were rough as they rubbed her soft flesh, but she didn't withdraw again. He wasn't hurting her, only showing ownership. She hated each stroke.

Ben reached across her and blew out the candle. In the darkness his voice came clear to her like the dropping of a trapdoor to a man at his own hanging. "Pull up your gown."

Bethanie hesitated. There was still time to change her mind. She could jump up and run out of his room. Ben couldn't even follow her. But she knew there was nowhere else to go and no one to turn to. She forced herself to follow his instructions.

This was to be it then. No words of love or caring. Maybe I'm better off without them, Bethanie thought. It was such words that had gotten her in this mess to begin with.

In silence, Ben lifted himself and slowly lowered his body to Bethanie. As his organ pushed into her unprepared flesh, Bethanie let out a cry of pain and heartbreak. Ben put his hand over her mouth to stifle any more sound as he pushed deeper. "It always hurts the first time, I've heard." His words were a cold statement brushing her ear.

His palm remained across her mouth as he took her.

Bethanie let the tears flow freely as her body remained stiff. She wasn't being raped, she reminded herself. She had come willingly to his bed. He was her husband doing what he had every right to do. Yet the pain of his thrusts blended with the ache in her heart.

Ben's body tensed, then collapsed on her. A minute later, he rolled off her and lay on his back, his only comment, "It won't hurt next time."

Bethanie pulled her gown down. "Don't ever cover my mouth again." It was a little thing, but Bethanie had to say it.

Ben turned toward her. "I will not, since you ask it. You will sleep in my bed from now on?"

Bethanie was surprised at the questioning tone in his voice. "Yes," she answered. He had doubted her word, or had he thought his cold lovemaking would drive her away?

Bethanie was aware that Ben didn't sleep for a long time. She wondered what this man, who treated sex as coldly as he did everything else, was thinking. Finally his breathing grew regular and she turned toward him. She studied his face in the dying firelight. In sleep he looked younger and more like Josh. Both brothers had the square jawline and short black beard. Only Josh had allowed the sun to tan his skin golden, whereas Ben's skin seemed a pale gray. Where Josh's features were strong, Ben's seemed hard, unyielding. Though Ben's arms were powerful like his younger brother's, his legs were thin, barely capable of movement and too weak to hold him up.

Bethanie scolded herself. She would think of Josh no more. She was Ben's wife in every way now.

When Bethanie awoke, Ben was gone. She dressed and went to the main room. He was, as always, at his desk working. She saw no change in his manner toward her, but she'd expected none. He left the house for the barns after breakfast without saying a word. Within minutes she heard his carriage pass.

At noon Ben returned. His face was clouded with thought as Bethanie moved silently around him. As she bent to pour his coffee, she caught him staring at her bodice. She reddened as she realized he must be thinking of last night.

Bethanie moved quickly away and returned to her chair.

"Beth." He sounded gruff, as always. "I've hired another girl from a nearby farm to help you out around here. You and Ruth are working too hard. She will come two days a week. Leave some of the heavy work for her."

"All right," Bethanie answered, trying to concentrate on her food.

"I don't want to see you doing the laundry or scrubbing floors on your hands and knees again," he ordered.

"All right." Bethanie frowned. "But I can handle the work."

Ben threw his napkin down. "Hell, woman, won't you let me be good to you?"

"I want no payment for what I did last night. It was my duty," Bethanie answered. She didn't want him doing anything for her. He would give her baby a name and a home. That was enough.

"I know that. I'm not trying to pay you like you were whoring. I'm only askin' for a little peace of mind. You're my wife, not a slave. If you can do your duty, I can do mine. You are mistress over one of the biggest ranches in Texas. You shouldn't be on your knees cleaning the floors." He pushed himself back from the table. "And for God's sake, make yourself some new dresses. Those are too tight. I don't want the hands gawking at you."

"The way you do?" Bethanie asked, hoping her words stabbed his cold heart deeply.

Ben swung around and rolled from the room. Bethanie heard the front door slam and Ben's voice yelling for Dusty to hitch up the buggy. Within minutes, she heard them driving away from the house, away from her.

She spent the rest of the day sewing and wondering if she'd gone too far. She ate dinner alone, knowing Ben must have preferred the campfire group to her company tonight. After sewing until her eyes could no longer focus, Bethanie undressed and crawled between the cold sheets of Ben's bed.

Ben didn't join her until well after midnight. He lowered himself beside her, making no attempt to touch her. The same scene was repeated each night for a week. He was cold, as always, to her during the day and lay without touching her each night. He made no comment about her new loose dresses, but Ruth said he had ordered more material brought out with the next supplies.

By Sunday, Bethanie was beginning to relax. Ben, for once, was in a good mood and even played a few games of checkers with her after dinner. They talked about horses, and both enjoyed the conversation. After saying good night, Bethanie retired to her bedroom to undress and Ben moved to his desk. As she combed her hair, she heard his chair in the hall. He paused at her door, but did not enter. She was thankful he had not insisted she share his bedroom. Here, she could dress in private. Perhaps he wanted the same privacy.

Ben pushed the door wide with his hand. "Come to bed," he ordered without emotion.

The muscles along her shoulders tightened and her mouth went suddenly dry. She usually lay waiting for Ben to finish his paperwork. "I'll be there shortly." She acted as if his order had been a request as she stretched her neck trying to get enough moisture to swallow.

Fifteen minutes later, Bethanie crawled into Ben's bed. He silently watched her. Bethanie tried to force a smile as she pulled the covers around her and turned her back to him.

Before she had time to warm the sheets beneath her, Ben's hand touched her shoulder. He pulled her firmly on her back and slid his hand along her leg until her nightgown was twisted at her waist. His hand moved between her legs and pulled them apart. Bethanie closed her eyes in dread and braced herself for what she knew would happen next.

Bethanie raised her hand to her mouth and bit back a scream as Ben pushed into her body. He didn't touch her breasts this time, and she was thankful. They were tender and growing larger from her pregnancy.

Ben's urge was soon satisfied and he rolled from her onto his side. He was silent for a moment, but she could hear his breathing grow regular. "I see how much you hate this." His voice was low in her ear. His fingers wiped the tears from her face. "Yet you don't complain. I admire that. You've kept your word and slept with me. Now I give my word. I'll not mount you but once a week. You need not fear me the other nights. Is that fair?"

Bethanie nodded as she pulled her gown over her legs. This duty of hers was humiliating and painful, but she could endure it once a week.

Ben propped his head on his elbow as he watched a steady stream of tears drifting down her face. "I know you may not believe me, but I have no wish to hurt you." Ben touched her hair in an awkward, calming gesture. He'd never been a gentle man, but his small action showed his concern for her.

Bethanie turned her face into his hand. "I know, Ben." Tears filled her eyes and ran in tiny rivers over her cheeks. Because there was no one else and she felt so all alone, Bethanie turned to this man beside her. She moved into his arms, and he held her for an hour as she cried. All the loneliness and fear she had felt these past weeks crumbled into tears. Ben never spoke, yet he patted her as a father strokes a heartbroken child. He held her until dawn, and no nightmares troubled Bethanie's sleep. The hazy dream of being awakened and running during the night didn't come while she slept so near her husband.

From that night on, Bethanie fell asleep on Ben's shoulder. He would turn toward her and open his arm in silent invitation. She was thankful he never tried to kiss her, or touch her other than hold her. True to his word, once each week he would satisfy his need. As the weeks passed, Bethanie surprised herself and no longer cried.

Chapter Eleven

Windy summer days followed one another into fall like a string of dried leaves follows a dust devil down a shriveled-up creekbed. The men of Weston Ranch fought the drought as valiantly as they'd struggled with the downpours of spring. Weather was never the topic of ideal conversation, and was often one of the many problems on Bethanie Weston's mind as she climbed from bed each morning and crossed the hallway to dress.

The north winds had begun to chill the morning air as Bethanie studied her reflection in the mirror for the hundredth time. Her stomach was rounded in the first display of motherhood. She knew she could keep the child a secret no longer. She had slept in Ben's bed for two and a half months and was now almost four months pregnant. But babies come early all the time, she reasoned, as she tried to pull in her abdomen. She'd made all her dresses loose and shapeless, but they couldn't conceal her for many more weeks.

"I'll tell him next week," Bethanie decided as she finished dressing. She tied her hair up into a bun and left her room thinking of breakfast. Now that the morning sickness was over, she found herself constantly hungry.

She enjoyed breakfast with Ben, as their time together aged. He was formal, as always, but liked talking about every detail of the ranch. The more she showed an interest, the more Ben explained ranching. Even the quiet evenings with Ben working at his desk while she sewed brought a calming peace across her mind.

Bethanie smiled as she walked across the polished floor of the main room. The morning sun darted through the crisp lace curtains and danced over each piece of rich wood furnishings. An open front door shot a triangular shaft through the room that ended at the base of the mammoth fireplace.

"Beth!" Ben shouted from the porch. "Beth, get out here!"

Bethanie hated being ordered, but had decided weeks ago that Ben meant no unkindness by his manner.

"I'm here," Bethanie answered as she stepped to the door. Squinting at the morning sun, she saw her husband before her. His face was now a golden brown, thanks to Dusty's outings. His hair curled slightly over his white collar and she wondered how he would react if she offered to cut it for him.

Ben watched her a moment, then stated, "Follow me." He pushed himself down the incline at the edge of the porch. Bethanie watched several ranch hands come out into the morning air and stand on the bunkhouse porch.

Ben moved to the barn as Bethanie followed, wondering what could be amiss. He stopped his chair beside the barn door and moved his hand up to the latch.

"Stand back," Ben yelled at Bethanie.

Just as she stepped beside Ben's chair, the barn door flew open. Two men ran forward with a beautiful smoky gray horse dancing between them. The huge animal pulled at the ropes about his neck and snorted as he tried to free himself of the pesky cowboys.

"Oh, Ben!" Bethanie laughed. "He's magnificent. I've never seen such a wonderful animal." She'd loved horses all her life, and knew this one to be a fine stallion. Just watching him prance brought a rush of excitement to her blood.

Ben smiled one of his rare lopsided grins. "It will take a month or so to break him for gentle riding. Then he's yours."

"What?" Bethanie turned to Ben, not believing his words.

"I bought him for you. No one else will ride him." Ben sounded aggravated that she doubted him. "I'll see you riding him in a month's time." He pointed at the horse as determination wrinkled his face.

Bethanie watched the spirited animal. She hadn't been on a horse since she married. He would be wonderful to ride, but in a month she would be too far along with the pregnancy. The image of her mother trying to help a woman who had fallen from a horse during pregnancy flashed through her mind. The woman had almost died from loss of blood and heartache over a stillborn child.

Bethanie's hand spread slowly across her abdomen. She realized she would protect with her life the child that grew unbidden within her. "No." She swallowed hard, aware of several ranch hands watching her. "No" seemed to be all she could force from her lips. She began to back away and saw the anger in Ben's face. All eyes were staring at her in disbelief. She couldn't just announce to everyone that she was pregnant. Yet, no one ever questioned Ben's word, and she was doing so in front of all his men.

Suddenly, she couldn't face Ben. She couldn't bear to see his cold hard eyes judging her and finding her wanting.

Bethanie turned and ran as fast as her long skirts would allow toward the house with Ben's angry shouts echoing around her. She paid no heed to his commands as tears blurred her vision.

She flew to her room and threw herself on the quilted

bedspread. The warm, peaceful room did little to comfort her now. Embarrassment burned her face as she buried her head in the pillows. She'd always dreamed of having such an animal, and now she couldn't ride him. What a magnificent gift given to her not by the man she loved, but by the man who thought he owned her. She'd tried to be a good wife, yet now she had humiliated him in front of everyone. In trying to give her baby a name, she'd managed to make everyone unhappy.

Bethanie didn't hear Ben's chair until it banged into her bedroom door, almost tearing the wood from its hinges. She lifted her head as he shoved his way into her room slamming the door behind him. She'd never seen him so angry. His face twisted with rage as he stopped beside her bed.

Ben yanked her into a sitting position. His long, strong fingers dug into her arms like an iron vise. "Why won't you take my gift?"

His powerful hands held her painfully. "Do you hate me so much?" He began shaking her. His narrowly controlled violence raged like a flash flood across the crevices of his angry features. "Do you hate the thought of being married to a cripple so much that you can't even take a gift from me?" Ben pulled her toward him until she could feel his words upon her face. "Why must you accept unwillingly everything I do for you?"

Bethanie was so frightened by Ben's rage, she hardly noticed his bruising grip. She'd seen him angry during the past months, but never uncontrollably as now.

"I know I'm not a full man," he yelled. "But by God, I've tried to be a husband to you."

Ben dropped his grip suddenly and pulled his hands back to his lap as if regretting having touched her. "I don't understand. You knew what I was when you married me, but you still act as if I am a jailor. Every time I get close to you, you endure my touch in distaste."

He rubbed his hands up and down his legs as if to clean the feel of her from his palms. "I can take no more, Beth. Part of me wants to beat you, and another part wants to hold you forever. I thought I'd make you happy with the damn horse. But you won't even take it; you hate me so." His dark brown eyes bore a sadness, a sorrow deeper than she could fully grasp. "I can't hold you, Beth . . . you're free to leave. I'll see you have enough money to go wherever you wish." He lowered his chin to his chest and shaded his eyes from her gaze.

Bethanie rubbed her bruised arm and slid to the edge of the bed. "No," she sobbed. She couldn't stand seeing Ben defeated like this. He was a proud man, and he'd done nothing to deserve such pain. She had been so wrapped up in her own loss of Josh she hadn't seen the fine, stubborn man before her. He was a strong man, who'd been trying to make her happy for months now. All his awkward efforts swam before her in her tears. The bedroom he'd insisted belong to her alone. The dresses. The hired girl. And now the horse.

"I won't leave." Her words were coming in gulps as the weight of her misjudgment settled upon her shoulders. "I don't hate your touch, Ben. I'm your wife . . . I don't hate you. I don't want to leave."

Ben raised his head. "Then why will you not accept the horse?"

"I want him, and I thank you for him." With forced effort, Bethanie leaned over and kissed his cheek. "I'll not leave you, Ben. You are a good husband and this is my home."

"Then why did you run away?" Ben asked in a skeptical tone. His thick eyebrows knotted together as his dark eyes watched her carefully.

"I wanted to wait until later to tell you," Bethanie began, her cheeks blushing red. There would be no other time; she must be honest now. "I can't ride for a while. I'm going to have a child."

"What?" Ben shouted, his knuckles turning white as he gripped the arms of his chair.

Bethanie placed her hands over his lean fingers as she sat eye level with him. "We are going to have a child." She bit back her lip as a twinge of guilt from her lie passed over her.

"How long have you known?" Ben interrogated, still not sure she was telling the truth.

"A few weeks," Bethanie answered, lowering her head. They had never talked about children. What if Ben didn't want any? She was suddenly aware of the hundreds of things married people must talk about she and Ben had never discussed.

"Why didn't you tell me earlier?" Ben asked. His hand moved to capture hers in a swift, startling action.

"I didn't know if you'd be pleased," Bethanie answered in a whisper.

"Pleased, pleased!" Ben's voice rose. "God, woman, I may explode with pleasure."

Bethanie looked up at him and was surprised to see him smiling. He looked younger and truly happy for once. He raked his fingers through his black hair and stared at the ceiling. "I've always wanted sons, but I never hoped . . . You've made me very happy, Beth." He thought for a moment, then laughed aloud. "You're right, there'll be no riding for you right now. I'll pen the horse until after the baby comes."

Bethanie smiled. "Thank you." She could not believe her news had made him so happy. "I'm sorry I embarrassed you in front of the men."

Ben seemed to have forgotten. "Forget it," he began, then shook his head. "No, don't forget it." A grin took any sting from his words. "Don't ever do that again. From now on, I want you keeping no secrets from me.

Understand?" His hand squeezed her fingers briefly. "So you don't want to leave me," he said to himself.

Bethanie wiped the tears from her eyes. "No, Ben, I want to stay." Ben must have thought she'd felt trapped here for these past months. If she were honest with herself, she had felt that way many times. But not now. Her garden was planted, her child was growing inside her. This was her home and Ben her husband.

Ben leaned closer and touched her face. "You kissed me," he whispered. "No one's kissed me since my mother died."

"But you've surely had other women?" Bethanie asked, amazed by his confession.

"Sure. Ones that charge by the hour," Ben answered. "Who else would want to sleep with me?"

Suddenly Bethanie understood this man beside her. He had never loved, never felt a woman's warmth. She hadn't thought of it before, but others had never touched him, and she'd fallen into the same pattern—partly because of his gruff manner, but partly due to the chair he was bound to. It must have been hard for him at first to endure his handicap and others' hands-off attitude. She lifted her head to cup Ben's bearded face. "When I sleep with you, Ben, I swear it's not out of pity or for a reward." She knew there was no pleasure in their lovemaking, but sleeping in his arms brought her comfort. His strong arms shielded her from the loneliness of her life here in this wild country, and her endless nightmare was held at bay by his presence.

Tears formed in her strong man's eyes. "I believe you. I'll not mount you while you're pregnant, Beth, if you'll stay in my bed." He was no longer demanding, but asking.

Bethanie smiled to herself. He was learning as much about women as she was about men. A man can ask for the world and a woman gives it willingly, yet let him demand and watch her withdraw. "I'll stay, Ben . . . When a baby moves inside a woman, another can feel it. Would you like that?"

"More than you know," Ben answered as he pulled Bethanie to him. "I hope I didn't hurt you." He moved his hands up and down her arms.

"No," Bethanie lied. "I'm fine. I should have told you earlier about the baby."

"Come here," Ben urged, pulling her into his lap.

"I'll hurt your legs." Bethanie tried to push away.

Ben laughed, "Nothing hurts them." He closed his arms around Bethanie as she sat in his lap, her head only slightly higher than his. "Let me hold my wife," he whispered as he pulled the pins from her hair and let it fall. "I like your hair down best. I remember that first day when you rode up and pulled off your hat. Your hair flowed wild and free like a cloud around you."

This was a side of Ben she'd never seen before. She felt warm and loved around him for the first time. Willingly, encircling his neck with her arms, she bent slightly and kissed his cheek once more as she felt his arms tighten around her.

"I'm not a man of fancy words," Ben said, clearing his throat. "I may never talk of this again, but I want to say it now. Beth, you're a strong, fine woman and you'll be a good mother. I want you to know that I'll take good care of you and the baby." He ran his hand lightly across her abdomen as if touching a miracle. "I hope you don't hate me for getting you pregnant so soon."

"No, Ben, I don't hate you." Bethanie couldn't bring herself to say she loved him. What a crazy set of morals she had adopted. She could lie about his child, but not about his love. Her child would have a name, a home, and a fine man to call father. Finally Bethanie said the only thing she could, "I'm happy about the baby, Ben. I want to give you many children."

Ben seemed satisfied with her comment. Holding her on his lap, he rolled the wheelchair into the main room.

Bethanie decided everyone on the ranch must have been waiting for them to come out. They all seemed to relax as they saw her riding on his lap.

"Break out the brandy, Ruth." Ben yelled loud enough for the hands on the porch to hear. "Give everyone a glass. We're going to toast the next generation of Westons."

Shock showed on everyone's face so completely that Bethanie decided she knew how the two-headed freak in the sideshow felt. Dusty broke first and ran to them, jumping like the child he was. "Bethanie, are you gonna have a baby?"

She blushed red. "Yes, Dusty, I'm going to have a baby."

"Wow, that's great!" Dusty whooped like a wild Indian

The others surrounded her and Ben with toasts and congratulations. Ben beamed with pleasure and shook everyone's hand, but his other arm never left Bethanie's waist. He held her tight even after everyone had gone back to work.

Bethanie pushed gently on his chest. "I have work to do, Ben."

Ben released her with a nod. "I'll see to your horse." He moved slowly to the door, his eyes never leaving her. "Throw some grub in a basket for Dusty and me, we've got a lot of ground to cover today. I'll see you late tonight." For a long moment he stared at her as if memorizing her face. Bethanie had the feeling he wanted to say more but could not find the words.

"Late tonight," Bethanie echoed as she moved into the kitchen.

Bethanie had just crawled into bed when she heard the familiar roll of Ben's chair in the hall. He moved into his dressing area for several minutes then came to his side of the bed. She listened to the low sound of him lifting himself from the chair to bed.

"Are you asleep?" Ben asked as he slid in beside her.

"No." Bethanie rolled toward his outstretched arm and snuggled into his chest.

"Beth," he whispered, brushing her hair back away from her face. "Did you mean it when you said you didn't sleep with me out of pity?"

"I meant it," Bethanie answered. She'd been unfair with Ben, but from this day forward she would try to understand him.

"I believe you. I'm not sure why you're here, but I know you wouldn't lie." He thought for a minute. "I know you're not fond of the intimacy between husband and wife, so I'll try not to overly force myself on you. Since you don't turn away when I hold you, I think it must not be me but the act that repulses you. I can accept that." He paused and rubbed his bearded chin lightly against her hair. "Beth, you make me very proud."

Bethanie strained and lightly kissed his mouth. "You're a good husband, Ben." For the first time, she reached to touch him, spreading her hand wide over his bare chest. His lean muscles rippled slightly under her touch.

"And you, woman," Ben whispered a little out of breath, "are my life."

Bethanie understood the man beside her better than she thought she ever could. Her hand slid slowly back and forth across his chest, touching the hairs in the middle before returning to the smooth muscles of his shoulders. She wanted to show him a fraction of the contentment she'd felt this day, knowing he was pleased about the pregnancy . . . knowing he wanted her child.

"Beth!" Ben said her name between clenched teeth as he grabbed her hand and held it firmly to him.

Bethanie turned to him. Even in the faint light of a single candle, she could see a touch of fire in the brown eyes of his strained face. She withdrew slightly. "Did I do something wrong?"

Ben's words reflected his pain. "I'll not be able to keep my promise if you touch me like that."

Bethanie laughed as she realized her power over him. She snuggled closer, pressing her full breasts into his side. Knowingly she wiggled her fingers free from his grasp. She moved her hand down his chest to the flat of his stomach. He made no move to stop her, so Bethanie timidly began to circle his abdomen with her fingers. She stroked lower with each round until she brushed the hard form of his manhood.

Ben made a low moan. "Woman," he said less firmly than before, "I gave my word not to touch you while you're pregnant."

Bethanie moved her hand back to his chest and circled in slow, wide strokes with her fingers. "And you are a man of your word," she commented as she moved slightly, allowing him to feel the softness of her breasts at his side.

"I am a man of my word, married to a cruel, teasing witch," he answered. "When I married you and agreed to celibacy, I had no idea how lovely you truly were." His voice lowered slightly. "When you first came to my bed, I thought I was dreaming as I had many nights before. I wanted you so desperately, but not if you were playing games."

"You almost frightened me away."

"Better that than have only your memory beside me. If you came, it had to be to stay. I could not watch you each day and have it otherwise."

Bethanie took his hand and lifted it to one of her

breasts. He held back, hesitant, as she pressed his palm beneath her fullness. He didn't pull away from her as she shaped his hand with gentle strokes. She heard his sharp intake of breath as she moved his fingers over the cotton material covering her nipple.

"I gave my word." Ben was obviously puzzled at her strange behavior. "You have always been a mystery to me. I guess I'll never understand women, but I'd like to figure you out. Why are you doing this, Beth?"

How could she tell him the reason, when she didn't understand herself? Perhaps it was because he wanted her baby, unlike Bethanie's own father, who hadn't wanted her. Perhaps, for the first time this morning she saw how much he cared for her. He'd been willing to let her go if she was unhappy. Or maybe it was just the knowledge that he'd never known love and she felt somehow years wiser. His loving could never be the raging forest fire she'd felt with Josh, but banked coals can warm the heart as well.

Bethanie moved her lips to his ear. "Are you saying you wish me to stop?" She pressed her mouth to his neck and kissed him softly.

"No, never." Ben's voice was ragged with passion now. "But I can't take much more."

"Then maybe," Bethanie whispered, "you'd best give your word starting tomorrow morning."

A deep laugh erupted from Ben as he pulled her to him. "Lord, what did I ever do to be given such a wonderful woman?"

Bethanie moved willingly into his arms, now unafraid to tell him the pleasing secrets only a woman can tell a man. The caring in his actions made up for the experience he lacked. Like the first time he entered her, Bethanie cried out, but this time with pleasure, and Ben smothered her cry with his kiss.

An hour later, as Ben cradled her in his arms, Bethanie

heard his breathing grow regular. She lay awake until the candle snuffed itself out in a pool of wax. She knew she'd never tell Ben the truth about her baby, not for the baby's sake, but for Ben's.

Chapter Twelve

"Allison's not gonna come, Beth!" Ben yelled in his usual voice that the entire ranch could hear. "I'll not have that weak, sniveling woman in my house again."

"It's my home, too!" Bethanie stormed as she leaned over the desk toward her husband. His brow was drawn in rage, yet the corner of his mouth turned up as he eyed the strained material across her bulging stomach. Bethanie patted her thick waistline and continued. "And she's my only relative."

"But it's the dead of winter." Ben lifted a finger as if thinking of a solid point.

"Then there will be plenty of men available to escort her. Besides, the Indians have returned to the Oklahoma Territory by now." Bethanie folded her arms over her ever-expanding abdomen. "Mike said he would go get Allison as soon as this storm passes."

"No!" Ben shouted, "I hate whimpering women."

"Yes," Bethanie insisted, just as the door to the kitchen swung open and Dusty wandered out, gnawing on a chicken leg.

He glanced at the two people he loved most in the world and lifted his shoulders as if to beg their pardon. His little-boy smile flashed white teeth. "You two at it again?" he asked, seeming to enjoy the glares they both gave him.

"Get out of here, Dusty," Ben yelled.

"No, stay, Dusty," Bethanie countered. "You're part of our family, and you should have some say on the subject." She'd grown to love the boy dearly, once she got all the dirt scrubbed off him. His brown hair always seemed an inch too long and his eyes a size too large for his face.

Dusty walked over and sat on the side arm of the couch. The snow outside was making him feel cooped up and restless. Unfortunately for Dusty, Bethanie used the opportunity to double up on lessons he'd missed over the summer. He was like a turtle in a box, always testing the limits, always looking for a way out. He enjoyed the company in the main house. The constant food supply seemed needed now for his insatiable appetite, but everyone knew he longed for the outdoors.

Ben threw his hands in the air. "Can I never win an argument? Look, even Dusty follows you, not me."

Bethanie laughed suddenly. "He knows better than to antagonize the cook, and you should know better than to cross a pregnant woman."

"Is that so, Dusty?" Ben grumbled.

Dusty smiled, unfrightened by Ben's gruff manner. "Partly, but mostly I've seen you two go at it all fall, and if Bethanie finds it worth arguing over, she's planning on winning."

Ben frowned at the boy. "What do you think we ought to do, Dusty? Should we bring Allison up from San Antonio in the dead of winter, or should we treasure our peace and quiet?"

Dusty pointed his half-eaten chicken leg at Ben. "I ain't exactly crazy about seeing Miss Allison, either. But you know you can't say no to Bethanie. Plus, Mike's had the packhorse saddled for two days in the barn. He's acting like a bull that got a hold of loco weed. I figure that makes your odds two to one."

"Oh, all right," Ben huffed. "She can come, but not until the baby's due."

Bethanie knew he was thinking of the last week or two in January and that would be too late. "Please, Ben," she pleaded as she turned toward him. "Let her come for Christmas."

"What?" Ben yelled.

"Stop yelling at me, Ben Weston. I can hear you fine. I'm pregnant, not deaf."

"Then hear me, woman. I'm the man in this house. Your cousin can visit, but only till the baby comes. Understand?"

Bethanie moved around his desk and kissed his cheek. "Anything you say," she whispered, knowing he had given in on every count.

"Dusty," Bethanie turned to the boy. "Play Ben some checkers while I put supper on the table. Maybe it'll cool his temper."

As they began a game, Bethanie moved about the dining room. Two more weeks until Allison would come. Her cousin had written begging to come, but the snow was delaying the trip. Bethanie remembered how hopeless Allison sounded in her letter. Times were hard for her since Martha's death. She had to grow up fast. Wilbur had departed midsummer with a cattle drive to make some quick money. Somehow, Allison had managed to run the hotel during his long absence. He hadn't returned in October with the other men, but had sent a message saying he knew a way to make some fast money up North and would see her soon. Allison sounded lonely and, judging from her questions, more than a little interested in Mike. It would be good to have her near when the baby came, and the hotel could easily be closed for a few of the winter months. With all the Indian attacks, there were very few travelers brave enough to venture as far out as San Antonio.

Bethanie touched her stomach and felt the child within her move. Never, if she lived to be a hundred, would anything feel so wonderful.

Three days passed before the sun began to melt the snow. Within hours the ranch transformed itself from an iceland into miles of slush and mud. While most of the hands trudged through the sticky earth to check on cattle, Mike prepared for his journey to collect Allison. He'd written to her during the fall, then proclaimed to anyone who would listen that he was in love enough to offer marriage. He'd every intention of doing so before her visit ended.

Bethanie watched him go. Mike was a fine man and would make a good husband for Allison. He'd told them already of his plan to buy a spread just to the north. Ben had offered to loan Mike enough money to buy the land in exchange for Mike's work as foreman for six years. Mike could use the years to start his own herd.

A dull pain in the small of Bethanie's back bothered her all afternoon. She knew it would be only a few weeks now before her child was born, maybe sooner. As the months had passed, the baby had somehow become more and more Ben's and less Josh's child. Though a part of her would always be somewhere with Josh, she allowed herself little time to think of him. Only during her quiet moments to herself did she dare think his name and again feel the pain of longing for his touch. He'd left his mark on her very soul and no amount of denial would erase it.

Bethanie pushed Josh once more from her thoughts as she helped Ruth clear the dinner dishes. Without warning an agonizing pain stretched around her abdomen like long, willowy vines. Bethanie crumbled to her knees by the windows. "Ruth," she whispered, fear reflecting in her voice. Bethanie glanced around, but Ben must be at his desk, out of sight from her corner of the dining area.

Ruth was instantly at her side. There was no need for her to ask why Bethanie called. Ruth knelt beside her, bracing Bethanie's body up with her own strength. "Relax, don't fight it, the pain will stop in a moment."

Bethanie couldn't reply. She nodded as sweat dampened her forehead. Ruth put a protective arm around her shoulder. "It's starting," she said simply. The older woman showed no sign of surprise or alarm.

"I'm afraid," Bethanie whispered as she let out a long-held breath. "I don't want Ben to know."

"You, afraid, Miss Bethanie?" Ruth chuckled in an uncommon laugh. "Why, you're the bravest woman I know. Didn't I hear how you fought off a war party of Indians single-handedly?" Ruth squeezed her arm lightly. "Don't you worry now. I've watched many women deliver. I know what to do when the time comes." She smiled, cracking her skin into thousands of tiny lines. "We've got a long night of work ahead, but I've never known you to be afraid of work. The baby will know how to come out. All I have to do is catch it."

"The pain is gone now," Bethanie answered as Ruth helped her to her feet. The housekeeper seemed as excited as if she were the grandmother.

"I'll get you into bed, then I'll make you a glass of that herb tea you like so well," Ruth whispered. "No need worrying the men just yet. They tend to get all antsy when a baby's comin'."

Bethanie crossed the large room with Ruth a step behind her. "I think I'll retire early, Ben," she said with more cheer than she felt.

"Fine, Beth, I'll read a while longer." Ben never bothered to raise his eyes from the book he was reading. He might grumble about Dusty having to spend too much time at schooling, but Ben anxiously awaited each box of new books.

Just as Ruth helped Bethanie into bed, another pain struck. This one was sharper than the last, like long, thin fingers strangling her middle. Bethanie lay back and tried to relax, but for the next two hours she marked time in the minutes between contractions.

"Beth." Ben bumped her bedroom door open. "I thought you were . . ." He stopped in midsentence at the sight before him. Bethanie lay in the bed she hadn't slept in for months, and Ruth sat beside her holding her hand.

"The time is near," Ruth answered Ben. Bethanie closed her eyes, as another contraction racked her body.

Ben rolled his chair to the bed and took Bethanie's other hand. "You should have called me," he scolded.

"I didn't want to worry you needlessly," Bethanie answered when she was able to speak.

"Worry me," Ben exclaimed. "My God, woman, you're having my child." His voice was rough, yet his touch gentle. "Isn't it too soon?" He looked at Ruth. "Could something be wrong?"

Ruth shook her head. "Babies come when they're ready, early or not. I've never known one to come when expected." She stood, leaving Bethanie to Ben. "I'll boil water to wash everything and tell Dusty to go break a branch off that willow out back." She was gone before Ben could ask any questions.

Ben wiped the sweat from Bethanie's forehead. "Are you all right?"

"Yes, Ben. Go back to your reading. It'll be a long night."

Ben shook his head. "I wish we lived close enough to go for a doctor. Would you like me to send a man to fetch one of the sisters?"

"No," Bethanie answered. "Ruth will help me." The last thing she wanted was one of those noisy sisters in the house. They might be the nearest women other than Ruth, but they'd never been interested in her except as a topic of gossip and she couldn't see having them here now.

Ben pulled the blanket up to her shoulders even though she was sweating from the strain of the last contraction. "I'll not leave you," he insisted.

"But, Ben," Bethanie scolded. "Men don't watch babies being born. It's not decent."

"Decent or not, I'm not leaving you." Ben drew his eyebrows together. "Do you think I could wait in the other room while you suffer in here? I love you too much for that."

Bethanie smiled. It was the first time Ben had spoken of love. Though his actions told her in a thousand ways, he was not given to pretty words. "All right, Ben," she said as another pain gripped her. His strong hand held her tightly until the contraction lessened.

The hours passed as the pains grew stronger and closer, finally coming almost one on top of the other. Bethanie's long hair was wet with sweat and Ben's face pale with worry.

Ruth moved about the room, keeping a fire going, changing towels under Bethanie as her water broke, and always encouraging her.

"Ruth . . . Ruth," Bethanie cried, "I have to push." The contractions were so strong she felt her insides might crumble from the pressure.

Ruth produced a short stick about the width of a fat cigar. "As the baby comes, bite down on this," she said. It was a short branch of the willow tree that had been stripped of all its bark.

Ruth lifted the sheet at Bethanie's legs and sat at the foot of the bed, waiting. Bethanie had to laugh even as tears of strain rolled down her face. Ruth looked as though she were waiting for a stage to arrive instead of a baby.

Bethanie felt the next contraction begin and put the stick in her mouth. One fear she'd had all during the pregnancy was that she might call Josh's name and not Ben's when in pain. She pressed her teeth into the soft wood. Now she would not cry out.

The pain grew, and Bethanie pushed with all her strength as she felt her entire insides sliding downward toward Ruth.

"I see its head!" Ruth shouted happily.

Bethanie glanced at Ben, thinking to see the same joy, but Ben's face was a dark cloud of worry. His face was twisted in agony, yet he looked wonderful to her now. He was here with her when she needed his strength. She knew he wasn't thinking of the baby, but only of her pain. In the moments between pushes, Bethanie squeezed his hand. Deep in his dark eyes she saw the love of a strong man. As she pushed again, Ben's face showed the same strain, the same pain as she felt. They were together as one, bringing their child into the world.

As she felt the tightening of another contraction, she rolled forward, grabbing her knees on either side of her huge bulk. She pushed as perspiration beaded all over her body, and the child emerged from deep within her.

Exhausted, Bethanie collapsed as Ruth lifted a tiny baby into the air. The older woman rushed across the room to the fire and began frantically working to clear the child's mouth and lungs of water. Seconds later, cries filled the room as Ruth wrapped the newborn tightly.

Ben held Bethanie as a chill overtook her. He yelled above the baby, each word showing his concern. "Ruth, is Bethanie all right? She's shaking like she's chin deep in snow, yet she's covered with sweat."

Before Ruth could answer Bethanie stopped shaking and cuddled close to Ben's arm. Ben wiped the long strands of hair from her face. "She's so pale," he whispered.

Ruth walked toward the new parents. "She's fine. She's quite a lady. I've seen women go through half as much with twice the trouble. She'll be needing her rest now, so she can feed this little screamer in a few hours."

Ben smiled down at Bethanie. "I'm a lucky man."

"No," Ruth corrected. "You're a lucky father." She laid the bundle in his arms. "She's tiny, no more than five pounds, but from her yells, I'd say she's sturdy enough."

Ben stared in wonder at the baby in his arms as Ruth moved around Bethanie, freshening the bed. Bethanie opened her eyes and turned to watch Ben with the baby. He examined the tiny hand like a man holding the world's greatest treasure. The baby's small fingers encircled Ben's thumb and pulled it toward her mouth. Ben laughed, all worry vanishing from his face.

Bethanie raised on one elbow. "I'm sorry, Ben, I know you wanted a boy."

"Who said?" Ben answered. "Look, Beth, isn't she the most beautiful girl you've ever seen? I'm so glad she's not ugly like other babies I've seen."

Bethanie looked down at her daughter nestled in Ben's arms. She had black hair and dark eyes from the Weston side. "What shall we name her?" she asked as Ben folded the blanket closer around her.

"I don't know. What was your mother's name?" Ben gave Bethanie only half his attention as he answered, "Mine was Ann."

"Mine was Mary, but I don't like Mary Ann much. My father was named after the ship that brought the first Shakers to America. They called him Mariah. I think my mother would have liked her first grandchild to be named Mariah."

Ben smiled down at the tiny baby. "Mariah Ann Weston. That sounds just fine."

Ruth, heavy-laden with soiled sheets and towels, stepped from the room. A sudden scream sounded in the hallway. "What are you doing sleeping there?" she yelled. "Get out of my way, boy!"

Ben and Bethanie broke into laughter as Dusty, rubbing sleepy eyes, stepped into the doorway. "I was waitin' for the baby," he mumbled.

"Well, come here." Ben beamed as he held up Mariah. "I'd like you to meet Miss Mariah Ann Weston."

Dusty took the bundle carefully, his expression exploding with joy. "Looks more like a squirrel than a girl." He looked up, frowning suddenly. "Sorry, I didn't mean nothing." He brightened. "She's gonna be a lot of work, I figure."

Bethanie laughed. "Not so much that we will have to drop your lessons."

Ben reached and pulled Bethanie closer to him. "I'm the happiest man alive. I can even see the future. Someday, Dusty, you and Mariah will run this ranch."

Bethanie squeezed Ben's arm before she fell into an exhausted sleep.

For six weeks Bethanie slept in her bedroom with Mariah in a cradle at her side. Her body recovered from the birth. Finally Mariah began to sleep all night, leaving Bethanie free to return to Ben's bed.

As she tiptoed on bare feet across the icy floor, Bethanie was reminded of the same journey nine months before. Who would ever have guessed Ben would have made such a fine father? He doted over Mariah almost as much as Ruth did.

Bethanie pushed the door open and saw Ben's sleeping

form in the firelight. He rolled over and squinted his eyes. "What's wrong, Beth?"

"Nothing." She stepped closer. "I've just come to sleep with my husband."

He was wide-awake now. "And do your wifely duty?"

Bethanie could see he was having trouble holding his features stern. "And do my wifely duty," she echoed, as she had months ago when she first came to his bed.

"Remove your gown. I wish to see my wife," Ben said as he folded his arms across his chest.

"If I don't, must I leave now?" Bethanie asked, slowly unbuttoning her gown. She let the garment fall slowly to the floor. Her skin glowed in the firelight and her breasts were full from nursing. She watched Ben as he devoured her body with his dark eyes. Her hair was flowing freely down her back. She knew the newly washed mass was shining golden red in the firelight.

His voice was thick with passion. "You are my wife, and you are a beauty." His hand gently touched her throat, allowing his fingers to slide along her body, stopping briefly between her breasts before continuing down. "Are you sure, Beth? It may be too soon."

"I'm sure, Ben." She smiled at his concern. Slowly, allowing him full view of her body, she circled the bed and lifted the covers on her side. As she moved beneath the blankets, Ben turned to study her.

"I missed you." He reached down and lifted her hands to his lips. Bethanie moved closer under the protection of his arm.

Chapter Thirteen

The nickname "Squirrel," which Dusty had given to Mariah Weston, stuck as the months passed. Allison came for a three-day stay before leaving to marry Mike. The newlyweds returned in a month, and with Ben's help, bought the spread bordering the Weston Ranch. After months of running a hotel in San Antonio, Allison seemed more than happy with her small ranch house. Bethanie was thrilled to have her cousin as a neighbor. She felt a sense of family surrounding her in this vast land unlike any she had ever known. Even Ben seemed to welcome Allison, seeing her as Mike's worry now and no longer a hindrance to him.

Ben drew Bethanie into the running of the ranch, more out of a need to keep her at his side than a feeling she would ever benefit from such information. Shortly after Mariah was born, they received a letter from Josh deeding his part of the ranch to Ben. Josh called it a gift to Mariah and future children, but Bethanie knew it was his way of saying he wouldn't return. With each day, her memories of Josh were more and more a misty dream. Ben was her reality. Josh was now more a fantasy hiding in the corners of her mind, waiting to drift into her thoughts, finally bringing more pleasure than pain.

Josh's next letter came just after Mariah's second birthday. He requested a great sum of money in exchange for half interest in a mine in Colorado. Ben sent the money without hesitation, commenting, "Josh wouldn't have asked if he weren't sure." Then he laughed. "We'll give our half back to him at the birth of his first child."

Bethanie turned away, never wanting Ben to see the sadness that filled her. Josh had been gone almost three years now. He would never know his first child, perhaps his only child. His memory would never leave the hidden place in her heart, no matter how far he traveled or how many years he stayed away.

One morning in April, Bethanie was thinking of Josh as she cleared the breakfast dishes wondering where he was. Two letters in three years were poor clues. The man Ben had sent with the money for Josh's mine had returned without any great wealth of knowledge about Josh's life. Josh was working hard far up in the mountains of Colorado, near a small town called Thomasville. Colorado seemed a world and a lifetime away.

Bethanie brushed the crumbs around Mariah's plate into her hand and lifted her head to allow the warm sun to shine on her face. The long, narrow dining-room windows allowed light to enter but weren't wide enough for a person to pass through. Bethanie loved this room because it welcomed the morning sun. When she and Ben grew old, they could sit here at the table and drink coffee while their grandchildren played between the two huge elms off to the left of the porch.

Dusty interrupted her thoughts as he burst through the front door with his latest box of books. The boy was now taller than Bethanie, with hands and feet two sizes bigger than the rest of his body. The first light shadow of a thin beard peppered down his sideburns. Bethanie had a feeling that as soon as he could grow one, he would wear a short, trimmed beard just like Ben's.

Mariah danced around Dusty like a butterfly. Her black curls bounced up and down just below her waist. "Dusty, please?" she screamed with excitement. "Please?" She knew only a few words, but they seemed to get her everything she wanted.

Dusty sidestepped Mariah, trying to keep from running over her. He might complain about her, but Bethanie could see the love and joy the tiny child brought him. "She follows me everywhere," he grumbled. "I found her just now in the barn."

"I know," Bethanie answered, only half listening as she took the books from him. Ever since Mariah began walking, she had been in Dusty's shadow. She was like a baby duck that bonds to the first moving thing it sees, then follows it everywhere.

"It ain't right, a man having to play nursemaid all day." Dusty pleaded his case as he followed Bethanie to the dining room.

"We'll talk about it after we read," Bethanie promised as she spread out the books.

"That's another thing. If I didn't have these lessons, I could be on the range with the other men," he complained. "I can read and write better than any hand on the ranch."

"We've been through this a thousand times. Ben and I want more for you." Bethanie knew his restlessness was due more to his love for the open range than his hatred of books.

Dusty slumped in his chair as he mumbled, "Never argue with a redhead."

Bethanie laughed. "You sound just like Ben." As she said his name, Ben's wheelchair rolled into the room.

Mariah jumped into her father's arms, crumpling the papers on his lap. "Daddy, ride. Daddy, ride." She squealed and pointed at Dusty.

"Listen, Squirrel, I told you I'd ask your dad, but I'm

supposed to be doin' Greek mythology today." Dusty smiled at Ben and shrugged hopefully. "It's so pretty outside; I'd like to take her riding. She could sit on the saddle in front of me."

"Go ahead, Dusty," Ben shouted above Mariah's squeals. "But stay in sight of the house. I need to talk to Beth for a minute anyway."

"Sure." Dusty gave a short salute before Mariah jumped into his arms. As he tried to pull her dress into order, Mariah yanked at his hat, completely destroying any style to the brim. "We'll be back in a while."

"But . . ." Bethanie began, then paused remembering how she'd loved riding when she was a child. "We'll have lessons later," she promised.

She turned back to Ben and was surprised to see wrinkles of worry cross his face. She moved beside him and touched his arm. "Dusty will be careful," she began, then realized the children weren't the cause of his alarm. He shook his head and touched his finger to his lips, cautioning her to wait until they were well out of hearing range.

Bethanie knelt beside his chair. "What is it, Ben?" she whispered.

"It's Mayson." Ben pounded his fist against the table. "I thought when we spoiled his plan to monopolize the cattle in Texas three years ago, he would give up."

"Ben, tell me!" She was as involved in the running of the ranch as Ben, and a sudden fear gripped her. Mayson was an evil man, capable of twisting the law, and most people, to his advantage. He made a great show of being a family man and a good Texan. He even counted among his friends judges and lawmen, but treachery followed him like a scent. Unseen, unheard, but always present.

Ben folded the paper across his leg. "I just got word that he's worked a deal with the renegade Indians who've left the reservation. They burn out small ranches; then Mayson moves in and sweeps the cattle off the land."

"That's terrible." Bethanie thought of Mike and Allison on their little ranch only miles away. If they were attacked, even if Ben heard the gunfire, they would all be killed before he could round up enough men to help. "Have they any proof it's Wes Mayson?"

"None." Ben shook his head. "But I'm organizing the ranchers now. We'll send word to Fort Worth. I doubt anyone will come on just a rumor."

Bethanie stood and nervously stacked the dirty dishes. These had been bloody years in Texas, and she'd prayed many times for a solution to the Indian problem. Though she felt safe here with as many as a hundred hands around and three sides of the house protected, the stories of attacks still frightened her. She'd seen too many ugly hulls of homes, burned to the ground while lives and dreams vanished like the smoke. Once a Ranger stopped by to talk with Ben. He'd pulled a string of scalps from his saddlebag, saying he'd taken them from an Indian who'd meant to add the Ranger's hair to the collection. Bethanie had been unable to take her eyes from the knots of hair, some blond, some brown, and some as black as little Mariah's curls.

Ben took her hand. "I'll send a man over this afternoon for Allison."

Bethanie nodded. "I'd worry less about her if she could be here, at least until the branding is over and Mike can be home." She smiled to herself as she thought of Allison and wondered if her tiny cousin was showing yet with child. Bethanie was happy for Allison and Mike and excited about the baby. Each day Mariah grew, Bethanie's arms ached to hold a baby once more. Maybe soon she would have another, but for now she would be satisfied to spoil the baby Mike had already informed everyone was a boy.

Gunfire shook her concentration, and she felt every nerve in her body jump to life. Mariah was her first thought as she ran for the door. Ben was behind her as Bethanie reached the porch. Another volley of gunshots thundered across the land as Dusty galloped toward the house. Mariah was nestled tightly in his arms.

Dusty swung himself from the saddle with Mariah tucked like a sack of flour under one arm. She laughed and wiggled with glee. "More, more," she cried as Dusty handed her into Bethanie's open arms. Another round of signal shots rumbled across the ridge as Bethanie hugged her child to her.

Dusty's face was pale, and his light brown eyes were alive with panic. "Indians!" He barely breathed the word over Mariah's yelling. There was no hint of the exciting adventure that had been in his eyes three years ago on the trip from San Antonio. He was too much a man now. He knew what was at stake.

Bethanie's face drained of blood as she tried to remember not to frighten Mariah. She lowered her to the ground. "Run tell Ruth how fast you rode the horse, darling." Before she finished the last word, Mariah was running into the house. Bethanie was unable to control the shaking that was overtaking her. She, like Dusty, had seen too much in the past three years.

Bethanie looked from Ben to Dusty. "They're not coming here?"

Ben looked knowingly at Dusty and nodded a silent command.

"No, Ben! Not here," Bethanie repeated.

Dusty bolted for the bunkhouse to find the few men left on the ranch. Most of the men were miles away with the spring branding. Another round of gunfire sounded and echoed off the ridge behind the house. The signal shots were closer.

Ben whirled his chair and headed for the gun rack. As

he pulled down rifle after rifle, Bethanie began to panic. "Ben, they wouldn't attack here . . . would they?"

"If they do, they're fools. The only way they could hit us is from the front. They'll lose ten or more to our one." He paused a moment to study her. "Now don't worry, Beth. I've got three men besides Dusty here. We can hold them off forever if need be. You and Mariah go with Ruth. She knows where to hide." Ben shoved bullets into the chamber.

"No!" Bethanie yelled above the clamor of cowboys entering the house with Dusty. They began frantically loading rifles. "I'm staying here with you. I can shoot."

Ben looked at her with a sudden rage, then softened before he spoke. "We have no time to argue this one, Beth. I want you safe with Mariah."

Tears were forming in her eyes, blurring her vision into a nightmarish scene. She could not leave him, not even to be with Mariah. Her place was with her husband. She had to make him understand. She shook her head, denying his command and moved closer to him. Her hand slid from the back of his chair to his shoulder. She belonged at his side.

"Beth," he whispered. "I'm a man, and I must defend what is mine. I love you dearly, but you have to stay with Mariah. I'd be less of a man if I couldn't protect my family." He pulled her hand from his shoulder and held her fingers tightly in his grip.

Bethanie knew she could argue no more. To do so would question his manhood. "But Dusty?" she cried.

"Dusty's old enough," Ben answered.

"But . . ." Bethanie began, as Dusty interrupted.

"I'm stayin' with Ben," he stated flatly, reflecting the strength of character within him. Now he must do what had to be done, yet he'd not even had his first shave. He set his jaw as he lifted his rifle. Bethanie saw a glimpse of the strong adult he would soon become.

Ruth came from the kitchen, a basket on one arm and Mariah under the other. She nodded at Bethanie, but her eyes showed her fright. "Kiss your daddy, Mariah. We're going on an adventure." As the child left Ruth's arms, Ruth lifted the old Walker-Colt from the bottom drawer of Ben's desk and began wrapping it in a towel.

Mariah ran to Ben and scrambled into his lap. He held her tight. Closing his eyes he pulled her head to his heart.

Mariah turned to Dusty. She held out her arms to him, and the boy lifted her tiny doll-like body. "Bye, Squirrel, see you later."

Bethanie knelt and kissed Ben. "I'll see you later, too," she whispered.

Ben's strong hands cupped her face as he looked deep into her eyes. "You're my life, Beth," he whispered in a low voice. Then, embarrassed by his words while others were around, he pulled away and moved back to the men.

Before she could change her mind, Bethanie followed Ruth out the back of the house to a small dugout used as a root cellar. The half-buried building was nestled in the cliff's edge. Ruth went in first and lit a lamp. As Bethanie stepped into the area, she was shocked to see Ruth removing boards from the back wall of the cellar. Within seconds, a dark opening, almost as tall as Bethanie, revealed the entrance to a cave.

Ruth picked up the basket with one hand and the lamp with the other. "This was here when they built the ranch," she explained. "It was Mike's idea to build the dugout in front. But for years, with just men around, no one ever used the cave."

Bethanie followed Ruth. Spiderwebs brushed her face as they moved several feet back to the natural tunnel. The moldy smell of damp earth and rotting burlap assaulted her senses as their shadows danced like deformed creatures with each swing of the lamp. She wanted to run back to Ben and demand to fight alongside him.

Anything would be better than hiding in this hole, waiting, not knowing. But Ben was right; they had to think of Mariah.

Ruth stopped after several yards. "The cave doesn't go back much farther. This is far enough to be able to leave the light on." She spread a blanket for Mariah beside the low light of the lantern. "I'll go back and close up the wall," she whispered.

Soon Ruth returned, and the women sat silently as Mariah played with finger shadows on the wall of the cave. The child finally grew bored and fell asleep.

Bethanie strained her ears as gunfire grew nearer. In the tomb of this cave, Bethanie couldn't tell if the shots were far away or echoes of constant firing only yards outside. Finally she could stand the suspense no longer. "Stay with Mariah," she whispered. "I'm going to try to look out." Ruth shook her head, but Bethanie stood and felt her way through the dark hole.

At the boarded-wall entrance, Bethanie slid only a few boards aside and slipped out. She heard shots, but they were close, near the house. Wild screams and shouts seemed to come from nowhere, as if carried on the breeze. She carefully stepped across the dirt floor and peered through the cracks in the wooden door.

"Where are the men?" Bethanie's mind seemed to scream the words silently, vibrating her head with hideous echoes.

She searched the grounds as horses ran madly past and dust flew like a whirlwind in the bright sun. She could see one side of the barn as a fire seemed to explode in the dry hay. Suddenly, a half-nude warrior, thick with paint, jumped from his horse and ran toward the dugout. The sun sparkled off the long blade of a knife he waved above his head. Bethanie stood paralyzed by terror as she saw his wild eyes and the flash of victory written across his face.

Where were the men? She prayed, knowing that they would fire and halt the brave's progress if they were alive.

Chapter Fourteen

Bethanie watched as the painted savage ran toward the dugout door. For a moment, her body seemed to be made of stone. Though her mind screamed for action, her muscles were incapable of following her command. The Indian slowed to signal a friend, and Bethanie suddenly took flight. She darted across the darkened half-cellar to the cave entrance. As the braves hammered against the door, Bethanie crawled behind the shelf. They might not have seen her, but it wouldn't take them long to figure out that the door to the dugout had been bolted from the inside. She hastily pulled the boards into place, concealing the cave's entrance, just as the intruders came hurling through the door.

Bethanie ran into the darkness of the cave, too frightened to care that the uneven rock edges were tearing her clothes. Gulping for breath, she reached the light of Ruth's lantern. As she knelt beside her sleeping child, Bethanie whispered to Ruth, "They're in the cellar."

Ruth grabbed Bethanie's arm, her eyes wild with fright. "They won't find the cave." Panic twisted the older woman's normally calm face. "But if they do, you must promise me one thing." She pulled the old Walker-Colt from her basket. "I was captured by Indians as a child. I saw what they did to the older women. Her hands were shaking as she handed Bethanie the gun. "Should they find the cave, you must shoot me before they take me."

"No!" Bethanie whispered as she heard the Indians rummaging in the cellar, already far too close.

"I beg you!" Ruth whimpered quietly. "Ben saved me years ago from them. I tried to kill myself later to keep from going crazy. Because I'm dark, everyone thought I was part Indian and treated me with the same disgust the Indians did." Tears broke from her wide eyes and ran in zigzag patterns down her wrinkled cheeks. "Ben promised me he would shoot me rather than allow me to endure the hell of capture again. You are his wife; you must fulfill his promise."

Bethanie could see Ruth was hysterical and incapable of reason. She must quiet the woman. Bethanie took the gun. "All right," she comforted. "I won't let them take you alive." For Ruth the fear was over, and she seemed resigned to accept the ending.

Ruth breathed deeply and leaned back against the wall of the cave. She closed her eyes as if resting after a long journey.

Bethanie had no time to think of Ruth's strange request, for she was too busy listening for any sound that might indicate the Indians had found the cave opening.

Time paused in long breaths as the women waited. Finally the noise in the cellar died down as the sound of gunfire returned. Bethanie's heart jumped. Somehow the men were fighting once more. Could the lull have been to catch the Indians off guard? The memory of the burning barn pushed away any such logic, but hope still grew even on barren soil.

Seemingly an hour of low thundering gunfire passed. Mariah awoke, and Ruth pulled a snack for her from the basket as calmly as if they were on a picnic. Bethanie's promise seemed to have eased Ruth, though it ripped at Bethanie's nerves like metal against stone. She feared her mind, or Ruth's, might snap at any moment, and she would scream, giving away their hiding place.

The gunfire stopped abruptly with a final round. An instant later, Bethanie heard rummaging in the cellar once more. She lifted the gun from beside her and placed it on her legs. They heard the soft, scraping sound of the shelves being moved away from the cave opening.

"Remember your promise," Ruth whispered.

Bethanie nodded, and turned the barrel of the revolver toward Ruth. With her free hand, she cradled Mariah's head into her side and covered the child's ear.

Ruth straightened and sat up tall, as one being honored.

"Bethanie!" a voice yelled from somewhere in the darkness. "Bethanie, are you there?"

A tidal wave of relief flooded over Bethanie. She laid down the gun and swept Mariah into her arms, then ran to the cave opening. She watched as the sun poured into the dusty storage cellar. Mike's blond hair glowed like a halo in the light. Bethanie shoved past the boards. She stepped over the body of an Indian, biting her bottom lip in horror. She pulled Mariah close and ran toward Mike. In an instant she and Mariah were smothered in his embrace.

"Bethanie. Oh, Bethanie," he cried. "We thought all of you were kidnapped. Thank God I remembered this cave."

Bethanie was laughing and crying at the same time as she hugged Mariah to her. It was over. The nightmare was over. She turned to Ruth and smiled. There was a bond between them now. They'd shared an experience, an insight into each other that would never be spoken of, but would hold them together for life. Ruth smiled and nodded toward Bethanie as if to confirm her thoughts.

"The men?" Bethanie suddenly remembered. "Was anyone hurt?"

Pain shot through Mike's blue eyes as if he'd been stabbed by her words. He grabbed her arm as she started to step away. "Bethanie, they all . . ."

She knew what he was going to say before the words formed. She wouldn't have admitted it, but she felt it. When the first firing stopped and Indians surrounded the house, she knew. Ben wouldn't have allowed them to enter the cellar if he had been alive.

"Ben!" Bethanie screamed as if she could call him back.

Ruth stepped beside her and took Mariah from her. Bethanie would have crumbled to the ground if Mike hadn't pulled her to him. "I'm sorry," he whispered. "We were too late. I'm sorry." Tears rolled down his tanned face. "We were so sure they'd never attack the big ranches."

Bethanie didn't want to hear the reasons. "No!" she screamed as she fought Mike with all her strength. "I must go to him."

"No, Bethanie." Mike couldn't hold her. The sorrow in his face multiplied as he watched her. "It's too late."

"It's not too late!" she cried as she bolted blindly from the dugout and ran toward the house.

The sun was bright in her face, and the smell of burning wood was thick in the air. Cowboys were everywhere, trying to put out small fires. Bethanie rushed past the bodies of Apache warriors in full war dress. Their rainbow-painted cheeks were now splattered with blood and dirt. Their dark, tanned faces bore no terror for her as they returned her look with dead stares, yet the sight of death vibrated around her in panic's melody. She ran inside the house, pushing tears from her eyes as she hurried from room to room. The house looked as though a tornado-force wind had swept through, overturning everything. The lace curtains across the dining-room windows were burning, charring the white wall. Bethanie turned away. She must find her husband.

Suddenly she saw Ben's empty wheelchair blocking the front door. She'd seen the chair empty before, but only when Ben was by her side in bed. Bethanie ran onto the porch. She froze at the sight before her.

Ben's body was roped spread-eagle between the two old elms, just off the porch. He was covered with blood, and his chin rested lifelessly against his chest.

"Ben!" Bethanie screamed until there was no air left in her lungs. She walked slowly toward him. As she stood only inches away, Bethanie put her arms about his neck, not caring that his blood soaked her dress. She placed her hands on either side of his bearded face and held him tenderly as though he were only asleep. "Ben, Ben," she whispered. "I love you."

As her heart melted in pain, she begged. "Ben, don't leave me." *He would hear her. He would come back to her. He was only asleep.* "Ben, don't leave me now."

She ran her fingers through his dark hair and smiled up at his sleeping eyes. "Ben, I love you," she whispered again, realizing how tall her man was.

A firm hand tried to pull her away, but Bethanie would not move. She wanted to be in Ben's arms, under his protection.

"Bethanie," someone said behind her, but she didn't want to hear. "We've got to cut him down," the voice kept repeating.

She watched as a man cut the ropes binding Ben's arms. As his body crumpled into the dirt, Bethanie fell with his weight. She cared nothing of the pain. She was still in Ben's arms.

Tears flowed, blurring her vision as her heart failed to accept what her mind knew was true. She could see all the times Ben had showed his love. He always respected her, always cherished her. Life couldn't leave him now. Not when she needed him so. She would refuse to allow this twist of fate she was being given. She would turn away from reality, now and always.

Mike pulled at her shoulder. "Please, Bethanie," he said, trying to lift her.

She wanted nothing from him or anyone. She wanted to be left alone with Ben.

A man yelled from the incline near the porch, "Mike, I think the boy's still alive."

Mike knelt close to Bethanie. "Help us with Dusty," he whispered. "If anyone can save him, it's you, Bethanie."

For a moment she looked at Mike as if he were a stranger to her; then a wail inside Bethanie shattered the crystal dream she had retreated into. As she watched the men drag Dusty's bloody body out from under the porch, reality hit in full force. She reached to kiss Ben's lips one last time. "Good-bye, my husband, my love." Then she turned and allowed Mike to help her up, forcing herself not to look back down at Ben.

Bethanie clung to Mike as men lifted Dusty's body from the dirt. His face was covered with blood from a head wound, and dark red stained his shoulder and leg.

"Get him into the house," Bethanie ordered. She followed, her face white with worry. If he were to live, much had to be done, and fast. The black gunpowder in the open wounds would kill him as surely as the bullets. She shoved her own grief into the corners of her mind. There would be time to mourn later.

Hours passed as Ruth and Bethanie nursed Dusty. His breathing was so weak, they thought they'd lost him several times. In all, five bullets were dug out of his flesh. Bethanie made an ointment to take the poison from his wounds. She was thankful to have something to occupy her thoughts and hands. Mariah stayed with the women and spent hours holding Dusty's limp hand. She finally curled up like a kitten on his covers and fell asleep.

After almost twenty hours of solid work, Dusty's breathing returned to normal, and he rested comfortably. His normally tan face was ghostly pale from the loss of blood. Sandy blond hair crossed his forehead atop a white bandage. Bethanie covered his chest with one corner of a quilt and Mariah's sleeping form at the foot of the bed with the other end.

Bethanie wandered into the large room and collapsed in a chair. Mike was working at Ben's desk, and for a moment in her mind, she saw Ben.

"Are you all right?" Mike asked. They were the same words Ben had asked her so many times.

"Yes," Bethanie answered, rubbing her palm back and forth across her forehead.

"I've been looking over Ben's will. Did you know he left the ranch to Mariah and Dusty."

"Yes," Bethanie answered, disinterested. They'd decided after Mariah's birth to set up the will that way.

"He left half a mine in Colorado to you with a note saying you'd know what to do," Mike added.

Bethanie opened one eye. Ben hadn't discussed the mine, but it seemed logical to her. She'd have to be the one to tell Josh of his brother's death. She could give him the deed to the other half of the mine then.

"He also left a sizeable bank balance in your name," Mike added.

Bethanie nodded. She really didn't want to think of money now. Exhausted, she leaned her head against the high wingback of the chair. Pretending she was in Ben's arms, she fell into a merciful sleep.

Chapter Fifteen

Dusty's body lay lifeless, half covered with bandages. The black ointment made from herbs and hog-bone marrow stained the white cloth of each wound, but blood was no longer pouring from the ripped flesh. Bethanie's hard work had paid off, for now; if his fever stayed down, Dusty would begin to heal. He'd lost so much blood in the past twenty-four hours, she knew any infection might yet take him beyond her care.

Mariah lay in a ball at the foot of Dusty's covers. Her long black braid circled her sunny face, making her look even more angelic in sleep. She refused to leave the room. In her childish way, she was as worried about Dusty as the others. She'd lost Ben; now she wouldn't leave Dusty lest he die. Bethanie smiled at Mariah's reasoning. To be truthful, she was doing the same thing by refusing to leave his side even though several of the others had offered to sit with him.

Bethanie watched as Dusty's brown eyes hesitantly opened. He looked around the room, confusion filling his young face. His mouth turned up in a hint of a smile as his gaze rested on Bethanie. "You're safe," he whispered hoarsely through dry lips. "And the squirrel?"

Bethanie nodded toward the foot of the bed. "She's fine." She could have guessed his first question would have been about Mariah.

Tears filled Dusty's eyes, and he fought to blink them away. The Indian battle was returning to his mind, and the pain showed in his golden gaze. "Bethanie . . . I saw Ben die." His voice was fighting childlike highness for control.

Bethanie knelt close and clasped his fingers. Their hands were almost the same size. She knew he must tell his story, or he would burst with pain inside.

"Bethanie," Dusty's grip tightened. "When the Indians starting trying to burn the house, Ben told me to get ready to run for cover under the porch. All the other men were dead or too near it to fire their guns. We waited for the last attack out on the porch, bold as you please. I heard Ben laugh as they started coming, like it was some kind of game he'd been waiting all his life to play."

Dusty swallowed hard. "As I ducked under the porch, he said, 'You're quite a man, son.' Then, just as they started firing again, I heard him say real low, 'Take care of Mariah for me, will you?'"

Dusty fought for control. "I didn't have time to answer. A bullet hit me in the leg, and I saw Ben slump forward with blood splattered all over his chest." Tears bubbled down Dusty's pale face. "I didn't have time to swear I would take care of her." His cries were coming in gulps of heartache only a child can feel. "I took another slug in the arm as I saw them drag Ben off the porch. He was already dead, but they started stringing him up."

Bethanie brushed his forehead with her fingers. "Hush now, Dusty. Don't talk anymore. You'll be stronger tomorrow." The boy could never know just how the knowledge that Ben was dead before they'd tied him to the trees was somehow a comfort to her.

"But I didn't tell Ben!" Dusty cried, turning his face into his pillow. "I can take care of you both."

Bethanie touched his sandy brown hair. "You didn't

have to tell Ben. He knew you'd take care of Mariah. Just as he knew I'd be able to take care of myself."

"He did?" Dusty rolled toward her, and pain tightened his face. His head wound made the slightest movement excruciating.

"Yes," Bethanie smiled. "He knew. Now rest."

Dusty nodded and closed his eyes. With a last squeeze of her hand, he fell asleep. Bethanie watched him turn an inch closer to a man. Mike would run the ranch for six more years; then Dusty would take over. It would have been Ben's plan, and it would free Bethanie to do what she knew she must.

The weeks passed into summer, and Dusty's wounds began to heal. His deep loss of Ben left its scar in the intensity of his golden brown eyes and the strong set of his jaw.

The warm Texas sun cast its morning light into her room as Bethanie stared at herself in the mirror. She knew, like Dusty, she would carry forever the grief of life without Ben. He'd been the rock she had grown to depend on, and now he was gone. She closed her mind to the pain, and as she had years ago under the porch of her aunt and uncle's hotel, she made a decision she knew would alter her life.

The woman who looked back from the oval mirror now seemed strong and self-assured. Her charcoal dress, though it brought out the luster in her red hair, gave an air of authority to her presence. Her green eyes had lost the wonder of a young, frightened girl, and now they burned with the coldness of reality. Even her carriage was that of a confident woman who could face any hardship. Bethanie only wished she felt as strong inwardly. She lifted her chin in determination and walked from her bedroom.

Without detour, she moved out the front door. Mike was standing on the porch talking with a group of new men he'd hired, both for the roundup and to protect the house. Bethanie knew any men who could pass Mike's standards were fine additions to the hands. Mike seemed to have an eye for sizing up people. He'd been able to see more character in Allison than others had, and he'd been right. Once she'd married, Allison had settled into the role of a warm and gracious lady.

As Bethanie stepped beside him, Mike raised his voice in formal introduction. "I would like you men to meet Mrs. Weston, the boss."

Bethanie nodded at the men. They were the usual assortment of cowhands that always seemed to appear near roundup time, except maybe for one large man near the back who looked a little out of place. He was cleaner than most cowhands, and the power in his shoulders seemed to tell of another kind of work besides ranching. But Bethanie knew it took all kinds to work a ranch this size. "Welcome to Weston Ranch, but I'm not your boss. Mike gives all the orders here." She could almost feel the release of caged air escape the men's lungs. They seemed relieved not to be taking orders from a woman, though she doubted any would have said so.

Bethanie turned to address Mike more than the men. "I'll be leaving in a few days when the cattle go to Colorado."

Mike's reaction exploded across his face. He lowered his voice, but the men were quiet as tombstones. His words carried in the silent air like fluffy cottonwood seeds in a summer breeze. "Bethanie, you can't mean this?"

"I'm going, Mike. Someone has to tell Josh about Ben, and I need time to get away and think." She shoved any other reason she might have to the back of her mind. How could she tell Mike that sleeping in the bed she and Ben always shared was painful each night? How could she explain that she must see Josh, even though her feelings were a blend of sorrow and caring with no small amount of fear mixed in?

"But it's dangerous." Mike's eyes darted around the air above her head as if searching for some printed reason in the clouds to make her stay.

"And here is safe?" Bethanie questioned.

Mike couldn't argue with a new widow about safety. The blood of her husband still stained the porch where they now stood. "I'll go and tell Josh. We've been friends for years."

"No." Bethanie's voice was low, but firm. "You're needed here with Allison about due. A man should be near when his first child is born. I want her to move in so Ruth can take care of her and the baby. Please stay here at the house until I return." She almost added, *"If I return,"* but there would be time for that later.

Mike ran his fingers through his sun-bleached hair in frustration. She knew he was out of reasons, but he was still not happy about her going. Before he could say more, one of the newly hired men stepped to the edge of the porch. Bethanie noticed he was the one she'd thought looked out of place when she had first walked out.

Bethanie turned her attention toward him, and to her amazement he drew away as if not wanting her to see him.

"Mr. Mike," he asked in a voice blended with a slight northern spice. "May I talk with you for a moment?"

Mike nodded and moved off the porch. Bethanie watched as the huge stranger stepped once more out of her gaze.

She followed Mike down the steps, intrigued and a little angry at the big man's action. As she stepped around Mike, her body went rigid at close sight of the stranger. He was tall and stone-solid in build. His hair was a white and sorrel blend that reminded Bethanie of the illogical mixture of snow and burning coals. But it was the left side of his face that shocked her. From his eye to his jawline was a scar that looked as if someone had pushed a white-hot poker into his cheek. His skin was twisted and deformed into the ugliest mutilation she'd ever seen.

The stranger turned his horrid profile away from her, and she could see the sadness in his eyes that her gaping reaction had caused. She would guess him to be in his middle forties, and he had not yet lost any of his youthful strength.

"I'm sorry," he began, not allowing Bethanie to see the scarred side of his face. "I had no wish to shock you, Mrs. Weston. I know I'm hell's version of ugly."

Bethanie sensed this man wanted no pity, so she tried to keep any trace from her voice. "I'm sorry to you, sir, for staring like an ill-mannered child."

"No need for apologies. I do try to stay out of the way of fine ladies like yourself. People call me Cain. Not many forget my name or wonder why I seek the solitary life after taking a look at my face."

"Nice to meet you, Mr. Cain. I hope you'll be happy here."

"Thank you kindly." The stranger seemed satisfied with her comment. He shuffled uneasily. "I wanted Mr. Mike to ask for me, but I might as well do my own askin' now." He straightened to a wide stance of a seaman and not the loose stand of a cowboy. "I already told him when I was hired that I don't know much about riding horses. But when I heard you talking about making a trip to Colorado, I thought of a way I could earn my keep. I've been there a few times, and I'm good with a team. I drove a freight wagon for Masters and his partners for a few years over by Raton Pass. I'd like to accompany you."

Bethanie could use a strong man to drive the team.

She'd heard of Masters and his dependable wagons. "I've one question first," she said thoughtfully.

Cain nodded with a frown as if he knew what was coming.

Bethanie remembered what Ben had told her once about every man in this country having a right to a few secrets. She would not ask Cain about his scar. "What's a man who's no good on a horse doing in Texas?"

Cain's face lightened with a smile, and he turned to show her slightly more than his profile. "I've been about everything a man can be, I guess. I thought I'd try wrangler next, but to tell the truth, me and horses don't seem to get along. I've been driving a supply wagon between Fort Worth and San Antonio for the past year. I'm sober and dependable; you can ask the freight company."

Bethanie glanced at Mike, knowing he would have checked out any man he hired. Mike nodded, "That's true. They couldn't speak highly enough of Cain. They were sorry to see him go."

Bethanie liked this man. There seemed an honesty about him. She knew she could look at him and not be troubled by the scar if he were a good man. "I'll talk it over with Mike," she promised, and offered her hand to Cain.

He seemed taken aback for a moment, as if he didn't know what to do. Then, slowly he touched her fingers. His "thank you" was so low that she could barely hear him. Bethanie smiled and turned back toward the house.

Chapter Sixteen

A week later, the air was dry and motionless as Bethanie watched Cain load her wagon for the trip to Colorado. Her beautiful smoky gray horse, Twilight, swung his head back and forth as if to resent being tied behind a wagon. Since the cattle drive was a small one, their wagon was also being used to haul supplies. Except for a few trunks of clothes, Bethanie was leaving Weston Ranch as she'd come. Mariah was her only treasure. Anything else could be bought when they reached Colorado. She wanted the household things to be left exactly as they were so that if she returned all would be the same.

Cain carefully arranged the trunks so that Mariah would have a place to play under the wagon's protective tarp. It would also provide enough room for Bethanie and her daughter to sleep during the trip. In the few days she'd watched Cain, Bethanie had learned a great deal about the silent man. He was clean and neat almost to an obsession. He wore no gun but carried a long knife that would stop any varmint, be it four- or two-legged, should he be challenged. He could crack a whip better than most men and handle a team like a man who had done so for years. She never heard him swear. He didn't chew or smoke and stayed mostly to himself. As she watched him now, Bethanie couldn't help but wonder what kind of life had produced such a man.

Mike came from the barn with a rifle slung over his shoulder. "Cain!" he yelled, "I want you to take this under your seat. I want these women well protected."

Bethanie moved up the steps to the house. "Michael," she said, half to herself. "You've already hired twice as many men as we need to move the cattle. We'll be lucky if we don't lose half of them to the mines when we get north."

Cain took the rifle and nodded to Mike. "I got all the supplies loaded. I can cook good enough to fix the first meal at dawn, but the men are on their own for the rest of the day."

"I've got a good man for trail boss. He'll take care of the men and herd. You just make sure Mrs. Weston and her daughter get delivered safely to the Weston Mine north of Leadville."

Before Cain could answer, Mariah ran out of the house past Bethanie to the wagon. She'd never been more than a few miles off the ranch, and now saw herself about to begin a great adventure.

Bethanie watched as Cain turned to greet her, making no attempt to hide his scar. Mariah seemed to accept his deformity without question or judgment. She gave him a quick hug, then began crawling over the boxes and trunks like a ground squirrel. Bethanie smiled and stepped into the house, doubting Cain would ever adjust to Mariah. He did seem to enjoy her company, however. The only time Bethanie had seen him smile was when he said the child's name.

Bethanie paused just inside the large main room and looked around, memorizing each wall. She felt a greeting as she had that first day in the warmth of the colors and the openness of the rooms. The bright mixtures of Indian and Mexican decor always seemed to cheer her. Then she saw the empty spot by the fireplace where Ben had always rolled his chair. There was no need for the open place now, but she doubted anyone in the house would ever rearrange the chairs. She knelt to brush her hand over the now highly polished floor remembering how angry Ben had been when he'd found her scrubbing.

When Bethanie looked up, she saw Ruth smiling at her from the kitchen door. "Ruth," Bethanie whispered the word as dearly as one might say "Mother." "I was just saying good-bye to the house."

"I understand." Ruth moved toward her. "I'll take good care of Dusty while you're away. I should have my hands full with him and Allison." She chuckled suddenly, in a hoarse, unfamiliar sound. "But then, I delivered one baby, I guess I can do it again."

Bethanie stood staring into the older woman's dark eyes, her look saying more than words ever could. They were bonded by joy and sorrow, closer than blood could ever tie. Words had never been needed between them, and they did not clutter the air now. "You'll keep up my herb garden?"

"Yes." Ruth's face was a mask of tightly held emotions. "You're thinking of not coming back. Thinking the pain would always be here." She was making statements, not asking questions.

Bethanie was little surprised at Ruth's insight. "I don't know," she answered honestly. "After I see Josh, I may go back East. I just haven't thought things through yet."

"You take your time." Ruth nodded as she tried to keep her hard exterior from melting into emotion. "Dusty and I will be here when you get ready to come home. I used to think if Ben died, I'd move on. But I know now this is my home and the only place I want to be. You'll find your spot, and I'm hoping when you do, it'll be here."

Tears broke from Bethanie's eyes and raced each other down her cheeks. She closed the distance between them and hugged Ruth.

The older woman patted her briskly on the shoulder. "Now, now, none of this crying. You're Mrs. Weston, a fine lady. Wouldn't do to let the men see you sniffling."

Bethanie nodded and stepped away. Before she could say more, Dusty hobbled from the bedroom. She turned and hugged him, avoiding putting pressure on any of his wounds. When she pulled away, she saw tears in his eyes.

Dusty brushed at her wet cheek with his thumb. "You know, Bethanie, you're right about why Ben told me to take care of Mariah and not both of you. 'Cause he knew what a great wife he had. He loved you. You were a real wonder to him. He told me once that when he saw you ride in all dirty and dressed like a boy, he knew you were the one for him. But he never thought you'd marry him, and when you did, he decided right then and there he was the luckiest man alive."

Bethanie couldn't speak for several seconds. She thought of what might have happened if she hadn't been pregnant and forced herself to go to Ben's bed. She might never have understood the man she married. She wished for the hundredth time that she had gotten pregnant again, but they'd never been so blessed.

Without words, Bethanie helped Dusty to the porch and watched as the men mounted for the drive. She ruffled his sandy hair. "You keep up with your studies."

"Sure," Dusty shrugged. "I'm starting to half like them anyway. I'll probably be so smart when you get back, you won't even know me."

Bethanie kissed his cheek as Mariah ran to his other side. She hugged him tightly.

Dusty laughed. "See you later, Squirrel."

"I love you," she yelled.

"I love you, too," Dusty answered more soberly.

Bethanie lifted her daughter and hurried toward the

wagon lest she change her mind about going. Within half an hour they were out of sight of the ranch and following beside cattle slowly moving north like a brown cloud hovering over the flat land.

The days of moving across Texas grasslands blurred together into endless heat and wind. Bethanie spent most of her time riding Twilight beside the wagon. Cain never wasted a word to her, but somehow never tired of listening to Mariah. He was already making coffee when Bethanie awoke each dawn, and quietly checking the perimeters of the campsite each night when she fell asleep. His cooking reminded her of childhood days, when her mother always made huge breakfasts that included desserts. Cain could even make fried apple turnovers in the campfire skillet that rivaled the memories of her mother's. The men enjoyed the early feast and were content to snack on leftovers at sunset.

Cain somehow found the time to make Mariah a rag doll family from bandanna handkerchiefs. She played with the tiny dolls constantly, making her days pass faster.

As they moved across the vast plains, the nights grew colder, but the days still burned the already dry prairie. Wood for campfires grew scarce. Cain used buffalo chips and twisted tufts of dry grass to supplement the sunflower stalks and fast-burning mesquite trees.

Bethanie watched as buffaloes moved in long brown clouds across the endless land. She found the creatures interesting, for they ran with a rocking motion, raising the front and back part of the body alternately. Mariah found them fun to watch, but Cain was always careful to keep the wagon at a safe distance. The buffaloes were wild and stupid. They detected danger by smell and not by sight, so all the men were careful to stay downwind of the hairy, cowlike animals. Twice in the days of cross-ing the plains, Bethanie saw wagons loaded down with buffalo hides. Several times they passed piles of decaying carcasses, but most of the plains were an endless sea of green.

Bethanie allowed the swaying grasslands and slow sunset to soothe her mind. The recent pain dulled to an ache within her heart. She needed the hours of mo-notony to rest, free from conversation or responsibility. Cain seemed to understand; perhaps he had heartaches of his own to remember. He cooked meals and made camp with his gaze never more than a blink away from Mariah.

As they crossed the sandy banks of the Canadian River, Bethanie began to wonder if she'd made the right decision to go to Josh. How could he welcome her when she brought him the news that his brother was dead? They hadn't heard from him for almost a year. At that time all he'd written about was working a mine and fight-ing off claim jumpers. He'd told of the past winter being so harsh it had killed off most of the cattle in northern Colorado. Ben had sent a letter promising cattle as soon as the snow melted and the trails were clear. He died before enough head could be rounded up.

Bethanie thought of Josh's last letter so many months ago. What if he'd made a new life for himself and wanted no part of her? He could even be married by now and have a family on the way. No. Bethanie closed her mind to such a thought. She would see Josh and tell him of Ben. If she could just see him one more time in her life, it would be enough. It might have to be. She had loved two men in her lifetime and been married to one. It was enough to ask of life.

As the drive neared Fort Union in the New Mexico Territory, the men began to tell frightening stories around the campfire. The safety of the fort that they all called the Queen of Forts seemed to loosen their tongues as well as their fears. Bethanie found the tales of a blood-thirsty halfbreed named Charley Bent the most upsetting. Bent's grandfather had been a kind country doctor, and then his father had operated a trading post before being named Indian agent. But Charley hated the white man and became a master of disguise, sometimes hiring on with wagon trains to protect the people against the likes of himself. Rumors about his whereabouts spread like grassfire. Some said after he failed at trying to kill his own father, he committed suicide. Others claimed to have talked with men who had seen him captured. But every-one's nerves were on edge, as if expecting to see him any minute.

The shadows became suspect. The call of wild turkey made cold sweat inch down everyone's spine. Even the lonely cry of coyotes along the breaks carved into Beth-anie's sleep like tiny knives whittle away at soft oak. Late each night she would pace the edges of the campfire hop-ing to wear herself down enough to sleep. As the outline of the fort came into view, she still could not shake the feeling of waiting for terror to strike.

Just after sunset, Bethanie was so lost in her fears that she didn't hear Cain silently step up beside her. "Don't take the stories too seriously, Mrs. Weston," he whis-pered.

Bethanie straightened on her three-legged stool and tried to make her voice sound light. "I know some of the stories are only tales. We have the same tales in Texas. When you live through hard times, they somehow change in the telling."

"I was here in '65 when the war ended and some of the Rebs came to fight Indians." Cain squatted on the ground beside her stool. "Locals called them Galvanized Yankees. They were the meanest, fightin'est group I've ever seen. They put a stop to most of the raids. Some stayed on to help Dick Wootten build that toll road over Raton Pass. Some came south and worked on Fort Union. Most tried mining as every man does who comes into the mountains."

Bethanie was surprised Cain was talking to her. These were more words than she'd ever heard him say. Perhaps the safety of night when she couldn't see his scar loosened his tongue. Maybe he felt she needed calming conversation. Either way, she was thankful for his low, steady voice. She listened to his stories of the early days until her eyelids grew heavy, and she excused herself to crawl beside Mariah, who was sleeping under the wagon.

Bethanie curved her body around her child and watched Cain's shadow in the firelight. Every night he would circle the ground around the wagon with his rope, believing snakes would never slither across it. Next, he would round up a load of wood to keep the fire going all night, even though the nightly chill would not freeze. Last, he always checked his knife and propped himself up so that he could keep a steady eye on her and Mariah. His actions tonight, as every night of the drive, brought Bethanie comfort and, she slept soundly knowing he was standing guard.

At dawn they left the protective shadow of Fort Union. The soil turned black, and piles of rocks jutted from the earth every few hundred feet. The cone hulls of long-dead volcanoes spotted the land on either side of them as they neared Raton Pass. Cain told of a man who had opened a toll road over the pass the year the war ended. Wootten's twenty-seven-mile road was the fastest route to northern Colorado.

As they reached the small settlement about dusk, Cain suggested going into town and finding a room for the night. The thought of a real bed and maybe a bath sounded heavenly to Bethanie. Cain said he knew of a woman who would wash all their clothes and have them ready by noon. Bethanie looked at all her dingy dresses. Even though she'd scrubbed them at the water crossings along the way, everything she owned was stained with the red mud from the Canadian River or the black dust of New Mexico Territory.

Bethanie rode over to the trail boss. "I'm going on into town. We'll catch up with you by tomorrow afternoon."

Williams smiled and gave a respectful tap on his hat. He'd been with the Westons for several years. He knew enough not to question Bethanie.

Within an hour, Bethanie and Mariah were checked into a hotel room and had ordered a bath. Cain had gone to see about the horses and laundry. He'd told her simply that he'd see her at noon tomorrow. Bethanie had learned to trust him over the past weeks, so her mind was freer from worry than it had been since Ben's death. She and Mariah took a long bath and ate dinner by the tiny fireplace while their hair dried. Mariah crawled up in Bethanie's lap and fell asleep. Bethanie sat watching the fire die down and let her mind drift from one thought to another.

She had just put Mariah into bed, when she heard a sound muffled by the hall carpet. Someone was walking past her door. Bethanie scolded herself. This was a hotel; of course there were people outside the door. But hadn't she taken the last room in the hall?

Another set of steps slowly passed the door. Bethanie lowered the wick on the lamp so that the room was almost black. She could see the light from the hall shining under the door.

A third person walked along the hall toward her room. The steps were louder, definitely those of a man. His boots were heavy and made an echoing thud as he drew closer.

Bethanie was wide-awake now. Half her mind told her it was nothing, as the other half demanded that she move around the bed to where she had left a gun by the washstand. Halfway round the bed, her muscles solidified suddenly as the footsteps in the hall stopped. A dark shadow blocked part of the light coming from the hall. Someone was standing outside . . . waiting.

She heard the unmistakable clank of a key against a metal lock. She held her breath as the knob rattled. To her horror the lock gave with a twist, and light fanned in around her. A stranger in buckskin bolted into the room. He was followed by two other sets of footsteps, and the light vanished with the closing of the door.

Bethanie's nightgown showed milky white in the darkness as she backed away. Her mind flooded with one thought. The gun!

Frantically, she jumped for her weapon, but a huge arm swung around her waist and pulled her to the floor. The grimy hand covered her half-scream as the man's two friends ran closer. The smell of cheap beer and tobacco assaulted Bethanie's senses as she fought violently. In answer to her struggle, his arm tightened and the large hand moved to cover her nose. Within seconds blood seemed to swell into her brain demanding she breathe. She stopped trying to hit him and concentrated on freeing his fingers enough to allow air to pass. He slid a muscular leg over her waist and grabbed both her wrists with one hand.

As he pulled her arms above her head she felt his laughter in her face. "Settle down, lady. We ain't gonna hurt you none."

He looked up at his friends. "See, I told you boys this would be the easiest way to get us a few head of cattle. Now we got somethin' to bargain with. You'll see how fast that trail boss hands over a hundred head."

Bethanie heard the two shadowy figures laugh. They

both made a high giggly sound of men who were long
into drink and short on brains.

The man on the floor used one knee to hold her down.
He held her hands tightly above her head. His weight
was pulling her gown dangerously low over her bust. His
hot breath stung the clean flesh of her throat. She could
see his eyes grow fiery with lust.

"I think we may have found more than we hoped for,"
he mumbled as he slid his fingers off her mouth to grab
the fullness of one of her breasts.

One of his partners sucked in air, whistling softly. "I
ain't never had a white woman," he snickered.

As the leader's hand pulled at her nightgown, Bethanie
drew needed air into her lungs and screamed with every
ounce of energy left. He abandoned his pursuit and covered her mouth once more.

"Why you . . ." he began as footsteps sounded in the
hall.

Before any of the men could move, the door exploded
open and Cain's shadow blocked the light from the hall.
The buckskin-clad man rose from Bethanie and was turning as a blow struck him at the side of the head. Bethanie
scrambled to Mariah's side. She lifted the half-awake
child gently and crawled under the bed.

The fight sounded as if a furious storm was raging
above them. She could hear the loud, drunken cries of
pain from the two smaller men and the powerful slam
of muscle and flesh colliding.

"Stay here," Bethanie whispered to Mariah. She
crawled to the washstand and lifted the gun. Cain was
strong, but the odds of three to one was not in his
favor.

Bethanie heard the clang of metal and saw Cain's knife
slide across the floor to the foot of the bed. The hand
that grabbed it was clad in buckskin. Bethanie peeked
over the bed and saw two men in a dance of violence

before her. The buckskin arm raised with the knife flashing silver in the night. As his arm plunged toward Cain's back, Bethanie raised the gun and fired.

Both men fell to the floor.

Chapter Seventeen

Bethanie dropped the gun on the bed and reached for the lamp. Before she could turn the key, light flooded the room from the hallway. People rushed forward in a noisy mass, drawn by the sound of gunfire. Mariah crawled from under the bed and scrambled into her mother's arms. Bethanie held her tight as she advanced toward the two huge men locked together on the floor. The stranger in buckskin was on top. He raised slightly and rolled off Cain as Bethanie neared. Blood spilled from his side and ran across his tan clothing like a tiny red river across sand.

Cain sat up. He slowly plowed his fingers through his thick, white-streaked hair and looked around at the three men he'd been fighting. The leader lay dead, his eyes staring up at the ceiling. One of his friends was unconscious near the fire, while the other whimpered like a wounded animal in the corner.

Bethanie knelt beside Cain. "Are you all right?"

Cain shrugged, his voice shaking slightly. "Don't worry about me, Mrs. Weston. Important thing is, are you and the child unharmed? If these men hurt you, I'll send them all to meet their Maker."

Bethanie noticed that none of the people filtering into her room seemed to think Cain was suggesting anything out of the ordinary. They seemed merely interested, not judgmental.

With a smile, Bethanie realized how welcome she'd felt to see this face she'd once thought was the ugliest on earth. "No, thanks to you, Cain, we're fine."

Cain retrieved his knife and slid it back into its Indian-made case. "Thanks to your shot, I'm alive." He thought for a minute. "There's a proverb in the Orient. When you save a man's life, it belongs to you."

"Couldn't we just call it even?" Bethanie touched his shoulder and felt the muscles tighten and withdraw. She made a mental note not to repeat her daring action.

"We'll call it even, Mrs. Weston, when it is." Cain's words were little more than a whisper, but a stubbornness blended among them.

A wiry man with a badge pinned on his vest wandered into the room as if it were a public place. He nudged the body of the buckskin-clad man with the toe of his muddy boot. Glancing up, the lawman seemed to recognize Cain and smiled out of a corner of his tight-lipped mouth.

Cain stood and grabbed the marshal's outstretched hand. "Good to see you again, Bill." Cain turned toward Bethanie. "This here's Marshal Hickok, Mrs. Weston. He used to ride shotgun when I drove stages for the Barlow-Sanderson Company a few years back."

The marshal removed his hat and nodded respectfully to Bethanie. "Please to meet ya, Mrs. Weston. Sorry these varmints bothered you and your daughter." He motioned for men to take the body out. "I'll see to 'um. Now you just rest easy."

"Thank you," Bethanie whispered, feeling extremely uncomfortable standing in her nightgown before everyone. She glanced at the small crowd and relaxed as she noticed all eyes were watching two men roll the dead man's body in a faded rag rug.

Hickok pulled the man's gun from its holster and spun the chambers. He held the gun to the light, then pulled a rolled ten-dollar bill from a chamber. "At least the fellow was considerate enough to pay for his own burial."

Bethanie had always heard of gunfighters leaving the chamber under the hammer empty to prevent accidental firing. A man could lose a leg from a black powder burn, even if the bullet only grazed the leg; but packing the empty chamber with money for the undertaker seemed morbid.

Marshal Hickok dusted his hand as if to rid himself of the dead man and turned back to Cain. "Good to see such a peace-loving man like you in these parts again. I knowed if you killed someone, he must have needed it powerful bad."

"I seen these boys downstairs drinking up courage and knew they were up to no good. That's one reason I bedded down close by."

Hickok patted his gun like a fat man pats his belly. "The territory's full of men like these three. Every one of them huntin' for that bloodthirsty half-breed, Charley Bent, ever since a five-thousand-dollar reward was posted on ever' tree from here to Santa Fe. But I heard a rumor today that he and his Dog Soldiers been killed by a group of Kaw Indians down by Fort Zarah. If that be true, maybe some of these bounty hunters will go back to farming and mining."

Bethanie was turning red from embarrassment down to her toes by now and wondered if the marshal planned on staying half the night to talk. She wished suddenly she hadn't sent her only wrapper to be washed, for even holding Mariah did little to cover her. She caught Cain's eye and thought he must have read her mind, for he put his arm around Hickok's shoulder and started moving him toward the door.

As Hickok turned to talk with his men in the hallway,

Cain looked back at Bethanie. "Good night, Mrs. Weston," he said. "I'll spread my bedroll at the foot of the back stairs. I'll be there if you need me again."

"Thank you." Bethanie thought of asking him to call her by her first name, but instinctively she knew he wouldn't approve. He was a man who valued his distance from people.

Mariah was too young to feel his withdrawal from the world. She ran holding her arms out to Cain. The huge man lifted her gently, as though she were a priceless treasure. She kissed his cheek and hugged him around the neck.

When Cain looked up, Bethanie thought she saw tears in his eyes. "I'll be near if you need me," he said as soothingly as a father would calm a frightened child.

Long days filtered by while the wagon moved through Raton Pass. Bethanie was amazed at Cain's stamina. Though he must have been twice her age, he never seemed to tire. The mountains grew huge and snow-capped. Forest covered the sloping land in thick shades of green with only scatterings of silvery aspens to sparkle in the emerald forest. Though the late summer days were mild, the nights now required a blanket.

Bethanie loved watching the countryside. After the flat land of Texas, this country quilted her scattered nerves together with its loveliness. The wind blended colors and smells fresher than she had ever known. Crystal streams of icy water crisscrossed the mountains as if in welcome to all visitors.

She saw signs of earlier travelers along the way. Sometimes the rotting frames of less sturdy wagons could be seen from the trail. Once Bethanie even noticed a faded banner across one of the wrecks. "Pikes Peak or Bust" was written in red. Black paint had been splattered across it announcing, "Busted, By Gosh." She couldn't help but think about all the men and women who had traveled here since 1849, their dreams no more at risk than her own right now.

As dusk brushed gold across the mountaintops, Williams, the trail boss, showed Bethanie her first view of Josh's home. Aspens nestled in a small valley and a huge white house stood guard at the edge of the trees. Though mining was a fever in this country, Bethanie couldn't help but think ranching would have to prosper in this beautiful valley, at least in the warmer months.

Williams, the trail boss, rode close to say his good-byes. The men were already turning the herd toward a large pasture farther north. Williams told her simply that Josh had bought the house the first winter he arrived, even though it was several miles from his mine.

Impatience struck Bethanie, and she kicked Twilight into a gallop. She'd waited all these weeks to see Josh. Though she'd told herself over and over she was making the trip to bring news of Ben's death, she now knew she had to see Josh again. She had to know if her constant memory of him was merely an innocent girl's dreams. She'd hidden away her ache for him in the darkest corner of her soul, but still the ache was there, as alive and real as it was the day he left. Though she'd been Ben's wife in every way, there was a tiny part of her that cried out for the wild, undefined love she'd shared briefly with Josh . . . a part she'd denied long enough.

She jumped from her horse and ran into the house without knocking. She was several feet into the hall before the sight that greeted her sent sudden shivers up her spine. Trash and broken furniture lay everywhere. Discarded whiskey bottles were scattered across the floor, making it resemble an alley behind a saloon more than a home. The large rooms were bare of any life or warmth.

Bethanie stumbled backward in horror. Dirt and

spiderwebs blanketed all but the latest deposits of bottles. The thought that Josh might live in such a wallow sickened her to the core.

"Whata ya want?" A shrill yell came from behind Bethanie.

Bethanie turned to see a fat woman with filthy gray hair hanging in long willow strands from a wrinkled face.

The crow-sharp voice sounded again. "I said, whata you want, dearie?"

Bethanie swallowed hard and tried to make her voice sound calm. "I'm looking for Josh Weston."

"Well, you can look all you like, but you ain't gonna find him here."

Bethanie couldn't keep the hope from her voice. "This isn't his house?"

"Sure this is his house, but he stays up at the mine. Don't come down but once in a while to sleep off a drunk. I'm the housekeeper, since some men broke in here a year ago and busted up the place. He wouldn't be too happy to know there's more strangers here, so suppose'n you tell me what you want and be on your way."

Bethanie could smell the whiskey on the housekeeper's breath, but she stood her ground. It would be dark in less than an hour, and she had no intention of sleeping outside. She stepped around the old woman and took the first two stairs. "Are there bedrooms upstairs?"

"Maybe there is, but this ain't no hotel, miss. I ain't got the place cleaned up from the last bunch of strangers who came in here drinking and fighting. So why don't you just be on your way before I . . ."

"Mrs. Weston." Cain sounded from the porch. "Mrs. Weston, are you all right?"

Shocked twisted the old woman's face into a thousand wrinkles. "Mrs. Weston," she whispered.

"Yes," Bethanie answered, her low voice bearing a ring of steel. "I'm Bethanie Weston, and I'd like to see if there is a room clean enough to sleep in." She moved up the steps. "Tomorrow we'll begin cleaning this place."

The old housekeeper wiped her hands on a filthy apron. A touch of worry blended through her bloodshot eyes. "Your room is at the top, Mrs. Weston. It's been closed off ever since I've been here, but Mr. Weston told me to sweep it out every once in a while."

Bethanie opened the door the woman indicated, fully expecting to see more trash. To her surprise the room was orderly, but dusty. All the furniture was draped with sheets, as if waiting to be unveiled. As she pulled the covers, she was delighted to find finely carved, delicate furnishings.

The housekeeper let out a long breath as Bethanie smiled. "I knew Mr. Weston was married, even if he never talked about it to no one in these parts. There ain't a man in the territory who would buy the things in this room unless he had a woman in mind. Besides, I see you wear the same kind of band he does on your finger."

Bethanie realized the woman's mistake. She thought Bethanie to be Josh's wife. She twisted the ring that had once been her grandmother's. If she told the woman of her mistake, there was a chance Josh would get the news of Ben's death before she could tell him. Also, she might get more work out of the old drunk if she believed Bethanie to be the wife and not just the widowed sister-in-law. Bethanie bit her lip and decided saying nothing was not really a lie. After all, she *was* Mrs. Weston, and she did own half of the mine. Cain eased the silence by bringing Mariah and the bags.

Though Bethanie was tired, she and Cain worked until midnight cleaning the bedrooms and hall. They scrubbed a room clean for Mariah and put her to bed before starting on Bethanie's room. The housekeeper kept disappearing, but Cain did the work of three people. Before they said good night he had hauled all the broken furniture that had lined the entry and halls outside to burn. As he walked toward the barn, Bethanie wondered at his unyielding devotion. It was as though he couldn't sleep without first seeing that she and Mariah were comfortable.

Bethanie bathed and crawled into her bed, smiling contentedly at the warm room around her. The fine oak furniture reflected the glow of the fireplace in golden tones of warmth. Whatever Josh's reasons were for buying this house and these furnishings she could only wonder, but the room made her feel at home. She dared to hope he would welcome her and not still resent her. She fell asleep feeling Josh was near for the first time in three years.

In the darkness of the house before dawn, Bethanie's nightmares returned. In her dream, the room was cold and barren. She heard shouts from outside. Suddenly her mother was yelling, "Run, Bethanie, run!" She climbed down from the bed. She was running for the woods behind her house, running until her lungs were on fire. She heard her mother scream behind her. Then she was falling, falling into blackness.

A cry of horror escaped her lips and woke her to reality. Bethanie sat up in the cold room and felt sweat bead across her body. Though it was only a dream, to her emotions it always seemed real. The dream never ended. She always woke at the same point.

She lit a candle and filled the room with shadows. Tears stained her eyes and she wished Ben were close. His presence had kept the dream at bay for so long; Bethanie had almost forgotten the hollow fear that echoed each pounding of her heart, each shallow breath. She rose slowly and dressed. There would be no more sleep for her tonight.

She pulled the blankets from the bed and noticed two chairs turned with their backs together by the window. They'd been against the wall when she first looked at the room, and she hadn't thought of moving them. As she draped the bedcovers over the chairs and opened the window, she couldn't help but wonder if Cain had done the rearranging. To her knowledge, he'd never been inside the ranch house, much less her bedroom back in Texas. Someone must have told him of her habit of airing all the covers every morning. A habit passed down from her Shaker mother. His thoughtfulness never ceased to amaze her.

As if her thought of Cain drew him to her, a light knock sounded at her door. Bethanie pushed the bolt back and opened it without hesitation. She knew it would be Cain. The housekeeper was probably sleeping off her drunkenness. No one else could have passed Cain to get to her door.

As always, he seemed nervous talking with her. "Mrs. Weston, I saw you open the window and knew you were up." He stepped back a few feet into the hallway. "The housekeeper left during the night. From the large bags she had, I'd say she took a bonus."

Bethanie shrugged and started down the hall. "I don't think we've lost much of a helper. I know finding someone to take care of this house must be a problem in this country, but it seems to me the house is better off without her."

When she turned to see if he agreed, Cain's face was twisted in agony. "I want to talk to you about that, Mrs. Weston." He knew she was watching him, and turned the scarred side of his face away from her. "I know my job was just to get you here, but I was thinking . . ."

Bethanie had to smile. Never in her life had she frightened anyone, yet she seemed to scare this man to within an inch of death. She had the feeling if she yelled "boo" at him, he would bolt like a wild colt. He looked like a rock of a man who'd never taken anything off anyone, yet around her, he was as jumpy as a rabbit in a dog kennel.

"I thought . . . if you would allow me . . . I could stay on around here and help out. This place needs lots of fixin' up and the barn needs a new roof . . . and the fence out back wouldn't hold a goat . . . and I could . . ."

"O.K., O.K., Cain," Bethanie laughed. "I would consider myself fortunate if you would agree to stay."

Cain let out a long-held breath. "Thanks, Mrs. Weston. I made some coffee in the kitchen. The trail boss told me there is a small settlement about five miles north. I thought if I left at daybreak, I could be back with supplies by noon."

Bethanie agreed and went to survey the cupboards. She saw Cain off, then looked around the house until Mariah awoke. They spent the morning washing hair and clothes. If Josh came home tonight, she would be more presentable.

True to his word, Cain was back by noon with a wagonload of supplies and tools. To Bethanie's surprise, a middle-aged woman climbed down from the wagon. Her clothes were little more than rags, but they were clean.

Cain pulled off his hat and began mutilating it with nervous fingers as he stood before Bethanie. "I met this woman in town," he whispered to Bethanie. "She was taking in laundry and not doing too well among these dirt-loving miners. I checked around and found out she was a widow and respectable. I was hoping you could see your way clear to hire her."

Bethanie got his point even before he said the word "housekeeper." She nodded first to him, then the woman. How could she tell Cain that she would have hired the woman herself if she'd met her first? The woman's face had little beauty in middle age, but her eyes reflected an openness of character. Her lips turned up in a smile even though her life couldn't have been an easy one.

Bethanie knew firsthand what it was like to try to make a living in a mining town. She offered her hand to the woman. "I'm Bethanie Weston, and I'd be delighted to have some help and company out here."

A bubbly smile covered the woman's plump face. "I'm Rachel, and I'd be glad to help for as long as you need me. I've heard of the Weston Mine, but I didn't know about a house. Josh Weston is kind of a legend around these parts. Some say he works night and day, never sleeping at all."

Cain started walking the horses to the barn as Rachel continued. "When your hired hand finished frightening me to death, I decided I didn't have nothing to lose by coming out to meet you. I've been having trouble keeping body and soul together since my husband died last winter."

Rachel patted Bethanie's hand. "Mr. Cain told me of your loss only a few months ago." The older woman heaved her chest as if fighting off sadness with determination. She looked toward Cain and changed the subject without hesitation. "I have the feeling Mr. Cain has a heart of gold to counter that ugly face. He even asked me if there was anything I needed at the store. Imagine a man thinking of a thing like that."

"I don't know what I'll be able to pay you." Bethanie realized she was probably being rash in replacing Josh's housekeeper. "But I'm sure it will be fair," she added. She already liked this woman who was free with her compliments and honest in her judgment of Cain.

By the time they had lunch, Bethanie knew Rachel was going to work out just fine. She doted over Mariah like a grandmother, and the child was delighted.

Everything was falling into place, but Bethanie still hadn't seen Josh. The uncertainty of his reaction gnawed at her self-confidence. If he didn't come home tonight, she knew she would have to go to the mine tomorrow.

Chapter Eighteen

Josh Weston waved good-bye to the miners as they climbed into buckboards. They were headed into town for their Saturday night fun. He knew that half, or more, would be out of money when they returned Sunday and wouldn't even remember where they'd spent their pay. But the men were in high spirits tonight. He only wished that he could feel their wild, carefree abandon. If he were being honest with himself, it had been some time since he'd felt anything.

Josh grabbed a clean towel and headed between the trees that hid the spring. Maybe feeling nothing was better than feeling pain. He smiled bitterly to himself. He hadn't even gotten drunk in weeks, so he must be getting better.

He stripped off his shirt and squinted watching the sun spread its fool's gold over the mountains. Trained for alertness, he heard a noise at the camp and laughed to think one of the men must have forgotten something in haste. Josh ducked his head low in the stream and felt the icy water wash away the dust of the mine.

He raised his head as a twig snapped behind him. Slowly, Josh turned around. His face was relaxed, but his hand hung ready at his gun handle. The past years had been peaceful, but he remembered a time when claim jumpers were as pesky as mosquitoes. A woman's form moved as gracefully as a spring breeze from the shadows of aspens.

Josh watched her slender body come toward him like she had a hundred times before in his fantasies. Her hair was red-gold fire and her eyes the green of new leaves. She was dressed in black, this time, in a riding skirt and boots. "God," his mind cried. "How could she grow more beautiful with each dream?"

Josh shook the water from his head and widened his stance. "Damn you!" he shouted in pain. "Go away and leave me alone. Must you haunt both my days and my nights?"

He watched her lips part in surprise at his outburst. He could see the hurt his words wrought in her expressive eyes. How could she look so innocent, as if she were unaware of the pain she caused him?

Josh stood and pulled the towel behind his neck. Every cell in his body wanted to run to her, but he had lived this nightmare of her disappearing too many times. "Damn, how I hate you," he hissed. "And I hate myself even more for wanting you."

He watched her head jerk to the side as if he had dealt her a blow. He had to face her straight on or go mad. Josh laughed without humor and fought to keep the tears from his eyes. His knuckles whitened from his grip on the towel. He must be cracking up. Maybe he had finally worked himself too hard. Usually he didn't see her except after several drinks.

He watched her straighten and saw a stamina in her crystal green eyes that he'd never seen before. She was different somehow from the Bethanie he remembered.

"I'm not a dream." Bethanie moved closer. "Or the nightmare you seem to think, Josh Weston, so stop yelling at me."

Josh watched her close the distance between them. He studied each line of her face, each curl of her hair. She was here, the same as he'd imagined for three long years. His heart began to thunder in his chest as he realized that his dream was, indeed, a reality. His mouth was dry, with words hung in his throat. He watched her move nearer and knew Bethanie was with him. But she wasn't the same. Somehow the years had made her stronger and more beautiful. How could she be more lovely than the perfection he left behind? Josh tried to hear what she was saying.

"I bring tragic news." Her eyes filled with tears and the sight tore into his heart. "I wanted to be the one to tell you." Her voice was little more than a whisper as she stood only inches away. "Ben was killed almost six weeks ago in an Indian raid at the ranch."

She was talking, telling him every detail of the day his brother died, but Josh couldn't get her words to sink in. He could only watch one lone tear roll down her face. He would have moved the very mountain they stood on if he could stop the tear's course.

Suddenly, the reality of her words registered like a bullet exploding inside his chest. Josh turned away from her, the pain of Ben's death plowing through his mind. Never in his longing for Bethanie would he have wished Ben harm. Never! Ben was his only kin, the brother he admired and loved.

Her warm hand touched his shoulder. "I know, I know," she whispered. "I loved him, too."

Josh whirled around and encircled her in his arms. He pulled her to him in a need to hold and be held. She ran her fingers over his wet hair and whispered softly, things mothers whisper to heartbroken children.

Bethanie's unhealed wound was ripped wide open again, and pain poured out with the same force it had the day Ben died. Held safely in Josh's strong arms, she was free to allow her pain to flow. They clung to each other for a long moment, sharing their grief.

Josh pulled her closer to him . . . closer than he'd ever allowed another to come. She felt so wonderful and soft in his arms. A faint scent of honeysuckle seemed to surround her. He buried his face into the silk of her hair. He'd been wrong to think numbness was better than feeling. Even the pain of sorrow was better than the walking death he'd lived these past three years.

Slowly, he moved his hand along her back, proving to himself she was real. She lifted her head from his shoulder, and he tenderly wiped a tear from her cheek. Her eyes closed as he cradled her chin in his palm. His thumb moved across her lips in a tender action that no amount of willpower could have stopped. He remembered the taste of her lips and the way they'd quivered at his anger when she'd told him she was married.

Heavy footsteps crashed suddenly toward them. Bethanie pulled away. Without turning she called out. "Over here, Cain."

Josh watched a huge middle-aged man emerge from the trees and freeze as if awaiting orders. The left side of his face was a mass of scars and his hair a blend of dark red and white. He was not a man Josh had seen before or would likely forget seeing.

"This is Cain. Mike hired him to get us here. I've asked him to stay on." Bethanie didn't turn her eyes from Josh as she continued. "Cain, I'd like you to meet Josh Weston, my husband's brother."

Cain nodded at Josh, but moved no closer. He reminded Josh of an untamed wilderness creature. He would go near humans, but not so close that he couldn't jump back before they advanced.

Josh nodded a greeting and watched Cain's reaction as he placed his arm around Bethanie's shoulder. The older man stiffened, not like a jealous lover but more like an alert watchdog.

Josh walked Bethanie back to her horse and said he

would be along later. She seemed reluctant to leave him, but she said nothing in front of Cain. Josh knew he had some heavy thinking, and maybe drinking, to do before he headed home. The way he felt about her hadn't changed in three years, and he knew what would have happened if Cain hadn't interrupted. By the look in her eyes, she knew, too, and that fact frightened Josh more than anything had in his life.

Bethanie lay awake most of the night thinking and listening for Josh, but he didn't come home. She tried to act as if nothing were wrong all the next day, but even Rachel could read her clearly enough to know something was amiss. They cleaned house all day. The work used up Bethanie's energy and allowed little time to think. By nightfall, Bethanie was too tired to wonder why Josh hadn't come home.

Just after she went to bed, she heard voices in the hall. Bethanie ran to the landing to see Cain holding Josh against the wall as Josh yelled obscenities at him in a drunken slur.

Bethanie ran down the stairs. "Cain," she shouted. "Don't hurt him."

"Hurt me, hell," Josh yelled. "I'll . . ."

Josh's words were stopped by Cain's fist at his jaw. She heard the pop of the older man's knuckles and the snap of Josh's lower jaw. Bethanie watched in horror as Josh slid unconscious to the floor like a huge rag doll.

Cain looked up with no hint of anger in his face. "Sorry, Mrs. Weston, but my hand slips when I hear that kind of language in front of ladies."

Bethanie had to smile. Cain was a poor liar. He wasn't sorry and his hand hadn't slipped. "Can you get him upstairs to his room? He can sleep it off, and we can explain the accident tomorrow over black coffee?"

She followed as Cain slung Josh over one shoulder and took the stairs two at a time.

He stopped her at Josh's bedroom door. "I'll see he gets to bed." Cain didn't wait for an answer, but closed the door in her face.

Bethanie spent another restless night tormented by the knowledge that Josh was only a wall away from her. She recalled the words he'd said to her when he first saw her at the stream. He'd said he hated her, yet love was in his eyes. Even as she'd held him to comfort his sorrow, her body had warmed at the feel of his muscular shoulders and the touch of his hands on her back. Had Josh felt the desire and also the guilt of needing her, even as they grieved his brother? Maybe that was why he had to be drunk to come back home.

Dawn filtered into her room, and finally Bethanie heard movement in the hall. She climbed from her bed as her doorknob twisted soundlessly. She waited, thankful for the bolt blocking the door. The footsteps retreated back down the hall. She shook herself awake. She was overreacting. It was probably only Rachel checking to see if she was still asleep. Or was it Josh? Or was Cain on guard just outside the door?

Bethanie dressed quickly and went downstairs. Rachel was already hard at work in the kitchen. Two dirty plates cluttered the table. "Mornin'," Rachel smiled. "You're the last one up. Cain and Josh have already downed a pot of coffee and gone off to look at the herd over on the north pasture."

"Cain and Josh?" Bethanie accepted the offered coffee.

"Sure," Rachel laughed. "Once that young man sobered up, they were thick as thieves. Mr. Weston is a gentleman, even if he did belt one on last night. He came down this morning and apologized to me right off."

Bethanie cleared away the men's plates and sat down

with her coffee. Rachel poured herself a cup and took the chair beside Bethanie. "They said not to expect them back until mid-afternoon. What part of the house should we tackle today?"

Bethanie had lost all interest in housekeeping. She drank her coffee and nodded at Rachel's chatter. Her bleak mood continued all morning while they worked. The weather seemed to mimic her emotions as clouds gathered and threatened rain.

By four, Bethanie could stand the house no longer and saddled Twilight. The clouds were now dark, and thunder echoed off the surrounding mountains. Mariah was busy helping Rachel make long curls from apple peelings. Bethanie promised a mothering Rachel that she would go only a short distance from the house. With her first taste of freedom all day, Bethanie kicked her horse into a gallop toward the north.

The woods were unfamiliar, and the wind whipped Bethanie around. Even the joy of riding was lost in her dark mood and the brooding weather. Why was Josh avoiding her? Maybe she had only brought him pain. Then, the sight of the doorknob turning flashed in her mind. Did he think he could come without knocking to her bedroom? She felt angry at him for thinking he could just take up where he left off, and angry at herself for knowing she would not only allow his advances, but welcome them.

Large drops of rain stung her face. She had ridden farther from the house than she'd planned. In a race to beat nature, Bethanie kicked Twilight into a run toward the barn. The storm opened forth a blinding rain as thunder crackled in victory. She gave her powerful animal his head and leaned low over him. If she hadn't been lost in her thoughts, she would have never been caught so unaware of the sky.

As Twilight galloped into the open barn door, Bethanie

allowed her cramped hands to let go of the reins. She leaned forward and patted the strong neck in a "thank you" to the animal for bringing her to safety.

Suddenly, powerful hands encircled her waist and pulled her off the horse with a jerk. She whirled to see Josh's face twisted in anger. "What kind of fool are you to be out in this?" he yelled above the thunder. The rain hammered against the roof like a thousand workmen. Shadows darkened the barn as clouds blocked the setting sun outside. Nature's storm was reflected in Josh's angry, dark eyes.

Josh's hands were still tight around her waist as he pulled her closer. "When I got back and discovered you were out in this storm I thought I'd go mad."

"I can take care of myself." Bethanie resented being thought of as incompetent.

"Don't ever do that again." Josh moved his hands to her shoulders. Though his words were hateful, his fingers were a caress.

"I'll do what I please, Josh Weston." Bethanie's anger at herself for being caught in the storm transferred to Josh.

"When did you get so sharp, woman?' Josh's words were a slap.

"About the same time you became a drunk," Bethanie answered, and saw her words had stung him also.

She pulled free, knocking herself off balance. Josh lunged to steady her, and they both fell backward against an empty stall. Josh swore and Bethanie screamed as the wood cracked, giving way beneath their weight. She fell against the packed earth, and Josh tumbled atop her. For a moment they lay face to face, staring at each other. Bethanie could feel his hard body covering her, their wet clothes doing little to hamper her sense of touch. His shoulders were wider, more muscular than she remembered. His dark hair was damp, covering his forehead.

In a flash of lightning, Bethanie could see it all in his eyes. She saw the need he had for her even though anger still clouded his smoldering gaze. As his chest pressed against her breasts, she could see the desire in his eyes. The longing, not for a night, but for a lifetime.

The instant shattered. Josh rolled violently off her as mighty arms jerked him to his feet. In a blink, Cain's hand reached to help Bethanie up. "I heard the crash. Are you all right, Mrs. Weston?" Cain glanced in rage toward Josh, and she watched his hands ball into fists.

Bethanie steadied herself. "I'm fine, Cain. It was just an accident." She looked over at Josh. The raw passion in his dark eyes embarrassed her. Were her feelings toward him as obvious? "I must get out of these wet clothes." Fire rose in her cheeks as Josh's eyebrows lifted slightly.

Bethanie turned and ran for the house. She thought she heard Josh start to follow, then stop. In that second on the barn floor, she had seen the promise in Josh's eyes. She could bolt her door tonight, but could she close her heart to him?

Josh took two steps to follow Bethanie before a mighty hand grabbed his shoulder. Rage flowed through him like water through a broken dam. He swung around blindly at the huge man behind him and plowed his fist into Cain's middle. Cain stumbled back a few feet in shock, then stood ready to fight.

"I've had enough of your interfering," Josh said as he swung and missed Cain's jaw by an inch. "You act as if I could do her harm. I don't know what you think gives you the right to protect Bethanie against me. I'll have no more of it." He swung again and heard a grunt as muscles bruised knuckles.

"You're a good man, Cain, but unless you're Beth-

anie's father, stay out of her life. I love that woman.
She's mine. No man is ever going to come between her
and me again while I'm alive."

Josh struck again, but not as hard. He realized that
Cain was not fighting, only blocking blows. As his fist
turned Cain's jaw, the man dropped suddenly to his knees
making no defense to block another blow. Josh stopped
his blow in mid-flight and knelt beside the strong man.
Cain's head rested on his chest in total defeat, not by
Josh's blows, but by his words.

"Cain?" Josh put his arm on the man's shoulder.
"What is it?" Could it be that Cain loved her, too? Josh
could not hate the man for that flaw. He had felt the pain
of loving her and not being able to have her.

Cain raised his deformed face to Josh. Tears fought
their way down his scarred flesh.

"I'll have the truth, Cain."

The older man nodded as if he could no longer hold
his lie within himself. He tried to speak but a sob tore
the words from him. Finally his voice won over a low
cry of pain. "I *am* her father," he whispered. "Though
I have no right to see her again, I'd give my life for her.
I'm her father."

Chapter Nineteen

Bethanie arranged the oak table in the large dining room for dinner. The house must have been beautifully stocked before vandals broke in and stole many of its treasures. All the linens and china seemed to be present, but most of the silverware had vanished. She searched every cabinet for candlesticks nice enough for the grand table. Finally she had to settle for an overturned china bowl as a base for three fat candles.

Each time she passed the wide bay window, Bethanie paused a moment. There was a magnificent view of the storm rolling over the mountains, but it was the barn that drew her constant attention. Josh and Cain had been in there for hours. Were they fighting, or merely waiting out the storm? The pounding of the rain against the house echoed the throbbing at her temple. She had so much to talk over with Josh. How would he react when he learned half of the mine was hers? His eyes had told her he still loved her, yet he had said nothing. Would he always see his brother's widow when he looked at her? Bethanie had known the minute she touched him that her passion for Josh was the same as it had been three years before. Even his angry words in the barn seemed to tell her he still cared.

As the rain slowed and dusk blanketed the mountains

in velvet, Bethanie heard Josh and Cain return. She paused outside the kitchen door, listening to the two men.

"I still think you should say something." Josh's voice sounded adamant.

As Bethanie pushed the door open silently, she saw Cain run his hand over a worried brow. "Some questions are better left unanswered."

"As you wish," Josh agreed, raising his head to observe Bethanie watching them. His gaze seemed to devour her with a long-denied thirst. Though his words were for Cain, his eyes never left her face. "Will you join us for dinner, Cain?'

"No." Cain backed away. "I'd like to eat in here with Miss Rachel, as usual."

Bethanie thought little of Josh's invitation, since she'd seen Ben do the same with many ranch hands. Josh, like his brother, treated all men equally regardless of position. Whatever had been the thorn between Cain and him, it must have been solved in the barn, for they were friendly enough now.

Josh offered his arm to Bethanie and they walked into the dining room. Dark eyes stared down at her as his free hand reached to cover her fingers. She felt his muscles tighten as her hand pressed into his damp shirt. He smiled as she shivered beneath the pressure of his touch. His pace slowed to a lingering walk. Could it be he wanted to savor this moment of nearness?

Josh pulled out her chair as if they were dining at a fine restaurant. "I bought this house from a lucky gold miner who hated the winters up here. When he sold it to me, there were more chairs," he smiled. "I seem to remember a housekeeper, too, but guess she got swept out with the broken furniture."

Bethanie liked the little game he was playing and decided to play along. "You might find her piled up with the broken wood behind the house. No doubt the candlesticks will be packed in her pockets."

"I guess so," Josh sighed. "But to tell the truth, this place never looked better than it does tonight."

Even before she looked up, she knew he was staring at her and not the room. She felt her cheeks redden at his compliment. His fingers lifted and brushed her jawline, then returned to rest lightly on her shoulder. The passion smoldering in his dark brown eyes said more than any words ever could. With great willpower, he made himself move away and take his seat opposite her.

Bethanie tried to bring up all the things that needed to be said between them, but, as always, words came awkwardly to her. Conversation seemed only background noise to the emotions she read in his eyes. He was caressing her with his gaze, brushing over every curve of her body, undressing her with his eyes even as she served dinner. She felt a fire burn from the core of her outward, blushing her skin with its warmth.

As if knowing of her distress, Josh talked of his luck buying old gold mines when gold was running out and the silver being discovered. His low voice was an embrace, and she had trouble following what he was saying.

As Josh talked, she watched his mouth move and wished she could touch her finger to his lips. The wonder of looking at him had not diminished in the past years. He was a handsome man, strong in body as well as character.

Leaving their plates of food almost untouched, Josh carried their coffee over to the huge fireplace. He pulled two chairs close to the hearth. They sat talking of nothing while each drank in the nearness of the other. Her gaze became hypnotized by his strong tanned fingers holding the fragile china cup. She remembered how gently those fingers had touched her body, and how quickly they'd been covered with blood when he'd slammed his fist into a tree at the falls after he'd learned of her marriage to his brother.

Bethanie heard Mariah cry out as they finished their coffee. She hurried up the stairs to her daughter. Mariah's room was across the hall from Bethanie's. It was large and airy with a small side room built for a maid or nanny. Rachel had claimed the space to be near the child even at night.

With Mariah in her arms, Bethanie returned. She wanted to reassure herself that with the reality of Mariah, the dream with Josh wouldn't vanish.

Josh had pulled off his boots and stretched his long legs out in front of him. Tears came to his eyes as he watched Bethanie and Mariah coming toward him. He slowly stood and leaned his long frame against the doorway.

"There must be no beauty anywhere else in this world," Josh whispered. "For it's surely all now within my vision."

Mariah looked up at Josh and joy filled her face. His resemblance to Ben seemed enough for her to welcome him openly. She moved into his arms willingly. For a few minutes, Josh didn't know how to handle such a wiggly bundle. He sat back and cradled her to him.

He stroked her black hair, the same coal color as his own. She lay her head against his chest, and after a few moments of nestling, fell asleep in his arms. Josh tucked her bare toes under the hem of her long gown and kissed her cheek. "She's wonderful," he said to himself.

He cradled Mariah as if holding a great treasure. "I have to ask, Bethanie," he whispered. "I've wondered all these years, is she mine?"

Bethanie moved beside him. She placed her hand on his shoulder and leaned close. "Does it matter?" she whispered, her lips brushing his ear.

Josh cuddled the sleeping child closer. "No," he answered. "It doesn't matter at all."

Josh stood and carefully carried Mariah up the stairs. He tucked her in bed and kissed her forehead. Bethanie felt tears flood her eyes as she watched him. He would never know he was kissing his own daughter, but somehow she felt now she must keep her secret in honor of Ben's memory. Bethanie smiled suddenly at life's funny turns. First, she wouldn't tell Ben the truth about Mariah and now she wouldn't tell Josh. Somehow, if she told Josh, she would be taking something away from Ben. She moved next to Josh's side and blew out the candle on the bedstand.

They stood in the shadows beside the bed for a moment. She could hear his breathing in the darkness. Without speaking they moved nearer to each other as if magnets were pulling them together.

Josh folded Bethanie gently against him. His fingers lifted her chin and turned her face toward him. "One thing does matter," he whispered as his lips brushed her forehead. "Are you mine?"

The dam of emotions Bethanie had held back, all the promises she'd made to herself about going slowly, vanished with his words. She returned his embrace as completely as if three years had never passed. She ran her fingers through his black hair and fought to keep from screaming out her joy.

Josh's lips found hers, and his kiss was as tender as the touch of first love. His hands roamed slowly over her back as if he feared he might frighten her away. She slid her arms around his neck and brushed the raven curls. Her lips blocked his moan as she pressed her breasts against his hard chest. There was a crying need between them. A need as vital as air to survive. A longing within each that only the other could fill.

As if from miles away, they heard steps coming up

the stairs. Bethanie spoke her thoughts. "Will you come to me tonight?" she whispered.

Josh pulled away as the steps neared. "Bolt your door," he answered in haste, as Rachel appeared at the door of Mariah's room.

Alarm showed in the older woman's eyes as she whispered, "There's a man downstairs and he's demanding to see you, Mr. Weston. I think there's some trouble at the mine."

Josh ran toward the hallway with Bethanie only a step behind him. She stood on the stairs as he greeted the dirt-covered young stranger. She forced Josh's last words, and the hurt they bore, to the back of her mind as she concentrated on the conversation below.

The young man's speech was coming in rapid gulps, telling of his long ride and of his fear. "There's been an explosion, Boss. Down in shaft three. Most of the men were already gone home when it blew. The few left say they ain't goin' down there." He stopped to breathe, and Bethanie saw his eyes enlarge as Cain entered from the kitchen. The stranger quickly turned back to Josh. "They say all the charges might not have exploded. I didn't know what to do, so I just came after you."

"You did right." Josh's voice was reassuring, but his movements were swift. He grabbed his hat and raincoat and started toward the door.

"Wait!" Bethanie cried. "I'm going with you."

Josh swung around as if he couldn't believe his ears. Passion still touched his eyes, but his voice was cold. "No, Bethanie, you stay here. I'll be back before morning."

Bethanie hurried down the last few steps, unafraid of his raised eyebrow and wrinkled forehead. "Rachel, get that brown bag out of the pantry. Cain, saddle Twilight for me." She looked straight into Josh's eyes. "I'm going with you, Josh Weston, and there is no way you are going to stop me."

"Why?" Josh asked as all the people around him ran to do her bidding. "What are you trying to prove, Bethanie?"

"I'm not trying to prove anything. If there are men hurt, I can do a fair job of doctoring."

"But the mine is no place for a woman." Josh's intelligent eyes were studying her. He did not miss the changes in her self-confidence or in the touch of authority in her voice.

"If you're there, I will be there, also." She wanted to add that she would never again hide from danger while someone she loved died, but he might not understand. Finally the only sensible answer she could think of came out. "Because I own half of that mine."

Her words hit Josh like a slap. His dark eyes turned mahogany-hard as he stepped away. "Is that why you came here, to tell me I now have a partner?"

Bethanie resented his cold words. Couldn't he see that if men were hurt at the mine she could be a great help? Didn't he realize she was not the girl he had left behind three years ago? She had nursed men after cattle stampedes and Indian attacks. *Well, if her owning part of the mine blurred his vision, so be it.* "Yes," she nodded as she put her coat around her shoulders and took the bag from Rachel. "And not a silent partner. Where you go . . . I go."

Josh opened the door in an exaggerated gesture. "Then by all means, Mrs. Weston, let's go."

They rode through the night in silence, mud muffling even the sound of hooves on the path. Bethanie wished she had told Josh about Ben's will from the first, but it hadn't seemed that important. Now, he thought she was coming with him because of the mine. How could she tell him that it was him she could not leave in danger?

She'd made up her mind the second she'd seen the fear in the young miner's face. She wouldn't wait in safety only to learn of Josh's death. If he died, it would be in her arms. Somehow, when this was over, she would make him understand. He might have told her to bolt her door from him, but she had no intention of doing so. The only thing that would turn her from him was his cold arms, and she'd seen too much fire in his eyes to believe he could ever turn her away.

As they dismounted at the mine entrance, Josh made no effort to assist her. He seemed to be pointedly ignoring her presence as he strode to the group of miners clustered around a fire. The night was so dark, and the crowd of men seemed like ghosts floating in the blackness.

The men, covered with rich black dirt, opened their circle to Josh, but their voices bore no welcome. The small campfire cast frightening shadows across their faces as they complained. Bethanie stepped silently behind Josh.

"We ain't taking a chance of there being more explosions," one man with massive shoulders shouted.

Josh pulled his hat off and ran his fingers through his hair. "Look, men, I left orders for everyone to stay out of shaft three until tomorrow. I was with Jackson when he laid the charges."

A cruel sound of hard laughter came from another miner. "Jackson is one of the fools who went down. Nothin' came up but dust and noise."

"But why, Blade?" Josh looked at the man who had just laughed.

"He's hungry for that bonus." The man shrugged. "You had a good idea to offer us a piece of any new strike, but some men take crazy risks for enough money."

Josh cursed under his breath. "How many men went

down with him?" Again his question was directed at the man he had called Blade.

"Four we think. We were all quitting for the day when they went down. The only reason some of us were still around when the shaft blew was 'cause we were waiting for the rain to let up."

Josh nodded as he pulled off his rain slicker. "Who'll go down with me? If they're alive, they'll be out of air by morning."

All the men seemed to back away a step except Blade, who crossed his chest with massive arms. "Four, maybe five fools already down there. Ain't no amount of money going to make us go."

"Look," Josh tried to reason. "I know where the charges are. All I need is someone who can hold a good light while I pull them out. Then we can dig through the cave-in."

"You get them charges out, and we'll help with the digging," Blade answered, and the others nodded in silent agreement.

Josh grabbed a lantern. "Who'll hold the light for me?" he asked as the men seemed to move back another step. "Damn it, men, we've got to try and help them." Still no one moved.

He jerked with surprise as a hand reached from behind him and molded around his fingers as he gripped the handle of the lantern. A golden band carved like the one he always wore glittered in the light. "I'll be right behind you," Bethanie whispered. "I can hold a light."

A rumble went through the crowd of men. Josh turned to face her. His features were in shadows, but she could feel his anger. There was no time to argue and no one else to go with him. She knew if he waited much longer, the chances of finding any men alive would be lost.

Josh nodded as the men mumbled in disbelief that a

woman would go into the mine. "After you, Mrs. Weston," Josh said, and heard gasps from several miners.

They moved through the dark hole, the lantern shedding light in a small circle around them. Josh clasped Bethanie's hand as they inched downward.

"Follow the tracks made by the ore carts, and stay between them. The ground is flat, and there's fewer rocks to stumble over."

"I've been in a mine before when I was a child. I don't mind the cold as much as the dark. I can take care of myself."

"You've been telling me that since we met. You'd think that I'd finally start to believe you." He turned a corner and the light flickered.

"The lantern won't go out, will it?' Bethanie asked, trying to keep her voice from shaking.

Josh squeezed her fingers. "I'd forgotten how you hate the darkness." He seemed to be piecing facts together in his mind. "You hate the blackness, yet you came in here with me. No half-interest in a mine drove you. You're afraid to leave my side. Afraid I'll die on you like Ben did." He drew a long breath as he pulled her closer. "And if I do?"

"Then we die together," Bethanie answered without hesitation.

"You're a complicated woman, Bethanie Weston. I may just have to stay alive a little longer to figure you out." He knelt beside a pile of rocks. "But first, I'm going to take out these explosives."

Bethanie held the lantern high as he worked, dismantling first one charge then the next. Finally they reached a blocked passageway, and Bethanie knew they were at the cave-in. Josh hammered into the rock pile, then listened. A faint sound came from the other side. He stripped off his shirt and began frantically digging. Bethanie flung her coat aside and pulled her hair back with her scarf. She knew she could only lift the smaller rocks, but she had to help. The thought of men trapped only a few feet away in total darkness sent cold chills up her spine.

After several minutes, Bethanie touched Josh's shoulder to silence his movement. She heard noises behind her, and turned to see Blade and several men.

Blade stormed forward. "We came to help dig. We figure if a man ain't afraid to bring his woman down here, we'd be downright yellow to hold back."

Josh straightened and winked at Bethanie. He wiped his forehead with his bandanna and stepped aside as others took his place.

Bethanie watched in wonder as the men moved the wall aside. A passage enlarged, and a shout rang out from both sides of the cave-in. Slowly the miners pulled their co-workers through the opening. Each, as if being reborn, cried and shouted with joy. The man named Jackson had a cut on his arm, but respectfully declined when she offered to treat his wound.

Josh slung his arm around her shoulder and brushed her hair lightly with a kiss as the men headed out. "You're quite a miner, Mrs. Weston. Better watch it, or the men will make a legend out of you tonight."

Bethanie could think of nothing to say. She didn't want to be a legend; she only wanted to help. Moving closer, she took comfort in his strong body beside her as they climbed out of the tunnel.

When they stepped into the open air, Blade was standing in front of the men. Most were mounted up, ready to head home, but they all seemed waiting for Blade to speak.

"Mrs. Weston." The huge man seemed suddenly shy. "The men and me would just like to thank you for what you did. We should've known the boss's lady would be brave. When we all seen your hand on that lantern and you wearing a ring just like the one that never gets off the boss's finger, there weren't no question who you was. We're mighty proud you're here."

Bethanie realized they all thought she was married to Josh. As she opened her mouth to correct Blade, Josh pulled her close. "I'm glad she's here, too, men. Now, let's all get some sleep, and I'll see you in the morning."

The men nodded and moved away, but Josh held her fast to his side. As the last man vanished into the night, Josh turned back toward the mine. "I wanta show you something before we head back."

Bethanie lifted the lantern.

"We won't need that, we're only going a few feet." Josh took the lantern from her hand and pulled her into the entrance. "I need to do something before we get back to the house, where you seem surrounded with protectors."

He pulled her into his arms. "Do I need protection?" she asked.

"Most assuredly," Josh answered as he jerked her hair free from the scarf. "I plan on finishing that kiss I started in the nursery."

Bethanie made no protest. She leaned against the cold wall of the mine. Josh's lips searched across her face to find her waiting mouth. His kiss grew deep as his fingers moved through her hair.

Finally he pulled away and whispered, "I swore I'd stop with a kiss, Bethanie. God, I burn with a fever for you, and the moment I seek to quench it, I find myself on fire."

Bethanie couldn't have put her thoughts into words. She'd longed for his touch all her life, and to have pushed him away would have been impossible. She moved her fingers slowly across his bare shoulder and into his thick hair. "I want you," she whispered honestly.

"No!" Josh muttered as she drew his mouth down to her lips. "No, Bethanie, we must stop." Though his words were negative, his entire body spoke of his need for her.

She could hear him saying her name as he brushed her lips, with his kiss. His hands followed her movements as she pulled her coat open in the blackness. She drew his mouth closer with one hand as she guided his fingers across her breasts. His touch circled over her mounds, setting fire to her even through her clothes. She let her fingers glide over his chest. His kiss deepened until the world began to spin around her. All the nights he'd been without her seemed to cry out in the darkness as he molded her to him, demanding and begging at the same time.

Josh pushed her against the cold wall of the mine as his body molded to her soft form. His breathing was rapid as he spread himself over her, pulling her hands out to the sides so he could feel every inch of her against him. She could feel the damp wall at her back and his warm lean body before her. He slid one leg between her thighs as his mouth took her lips savagely. She made no protest, but openly accepted his demanding body. Buttons flew in the darkness as he pulled her blouse open and pushed her camisole from her shoulders. His hand moved slowly down her neck and between her breasts. Bethanie cried out in joy as his rough hand pushed the cotton away from her waiting nipples. His mouth moved like liquid fire down her throat to her breasts. He pulled at her clothes recklessly, trying to feel more of her against his bare chest.

"Josh," she whispered. "Josh, my love."

Josh's voice was slow with passion. "Do you want me, Bethanie? Does your body cry for me the way my soul has cried for you every night for three years?"

"Please, Josh, please love me."

Josh's fingers moved along her flesh. "Love you . . . or satisfy you?" His mouth came down hard against her lips. Bethanie pushed away, but his kiss demanded response. He was being cruel, and she knew he was punishing himself more than her. She stopped struggling and accepted his harsh loving even as he bruised her flesh and lips.

Suddenly Josh pulled away. "Stop me, Bethanie. Don't let me hurt you." There was pain in his words.

Bethanie reached and cupped his face with her hands. "I can't; I never could."

Josh's lips returned to her mouth with great tenderness. "I'm sorry," he whispered into her hair. His fingers slowly moved over her body erasing any pain he might have caused. She welcomed this gentle loving as she had welcomed the other loving, with all her heart.

Josh gently pushed her from him. His voice became raspy with passion. "We must stop. I'll not take you on the floor of this mine. I'll not."

Bethanie stood back confused. Had she been too forward? She knew even now as he moved away that if she touched him, he would come to her again. He hadn't spoken of love. Why was it she could always manage to do what was right and proper, except where Josh was concerned? With him there had never been caution. There was never a slow time or indecision. He was as much a part of her as her own limbs. To deny him would have been to disown herself. Yet, he'd told her to bolt him out, and now he pulled away.

An hour later, Bethanie fell exhausted into her bed. Josh hadn't spoken on the ride back and had left her at the door while he took care of the horses. She'd not been ashamed to love him years ago, and she wasn't ashamed now. Josh must have told her to bolt the door because he questioned the feelings he had for her. He didn't even want the housekeeper or Cain to know that he loved her. Or was it only lust? Had it always been only physical on his part? For the first time since she married Ben, Bethanie felt dirty. Dirty like she felt when people had yelled names at her and her mother.

She tried to sleep, but his words kept echoing in her mind. She could hear Josh pacing in the next room. The rest of the house was quiet with sleep, but still he paced. A slow rain pattered on her window, and still Josh paced. Finally the dull rhythm lulled her to sleep.

The fire in her bedroom had died down low when Bethanie's dream returned. She was running, running from the shouts. Fighting her way through the darkness. She heard her mother scream. Then she was falling into the darkness.

Josh's voice pulled her back from the nightmare. "Bethanie, Bethanie," he whispered. "Are you all right?"

Bethanie opened her eyes to see him standing above her. His hair was tossed and he wore only pants. There was no sign that he'd been asleep. He leaned closer, wiping the cold sweat from her forehead.

"I had a nightmare," Bethanie answered. Then, unable to hide her honesty, she shook her head. "I've always been afraid to be alone at night."

Josh pulled her to him with a low moan. "You're not alone, darling. I'm right here."

"But . . . you don't want me." Bethanie fought the tears. "You told me to bolt my door."

Josh laughed as he turned her face toward an open space between her room and his. "I knew I could use a secret panel if you needed me. I put one in the wall between the rooms when I moved in, just like the sliding wall at the hotel in San Antonio. I guess I was hoping someday you would just appear again. I was planning to tell you about it when Rachel interrupted us earlier." He pulled away, but his hands still rested on her shoulders. "I was determined not to come to your room tonight, but when I heard you crying in your sleep, I couldn't stay away."

Bethanie brushed his dark hair from his forehead. Her gentle action brought pain to his deep mahogany eyes. "Why, Josh? Why do you push me away? Why were you so cruel in the mine?"

Josh stood and turned his back to her. She could see his hard muscles, golden in the firelight. His words were low and deep with pain. "Because I can't even look at you without wanting you. I'm afraid if you knew how much I need you, it would frighten you away forever. I don't think I could live if I lost you again.

"Then you do want me?" Bethanie asked as she climbed from the bed and stood beside him.

"No, I don't *want* you, Bethanie. It went far beyond that the moment I touched you at the spring. I need you, as a dying man needs absolution." He turned and his eyes were filled with longing. "I *need* you not for just the nights, but for the mornings as well. Without you I'm hollow, incomplete."

"Why didn't you come to me?" Bethanie moved her hand to his hard chest and brushed his flesh with her fingers. She loved the way his muscles tightened to her touch. She caressed his shoulders, then drew slow lazy circles to his waist. Smiling in the moonlight, she repeated the action and heard his breathing grow ragged.

Josh's voice was a low agony when he finally spoke. "I swore to myself I would give you time. I didn't want to hurry you into anything."

Bethanie brushed her fingers lightly along the band of his pants and saw the fire in his eyes begin to smolder. She touched her lips to his ear as she whispered, "From that rainy night in the cave, a part of me has always belonged to you. There is no right or wrong, no fast or slow between us. We belong to each other as truly as the moon and stars belong to the sky."

Josh's hands moved around her waist and pulled her to him. "God. I love you beyond a state of madness, Bethanie. You feel so perfect in my arms."

As his lips found hers, Bethanie felt the passion of his need. She pressed close to him and began to sink into the ocean of fire that surged within her. His hands possessed her with each searing touch as his kiss branded ownership over her. He pulled her gown open in haste. His lips moved down her throat to the valley between her breasts. Bethanie felt weak from his touch . . . his power over her.

Then his actions slowed, as if he wanted to savor each touch, each kiss. He lifted her in his arms and moved across the room to where the open panel stood. Kissing her ear, he whispered, "I want to make love to you in my bed, where I've dreamed of you so many nights."

"You're not angry any longer?"

"I was never angry. I only feared that you didn't want me as completely as I want you."

He undressed her slowly, driving her mad with his gentleness. When she lay nude across his huge four-poster bed, he leaned above her, studying her in the firelight. Tenderly, his hands explored her body, brushing each inch of her skin until she thought she would die from the pleasure. Eventually, his trail ended at her breasts. His thumbs covered each rosy peak, gently circling. His mouth teased her lips with light kisses until she cried out for more.

"Bethanie." His voice was low with passion. "Bethanie, say you love me." His hands slid down her stomach and across to her hips. He turned her toward him, and she felt the length of his body beside her. "Do you love me?"

Bethanie answered without words, by moving into his embrace. Both his hands rested on her hips as he drew her even closer to him.

Her arms encircled his neck as he asked, "Tell me you need me. Tell me, my silent Bethanie, that you want me. That you've never stopped wanting me. Tell me that I've haunted you as your touch has haunted me."

Bethanie could not speak. What he said was true; he had always been a part of her. She did need him and want him. He was the passion of her soul. Closing her mind to the fact had not made the need for him go away. Like a mother loving two sons, she had loved both Ben and Josh, but in different ways. Be it right or wrong, she loved them both. Her love couldn't be measured like a commodity to be divided. She loved them each with all the love she had, with a total love for both.

"I love you, Josh. I've loved you from time beginning, and I'll go on loving you as long as my spirit lives." She kissed his eyes. "I could no more bolt you out than I could lock out myself."

He made love to her then, with a sweet union of bodies and minds. All the pain and loneliness he'd known was burned in their fire for each other. In the quietness of their loving, he thought he must be dreaming, but with each new peak, he knew no fantasy could be so wonderful as Bethanie in his arms. As she had years ago in the cave, she said not a word to him as the night aged, but let her body speak the volumes of her love.

When light drifted into his room, Josh woke her with loving kisses. "Bethanie," he whispered. "I've one more question. Will you marry me?"

Bethanie opened her eyes and smiled. "I'll think it over," she said as she stretched beside him.

He laughed and popped her on the backside. "I'm not letting you out of my sight until we're married, so you might as well say yes or you'll be kept a prisoner here forever."

Bethanie moved beside him again and watched fire touch his eyes. "Does the guard serve meals?"

"I serve all your needs, madam," Josh laughed as he pulled the covers over them, blocking out the sun and the world for another hour.

Three weeks later they were married by the circuit minister, with Rachel and Cain acting as witnesses. As the days passed a joy filled Bethanie's already overflowing heart when she realized she had once again married while already with child.

Part II
Texas, 1886

Chapter Twenty

Dusty Barfield pulled his collar an inch higher and turned his bearded face away from the freezing wind. He'd been riding the border of the Weston Ranch for twelve hours, and encroaching night was forcing him toward home. He knew Ruth would leave a meal and probably a washtub for him by the warm hearth as she had on cold nights for almost twenty years. Dusty nudged his mount faster as he raced the darkness. He was looking forward to a warm fire. If he finished the bookwork in time, he might even get a few hours reading in before sleep demanded its due.

A shadow moved along the horizon, halting Dusty's progress and wrenching an oath from his lips. He swung from the saddle and knelt beside the carcass of one of the prize heifers he'd bought last spring to improve his herd. The cow's throat was slashed, just like all the others he'd seen this week. Frozen blood covered her legs, telling of a slow death for the cow. She could have staggered a mile from where she'd been cut, and it was already too dark to follow the trail. The butcher would be long gone, having soundlessly knifed into the Weston Ranch.

Dusty stood and swore once more in frustration. He could fight any enemy in the open, but this senseless slaughter of his cattle was slowly unnerving him.

A sudden movement in the brush snapped Dusty

around. His hand pulled the Colt from his leg in a fluid action. His body went rigid with all attention following the barrel of his gun. A calf, not more than two days old, struggled past the bushes and waggled toward the corpse of its mother.

Dusty laughed in relief as he replaced his gun. "Well, looks like our knife killer missed one of my herd." He lifted the newborn across his saddle and tied its legs underneath the horse. "I'll give you a ride back to the ranch, and we'll find a milk-cow that doesn't mind having an extra for dinner."

It was well after dark by the time Dusty found the calf a willing substitute mom and made it back to the ranch house. He knew Ruth would be asleep in her room, so he stripped down and washed in front of the fire in the main room.

"The old house seems filled with ghosts tonight," Dusty said to himself. "Guess that's why I built my cabin. It just never seems right to sleep here with all the memories." He laughed as he realized he'd said his thoughts aloud. "I've spent so much time alone, I'm starting to talk to myself. And answer."

Dusty shook his damp hair and moved with determination toward the records. He nibbled at his supper and worked over the books. Long after midnight, with only a blanket pulled around him for warmth, he stretched his long body out on the couch and fell into exhausted sleep.

The train pulled into Fort Worth for a few hours' layover as dusk spread over the flat land like thin golden paint. Mariah Weston straightened her back, refusing to surrender to the fatigue that flooded her body. She was two months past twenty and woman enough to carry herself like a lady even in these dire surroundings. She was no wide-eyed child on a first outing. She had ridden horseback, with her parents and four brothers, to San Francisco and spent a year traveling Europe in style. Her grace spoke of finishing-school training, but the strong set of her jaw could only have been Weston-bred.

She was not wild like her middle two brothers, or serious and bookish like the other two, but Mariah had her dream, and she aimed to see it come true. She'd always been pampered, as the only girl among four brothers. She was short by Weston standards, with velvet-black hair and dark brown eyes that could make almost any male heart beat faster. As she had grown to womanhood, she'd found herself constantly courted thanks to both the scarcity of women in Colorado and the common knowledge that the Weston mines were worth millions. She'd begun construction on a wall around her heart on her sixteenth birthday when an anxious suitor had declared his love and in the same breath asked what percentage of the mines she would someday inherit.

Mariah knew she would never be happy unless she was more than a prize some man won. She had the strong blood of pioneers flowing in her veins. She planned on blazing a trail few women had tried. If her aim was true, she would reach her goal in a little over two years and be Dr. Mariah Weston. Boston University Medical School had already accepted her as one of seven women to start the fall classes. Now, only one problem remained to be solved, and it waited at the end of this train ride. Her half of the Weston Ranch must be sold.

"Miss Weston?" A young man only a few years older than herself interrupted Mariah's thoughts. Dressed in an Eastern-style suit, he swayed in the narrow aisle beside her seat. "You are Miss Mariah Weston?"

"Yes," Mariah answered. Though she smiled up at the man, she didn't miss Cain's watchful eyes open slightly as he faked sleep in the window seat opposite her. She could tell from the twist of the old man's lip that he had sized up the intruder and found him wanting, as well as harmless.

The stranger removed his round derby hat to unleash a bushel of curly brown hair. "I'm Elliot Mayson, son of Wes Mayson." When Mariah gave no sign of caring, he continued. "My father has a ranch south of the place where you were born. My mother died when I was born, but my father says he's known your mother and father since before you were born." He looked as if he were waiting for her to acknowledge his statement.

The train jolted slightly, swaying Elliot closer to her. He smelled of damp wool and dust. And, Mariah thought to herself, insincerity.

Mariah smiled sweetly as she twisted a strand of her coal black hair. She decided she would play along. She had been successfully fending off admirers since she was fifteen. She could have this dude for breakfast, and even Cain knew it, or he would've been at her guard like a hungry watchdog. But she knew nothing of the Weston Ranch, and this young man might be just the one to enlighten her on a few points.

"Please," Mariah spoke, her voice as soft as a spring breeze even on this cold train. "Won't you sit down, Mr. Mayson. I'm sorry I don't remember your family, but you see, I left the ranch when I was two years old."

Elliot's head bobbled happily as he took the seat next to Cain. He frowned as the old man grunted, and reluctantly moved over. "Is he with you?" Elliot whispered as he balanced his hat on his knees and looked as though he were waiting for a camera to snap.

"Yes," Mariah smiled. "Cain's relaxed appearance is deceiving. I wouldn't wake him if I were you."

Elliot took the warning to heart and moved as far away as he could from Cain. "My father sent me a wire, as I started home from college, telling me you'd be on this train and asking me to offer you my gentlemanly protection. I've heard him talk of the Weston Ranch and your father, Ben Weston, all my life."

Mariah had to smile. The day she would need this greenhorn's protection would be the day her four brothers disowned her. She might be petite, but Lord help the man who crossed her fiery temper or her right fist.

Elliot seemed to take her smile as approval and relaxed a little. He crossed his legs in a manner that, while not feminine, destroyed any hint of masculinity in his long frame.

In the three-hour train trip that followed, he told Mariah as much as he knew about the Weston Ranch, and most of it was bad. Elliot described the man who ran the Weston land as being hard to reason with. Though Elliot admitted Dusty Barfield's men were fiercely loyal, he said that Dusty would never work with Elliot's father on any business deal, even when it promised to be highly profitable.

Mariah frowned when Elliot said he believed the Weston Ranch was in deep financial trouble. Though he admitted the past winter had been the worst since Austin settled Texas land, Elliot seemed to think all the blame lay on the ranch's foreman and half-owner. He told Mariah of how Dusty wouldn't sell his cattle to Elliot's father and thousands of beef had frozen on the open range.

Mariah knew there was another side to Elliot's tale. She had learned long ago that people who need to build themselves up by tearing away at others usually don't stand very tall.

A few hours before dawn, the train pulled into the deserted station. The town was dark and unwelcoming. Mariah could make out a line of stores and a church. A yellowed campaign poster promoting John Ireland, "Ox-cart John," for governor waved in the wind as the whistle blew and the train moved on. Cain disappeared into the shadows to find a carriage, and Mariah wished suddenly she had sent a message of her arrival.

Elliot Mayson continued talking as if he had nowhere to go. Finally, when he saw Cain returning, he bowed his good-byes and suggested he talk with his father about Mariah's problem. "Perhaps," he volunteered as he helped her into the carriage while Cain loaded trunks, "I might persuade my father to buy your half before the ranch goes completely under."

Mariah nodded, only half listening. She had traveled this far hoping to sell her part to Dusty for whatever he considered a fair price. Though she only vaguely remembered Dusty, she needed money . . . her own money . . . fast. If the ranch was in as much trouble as Elliot said, maybe his father would be her only way out.

Cain rocked the rented buggy as he climbed in and took the reins. "That boy reminds me of one of them pastry things you gave me once in France. Real pretty on the outside, but full of sugar-sweet mush inside."

"Elliot the Eclair," Mariah laughed. She put her hand through Cain's arm and leaned against him in a trusting gesture. "Tell me, Cain." Her voice reflected the open honesty they had long shared. "Do you think what he said about the ranch is true?"

Cain was silent for a long moment. "I wouldn't put too much faith in his words. Your dad died before I came to the ranch, but I figure if your mother married him, he must've been quite a man. I don't think he'd have left this Dusty half a ranch if the boy was dim-witted."

"That's true." Mariah nodded to herself in the darkness. "But Mother speaks of Dusty as a boy. He must be thirty or more by now."

Cain drove the rented team with only the guide of moonlight. "Wait to make a judgment, child. As far as that Mayson boy goes, I wouldn't listen too long to the

music of a magpie. Why don't you try to get some sleep.
It'll be dawn before we get to the ranch."

"If you're too tired, we could stop for a while." Mariah
scolded herself for forgetting Cain's age. He was too old
to be traveling around the country, but her Uncle Josh
never allowed her to travel without the huge, silent man.
He was her constant guardian and often her only confi-
dant.

"I slept on the train," Cain answered as he tucked a
blanket over her shoulders.

"Sure," Mariah yawned as she closed her eyes. Cain
probably hadn't missed a word Elliot Mayson had said.
She laughed suddenly to herself, thinking how her future husband would react when Cain went along on
their honeymoon. When she had gone away to school,
Cain would see her to the door, then be waiting when
she got out for vacation. He had made the trip from
Denver to Boston twice for her every year of school.
The old man loved her brothers, but she had the feeling
he would die for her without hesitation, or kill anyone
he thought might harm her

Chapter Twenty-one

A golden dawn was breaking over the cliffs behind the ranch house as Cain stopped the buggy. "We're on Weston ranch land," he said emotionlessly as he touched Mariah's shoulder.

She rubbed her eyes and looked at the wide adobe house nestled among a grove of trees at the foot of a cliff. A faraway memory drifted into her mind as she studied each building, each path, each tree. Mariah shook her head; she had been too young to remember much. She couldn't tell if her memory now was real or only a shadow of her mother's description of the ranch. She could see the root cellar where they'd hidden the day her father had been killed. To the left were the barns and bunkhouse just like her mother had described. Out front stood two huge elms where her father had been tied and murdered by the Indians almost eighteen years ago.

"Looks like they've added a wing off to the left of the main house since I was here." Cain spoke as if it had been only a few months and not years since he had seen the ranch. "I don't remember that porch swing, either."

"Let's go." Mariah swallowed the lump in her throat. She was suddenly anxious to get this over and leave. She couldn't tell if it was because her memories here were bad memories or if she was afraid to grow too fond of a place she must sell in order to reach her goal in life. As they neared the house, Mariah set her mind on her future dreams.

Cain let her out at the porch and said he would take care of the team. Mariah slowly walked the steps and opened the door without knocking. This was half her house after all, and she planned to look around a little before anyone was awake. The element of surprise would aid her in more clearly picturing the problems.

As Mariah walked into a huge room, her eyes blinked to adjust to the shadows. She could see a study area with books and papers piled everywhere. A dining room was off to the right, with a dirty place setting abandoned beside a small mountain of papers. As she moved into the center of the room, she saw a wicker wheelchair pushed close to the fire. Clothes lay across the chair, and a watch was piled on top of the clothing. Curiosity drew her to the chair.

Mariah reached to touch the high cane back when something on the couch moved. She jumped in surprise as a man rolled over in his sleep. He was nude from the waist up, and a sandy brown beard framed his features.

Mariah moved closer. His hair half covered his sleeping eyes, but she could tell he was young, though several years past a boy. His chest was scarred in two places that she could see, but the marks only seemed to add character to his perfection. His shoulders were broad, but his waist and hips promised to be narrow beneath the Indian blanket across him.

The morning sun touched his body as if spotlighting him. She had been around men all her life, but this sleeping, darkly tanned man drew her close appraisal. Her gaze traveled slowly down his chest to where the blanket pulled across just past his navel. Mischievously, she wondered if the rest of him were as tan as his top half. Smiling, she thought of how shocked her mother would be at her outrageous question.

A low male voice shook her to the core. "If you're planning on robbing me, all I have on is the blanket. If this is a social call, it's a bit early."

Mariah's gaze quickly traveled back to the man's face, and she looked into the deepest golden eyes she'd ever seen. She stumbled backward over the wheelchair and almost fell. Her hand caught the watch an inch before it hit the floor. He made no attempt to stand and help her, for which she was grateful. Her curiosity to see the rest of his tan was not as strong as she might have thought. She pulled herself up to her full five feet. "Do you live here?" she asked, trying to sound formal.

"No." The stranger's words came low and slow, almost like a gentle touch. "I only fell asleep while working late on the books last night." His eyes were watching her with an intensity that made her uneasy.

"How about you?" He winked. "You live around here . . . or just fall out of heaven a moment ago?" he asked as he sat up and ran long fingers through his brown hair.

Mariah's bottom lip protruded slightly as it always did when she realized a man was making fun of her. Who did this bookkeeper think he was, sleeping nude in the main room and then questioning her, the owner?

"I'm Mariah Weston, and this ranch is half mine." She handed him the watch as she talked, and wondered what the initials "S.J.B." stood for. "I came to see a man named Dustin Barfield, who lives here."

The man seemed to be in no hurry to call his boss. "You know Mr. Barfield, do you? Plan on helping him run this ranch?"

Mariah straightened the wrinkled pleats of her skirt. "Yes, I know him, not that it's any of your business, but I plan on seeing him about selling the ranch."

The stranger leaned his head back and closed his eyes as if needing time to digest her words. She studied him, realizing her decision could mean his job. Then Mariah suddenly realized the chair must belong to him. Of course, that would explain why he slept here and why he'd made no move to stand.

When he said nothing, Mariah sat on the hearth opposite him and tried to think of something to say. "I'm . . . sorry I fell over your chair," she mumbled, hating herself for being so dim-witted. "Can I do something for you?" She hoped he didn't suggest she help him into the chair, for he looked almost double her weight.

He opened one eye and stared at her. She felt sorry all over again that he was crippled. He looked so strong as he leaned forward and rested his forehead on his palms. His words seemed spoken more to himself than her. "You can tell me why after being here five minutes you want to sell this place?" he asked.

Mariah's anger touched her words. "I don't see that it is any of your concern." When he didn't fire back or argue, Mariah felt strangely guilty that she had snapped at him. He probably hadn't been around many women out here and wasn't trying to be unkind.

The man stretched, pulling his shoulders back into a mass of tight muscles. Mariah lowered her eyes but continued to watch him through her eyelashes. He was the most handsome man she'd ever seen. She liked his voice, even now with the hint of anger in it. "Look, Mariah Weston, I'm not worth much after two hours' sleep and no coffee. Why don't I make us a pot and we'll talk?"

"No!" Mariah almost yelled. She was thankful to hear Cain coming up the steps. "I'll make the coffee." She turned to see Cain blocking the door as he squinted, trying to see in the dim light. "Cain, will you help this man get dressed while I make the coffee?"

Both men said "What?" at the same instant, but Mariah was already halfway across the room. She guessed the kitchen would be on the other side of the dining room. She certainly wasn't going to stay around explaining to Cain that this nude man was crippled. She could just guess what questions the older man might ask.

As she opened the kitchen door, she saw an aging woman by the stove. A pot of coffee was boiling on the fire. The warm smell filled the room with welcome as the old woman turned and smiled. "You don't remember me, child, but I brought you into this world."

Mariah moved closer. "Are you Ruth?"

The old woman nodded. "That I am."

Mariah laughed as if a storybook character she'd heard about all her childhood had suddenly come to life. She crossed the room and put her arm around Ruth in an affectionate hug. "I've heard Mother talk about you all my life."

Ruth placed her aging hands on Mariah's shoulders and pushed her to arm's length. "Let me look at you, child." A smile rippled from her lips across gray-white cheeks. "My, my, you've made a fine woman. You have your mother's nose, I think, and the Weston hair and eyes. I knew you were a keeper the minute I cleaned you up."

Mariah laughed, feeling suddenly very much at home with this woman. "You should see my brothers. Mother had one son a year the first four years she was married to Uncle Josh. She named them after the first four books of the New Testament: Matthew, Mark, Luke, and John. They all look just like Josh, except the youngest. He has Mom's red hair. The others tease John that Mom stopped for fear she might have another carrottop and have to name him Acts."

Ruth pulled cups down from the cupboard. "I'd like to see your mom. She was quite a lady, even when she was no more than your age. The day she walked into this place I knew both the Weston boys loved her."

Mariah looked surprised. "You mean Uncle Josh loved her even before she married Dad?"

Ruth nodded. "They both loved her. But for reasons long buried, she married Ben. They were very happy when you came along. I thought this house would explode with joy. Is Bethanie happy now?"

"Yes," Mariah answered without hesitation. Josh and her mother were loving parents. She'd grown up seeing the special way they looked at each other, even when they disagreed. She'd often thought she would give anything to have that kind of love with one man, and apparently her mother had found it with two.

"We'll visit more later," Ruth said as she handed Mariah the serving tray. "If you'll take the men coffee, I'll air your mother's old room and draw a bath for you. I know you must be bone-tired. The bedrooms in the new wing have all been empty since Mike and Allison moved to their ranch, but I think you'll feel more at home in Bethanie's room."

"Thank you." Mariah nodded, remembering something her mother had once said about Ruth. The woman knew everything going on in the house and usually outguessed everyone's needs. As she took the tray of coffee, she had no doubt Ruth retained her talent.

Mariah moved through the door hearing the unfamiliar sound of Cain's laughter. She looked up to see him standing beside a tall man dressed in tight denims and a white shirt open down the front. Golden eyes turned to watch her as she moved into the room.

"I thought . . ." Mariah tried to stop stumbling over her tongue as the now wide-awake cowboy moved on sure feet toward her. "I thought . . ."

"Cain and I just figured out what you thought." He took the tray from her and set it on the dining table.

"When I said the chair was mine, I was incorrect. It is half mine . . . as is everything in this house."

Mariah decided to work on one new fact at a time. "Then, why a wheelchair?"

Dusty poured a cup and handed it to Cain. "The chair was your father's. Don't you remember?"

"No." Mariah looked at Cain. "My father wasn't in a wheelchair. If he had been, someone would have mentioned it, or I would have remembered."

"Your father was a strong man. I guess the fact he was in a chair never seemed important to anyone," Dusty replied.

Cain nodded. "I was hired just after he was killed. I remember a slanted side on the porch for a chair to go down."

"All right." Mariah pushed the offered cup of coffee away. The realization of how little she knew of her mother and their life on the Weston Ranch hit her like a blow. "Then if the chair is half yours, you must be Dustin Barfield."

"Guilty as charged." Dusty lifted his cup and drained half the hot liquid. "It's really amazing what powers of reasoning a finishing school can teach even a bit of a girl."

Mariah's temper flared. "I'm not a bit of a girl. I'm a woman, and I'll thank you to stop treating me as if I were a child. I've been on my own, doing what I please for some time now."

Dusty's words were cold and low. "I'll tell you one thing you're not going to do, Mariah Weston. You're not going to sell this ranch."

"I damn well will if I please. I happen to know that a Mr. Mayson is already interested in making an offer."

"Over my dead body," Dusty hissed.

"I doubt that will be one of the terms." She moved

toward the far hallway where she had seen Ruth disappear.

Dusty slammed his cup hard against the table. "You're not Mariah Weston. You haven't got an ounce of Bethanie's softness or a hair of Ben's brains. I should have you arrested as an imposter."

Mariah whirled to face him, her hands clenched in rage. "No, I'm not my parents. I'm me, my own person. I'm going to sell this ranch, take the money, and do what is important to me. This ranch may have been their love and home, but it's not mine. I have my own dreams, and I'm going to see them through. No cowpunching clod who's never been off the ranch is going to tell me what I can and can't do." She took a quick gulp of air and smiled at Dusty's shocked face. "Now, if you will excuse me, I am going to take a bath and go to bed. You may not sleep here, but I do."

As she moved down the hallway, she heard Cain say, "She's a firecat, son. You best stay out of her path."

Mariah stepped into the room Ruth was cleaning and heard the sound of Dusty laughing. Anger poured through her veins like hot wax. She was tempted to go back and give both Cain and Dustin Barfield a piece of her mind. She was not some schoolgirl to be manipulated at will. She had her dreams too, and she would not give in without a fight. The memory of Dusty's golden brown eyes, alive with rage, flashed in her mind. She could see he wouldn't be handled lightly either. Well, if it was to be a fight, then fight she would.

Chapter Twenty-two

Shadows crept in long strides across her room when Mariah awoke. She sat up and stretched, loving the feel of having finally slept in a bed after days of travel. She pulled her long ebony curls on top of her head and breathed deep of the wonderful smell of bacon frying somewhere in the house.

A light tap sounded at her door. Mariah turned lazily expecting to welcome Ruth. To her surprise, she watched the door swing open to reveal Dusty's frame leaning against the doorfacing. He was dressed in black pants and a spotlessly white shirt. His dark vest seemed to emphasize his slim waist and broad shoulders. He slowly rolled up one of his shirtsleeves in an absentminded gesture. The white, starched shirt contrasted dramatically with his tanned, muscular arm.

"Evening, Miss Weston," he smiled as if he had forgotten their bitter words. "It's almost dark, but I thought you'd probably like a little breakfast." She watched as his golden eyes dropped to her bare shoulders. His gaze warmed her flesh as his vision moved lower to the tight-fitting silk of her camisole.

Mariah jerked her arms down releasing her curls to tumble around her shoulders. She pulled a colorful quilt over her half-exposed breasts, wishing she had taken the time to unpack a modest cotton nightgown. Anger warmed her cheeks even more. "Sir, I'm not dressed," she said, knowing he was fully aware of the fact. "I'd thank you to close my door."

Dusty shrugged. "Fair's fair. I wasn't dressed this morning and that didn't seem to stop you from confronting me. Anyway, I happen to be standing on my half of the hall." His smile was smug and his eyes full of challenge.

Mariah jerked the quilt around her and rolled off the far side of the bed onto her bare feet. She stormed toward him in an angry huff.

Dusty stepped back in mock fear. "Don't go on the warpath. I just thought you'd like some breakfast before dark."

"I will," Mariah answered as she slammed the door. "When I get dressed."

As the sound of the door echoed through the house, Mariah heard Dusty's laughter from the hall. "Ten minutes, Miss Spoiled Brat, ten minutes."

Mariah dropped her quilt and moved over to her trunk. She rapidly dug to the bottom and found her riding skirt and blouse. She was not going to bother dressing for dinner with this cowboy. If she'd brought a pair of pants, she would have worn them. She pulled her hair back and quickly braided it into a long thick plait.

Wrapping a red sash around her small waist, Mariah stood before an oval mirror. She studied her reflection for a minute. Her waist was tiny and her breasts a bit too full, she thought. She had been told all her life that she was beautiful. Most of the men she knew treated her like some dainty ornament. Maybe that's why it was so important for her to make something of her life. She wanted to be more than a doll. She wanted men to see her as a person. More than anything, she wanted what every man already had; she wanted to be in control of her own destiny. The medical school at Boston University would be her start.

Mariah smiled to herself and nodded at her reflection. Here on the Weston Ranch, she was taking the first step to her goal. She would sell the ranch and pay for more schooling. By the time she ran out of money, she would be one of a handful of women physicians in this country.

Satisfied with her hurried grooming, she moved gracefully down the hall, surprised that Dusty wasn't standing outside her door waiting. She followed the delicious smell of bread baking to the dining room. The table was set with beautiful china and linens, but no one was about.

As she reached to brush the centerpiece of bluebonnets, the sun seemed to add a golden glow to the entire room. This country was so isolated and uncivilized, yet nature seemed to try so hard to shine.

Dusty stepped through the kitchen door with his arms loaded down with plates. "I cooked you bacon and eggs with gravy and biscuits."

"You cooked?" Mariah questioned.

"Nothin' fancy like you must have had in Europe or back East. But I work here late at night, and I had to learn to cook or starve. Ruth likes to go to bed and get up with the sun." Dusty set the plates of food on the table.

"How did you know about my travels?" Mariah asked as she studied him.

"Letters from your mom mostly, and I had a long talk with Cain before he turned in." Dusty winked at her in a disarming gesture that warmed her to the core. "You seem to be his favorite topic of conversation."

"Cain is suddenly becoming as gabby as an old woman," Mariah muttered.

To her surprise, Dusty moved behind a chair and pulled it out for her. She was glad to know he wasn't totally void of manners here at his ranch in the middle of this half-wild state.

Taking her place, she felt Dusty's shoulder touch hers as he leaned close behind her. His words were so low in her ear she wasn't sure he was aware he spoke them. "It's nice to have you home, Mariah."

Mariah turned her head toward him, and her cheek brushed the side of his beard. She wanted to say this was not her home, but didn't have the heart to start an argument again so soon. "You might have more women to dinner, Mr. Barfield, if you'd consider shaving."

Dusty straightened and rubbed his furry jawline with his thumb. "You think so?" His words sounded serious, but his eyes twinkled golden with mischief. A maverick eyebrow shot up, giving him the look of a pirate. "I've had this for so many years I might not recognize myself clean-shaven. But who knows?" He tugged at her braid lightly. "There are bound to be a few changes around this place."

He slid into the chair across from her and began handing her dishes. Within a few minutes, Mariah found her plate filled with a huge breakfast. She ate like a hungry field hand instead of a small woman who had spent the day asleep.

After several bites, Mariah looked up to see Dusty sipping his coffee and watching her with an easy smile brushing his full lips. She wished suddenly that she'd met him somewhere else and he'd not been the one her father had made half owner of this ranch. She would've liked getting to know him and playing the flirting game she always played with men. She smiled back, and then continued eating.

When Dusty finally spoke, his words sounded rehearsed. "It's dark, but I thought you might like to ride up to the ridge and watch the stars come out. That is, if you still love to ride?"

Mariah poured herself another cup of coffee. "That would be wonderful. I could use the exercise." While she sipped her coffee, Dusty played with a biscuit on his plate but made no effort to take even one bite. He was watching her every move. Mariah tried to figure out if he was quiet or shy. He was so unlike all the men she'd met before. No one must have schooled him in the art of keeping lively conversation going. She found his silent attention both flattering and relaxing.

Finally he stood, "I'll go saddle a few horses while you finish . . . unless you would prefer to ride with me like you used to do?"

Mariah smiled. "I think I'm old enough for a horse of my own. You might be surprised. I might just ride better than you."

Dusty walked toward the door. "That'll be the day, when a schoolgirl outrides me." There was a hint of challenge in his voice.

"I'm not a schoolgirl," Mariah shouted after him, but there was no anger in her tone.

"So I noticed." Dusty glanced at her as he grabbed his hat and coat off the rack by the door. His eyes dropped briefly to her blouse before returning to her face. A lazy smile spread over his handsome features. She knew he was thinking of the way she had looked earlier, with only her camisole to cover her.

He was gone before she could answer. Mariah leaned back in her chair and smiled. She had first thought this Dusty might be a problem, but maybe there was a way around him, and it wasn't with arguments. She rose slowly and went to fetch her coat. Yes, she thought, she would handle him as she'd handled men all her life. She'd never encountered a man who wouldn't give in after one of her smiles. Even Uncle Josh would have allowed her to go back to school and work for her goal if her mother hadn't insisted against it. Mariah knew her mother wanted to protect her from the pain of being an outcast as the only woman enrolled in medical school. But Mariah had a mind of her own, and she planned to reach her goal without any outside help.

Mariah stepped out onto the porch as Dusty brought up the horses. The evening glowed in shadowy blues as a full moon hung like a huge milk glass dish in the cloudless sky. She moved silently behind Dusty as he tightened the girth on a chestnut mare. She hesitated a moment before reaching to rest her hand on his arm. He'd been so nice this evening, she hated to manipulate him. But a woman had to use what weapons she had to fight to be equal. "Thanks for suggesting a ride," Mariah whispered as he turned toward her. His face was hidden in shadows, but she felt the muscles in his forearm tighten beneath her fingers.

She slid her hand up his shirt to his shoulder feeling his flesh tighten to her light touch. "Help me up?" She moved closer, fully aware how her nearness was affecting his breathing. She smiled to herself. This was going to be easier than she thought.

Dusty's hands went around her waist slowly. He pulled her closer, then lifted her effortlessly into the saddle. She looked down at him, his hands remaining around her waist. Then, as if not wanting her to read his thoughts, Dusty turned away and said roughly, "Let's ride."

Before he could reach his horse, Mariah kicked her mount into action. She rode across the open land, laughing as Dusty yelled for her to wait. It was several minutes before he caught up with her. "Slow down, Mariah," he yelled. "When I said a ride, I didn't mean a race."

Mariah pulled her horse up and slowed to a walk. "I'm sorry if it's too much for you. I should have remembered your age."

"My age?" Dusty laughed. "All right, kid, I'll race you to the elms at the edge of the ridge."

Before the last word was out of his mouth, Mariah was already two lengths ahead of him. She shoved her hat off her head and laughed as the wind whistled by her face. They rode hard as the moonlight danced across the land. Dusty passed her less than a hundred feet from the trees. He jumped from his horse and turned to greet her, his arms folded as if waiting.

Mariah reined her mount beside him, laughing with the pure joy of riding. He reached for her without hesitation and pulled her to stand beside him. "Glad you finally got here, kid," he said, out of breath.

Mariah put her arms around his neck in a loose hold. "I'll guess I'll have to pay up. What is the usual bet here in Texas?"

Dusty's sudden loss of breath had nothing to do with his vigorous ride. He moved away slightly and straightened into a tense stance. "I never make bets with kids."

Mariah found his shyness unusual and refreshing. She knew he was attracted to her; those golden eyes couldn't lie so blatantly. She stepped closer and locked her hand gently over his arm. As they strolled toward the ridge's edge, Mariah asked, "Do you really think of me as a child?"

Dusty didn't answer, but bent his elbow to accommodate her touch. His words came slow in the night air. "The stars look huge from this spot. On a clear night like this, you can see miles just by moonlight."

They walked beside a thick shelter of trees. Dusty's low voice blended with the whispers of the leaves around them. "Years ago, when Indians were a problem, we kept a man posted over there by the trees. Nowadays only an old-timer named Willie sleeps out here."

Mariah tugged at his arm and he stopped. "Dusty," she asked again, "do you still think of me as a child?"

As he turned toward her, his arm brushed the material covering her breasts. "I . . ." He seemed to be unable to finish. His face was hidden in shadows, but his voice seemed lower than before. "I think . . ."

Mariah smiled to herself. She knew if she could get him to admit she was an adult, the battle would be half won. But she was unprepared for this quiet man's action. In the swiftness of a snapping twig, he bent toward her, capturing her lips with his kiss.

Mariah had been kissed several times by daring suitors, but nothing compared to Dusty's kiss. His long fingers clasped over her shoulders pulling her to him full length. His mouth pressed hers in bruising need. As she tried to protest, his tongue parted her lips to taste the inside of her mouth. Mariah tried to move away, but couldn't break free from his powerful hold. As her heart pounded moments into eternity, she felt herself sinking into his embrace. The wall she had built so carefully to allow no man near was slowly sinking into quicksand.

All thoughts drained from Mariah's mind as she tried to stay afloat in the flood of sensations that swept over her. Her fingers rose to his chest, and even her effort to push him away became a tender embrace. His hands moved down her back, pulling her close and burning her forever with his fire. He wasn't playing with the same set of rules, she suddenly realized. He wasn't playing a game at all.

Mariah pushed her palms up his chest and across his shoulders to touch his hair. Her fingers ran through his sandy curls, and she felt herself melting into him as wax liquifies in the sun. His kiss deepened from a fiery explosion into a gentle need that she could no more have turned away from than stop her heart's pounding.

Gently, his kisses lightened to a feathery touch upon her lips. They rippled like silent whispers of desire over her face. Mariah closed her eyes as she realized he was slowly lowering her from the sky back to earth. The knowledge that she didn't want to return, but longed for him to kiss her again, blanketed all other thoughts.

Dusty's lips slowly crossed her cheek to her ear where he whispered, "That should answer any question as to whether or not I think of you as a child or a woman." As his words registered, he stepped away, ending his embrace.

Mariah felt the chill of his withdrawal both on her body and in her heart. The knowledge that his kiss had been a demonstration frightened her. She'd fancied herself as always knowing how to handle the opposite sex, and now she knew that she had only been dealing with boys and doting old men. This man wouldn't be managed so easily, if at all. Anger, at herself and him, balled her fingers into fists. Before she took time to think, her right fist flew through the air and landed solidly across his jaw.

Dusty staggered slightly but easily dodged her left hook that followed an instant later.

Mariah's voice was cold as she fought hard to control her anger. "Don't ever force your advances on me again, or I'll see you dead."

Dusty rubbed his jaw. "Mariah, it will be a cold day in hell before I ever force you to do anything. But don't lie to me or yourself. You wanted, even begged, for that kiss. What happened between us was no taking, but a giving of both."

Mariah knew he spoke the truth, but the truth was only a cup of water over her prairie fire of anger. "Then don't ever kiss me again."

"I'll not make that promise." Dusty grew nearer, his face pale in the moonlight. "But I'll tell you this, Mariah Weston. Someday you'll beg me to kiss you again. For the feel of my arms will haunt your dreams from this night on." He turned and swung into his saddle. "As the feel of you will haunt me."

He disappeared into the trees before Mariah could answer. She rode back to the barn and unsaddled her own horse. The house was quiet as a tomb. Mariah knew Dusty wouldn't return tonight. She remembered he'd said this was not his home. She hadn't even thought to ask him where he slept. Did he sleep out under the stars during these cold nights? Or in the bunkhouse with his men? She wished she knew where he was, for there also were her thoughts.

Chapter Twenty-three

Mariah wasted her time trying to sleep as the full Comanche moon followed a path across the sky. When she did lapse into fitful dreams, the memory of Dusty's body pressing against her returned. She'd wake to find her skin cold for need of the fire he had ignited. At first light Mariah gave up the tossing and climbed out of bed. She dressed slowly with meticulous care, even pulling her hair into a mass of black curls above her head. Standing in front of the oval mirror, she admired her reflection with honest satisfaction. The image of a confident, fashionable young woman stood before her. No evidence of the bewildered, naive girl showed on the outside. She could face today, and Dusty Barfield, straight on as she had faced all the problems of her life.

Mariah spent the morning visiting with Ruth and wandering around the ranch house. The rooms that had been added to accommodate Mike and Allison's ever-growing family during their years on the ranch were quiet now, waiting for the next generation. They left Mariah feeling hollow, like visiting an empty nursery of a childless couple.

Mid-morning, Ruth joined Mariah for coffee. The old woman explained that everything in the original wing was the same as it had been when Ben and Bethanie lived there, with the exception of a few rugs.

Mariah discovered that Ruth talked only of subjects she wished to. The old housekeeper often chose to ignore questions as if she hadn't heard them.

After coffee, Mariah began examining all the ranch books which she found in order on top of the massive desk. Only one drawer was locked to her curious digging. Every fact about the ranch over the past ten years had been carefully documented in a clear, bold handwriting. There'd been good times and hard times, but always the bookkeeping looked complete. When times were good, Dusty had used the profits to improve the ranch. When times were hard, he'd crossed his own salary off the chart to help pay bills. She was surprised to see that he paid himself only the same as the hands. Never more, even in the best of times.

Just after ten, a knock sounded at the door, rattling like some huge woodpecker gone crazy on the porch. Mariah's brave front was a wasted effort as she greeted only Elliot Mayson. He seemed a faded substitute of the man she'd expected. Elliot was dressed in a wool, Eastern-cut suit that seemed to have shrunk a size since he'd put it on. His round hat has been replaced by a wide-brimmed Stetson, making him seem like a crossbreed of East and West.

"Miss Weston." He smiled with a mouth blessed with too many teeth. "I hope you don't find me presumptuous to call on you unannounced. I wanted to check on your welfare as well as invite you to go for a ride this magnificent morning."

Mariah's smile vanished as she noticed he drove a buggy. She loved horses and would rather ride bareback than in a buggy. She recovered enough to invite him in for tea. As she turned to fetch refreshments, she saw Ruth coming from the kitchen with a tray already made.

Mariah gracefully served tea and listened to Elliot chatter for half an hour. He seemed never to tire of telling her of all his accomplishments. He reminded her of the young men who came to her school for Sunday teas. He saw himself and his ever-changing emotions as life's most interesting subject. By the time they set off in the buggy, Mariah's head was pounding from the hammering of his precisely pronounced words and the flood of his extravagant vocabulary. She even mused that Elliot's father may have sent him away to school to lower the chatter level.

She sat quietly, her fingers intertwined to keep from taking the reins away from his incapable hands. They bounced over the land she'd galloped across the moonlight with Dusty. Now the sun was high, and the cold breeze only served to stir the dust in her face.

Finally Elliot pulled the buggy under a clump of trees at the edge of the ridge, not a hundred yards from where she had stood with Dusty looking at the stars.

Elliot helped her from the buggy as if she were senile and incapable of any actions on her own. He patted her hand as they strolled among the short shadows. He rambled on several minutes before seeming to find his direction. "I've talked with my father, and he is very interested in making you an offer. If he can buy your half, he will split the ranch."

Mariah didn't respond. She had to sell her half of the ranch to get the money for two years of schooling. But she still clung to the idea that Dusty would make her an offer. Even his behavior last night didn't alter the fact that she'd feel guilty about causing the demise of the Weston Ranch.

A rustling among the trees drew their attention. Elliot stiffened as a lone rider broke from the green mass and rode toward them. Mariah didn't have to look at the intruder's face to recognize Dusty's strong, lean body in control of his powerful horse.

Dusty stopped several feet from her and shoved his

hat far back on his sandy-brown hair. Mariah felt a smile crawl out of her planned pout, for Dusty's face was clean-shaven. He looked younger without a beard, but the strong line of authority still set his jawline. She thought she also saw a hint of jealousy touch his golden eyes as he studied Elliot.

"Morning, Mr. Mayson," Dusty nodded toward Elliot, then turned to wink at Mariah with a bold gesture that drew blood to her cheeks.

"Good morning, sir. I almost didn't know you without a beard. Can't say I remember ever seeing you without one. But then, I don't see you that often." Elliot seemed to make no attempt to hide his displeasure. "We were just enjoying a pleasant ride." When Dusty made no action to move on, Elliot added, "Alone."

Mariah studied Dusty carefully. He would had to have been a complete idiot not to get Elliot's point, but still he sat in the saddle as if he were watching a sleeping herd and had nowhere else to go. Mariah couldn't help but study the two men. Though Elliot was at least eight years Dusty's junior, they were very nearly the same size. However, Mariah knew Dusty's shoulders were wide with muscles while Elliot's had been created by a tailor.

She could see the circles under Dusty's eyes, and knew he'd been awake most of the night also. His voice was matter-of-fact. "I thought I'd ride out and tell Miss Weston that Allison and Mike are at the ranch." His next words were cold. "That is if she's finished with her . . . comparisons."

Did Dusty think she brought Elliot here to get him to kiss her? Anger rushed in her veins, but a smile froze across her face. "Please tell Allison and Mike I will be along directly, as soon as I complete a little study." There was no mistaking the master-to-servant tone in her voice.

Dusty's face clouded in anger, and Elliot's went blank

in confusion. Before she could say another word, Dusty kicked his horse and left in a cloud of dirt.

Mariah turned her back and wished she hadn't been so bold. She'd ordered him around like he was beneath her station, then hinted she might complete the comparison he'd suggested. Why couldn't she stop striking every time he provoked her? His image of her must be growing more distorted from the truth each time they met. He must think her a mindless brat. Why didn't she let him see her other side? But how do you tell a man you're deeply concerned about people and want to help them, when you've walloped him in the jaw and threatened to kill him the night before. How do you share your dreams with someone who only wants to see your flaws?

Elliot's smooth hand touched Mariah's arm. "Are you all right, Mariah?"

For a moment she thought he was actually interested in her welfare, but he continued with a list of negative feelings he bore toward Dusty which ended with, "My father will hear of his rude behavior."

"Does your father know of all you do?" Mariah asked, only half interested.

"Well . . . no." Elliot seemed upset by her question. "I did tell him I was coming here today, but . . ."

Elliot was gaining her full attention for the first time since they met. "Did your father send you the way he sent you to meet me on the train?"

"Well . . . he is very interested in buying your part of the ranch. But I assure you, Mariah, I would have come with or without his approval." His eyes looked beyond her to the invisible future only he could envision. "When I think about what a surprise it would be to him if I closed this deal for him. I would just walk in and hand him half of a ranch he's wanted all his life."

Mariah relaxed and added another brick to the wall around her heart. Elliot was only interested in her for the ranch, just as the others had been interested in her for the mines. He wanted to buy her half to prove something to his father. Even though it was a little disheartening to her ego, as least she could handle him knowing where she stood.

Elliot talked and pleaded all the way back to the ranch, until Mariah agreed to have a decision about selling by the following morning. She disliked being pushed almost as much as she hated his constant pampering. He, however, paid no attention to her withdrawal and continued to grow more bold with each touch, even going so far as to place his arm around her shoulder as he said his goodbyes on the porch. The idea that she wasn't attracted to him would never have crossed his conceited mind.

When she opened the door, she was bombarded with half a dozen blond-headed cousins. Mike and Allison's two oldest children were away at school, but Mariah wondered if anyone ever stopped to count and notice they were gone. For several minutes she hugged and laughed as they all tried to talk at once.

Just as the clan settled down, Dusty opened the door and the hugging ritual began again with even more vigor. From the way he teased and complimented each one, Mariah knew he must have long ago been accepted as part of the family. Though she'd seen most of the cousins when they had visited Colorado every few years, Dusty seemed more a part of the family.

Mariah spent the afternoon playing with the children and chatting with Allison. Her second cousin, whom Mariah called Aunt Allison, was a bubbly, plump woman who always seemed to beam whenever Uncle Mike was near. Mike had served several years in the Texas House of Representatives, and Allison had always packed up all the kids and followed him to Austin while the House was in session. Mariah smiled now just thinking of what the long train ride must be like with all these children.

Aunt Allison laughed as she rocked her youngest. "This one makes an even dozen, and we think that's just about right. I grew up an only child and think there is nothing grander than a house full of children."

Mariah smiled at Dusty, carrying a serving tray, as he dodged two boys running through the house. He carefully maneuvered past the girls who sat in a circle on the floor, and set the tray in front of Mariah. "If you'll serve tea, Mariah, Ruth has lemonade in the kitchen for all the children."

His announcement caused an instant scramble out of the room by everyone under the age of twelve.

As Mariah handed him a cup of hot tea, Dusty's hand touched her fingers. She glanced up and found his eyes dark and unreadable. His finger slowly ran the length of her own, then he withdrew to slowly run his same finger along his bottom lip. Mariah found the action, though simple, intoxicating to her imagination. She was sorry when he moved away to the desk and began a long discussion with Mike.

After dinner, Mariah moved gradually closer to the men huddled around the desk. Dusty had been thumbing through one volume of a law book for ten minutes and didn't even seem to notice as she moved within hearing distance. His hair half covered his eyes, and Mariah found herself wanting to brush aside the light brown mass.

"I could understand," Dusty said, "if it were some drifter or Indian who needed food, but the cattle I've found were simply killed and left to rot."

Mike nodded. "We both have a pretty good idea who's behind this mess. He'd like nothing better than to bankrupt the Weston Ranch and then step in and buy it for next to nothing."

"I'll never give up." Dusty spoke the words as fact.

"I know, but you'd best be on your guard. I've got to

leave for Austin in the morning, and I don't want you getting into any trouble while I'm gone."

"I've never gone looking for a fight." Dusty stood as Mike began motioning his family toward the door.

"Yeah, and you've never backed down from one either, Dusty, and that worries me."

"I wish I could go with you this time, Mike." Dusty caught sight of Mariah as she stood nearby. He offered her his arm as they followed the guests to the porch. "But things are pretty busy right now."

Mike didn't follow Dusty's gaze. "I understand, but it's always good to have you and that mind of yours with me in the capital. Time was when all you needed to fight the bad guys was a good gun and a strong horse. Now it's young men like you with a knowledge of the law who will win out."

The two men shook hands in a friendly farewell. Children piled into the wagon as Allison hugged Mariah goodbye.

Mariah and Dusty stood on the porch and waved to their guests as the sun set over the ridge. She watched as their buggy moved out of sight and wished they hadn't stayed so long. She needed to talk with Dusty.

When she turned around, he'd disappeared into the house. Mariah decided now was the time. She would simply tell him she must sell her half of the ranch and ask him if he would like to buy her out. It shouldn't be that complicated, but somehow, with Dusty, nothing seemed simple. Even a kiss.

Mariah found Dusty clearing the table from the huge meal Ruth had prepared. She once again wondered at the kind of a man who would even think of the dirty dishes.

Dusty looked up as she neared. "I thought I'd clean these for Ruth. The dinner was a lot of work, and she shouldn't have to face these in the morning."

"I'll help," Mariah volunteered.

Dusty smiled and tossed her a towel. "I'll wash and you dry. Try to keep up."

Mariah laughed. She'd enjoyed being around Dusty with all the others present. He hadn't seemed so shy. As they worked she decided to keep the conversation light. She asked questions about the ranch and when she was born. He told her about the days he worked planting her mother's herb garden and how Ruth still practiced all the mixtures Bethanie had taught her.

Mariah tried to explain her love for helping others. She told him of ways her mother's doctoring and modern medicine could be combined to save lives. Dusty seemed to enjoy Mariah's accounts of her and her mother having traveled, sometimes miles, to help the sick or hurt.

Before Mariah realized where the time had gone, the dishes were finished and Dusty was standing at the back door. "You're a pretty good hand for a spoiled brat," he teased.

"And you continue to amaze me with your skill in the kitchen. You didn't break a dish." Mariah laughed.

He leaned against the open door as if reluctant to leave. His eyes grew darker as she moved to enjoy the night breeze with him. She knew he wanted to kiss her again. Or at least she thought he did. Dustin Barfield was a hard man to read.

"Dusty," Mariah reached to touch him, then pulled back. "I need to talk to you about selling the ranch."

She watched a muscle tighten in his jawline, and she moved a few feet away. How could he listen so openly before and now close up? Maybe if he understood her need for the money?

"You're not still thinking of selling." A hint of anger blended in his words.

"Yes." Mariah tightened her hands into fists. She was tired, but she could still stand up for what she had to do.

Dusty watched her for a long moment. "We'll talk

about it in the morning." His tone sounded as if he were ordering a bothersome child to bed.

"No, Dusty, we must talk about it now." Mariah protested. He couldn't just avoid her every time the subject came up.

"I will." Dusty was trying not to yell. "But not now, not tonight."

Before she could answer, he stepped out of the house and vanished into the black night without an explanation. Mariah stormed to the door. She hated the way he walked out on a fight. She closed the door and locked it, wishing she could do the same with her emotions.

Mariah paced her bedroom for an hour, organizing her thoughts. Tomorrow she'd be ready to face Dusty and talk him into buying her half of this troubled ranch. Getting through medical school was more important than watching a herd of cattle grow fat for slaughter. Her dreams were just as important as his, and she would make him see it even if she had to tie him down to get him to listen.

When she finally retired, she was exhausted, but the feel of Dusty's touch still haunted her dreams with a longing she could not deny.

In what seemed like only minutes, Mariah opened her eyes to the gray light of a rainy morning. That sick feeling of having overslept flooded over her. She threw on her wrap and ran out into the hallway. She flew down the corridor and into the huge main room, where a mantel clock ticked away, heedless of her panic.

"Nine-thirty!" She stomped her bare foot. She'd planned to talk with Dusty for at least an hour before Elliot arrived. Now she would have less than thirty minutes.

"Something not going your way, princess?" A voice sounded from behind her.

Mariah whirled to find Dusty sitting at the desk. Papers were scattered in front of him, telling her he'd been working for hours already. She pulled her wrap closed. "Give me ten minutes to dress. I have to talk with you."

Dusty smiled and leaned back in his chair. "How about talking while you get dressed? That would save time."

Mariah shook her head and ran down the hall. "Five minutes and I'll be ready."

She flew into her room and grabbed the first skirt and blouse she found. Within five minutes she'd dressed, washed her face, and combed her hair into long waves down her back. Her simple blouse buttoned down the front with a bow tied at the neck, and her navy skirt was full and long. Her brothers teased her, saying she looked like a schoolteacher in those clothes. Mariah hoped the air of authority carried over today, for she had many decisions to make.

Tying her hair back with a ribbon, she hurried into the main room. Dusty hadn't moved from his place. He stood as she neared and held out his hand toward the dining area. "Ruth made some coffee and cinnamon rolls. We can eat while we talk."

Mariah nodded, following him to the table. As he pulled out her chair, his hand brushed her shoulder lightly. She jumped at his touch. She knew this was just the calm before the storm that would hit as soon as they started talking. Suddenly she couldn't remember any of the words she planned to say.

"Dusty, we must talk," she began.

"We can talk, but not of selling the ranch. I won't, and that is final. I've got enough problems without any thoughts about selling." He was standing behind her, but his words echoed with tightly held anger.

Mariah resented his condescending tone. "We *will* talk about the selling of this ranch. I'm half owner and am getting sick and tired of being talked to like some child."

"Then stop acting like a spoiled brat and see the whole

picture. You can't sell your half of the ranch on some whim."

Mariah stood and faced him. "I'm not a spoiled brat and this is not a whim. Elliot will be here in a few minutes, and I'll show you what I can do." This wasn't going the way she'd planned at all, but there seemed no reasoning with Dusty. He was as headstrong as he was handsome. And right now she hated him for being both. He was confusing her more than anyone had in her entire life.

"You'll . . ." Dusty stopped as they both heard a buggy approaching. Both turned to see Elliot rein up as the clock chimed a quarter to ten.

Dusty suddenly jerked Mariah out of sight of the windows. "He's an eager one." His hands were tight around her arms. "Mariah, there's so much you don't understand."

Mariah pushed him a few inches away from her. "I'm sick of being treated this way. I plan to sign Elliot's papers and be done with this mess. You can just work out the details with your new partner."

Dusty's face twisted in frustration. "Don't see him." To her astonishment, his words were almost a plea.

"I'm sorry," Mariah answered. She knew if she put her decision off any longer, it would be even more difficult. What did it really matter to Dusty if the ranch were half owned by her or someone else? "Unless you plan on kidnapping me, I'm going to talk with Elliot."

Mariah had taken three steps toward the door when Dusty's arm captured her waist. With a cry of frustration she twisted to strike him, but his movements were lightning accurate. Before she realized what was happening, he tied a dinner napkin over her mouth. As she struggled in disbelief, he pulled her hands behind her, yanked the ribbon from her hair, and bound her hands. When he turned her to face him, she kicked as furiously as she could, but her skirt buffered each blow. Panic flowed in Mariah's blood as she feared he must have suddenly gone mad.

"I'm sorry," Dusty whispered as Elliot's knock pounded on the door. "I . . . can't let you meet with him."

Ruth entered silently from the kitchen. Mariah turned wide-eyed toward the old woman. She silently pleaded for help, but to her horror, Ruth only looked at them like they were children playing some harmless game.

Dusty bent and lifted Mariah over his shoulder like a sack of grain. "Answer the door, Ruth. Give Elliot Mayson some coffee, and tell him I'll be with him in a few minutes."

To Mariah's horror, Ruth nodded as if kidnapping were an everyday occurrence in this household. Dusty ran to the back door as Elliot's hard knock sounded again. He moved her outside, and within seconds they were hidden in the trees behind the house. Mariah had never been so terrified in all her life. She could see only the ground as he crisscrossed among the trees. She could hear the bubble of a waterfall, and was thankful she hadn't suggested drowning as a means of solving Dusty's problem.

Dusty twisted her in his arms until she was cradled like a child. She looked up and was surprised to see no anger in his face, only worry. He held her close as he moved, and Mariah was very much aware of his hand just below her breast. She struggled suddenly, and his grip tightened, moving slightly higher. Mariah froze as her emotions seemed locked on a fast-moving carrousel with first one then another coming to the top. His hand didn't return to below her breast but remained with his first two fingers pressing against her softness. The ribbon binding her hands cut painfully into her wrists. She could hear his heart pounding in her ears as he carried her into the shadow of the aging trees.

The maddening sensation that she wanted him to press his hand higher frightened Mariah far more than the fact she was being kidnapped.

He moved between closely bunched trees as Mariah caught sight of a cabin. The solidly built cabin was completely hidden in the clump of trees beneath the ridge. The low-hanging clouds seemed to close over the treetops, blanketing them from the rest of the world. No one, unless he knew the cabin was among the trees, would ever guess its existence.

"I thought I'd show you my home while you're visiting," he whispered as he kicked the door open. "Now seems an ideal time."

Chapter Twenty-four

Dusty stormed across the cabin and tossed Mariah onto a bed. The cloudy day offered little light to the room. Mariah blinked, trying to draw the room into focus as he retied her hands around a corner post of the four-poster bed. The room looked more like a study than a house, with books lining three of the walls. She knew this was Dusty's place, where he slept and where he went to be alone. The worn, overstuffed chair by the fire told of a great love for reading, just as the chair's solitude told of few visitors. Even in her fright, Mariah was fascinated by the man who must live here. She could see every kind of book, from the first-readers gathering dust on the top shelf, to a row of law books stacked on a desk in one corner. Could the person who must spend hours treasuring these books possibly be the same man who was kidnapping her?

After Dusty finished tying her hands, he removed the gag slowly, trying not to tangle her hair. He leaned her back amid several layers of colorful quilts. A smile of victory touched his lips, yet worry still shadowed his eyes. "Scream if you'd like, but the waterfall will drown out any noise before it reaches the house."

Mariah jerked her face free of his grip. "Let me go, or I swear I'll see you hang for kidnapping."

Dusty tried to keep his voice calm. "I built this place with Mike's help the year after you left."

Mariah pulled at her bonds. "I'll carve your name on a tombstone myself, Dustin Barfield."

Dusty continued as if he hadn't heard her threat. "I doubt if anyone but Ruth and Mike knows where it is, so you'll be safe here. The trees are so thick no one would guess there was a cabin out behind the main house."

"Safe!" Mariah screamed. "You're the only one I need to be safe from. In a few minutes Cain will notice I'm missing, and he'll tear this hideout of yours apart."

Dusty shrugged. "Cain left for town before daybreak. Said he'd be back later. Now, if you're comfortable, I need to get back to that weak-kneed boyfriend of yours. I wouldn't want to keep the son of Wes Mayson waiting."

Mariah knew she had to keep Dusty here longer. The more time he spent away, the more worried Elliot would be, and hopefully the more suspicious. "My hands are too tight," she complained.

Dusty leaned over her to check the knots. "They aren't cutting off your circulation. You'll be fine, and I'll be back in half an hour to untie you."

As he stood to go, Mariah cried, "Wait!"

Dusty looked at her with one eyebrow raised, as if guessing her next game. "What now?" he asked.

Mariah said the first thing that came to mind. "You said you would kiss me if I asked you to. Well, I'm asking."

"Now?" Dusty shook his head, then laughed as if she had suddenly lost her mind.

"Now," Mariah insisted. "I want to know that it was just the moonlight the other night and nothing more. I want to know kissing you means nothing so that when I kill you I'll do so without any questions."

Dusty sat on the bed beside her. "All right. It's not

exactly the begging tone I had hoped for, but knowing you, I might wait a long time for a soft 'please.' " He moved slowly toward her, a smile lifting the corners of his full lips. His mouth brushed hers lightly at first. Mariah lay frozen, waiting. His tongue tickled the corner of her mouth, then he whispered, "I'll kiss you now, Mariah, but you have to kiss me back." His lips were at her cheek, moving slowly to her ear. "I'll show you what no Eastern-educated fool like Elliot Mayson will ever know, but you have to meet me halfway. For in the middle lies . . . paradise."

His words tickled her ear as his fingers slid lightly along her from her shoulders to her waist. She turned willingly toward his mouth and felt his lips meet hers. His mouth was gentle and tender as his hands continued to caress her sides, creating a tidal wave of fire within her. She swayed back and forth and felt his fingers brush the sides of her breasts in their journey. A sigh escaped as she opened her mouth, allowing his kiss to deepen. His tongue moved slowly inside to taste, his hands crept an inch farther up the sides of her breasts. Each movement slightly increased in pressure, and Mariah's pleasure climbed. Never had she been so kissed or so touched by a man. A yearning deep within her grew like a hollow ache and spread over her body. She wanted more, but with each touch the ache grew into a greater need.

With hesitation, she returned his kiss, following his lead. He pulled his mouth free and moved to her neck, kissing the spot where her pulse pounded. "Mariah . . . Mariah," he whispered into the hollow of her neck.

"No . . ." Mariah cried with a sob, fighting her body for control. "No, stop," she whispered as his hands moved along the sides of her breasts and his lips moved down her throat.

"Where should I stop loving you, Mariah?" Dusty's voice was low in passion. "Here?" He moved his hands to her waist and spread them wide over her abdomen. "Or here?" he whispered as his fingers moved up to trace under each of her breasts. He knotted the material of her blouse tightly in his fist. His action revealed the clear outline of her bust.

His mouth moved to her ear, and his teeth tugged at her lobe before he whispered, "Or here, Mariah?" His thumbs brushed with loving strokes over the thin material covering her breasts.

She said the only word her body would allow. The only word her lips could form. "More."

Dusty returned to her lips then, with a passion she'd never tasted before. His kiss was afire with need as he slid his body down beside her on the bed. His hands no longer moved in smooth strokes, but explored freely over the silk of her blouse. Mariah twisted and felt his hand cover her breast. He groaned, as if in pain, but didn't pull his hand away. Slowly his fingers began to caress her, and with each movement Mariah's pleasure grew.

His kiss transformed from tender to demanding, and Mariah loved each version. She could barely breathe as his hand flattened over her heart. Then, his touch was gone and she tried to cry out for its return, but his lips stopped any sound. She felt his fingers at her throat as he pulled the blouse bow free. His hand moved down her front, unbuttoning each barrier in his way as his kiss continued. He lovingly slid the material open and shoved her camisole up. His hand moved onto the silk of her warm, waiting flesh.

Mariah thought she would die with pleasure as his strong fingers touched her burning skin. He caught her pointed flesh between two of his fingers and tugged slightly, breaking the kiss as she moaned with each tug. Mariah closed her eyes as his magic worked over her. The fire within her was growing with each action, and yet the need for more equalled each pleasure.

Just as she thought she could endure no more joy, she felt his mouth close over her flesh. His tongue circled her nipple and she cried out. He moved from one to the other silky peak as she swayed beneath him. He slowly tasted his fill of her yielding flesh, and she knew her breasts swelled in welcome. A low cry escaped her lips. A cry of need only lovers understood, only lovers can quench.

When his mouth finally returned to her lips, she hungrily showed him of her pleasure. He took his time as she practiced kissing him. He would allow her long moments to experiment before he would pull her closer and demonstrate his passion once more. Always he touched her breasts as if accompanying their kiss with the waves of fire his hands brought. His tongue would plunge deep as his hands gripped possessively, then his kiss would lighten to a feathery touch and his fingers would brush across her so softly she would feel herself floating in desire.

Finally, when her breathing was coming in short gulps, Dusty moved over her. He lowered his slender body like a blanket. She could feel his legs through their clothes on either side of her limbs. As he slid down, she felt his belt buckle push lightly into her abdomen. He rested his head between her breasts and moved his fingers from where her arms were tied down the outside of her body. He pushed the mounds gently together until her flesh was touching either side of his face. Mariah could feel her heart pounding beneath his head, and his hair tickled her skin as his mouth moved slowly back and forth.

Mariah knew she was sinking fast. If she didn't stop this madness, she knew she would be unable to stop. "Please," she begged to herself as well as Dusty. "Please, stop."

His hands now gripped her waist tightly in a brand of ownership. He pushed at the material of her skirt. The waistband buttons snapped as the skirt slid a few inches off her waist.

"No," Mariah cried, as the pleasure of his hands brushing her flesh blended with the last hint of sanity in her mind.

Dusty pulled away slightly. "Mariah, I love you. I love you beyond reason. Beyond any feeling I've ever had in my life. When I awoke the other morning to find you standing before me, I thought I was dreaming. You belong to me and this ranch."

An ounce of reason returned to Mariah's brain. "I belong to no one." She hated the thought that anyone would ever think they owned her. She must stop this insane pleasure before she lost her mind.

Dusty's fingers circled her breasts, and he smiled as Mariah's lips parted in a silent sigh. "Tell me you don't want me, Mariah. Tell me my touch doesn't set you on fire, and I'll back away. You may deny you love me, but you cannot deny you want me as much as I need you."

Mariah twisted away from him. She could not deny him, but anger of his power over her body sobered her mind. "If you've finished raping me, would you untie me?"

Dusty's golden eyes darkened, first in frustration, then anger. His hand raised above her as if on a quest to prove her wrong, then dropped in a fist among the quilts. He rolled away from her with a frustrated sigh. He jerked out his pocket knife and cut her bounds. "I wasn't raping you . . ." She could hear the hurt in his words.

Mariah jumped off the bed and pulled her clothes together. "What do you call it when you tie a woman to your bed?"

Dusty shook his head in disbelief that she could even think that what he'd done was rape. She could see the questions in his eyes. For perhaps the first time in his life, this strong man was questioning himself, doubting himself. "But . . ." Frustrated, he dug his fingers through his light hair.

Mariah was furious at Dusty and at herself. She knew what had happened had been jointly wanted, but she grabbed the first weapon at her disposal, his doubt. "I should shoot you for what you just did to me. No man has ever taken any of the liberties you did."

It bothered her that he might have been doing what he did to save his ranch and not out of any feeling for her. Every man who'd ever courted her had done so with other goals than just loving her. Hadn't Dusty kissed her only two nights ago just to prove a point? "Did you think you could paw me a little and get me to forget about selling the ranch? Well, you were wrong. You can hold me here for days and make my head swim with your kisses, but I still will sell my half of the ranch."

"Paw you! Paw you!" Dusty rose and stormed to the door. "Is that what you think I was doing? I could have sworn you asked me to kiss you."

"A kiss, no more."

"Don't lie to me, Mariah. You asked for more."

"No. You took more."

"My God, have you no heart?" He grabbed a low ceiling beam with both hands and pushed as if to move the house. "Could I have been so wrong about you? Could a woman with such passion have only a cold stone inside her for a heart? I was loving you, Mariah. Loving you for no motive than to bring you pleasure."

"You kidnapped me. You tied me to your bed and took what you wanted while I protested. Now you expect me to believe you did so to make me happy?"

"I was loving you."

"You were taking."

"No!"

"I hate you for what you did!"

Dusty pulled the door open with such force the win-

dows on either side of it shook. "To hell with the ranch
and to hell with you, if you believe that. Go. Get out of
my sight. Sell the ranch, I don't care anymore. Do what
you want, but get out of my life. I don't ever want to
see you or touch you again as long as I live."

His words hurt her more than if he'd hit her. She ran
out the doorway, fighting to keep from crying. Rain was
falling so softly she hadn't even heard it. Even outside,
its splattering seemed dwarfed by the thundering of her
heart. As she picked her way through the trees, Mariah
let the tears run free. A huge lump grew in her throat,
making her breathing shallow as each tear burned its way
down her face. She felt her heart tearing apart with each
step she took away from Dusty. How could he have made
her feel such passion and yet not take the time to understand her? She had a right to her dreams just as he did,
yet every time she'd tried to talk to him about her plans
he'd refused to listen.

As Mariah passed the waterfall, she crumbled onto the
wet grass and cried like she'd never cried before. Huge
sobs were drowned out by the falling rain as it washed
her cheeks clean after each tear. Her fingers clawed at
the earth and pulled handfuls of sod into her fists. She
slung the wet dirt from her as if she could throw out the
pain that mounted in her chest.

Chapter Twenty-five

Mariah lay in the wet grass beside the waterfall and cried until all her energy drained. Soaking wet, she finally gathered the strength to stand, then trudged toward the house. The clouds unleashed a torrent in downward waves, slowing her progress and making each step an effort. She knew Elliot would be long gone, but she didn't care. There would be other days to worry about selling the ranch. All she wanted now was to slip into a hot bath and forget everything that had happened this morning. She didn't want to think about Dusty or the feelings he'd set alive within her.

As Mariah neared the back of the ranch house, she saw Cain bolt from the doorway and run toward her. Worry covered his face as he yanked his parka off and held it out to her.

As he reached her, Mariah collapsed in the old man's arms. She was too cold and wet to move another step. He lifted her as he had all her life and comforted her with his strong arms. As always, he asked no questions. His kindness and devotion were unconditional. He carried her toward the house while protecting her with his body from the rain.

Mariah lifted her head as he swung her into the kitchen. There, to her surprise, stood her mother talking with Ruth. Bethanie turned at the sound Cain made, and Mariah saw concern fill her mother's beautiful face. Cain lowered Mariah to the floor, and Mariah ran into Bethanie's arms. Gone now was the self-confident woman she thought she had become. With a sob, she realized what Dusty must feel everyday with no family around him. He had no one to turn to during life's storms. No arms to comfort him.

Bethanie held Mariah tightly. Her voice was soft as she spoke to the others. "Ruth, put some coffee on and water for a bath. Cain, put a tub in my room and light the fireplace. We've got to get her out of these clothes before she catches her death of cold."

Mariah followed her mother's orders, and within half an hour was soaking in a hot tub with a half a pot of coffee to warm her insides. No one asked any questions about where she'd been, and Mariah was thankful for their silence. She watched her mother rock in a creaking Bentwood rocker by the fire. Bethanie seemed a hundred miles away, as if reliving the past. Mariah saw her mother as a quiet woman who always seemed to know what was right to do. She was greatly loved by everyone who knew her, and considered one of the most beautiful women in Colorado.

"Why did you come?" Mariah asked quietly.

"Cain wired me. Josh couldn't get away for a few days, so I took the train alone. It was time I came back for a visit, and I wanted to face the memories without Josh."

Mariah relaxed against the side of the tub. It was unlike Cain ever to interfere. Did he think she needed help with Dusty or with selling the ranch? She watched her mother rocking and wondered if another reason brought her here after all these years.

"Mother, what are you thinking?" Mariah asked, knowing her mother would never share her thoughts without being asked. The long pause that followed left

Mariah to wonder if, even now, her mother would open up with her feelings.

Bethanie smiled and leaned forward in the rocker. "I was thinking, your father asked me to marry him in this room. We were married that night."

"Did you love him very much?" Mariah asked. She wanted to add, "As much as you love Uncle Josh," but couldn't bring herself to be quite so direct.

"Not at first," Bethanie answered honestly. "But I think he loved enough for the both of us. As the time passed, I grew to love him. He kept proving his love to me until I couldn't help but care for him."

Mariah asked quietly, "Proving he loved you . . . physically?" She knew she was on untrod ground and doubted her mother would answer such a question even as the words passed her lips.

"No," Bethanie surprised her daughter with her honesty. "You can show someone you love them with physical actions, but you prove it by what you do outside the bedroom. He was willing to protect me with his name and his life. What more could any woman ask of love?"

Mariah wasn't sure she understood what her mother was saying. She climbed out of the bath and wriggled into her nightgown. Though it was mid-afternoon, she felt ready for bed. The low, brooding clouds made it seem like twilight.

Mariah watched as Bethanie stood and moved to the old oval mirror. Her mother brushed the carved frame in a greeting.

"Mother," Mariah whispered. "Should a woman give up everything for the man she loves?"

Mariah watched pain touch her mother's reflection before she turned and faced her daughter with a carefully masked face. "I don't know, Mariah, but if you give up beliefs, dreams, or . . . principles you're not the same person that other person loves."

The sound of horses suddenly broke the quiet mood of the house. Mariah slipped on her dressing gown and followed her mother to the porch. They watched as watery gray figures moved near.

Bethanie and Mariah stood under the protection of the long roof as rain dripped on a dozen men on horseback. The horses were winded and huffing smoky puffs into the gray-wet air. An overweight man with a badge pinned on his rain slicker approached the porch in wide, splashing strides.

"Mrs. Weston, you may not remember me, but I'm Sheriff Harris." He tipped his hat slightly, spilling water down the front of his coat.

"I remember you, Sheriff." Bethanie's voice was guarded, telling Mariah her mother didn't trust this man. Bethanie Weston always carried her chin in a graceful tilt that seemed to demand respect. "What may I do to help you, Mr Harris?" It was obvious to all that she pointedly neglected to use the man's title.

Harris reached the porch. "We're looking for Dustin Barfield."

"I haven't seen him today," Bethanie answered. Mariah noticed her mother volunteered no information or offered to let anyone else answer the question. "What do you need to speak to him about?"

The sheriff puffed up like a water-soaked toad, apparently proud of his mission. "I plan on arresting him for the murder of Elliot Mayson."

Mariah gasped and felt Bethanie's hand touch her arm. She glanced at the frozen profile of her mother as the sheriff continued. "We found Elliot's body two hours ago halfway to town. He was still warm, with Dusty's slicker over him. Guess the murdering fool didn't remember having his initials on the inside of the parka."

Mariah fought to draw air into her lungs. "What time

was Elliot murdered?" She held to her mother, facing herself for the blow of the sheriff's words.

The sheriff shrugged. "Sometime after ten. We found the body about eleven."

Mariah let out a long breath. She knew Dusty was with her during that time. Before she could tell the sheriff, she saw Dusty coming from the barn. His clothes were plastered against his lean form, and his head was down against the rain.

The sheriff stepped off the porch and motioned for several men to dismount. His husky voice rumbled across the yard. "Dustin Barfield, I'd like to ask you a few questions." The sheriff's words were echoed by the rolling thunder of the low-hanging clouds.

Dusty looked up, and his frown told Mariah he was in no mood to be bothered. The rain was blocking his view of more than a few feet. He started to walk around the sheriff as if the lawman was no more than a hitching post.

"Where were you this morning?" Sheriff Harris yelled.

Dusty's vision darted to Mariah and for a moment she saw hate touch his golden eyes. Could he really think she would turn him in for kidnapping? Or worse?

"None of your business," he answered the sheriff in a hiss, his eyes never leaving Mariah.

Several men moved to form a ring around Dusty. The sheriff smiled as he jerked Dusty's arm. "I'm making it my business, mister. Elliot Mayson was murdered today, and I think you had something to do with it."

"What!" Dusty yelled, then laughed with relief that only Mariah could understand. He glanced back over toward her as if to apologize.

The sheriff seemed tired of their chatter in the rain. "You're under arrest for the murder. I know there's been bad blood between you and the Maysons ever since Ben

Weston was killed, but shooting his son is no way to solve anything. Where were you this morning?"

"I a—I was alone. I overslept," Dusty answered, then turned to walk away.

Before Dusty moved two feet, men closed around him. As he resisted their grip, the sheriff moved in. The fat man spread his lips thin over his teeth and barked again. "There ain't a rancher in Texas who sleeps past sunup. So don't lie to me. Now once more, where were you this morning?"

Dusty slung his wet hair out of his eyes and pulled at the men who held him. "I was alone." Though the words were low, they were said like an obscenity tossed in the sheriff's face.

The sheriff reacted to the words as they were meant. He slung his fist up and clipped Dusty across the chin. Dusty's head jerked back from the blow of Harris's knuckles. As his chin lowered, the sheriff's other fist pounded into his stomach with so much force that the men who were holding Dusty almost lost their balance.

Dusty silently took the blows. He twisted in pain only as he heard Mariah cry his name as if she were being torn apart with each blow.

The sheriff laughed as he landed his knuckles into Dusty's face. "You've been a smartass pup ever since you took over this ranch. I figure it's about time someone took you down a notch or two."

Bethanie held Mariah back as they watched Dusty take blow after blow before he fell to his knees suspended between the two deputies. Each hit on Dusty's body tore at Mariah's heart. She wanted to stop the men, to run and protect Dusty from the blows with her own body, but her mother's hands held her tight to the porch. Mariah turned to her mother in anger. But, to Mariah's astonishment, Bethanie's vision wasn't on the fight, but on Cain. She watched as Bethanie nodded slowly toward the older man, and Cain melted into the rain at the edge of the porch.

Mariah knew Cain could do nothing against a dozen men, but she could stand no more. She bolted down the steps and confronted the sheriff. "Stop!" she yelled. "He was with me. He couldn't have killed Elliot Mayson. He was with me!" She knelt in the mud in front of Dusty. His face was down, but she could see blood mixing with rain, dripping onto his shirt.

The sheriff grabbed a handful of Dusty's hair and pulled his head up. Mariah swallowed a scream as she looked into Dusty's half-conscious eyes. "Were you with her?" Harris interrogated above Mariah's cries. "There'd be a reason for a man to stay in bed all morning."

Dusty's mouth was bleeding, and his left eye was almost swollen shut. "No," he answered between gritted teeth. "I didn't kill Elliot, but I was alone this morning. I wasn't with her."

"Too bad, Barfield. You could've had an alibi at the cost of this lady's reputation. You must dislike your partner pretty bad, not to let her lie to save that no good neck of yours."

"I'm not lying!" Mariah cried above the rain, but no one listened. They tied Dusty atop a horse and headed out.

As the sheriff passed the porch, he tipped his hat to Bethanie. "I'm leaving Hank here to see your daughter doesn't come to town tomorrow and mix up the trial."

"That will not be necessary," Bethanie answered.

"In fact, I better leave a couple of men to see that no one from this house is at the trial. I want to get this over fast and have the hanging by tomorrow night. Wouldn't do to let it fester and have two of the biggest ranches in Texas fighting each other."

Mariah ran beside Dusty's horse. "Please tell them where you were," she begged.

"No," Dusty answered. "I was alone. Stay away from me." His words were sharp, but his eyes seemed to be pleading.

Mariah walked back to her mother as the horses faded into the rain. "How could he hate me so much?" she cried.

"Or love you so much?" Bethanie whispered. "The sheriff is one of Mayson's men. If he thought Dusty had an alibi, he might try to eliminate you. I know he'll do whatever he thinks Mayson wants, and so does Dusty."

"We must do something!" Mariah pleaded. She couldn't just let these crazy men carry Dusty off without a fight. There had to be something she could do.

"We will, Mariah. Cain will follow them and keep an eye on Dusty. When the time is right, we'll do something."

To Mariah's horror, Bethanie turned to the two men left to guard them, and said, "You men might as well come in out of the rain and have some hot tea." As they walked inside, she turned to Ruth. "Make us up a pot of that herb tea from the leaves of the purple nightshade plant and add a little whiskey for sweetener. That should help the chill."

Mariah pulled her mother back a few steps. "I've always had trouble remembering all your herbs, Mother." Mariah's voice carried only to Bethanie's ears. "But the nightshade plant won't help the chill."

Bethanie touched a finger to her lips as Mariah whispered, "The nearest I remember it's a sleeping agent."

Bethanie nodded slowly with an angelic smile touching the corners of her mouth.

Mariah glanced toward Ruth. The old woman never batted an eye as she disappeared into the kitchen to follow Bethanie's instructions. Mariah watched as her mother invited the men to rest by the warm fire.

Chapter Twenty-six

Mariah paced the polished brick floor of the ranch house, as her mother sat quietly facing their guards. Mariah's mind was screaming to take action. The vision of Dusty's bloody face kept flashing through her brain like a scene of horror blinking past a window of a swiftly moving train. She wanted to strike out and not wait for the slow-acting herb to do its work.

Mariah watched the sheriff's two men. They seemed ill at ease. They were rough ranch hands, not accustomed to the gracious attention Bethanie was now paying them. They gladly accepted the offered tea, thankful for a diversion. Their huge, dirty hands seemed deformed as they gripped the china cups. Ruth brightened their spirits by lacing each cup with a generous portion of brandy.

As the moments ticked away, Bethanie refilled the men's cups repeatedly while her own sat untouched. They didn't seem to notice that she offered no cup to Mariah. Bethanie's soft voice played like a melody as she acted out the role of the perfect hostess. "We like to add a little herb to our tea. It adds a sweet taste and takes the chill away."

Mariah was amazed at how easily her mother lied to the men while pouring a tea so heavily blended with sleeping potion. Mariah yawned just from the smell.

The two men tried to fight their drowsiness but bobbed

like two swollen corks in a barrel of whiskey. Their faces grew flushed from drink and Ruth's constant stirring of the already warm fireplace. Mariah heard her mother begin to hum an old Shaker melody used years ago to rock her children to sleep. She watched as both men leaned their heads against the cushions and began to snore in unison.

Bethanie whispered as if she were saying words to the song she had been humming. "Get your riding clothes on, Mariah."

Mariah moved to her mother's side. "Should we tie them up?" she whispered.

"No," Bethanie answered calmly. "We'll probably be back before they awaken."

Mariah nodded. Without another moment's hesitation, she ran to her room and dressed in her best riding clothes. If she was going to proclaim to the town that she was a wanton woman by going to a man's cabin alone, at least she'd be dressed like a lady for her own downfall.

Bethanie was standing at the huge oak desk when Mariah returned. Her mother had changed into a charcoal split skirt and a white high-collared blouse. Mariah watched as her mother reached behind a book and pulled out a key.

Bethanie unlocked the bottom desk drawer. She pulled out an old Walker-Colt handgun and laid it gently on the desk as though it were a treasured keepsake. Mariah didn't have to ask. She knew the long Walker-Colt had belonged to Ben Weston. She'd heard her mother tell the boys the story of how Sam Walker had given the gun to Ben after he'd been hurt fighting bank robbers.

"After you were born, Ben always locked up his extra guns. With all of Allison's kids around, I guess Dusty continued the practice." She lifted two gunbelts already heavy with guns and a full belt of bullets from the large drawer. "This was Dusty's when he was a boy. See if it fits you."

Mariah had been around guns all her life and could shoot as well as any of her brothers, but she'd never worn a gunbelt. She started to laugh and suggest her mother might be overdoing it a little, but the image of Dusty's bloody face erased the thought from her mind. She strapped the belt around her tiny waist and checked to see that every bullet loop and each chamber of the gun was full.

Ruth joined the women. She kept her eyes on the two sleeping men by the fire as she spoke. "The horses are ready, Bethanie. I think I should tell you that when Elliot Mayson came by this morning, he took one look at the sky and asked to borrow Dusty's slicker that was hanging by the door."

Bethanie raised a questioning eyebrow as she buckled her gunbelt as tightly as she could over her hips. "Did he put it on?"

Ruth began nodding her head as if following Bethanie's train of thought. "I watched him put it on before he climbed into the saddle. That was the first time I ever saw him ride a horse, but I guess a wagon would have gotten bogged down in all this mud."

Bethanie's face saddened as she whispered her next question. "How big a man was Elliot Mayson?"

Ruth's words were slow in coming. "About the same size as Dusty."

Before Mariah could ask any questions, Bethanie turned and lifted an ancient leather saddlebag from the corner. She knew it contained her mother's medicines. She'd seen her mother carry a bag just like it for hours as she moved from house to house during the Fever of '80. There must've been a hundred times during her childhood that Mariah had awakened to see her mother leaving with the bag to tend the sick or dying. Cain always traveled at her side on her nursing missions, but today Cain had disappeared into the fog.

"Cain," Mariah whispered. "Where is Cain?"

Bethanie's answer was quick and honest. "He'll be in town by now, staying out of sight until we need him." She moved toward the door. "Before we leave, Mariah, I must ask you one question. How far are you willing to go to save Dusty Barfield's life?"

"As far as it takes," Mariah answered.

"Even if it's dangerous?" Bethanie worded her question carefully. "Even if we must step beyond the law?"

Mariah thought of Dusty's speech in the cabin when he told her he never wanted to see her again. Her mind clearly recalled the hatred that had been in his face. In a breath's length, Mariah envisioned his face as she'd last seen it, bloody and bruised. Her heart tore remembering the crimson stream dripping from his lips . . . the very lips that had kissed her with more passion than she'd ever known. She could almost hear him whispering his love for her.

Mariah jerked on her jacket with determination. "I'm going to help Dusty if there's any way in heaven, Mother. Even if it steps beyond the law."

Bethanie nodded toward Ruth as she pulled her coat on. "I left the old Colt for you if those two should wake up."

Ruth followed them to the porch. "I wouldn't want to shoot anyone, but I could sure club them with it if they so much as open an eye."

Bethanie and Mariah smiled at Ruth's ethics. They left the house just as the rain slowed to a pathetic spattering, but the air was soup-thick with moisture. They rode north toward town at a pace few men could have equaled.

As they neared the long string of buildings that marked the town, Bethanie pulled her horse in close beside Mariah. "I'll be with you whatever you do."

Mariah smiled. "Thanks."

The townspeople turned to stare at them as they rode down the street. By the time they reined up in front of the sheriff's office, there was a small parade behind them. A deputy, who came out to greet them, seemed hesitant to speak in front of the crowd.

"Sheriff's gone to get the judge. He'll be back in an hour." The deputy stammered while trying to manage the tobacco wad in his mouth.

Mariah walked up the steps with her mother only a few feet behind her. "We are here to nurse the prisoner."

The deputy hesitated.

Mariah lifted her stubborn chin. "Surely you're not afraid of two women?"

"No, but I thought the sheriff said you two would be staying at your ranch. Don't know if he'd like it none that you're here to nurse the prisoner." The deputy was having trouble making a decision. The more nervous he became, the more he chomped down on the huge brown mass of tobacco in his jaw. Finally he held his hand out and took Mariah's gun. "I reckon it's all right for one of you to go in. But jail ain't no place for a lady." He leaned sideways and spit a brown rainbow off the corner of the porch, sending several onlookers jumping backward in disgust.

Mariah took the medicine bag from her mother. She noticed Cain standing in the crowd. Her small army was all present. It was time for her to advance. Mariah turned to the deputy. "Now, may I pass before the prisoner's cuts get infected?"

The deputy snickered. "All right, but he ain't gonna be alive long enough to get no infection. He'll be swinging from a tree before the moon rises."

Mariah tried to ignore his comment as she marched inside. Her insides might be jumping like a jar full of red ants riding in the back of a buggy, but she would show no fear to this man.

The office was filled with cigar smoke and the smell of a few too many unwashed bodies. Coffee bubbled on a huge dilapidated Franklin stove in the center of the room. Cells lined the back wall with all the doors open except one. Mariah moved around the score of deputies to the one locked door. She stood on her tiptoes and pressed her face against the tiny window at the otherwise solid door.

At first she could see nothing in the dark hole except the smoky strands of light forming a triangle against one wall. The floor was covered with dirt and straw. A cot bordered the wall farthest from the light.

As her eyes adjusted to the light, she watched Dusty roll toward her on the cot. A small cut on his cheek was still bleeding, and his left eye was swollen almost closed. She saw no pleasure in his face as he looked at her, only pain.

The deputy unlocked the door and held it open for Mariah. "Don't try nothing funny, miss."

Mariah gave him a look she saved for the lowest of mankind. "I'll need clean, hot water," she ordered.

The deputy was used to taking orders. He nodded and locked her in the cell.

Mariah knelt beside Dusty. She pulled her riding gloves off and opened the medicine bag.

"Why did you come?" Dusty lay back and stared at the ceiling. "I thought you were safe back at the ranch."

Mariah spread ointment on a cloth and began treating Dusty's cut. Her actions were gentle, but her words were sharp. "We came to help."

"We?" Dusty turned toward her.

"Mother and I," Mariah whispered as a man opened the door and set a questionably clean bowl beside her.

Dusty closed his eyes and lay back. "Dear God, Bethanie is here. If I'm not hung tonight, Josh will kill me for putting the two of you in danger."

"You didn't put us into anything. We came on our own free will."

Dusty rolled to face her. "And your free will may be the death of you both. This is not a game we're playing in a schoolroom. The sheriff has gone to get the judge, who just happens to be at Mayson's house. It seems he's an old friend, and they were having some big meeting there this week."

Mariah ran her hand along Dusty's ribcage and felt his sharp intake of breath as she passed over two ribs. "Pull off your shirt," Mariah ordered as she dug into the bag.

Dusty leaned forward and pulled his shirt off without an argument. He seemed hard-pressed to keep his breathing steady as Mariah moved her hand along his ribs. "I don't think any bones are broken," she whispered only a few inches from him. "I think I need to wrap those bottom ribs."

She forced her eyes to stay on her task. She knew if she looked up, he would read her thoughts. The feel of his flesh sent heat through her body and centered in her cheeks. She could feel his warm breath in her hair.

As she rolled a strip of bandage around his lower chest, Dusty asked in a low voice. "Mariah, why did you come?"

"You were wrongly arrested and hurt," Mariah answered, trying not to let him know how much his nearness affected her. "I plan on being a doctor in two years. I can't bear to see someone suffer."

Pain reflected in Dusty's words. "Not even someone who kidnapped you and tried to rape you?"

Mariah looked into his golden-brown eyes. "Not even someone . . . who says he hates me and never wants to see me again."

The feeling that passed between them was as real as anything tangible in the room. Dusty didn't move toward her, but his eyes caressed her very soul. Mariah moved her hand lovingly back and forth along the bandage, feeling his heart pound beneath the dressing. No matter what had been said between them, no matter how far apart they were, what she felt for this one man could never be duplicated or contrived. She realized she loved him and would give her very life to help him.

Without breaking the spell, Dusty moved his hand up to touch her hair. His thoughts became words. "Mariah, you must go."

Mariah shook her head, brushing the side of his hand with her cheek. "I will not."

The guard rattled the lock before Dusty could say more.

Mariah stood and faced the guard. "He needs more medical attention. He needs to be moved to a doctor."

The deputy shook his head. "Ain't that much time. He'll be dancing in the air before dusk. The judge and Mr. Mayson arrived a few minutes ago and are setting up over in the saloon now." The deputy snickered. "I figure a trial like this ain't no place for ladies like your mother and you. I'm to keep you here till it's over." His head nodded uncontrollably as if he had some plans to keep them amused while everyone was at the trial.

Dusty followed Mariah a foot outside his cell door. As the deputy moved closer in alarm, Dusty caught Mariah's arm and swung her around into his embrace. Over her head, he spoke to the deputy. "Don't mind if I kiss a pretty girl good-bye do you, Smith?"

The deputy laughed and stepped back a few feet. "Well, be quick about it."

Dusty pulled Mariah into his arms with a sudden force, but there was no passion in his kiss. As his lips pressed against her mouth, she felt his hands slide to her gunbelt and pull her hips toward him.

When he broke the kiss, he moved to her ear and whispered, "Slap me hard, my love."

Mariah felt confused and embarrassed in front of the men. This was no last kiss from a man about to die.

When she didn't respond, Dusty bit down on her bottom lip and laughed as she jerked away in pain.

"What's the matter, my little spoiled brat? You never been kissed by a man before? I guess you'll cry rape again the minute I'm dead and name the bastard after me."

Anger boiled in Mariah as she heard the deputies in the room laugh at Dusty's crude remark. Her right hand was flying through the air before she thought. The slap she delivered seemed to be far more powerful than she intended, for Dusty staggered several feet across the room, almost colliding with the old stove and sending hot coffee in every direction.

She dropped her hands to her side in confusion at Dusty's strange behavior. Her fingers rested along empty slots in the gunbelt. Several bullets were missing. Understanding dawned on Mariah as she glanced toward the stove Dusty had almost fallen into. *The stove is full of bullets,* her mind shouted.

Mariah grabbed the medicine bag and stormed toward Dusty. Her face was frozen in anger as her heart laughed in hope over the reckless scheme Dusty was planning. As she neared, he backed away from her toward the front door. Mariah pushed at his chest with her finger, and he moved into the light. "You lying, no good ranch hand. What makes you think you have the right to kiss me? I'm not one of your stupid farm girls that you can kiss at will."

Mariah had backed Dusty to the door opening with

the deputies laughing at the lovers' quarrel they were watching.

"Sure you fight," Dusty yelled. "But you melt like butter when touched. Tell me, love, how often do you melt into the arms of others?"

"Why you lying . . ." Mariah froze as shots exploded from the office behind her. Men dove in every direction for cover as more shots followed, ringing off the walls of the sheriff's office.

Mariah felt Dusty pull her violently toward the horses Bethanie was still holding. He swung Bethanie onto her horse first and slapped the mount into action. Dusty climbed up behind Mariah just as men came running from the office yelling for them to stop. Within seconds, they were at full gallop three lengths behind Bethanie.

Bethanie led them past the general store which marked the corner of town. Mariah saw Cain step out from the shade of the last building and nod toward Bethanie as she rode by. His massive muscles strained as he shoved a wagon loaded down with supplies toward the center of the street. Dusty threaded the horse Mariah and he rode through the last free space before Cain closed the street to anyone who might follow.

Dusty reined the horse and leaned low to Cain. "There's a cabin along the far north ridge. Meet me there after dark with supplies."

Cain nodded as Dusty kicked the horse into full gallop trying to catch Bethanie.

They rode south until the sun began to set, then they doubled back north. Dusty led them over the rocky slopes and through swollen streams in an effort to prevent anyone from following.

As they slowed through a ravine to rest the horses, Dusty held his hand out to Bethanie. "Bethanie," he whispered as dearly as one might call out the name Mother. "Bethanie, you are more beautiful than you were before you left here. You still ride a horse with the stamina of a drover and the grace of a lady. Glad as I am to see you, I wish you were safely back in Colorado."

Bethanie smiled at the touch of little boy she would always see in this man. "Cain wired me. I had to come."

Mariah asked, "Why? Because I was planning to sell the ranch?"

"No," Bethanie answered. "That would be between the two of you. I came for another reason. Dusty will remember my uncle in San Antonio. Cain heard word he is back in Texas. I understand he is sick and dying, but he may still be evil enough to try and do harm."

Dusty's hold around Mariah's waist tightened slightly as he explained. "Wilbur's his name. He's Allison's father, but Mike ran him off years ago. The way I remember him, a lower lying thief never lived."

"True." Bethanie released Dusty's hand. "But I must ask him one question. He's the only man alive who knows where my father might be. I've denied it all my life, even to Josh, but there has always been a tiny need in me to know if the man who caused my mother a life of pain is still alive."

Mariah wanted to ask her mother so many questions, but now was not the time. She could tell by the pain in her mother's voice that Bethanie had never quite recovered from her childhood as an outcast. She understood why Bethanie was so protective, and loved her mother for it even though she didn't always understand.

Dusty fell back into the shadows behind Bethanie's horse as they headed north once more, slowly letting the horses pick their way by moonlight over the uneven ground. Mariah cradled into his arms.

"Where will you go?" she whispered, knowing her mother was too far ahead of them to overhear.

"I could go to my cabin behind the main house. I'd

probably be safe there, but it might mean putting you in more danger."

Dusty moved his hand under her coat. He slowly brushed his fingers over the silk of her blouse. Mariah leaned closer and turned her face until she could brush her lips against his throat. Dusty moaned slightly and moved his hand up to touch the material over one of her breasts. His action fueled a fire in Mariah that had been burning since the night he'd first kissed her.

Dusty's voice was thick with passion. "Maybe I'll go west into the territories. Will you go with me if I ask you, Mariah?" As he spoke, his fingers parted her blouse and moved in under the material to touch her bare flesh.

A thousand conflicts battled one another in her mind, but her heart would let her give only one answer. "Yes," Mariah whispered, "I'll go with you."

Dusty turned her slightly and lightly kissed her lips. "I love you too much to ask you." His voice broke slightly. "I have to go alone."

Chapter Twenty-seven

Night blanketed the Texas landscape in black frosty wool. Bethanie watched as Dusty helped Mariah down from the horse. By the time he turned to assist Bethanie, she was already standing beside her mount. The night seemed fluid with sounds. Ruth's stories of a madman slaughtering Weston cattle for no apparent reason filled Bethanie's thoughts now. A man strong enough to slit a knife deep into a cow's throat would make quick work of two women traveling through the darkness.

"Did you hear anyone following us?" she whispered.

"No." Dusty's voice matched Bethanie's low tone. "But the ground is so soft with rain, they could be half a mile back and we wouldn't hear 'em."

Bethanie unbuckled the gunbelt. "Dusty, take this." She handed him the holster, knowing he'd need the weapon more than she would. She pulled a rifle from its sheath on her saddle. The metal barrel made a swishing sound against the leather-fringed casing. The sound echoed and joined with the wind as it rustled the dew-thickened leaves.

Bethanie watched as Dusty's shadowy figure led the horses between nearby cottonwoods. He drew his Colt and silently moved toward the cabin in the center of the small clearing. Smoke twisted from the chimney, rooting its way into the heavy, foggy sky. No other life seemed near. Bethanie held her breath, for this might yet prove a trap. She edged nearer to her daughter.

Bethanie swelled with pride as she watched Mariah standing erect in the face of danger. Mariah carried a rifle over one bent arm with the cool caution her father might have shown in danger. There was a Weston breeding of strength in Mariah that would allow her no show of fear, yet, as her mother, Bethanie could see Mariah bite the corner of her lip in worry.

Dusty reached the edge of the planked porch just as the cabin door swung open with a bang. A huge shadow blocked the firelight's exit into the blackness. Both women released entrapped air in relief as Cain searched the darkness for visitors.

"Cain!" Mariah exclaimed as Dusty lowered his gun. Bethanie stepped back to claim her medicine bag as Mariah hurried toward Cain and the safety he offered. Bethanie smiled. Mariah was a headstrong and self-assured woman. She bore none of Bethanie's hesitance or fear of life.

Cain sighed with relief. "Get yourself in here, girl, before you catch your death of cold. I got a good fire going and coffee boiling." He moved toward Bethanie and the horses. "I'll feed the horses. You go on in and warm up."

Bethanie nodded toward Cain as he took the reins from her cold fingers. He always seemed to be there, ready to help. He divided his time between Mariah and her, but Bethanie knew he usually went with Mariah because he felt Bethanie would want him to. Many times over the years she'd tried to remember something she'd done to earn such undying devotion, but she could think of nothing. Bethanie patted his shoulder gently, the only gesture of warmth he'd ever allowed from anyone except Mariah.

Cain accepted her action with a stiff nod. "I'll stay on

the porch and keep an eye out while you rest a few minutes. Ruth posted a man on the ridge by the ranch. If
riders come near the ranch, he'll fire three shots. I'll stay
out here in case they come from the other direction."

Bethanie moved toward the house with a tired body
and an aching heart. She knew they must make plans,
yet all the alternatives looked bleak. If they tried to fight,
Dusty might be dead before all the facts were known. If
he ran, he'd be a wanted man the rest of his life. She'd
seen a few men in the mining towns who were on the
run. They were always in a hurry to move on and jumped
at every sound. She couldn't bear to think of Dusty as
never being able to settle down. If he ran, he'd forever
be an outcast. She fought back tears as she moved inside,
suddenly wishing Josh were with her.

The cabin was little more than a line shack, probably
used only during roundup. They would be safe here for
an hour, maybe two.

Dusty handed Bethanie a cup of coffee. She looked
up into his strong face. She hadn't seen him in years,
yet she knew he wasn't the type of man to shoot Elliot
Mayson in cold blood. Her mind turned back in time to
those days when she'd tutored Dusty. The lovable, scruffy
boy had vanished and long ago been replaced by the
strong, handsome man before her. He was tall, with lean-
hard muscles from spending hours each day in the saddle.
His hair was a little longer than stylish, with sunbleached
strands, and his eyes had a mature wisdom in their
golden depths that could have developed only through
years of making his own decisions. Something about the
stubborn set of his jaw reminded her of Ben.

Dusty smiled at Bethanie and gestured toward Mariah.
"The squirrel turned out all right, didn't she?"

Bethanie's laughter relieved some of the tension in her
tired body. "Yes. She's quite a headstrong woman. Has

she told you she'd planning on going to medical school even against my advice?"

"All I knew until today was she wanted to sell the ranch. It makes sense she would want to heal people, third generation. Your mother healed Josh during the war, you saved my life after the Indian attack, and now Mariah. I only wish she'd told me the reason she needed money earlier."

Dusty moved behind Mariah and placed his hands lovingly on her shoulders. Bethanie admired his unembarrassed show of caring. He looked at Bethanie over Mariah's head and added, "Mariah is Weston born and bred, so she can handle medical school."

Mariah twisted in his hold. "Stop talking about me as if I'm some dim-witted little sister who can't follow the conversation, or I'll put your only good eye out of commission." Mariah brushed her fingers lovingly over Dusty's bruised cheek. "And while we're talking for once, let me make one thing clear to you, Mr. Barfield. I don't have to explain my actions to you or anyone else. But, when I have tried, I seem to remember you as a poor listener."

Dusty groaned and pulled her hand to his chest. Though his words were cold, his hand spread her fingers caressingly over his heart. "It's too bad, along with Ben's courage and Bethanie's beauty, you couldn't have inherited some of Ruth's silence."

Passion and anger were warring across Mariah's face. "Too bad you've lived with cows so long you don't know how to carry on a conversation. I would gladly have told you about medical school if you'd have given me the time, but you were too busy second-guessing me." Mariah pulled away from his touch.

"Second-guessing you? The only thing I can depend on you doing, Mariah, is doubling up that fist every time you get angry." Dusty's knuckles were white as they gripped his gunbelt to keep from reaching out for Mariah. "I pity the man who's stuck with you. He'll need your medical attention after every fight."

"And I feel sorry for the woman who marries you. She'll be talking to walls for company in less than a month." Mariah turned her back to Dusty and moved closer to the fire, but not before Bethanie saw a tear sparkle from her daughter's cheek.

Bethanie could just imagine what the past few days at the ranch must have been like between these two. Mariah would always give as much as she took in love as well as a war, and certainly both were thick in the air between them. Bethanie interrupted. "We haven't got much time. It won't take the sheriff long to round up enough men. Most will follow our trail south, but a few may double back thinking we've tricked them."

Dusty nodded and slowly moved to stand behind Mariah. She stiffened as he touched her shoulders, but she didn't pull away. Dusty directed his words more to himself than to the women. "We can ride down to the ranch house, and I'll leave you two there. I can take the back trail up the ridge and head north to Fort Worth. I know a few Frenchmen who might help me get lost."

Mariah shook her head. "You can't just run. We've got to stand and fight. You can clear yourself in time."

"That's just it." Dusty kicked at the fire with his boot. "I haven't got time. If I stay, there will be a fight, and men on both the Mayson and Weston ranch will die. If I'm caught, they'll hang me on the spot without a trial, not that one would help much with Judge Carr on the bench."

Bethanie paced the dusty floor. "Josh should be on his way here by now. I wouldn't be surprised if he took the next train out after reading the note I left him. I would have waited for him, but I was afraid my uncle would be gone before I got a chance to talk with him. I have to ask Uncle Wilbur one question." Bethanie rubbed her forehead, pushing a strand of golden-red hair away from her face. "Josh still has friends in Texas. He can investigate, then set up a fair trial."

"Maybe." Dusty shrugged. "By tomorrow morning I'll have a price on my head, dead or alive. My only chance is to get to Fort Worth fast. There's a little French settlement not far from there called Dallas. The folks are mostly artists, scientists, and tradesmen. I've heard that they'll hire anyone who knows anything about ranching and farming to teach them. They set up a new camp last summer across the Trinity River. I could get lost there and still be close to home."

Mariah stood. "I'll go with you," she stated firmly.

Dusty's face reflected Bethanie's shock at Mariah's statement. He cupped Mariah's chin in his palm, a slow smile spreading across his lips. Their angry words seemed forgotten as their world narrowed to include only each other.

Bethanie didn't move a muscle. She wanted to cry out for her daughter to stay and be safe, but suddenly, more than ever before, she realized Mariah must make her own choices. As her mother, all Bethanie could do was stand beside her decision.

Dusty drew Mariah into his arms and held her tightly. "No, darling," he whispered. "No. I can't take you into danger, even though the thought of you by my side is intoxicating."

"I am going with you!" Mariah pushed away from him slightly.

"No. There are things that must be done no matter how two people feel about each other. I couldn't put you in danger. It would tear away at the very rules I believe in. No matter how we feel about each other, we must think before we act."

Bethanie turned to face the windows as Dusty's words

tore at her heart. She understood Mariah's sobs, for she had cried at almost the same words once spoken to her twenty years ago. Josh had broken her heart with his words of honor, yet she knew she wouldn't have loved him so deeply if he'd shown less strength. Bethanie only prayed Mariah would have the understanding it had taken herself years to develop.

Before Bethanie had time to say any words of comfort, Cain opened the door. His tone was as cold as the air he let into the tiny room. "Riders coming from the north."

Dusty headed toward the door. "Let's race for the ranch. I can hide in the cabin, then take the back path over the ridge."

Bethanie hurried to the porch. "Mariah, take my horse. You'll make better time riding single. We'll slow them down as much as we can. When they've gone, I'll return to the ranch house with Cain."

Mariah nodded, and she climbed into the saddle. Tears stained her cheeks. "Be careful, Mother."

"I'll be with Cain" was Bethanie's only reply. She knew Mariah and Dusty needed a few minutes alone to say their goodbyes. She watched as Dusty and Mariah moved silently down the ravine to the south of the cabin. The mud muffled the sound of their horses' hooves. They would be a mile or more away before the men, arriving from the north, could thread their way through the trees to the cabin.

Bethanie returned to the house and sat down to wait by the fireplace. She pillowed her head against the warm leather medicine bag and watched as Cain paced back and forth on the porch. The minutes dragged by and Bethanie's eyelids grew heavy. She hadn't slept on the train ride last night, and today had been endless. In her tired mind, her surroundings and her dream danced together as one. Slowly nightmare blended with reality, and they were one. She was a child again in a tiny cabin. She could hear horses coming and men shouting . . . yelling something she couldn't understand. She saw the shadow of a man walk in front of the windows as other men with torches rode up to her house. The men were arguing with the shadow on the porch. In her dream, Bethanie knew they were yelling at her father. She climbed down from the huge bed.

Bethanie jerked awake as a round of gunfire shattered her nightmare and brought her to reality. She ran to the door to see men on horseback surrounding the porch. Every other man carried a torch and all had their guns pointed toward her. She recognized the deputy whom Dusty had called Smith and a tall, thin man wearing black. The thin man might be twenty years older than the last time she'd seen him, but his snakelike quality had not mellowed. Bethanie would have known Wes Mayson even if he had been farther into the shadows with the rest of the men.

Bethanie glanced around in panic looking for Cain. It took endless seconds for her to realize that the crumpled dark form on the steps was Cain's body. Bethanie ran toward him in blind outrage as several of the men dismounted.

The deputy's whine sounded in the darkness. "I told him to identify himself. What was I supposed to do? Wait around all day for him to speak up?"

One of the men moved up behind Bethanie. "Hell, Smith, I don't think the bastard was even armed." He squatted beside Bethanie, showing only mild interest. "Is he dead?"

Bethanie ran her fingers along Cain's scarred throat. The pulse was weak, but steady. "He's still alive. Get him inside." Her hands were shaking as she pulled at his side to lift him and felt warm blood run over her fingers. Cain's blood.

Several men moved closer, offering reluctant assistance. They carried Cain into the cabin and laid him on the dirt-covered floor. Bethanie was so upset, she barely noticed several men shuffling into the cabin, watching like a gallery at a school play. She laid her rifle beside Cain and tried to remember what to do to help him. Tears flooded her vision as she examined his wound.

In the firelight she could see blood oozing from a wide hole just above Cain's belt buckle.

"It's a gut wound," someone said as Bethanie tried to push Cain's blood back into his body with her hands, but there was no way to stop the flow of his life slipping through her fingers.

She knew there was little she could do for a bullet to the stomach. There was little anyone could do. All the times this man had saved her life came flooding into her mind. For almost twenty years he'd been there as a strong wall against harm's way.

Mayson's black boots appeared at her side. "Sorry about your hired hand, ma'am, but we're in search of a man who killed my son. You left town with him a few hours ago, so where is he?"

"He's not here," Bethanie answered as she pulled a bandage from her medicine bag.

Mayson turned and gave orders for everyone to search the area. A few minutes later when Bethanie raised her head, only Mayson, Smith, the sheriff, and a large man dressed in a heavy fur-lined coat remained in the room.

Smith patted his gun handle. "Whata we goin' ta do about this man, Mr. Mayson?"

Bethanie turned in anger. Her voice was low and cold as ice. "I'll see you're tried for murder if he dies, so you had better pray he lives."

The sheriff shook his head. "He ain't going to live. He's gut shot, lady. He'll be dead before we could get him on a horse."

Smith began sweating like a wool-clad pig in summer. "I'm not gonna go to jail for killing nobody. It were just an accident, like this morning.

Bethanie sensed the deputy had said more than he meant to and faced the whining fool. "What accident this morning?"

The deputy darted a hesitant glance at Mayson. Smith was mindless with fright at his slip of the tongue. "I didn't know Elliot Mayson would be wearin' Dusty's slicker. It was raining, and Dusty and Elliot looked the same from a distance."

"Shut up, you fool!" the sheriff yelled as he slammed his rifle butt into the deputy's face.

The sound of cracking teeth ground with the deputy's high-pitched whimper.

Bethanie looked toward Mayson and saw no surprise in his face. The deputy's confession was no revelation to this cold, power-hungry man. He wanted Dusty dead. She knew without asking that he'd ordered Dusty shot this morning. When that hadn't worked out, the next plan must have been to blame Elliot's shooting on Dusty. Either way, Dusty was a dead man and Mayson moved in on the Weston Ranch.

Mayson looked down at her with eyes incapable of anything other than greed. "The question appears to be, Mrs. Weston, now what do we do with you? You know too much ever to be allowed to leave this cabin."

The dark form wearing a heavy coat moved into the circle of light from the fireplace. Bethanie caught her breath in her throat as she recognized the aging face of her uncle. His features were twisted now, reflecting the evil life he had lived. His skin was pale, almost transparent with poor health. A cancer sore crawled up his neck and onto his face like a weed growing just under the skin. He had the look of a man who walked only one step ahead of death and who was tiring from the constant effort. Even though the room was warm, he hugged his coat as if his body could no longer hold any heat.

"Bethanie." Wilbur's voice was raspy. "I've waited a long time to see you again." His watery eyes traveled over her, tickling her flesh like a hundred tiny spiders.

Bethanie was no longer the child who cowered at his lusting stares. "Wilbur," she answered. "Hell must have spit you out from the looks of you. Not even the devil could stand the stench of your evil soul."

Wilbur laughed. "I'll live long enough to see you dead, my girl. You see, you have no Weston men around to protect you. They were fools anyway. Even when I told them you were a worthless bastard child, they both took turns marrying you. Tell me, my little niece, did they take turns bedding you also?" His laughter was cruel. "I thought you might have enough passion for the cripple, but never for the younger man. Did he leave you, and that's why you came crawling back to Texas?"

Bethanie stood and straightened her shoulders. "You are the reason I came back to Texas," she answered. "I have heard you know of my father."

Wilbur laughed again and moved closer. "I haven't heard from him in twenty years. He's dead by now, no doubt of some disease your whoring mother gave him."

As Wilbur grabbed for Bethanie, a shot rang out through the cabin. Wilbur jerked backward in pain. Blood seemed to explode across his chest. He pulled at his coat as if for protection from the pain. Life passed from his eyes even before his body hit the floor. His large form jerked once in reflex action before flattening into a pool of his own blood.

Bethanie pulled her gaze away from Wilbur's body and looked behind her. Cain lowered the rifle back beside him where Bethanie had placed it.

Cain's words were a whisper, but they resounded off

the walls of Bethanie's mind. "No man talks of Mary like that . . . and lives."

The way he said her mother's name was like a prayer on his lips. The pieces of her life's puzzle began to fall into place around her. Tears clouded her eyes, and she moved to cradle his head in her lap. "You knew my mother," she whispered, her tears raining on his face. She didn't care that Wilbur died without telling her about her father. Her heart had reasoned out the answer the moment Cain spoke her mother's name.

"I knew her . . . loved her," Cain answered. "One night men came to burn us out. I stood before them without a gun. They couldn't kill me so they burned a torch into my face . . . threw me into the river for dead." He gulped, fighting to make the words come out above his pain. "I lay near death for months miles downriver. When I could walk, I thought she would never want to see me again. I tried . . . to run from this face and the pain I had caused her, but I could never run far enough. When I came back it was too late, she had taken you and moved. I followed, but always too late . . . till Texas."

Bethanie held Cain to her. Even through her tears she could see the life slowly leaving his body. "Why?" she cried. "Why didn't you ever tell me?"

Cain raised his huge hand to her face. "I had to . . . earn your love," he whispered. "A man never had a finer daughter. Every time I watched you care for the sick or sing an old Shaker song to your children, I was a little nearer to my Mary. I could have asked for no greater life."

"Father," Bethanie cried as she cradled his head in her arms. A loud thud sounded at the door, as if a log had been wedged to keep it closed. She looked up to find Mayson and Smith gone. She smelled kerosene, and in an instant knew what was happening. "Father!" she cried again. "They're burning the cabin."

Cain's face was pale. He barely had the energy to open his eyes. "Run, Bethanie. You must . . . back window. Run!"

"No!" Bethanie cried as his dying breath blended with the words in the nightmare that had haunted her all her life.

A torch flashed like a flaming comet, then hit the porch. Another followed in repetition. The old wood caught fire like straw. Bethanie clutched Cain's head to her like a frightened child. His hand fell lifeless to the floor. She knew he was dead, but she couldn't let go. She'd wanted her father all her life, and now she learned he'd always been at her side. There were so many things she wanted to say to him, so many words that needed to be said. She wanted to be a little girl again and have both a mother and a father to love her. She wanted to tell him that her mother never stopped loving him all her life . . . as he'd never stopped loving Mary.

Flames licked the windows and the room grew bright as day, but still Bethanie would not let her father go.

The nightmare seemed clearer now. Her mind had refused to remember the night her father left, and her mother would never talk of it. Bethanie's mind whirled with a thousand questions. Why had her mother never spoken of him? Why had Mary run from the house that night and not stayed with her husband if she loved him so much?

Bethanie heard crackling above her as the roof caught fire. The noise seemed to crystallize the answer in her mind. Her mother had run into the woods that night with Bethanie, for the same reason she had hid in the cave with Mariah.

For the same reason she must run tonight. For her children!

Bethanie kissed her father's lifeless cheek farewell. She moved her hand along his scarred face and didn't feel the deformed skin. "Good-bye, Father," she whispered.

Without looking back, Bethanie crawled across the floor to the back room that was little more than a shed built onto the one-room cabin. She pulled her coat over her hair as part of the roof fell.

Silently, Bethanie slid through the window and rolled onto the ground. The fire noisily gobbled up any sound she might have made. She scrambled to her feet and ran down the ravine toward the cottonwoods growing at the bottom.

Darkness engulfed her and she stumbled. Bethanie felt herself falling, falling into the blackness.

Chapter Twenty-eight

Mariah followed Dusty through the ravine for half a mile. The night was almost black with clouds bubbling like dark molasses across the sky. At times she had to follow him by the soft murmur of hooves in front of her. The cottonwood and elm trees reached for her in the darkness, trying to pull Mariah's tired body from the horse.

Finally Dusty began to climb out of the muddy, wooded area. "We'll be home in a few minutes," he whispered back to her. "The man on the ridge has spotted us by now. He would have fired if it wasn't safe to move in."

Mariah nodded. All their problems kept rumbling through her mind. Right now nothing sounded better than "being home in a few minutes." As soon as she spotted the tiny light of the Weston Ranch, Mariah broke into full gallop, with Dusty close behind her.

They reached the porch just as the door swung open and Josh Weston ran out, flanked by two sons already almost his height. Mariah bolted from her mount and flew into the arms of her family.

Laughing, Mariah turned toward Dusty. She didn't miss his slightly raised eyebrow as he looked from one of the younger men to the other. "Dusty, I'd like you to meet two of my brothers, Mark and Luke."

Dusty looked relieved and hurried forward with a handshake.

Mariah nestled under Josh's open arm as her middle brothers introduced themselves to Dusty. They looked so much like Josh, she couldn't believe Dusty wouldn't have known who they were on sight. Matthew, the oldest, might be content to study and read, and John, the youngest, was always off doing his own thing; but she would have bet money that the two middle brothers, Mark and Luke, would be with Josh. The two were at that awkward age between boys and men, but they never lacked for adventure in their souls.

"How are you, Mariah?" Josh asked as he squeezed her shoulder. He was a handsome man with silver-gray sideburns and tanned smile lines around his mouth. She could hear the touch of worry in his tone as he searched the darkness for his wife.

"Mother is at the cabin on the north ridge." Mariah watched as her words saddened his face. "With Cain," she added, knowing her last words would ease his mind. Josh had been a wonderful father to her for as long as she could remember, but his thoughts were always with Bethanie.

Dusty pulled free from the boys and turned to face Josh. "It's good to see you again," he said simply as the two men shook hands.

Josh smiled. "It's been a long time since you blackmailed me into taking you out of San Antonio, kid."

Dusty pushed his hair to one side of his forehead. "Appears I'm in trouble again. When I left San Antonio, I had nothing to lose." Dusty looked at Mariah, and Josh would've had to have been blind not to see the warmth in Dusty's eyes. "I wish I had time to stay and visit, but I've got some hard riding to do tonight. Mariah can tell you the details while I go pack a saddlebag."

"Ruth already told me what happened." Josh touched

Dusty's shoulder. "We'll get this straightened out, but i
may take a few days."

"I'll keep in touch." Without another word, Dusty
moved away from the house toward his place out back

Josh leaned against the porch post as he stared out ir
the direction of the north cabin.

Mariah kissed Josh on the cheek. "I have to talk to
Dusty."

Josh nodded, only half listening, and Mariah slipped
into the shadows to follow Dusty.

She caught up with him in the clearing by the water
fall. "Dusty, please don't go." Her cry was almos
drowned out by the falling water.

Dusty turned to face her, but his features were in shad
ows. "I have to, Mariah."

"Then let me go with you?"

"No."

"But . . ." Frustration and anger boiled in her vein:
at the helplessness of the situation. He had done nothing
wrong, yet he was being hunted like an animal. She
wanted to strike out at the world, but instead suddenly
began pounding on Dusty's chest with her fists.

Dusty grabbed her wrists and pulled her close to him
She could feel his body through her clothes as he molded
to her. "No argument, Mariah. Something tells me you've
gotten everything you've ever asked for, but not this time.'

"I'm not spoiled. You see only the part of me you
want to see."

"Like hell you're not. I remember when you were two
you already had everyone wrapped around your finger
including me."

Mariah knew part of what he said was true. She'd had
an easy life, surrounded by people who loved her. Maybe
as a doctor, she could pay everyone back for the kindness
she'd known all her life.

"Let's not argue, Dusty. This mess will be cleared

p in a few days, and I don't want to be sorry for what
said to you in anger." Mariah ran her fingers into his
air and pulled his face down close to hers. "I don't
want you to go without saying one thing to you." Her
ips were almost touching his mouth.

"Don't say anything, Mariah." Dusty could stand the
nearness of her no longer. He lowered his lips to Mariah's
nd kissed her with all the tenderness in his soul.

When he was able to, he whispered against her moist,
rembling lips. "Say no words of anger or of love,
Mariah. It would make it harder for me to leave. Only
et me hold you one more time and dream as I have since
he moment I saw you that you are mine."

Mariah pulled his mouth to her lips and kissed him
gain. She loved him and would all her life. Her actions
would tell him, if her words could not. There was no
holding back with this man, in anger or in love.

Neither reacted for a moment after they heard Josh
shout. His cry seemed unreal in the damp night air. Dusty
umped first, pulling Mariah toward the house before she
ealized what was happening.

"Fire at the north cabin!" Josh shouted as Dusty came
round the corner of the house.

"Mother!" Mariah screamed.

Josh's features tightened. "Luke! Saddle the horses
ast. Mark! Roust the men out of the bunkhouse. Mariah!
Bring blankets in case anyone's hurt."

Dusty ran to his horse with Josh only a step behind
him. Josh grabbed Dusty's shoulder just before he
mounted. "Dusty, everyone within thirty miles will see
he fire . . . including the posse."

"I don't care." Dusty jerked free of Josh's hold. "I've
got to go."

Josh nodded and mounted the horse Mariah had ridden
earlier. Both men were at full gallop within seconds.

They had disappeared into the darkness before Mariah and her brothers had time to carry out Josh's orders.

Mariah rode toward the burning cabin with dread welling in her heart. Her mother or Cain might be in the fire! Dusty might be caught! Her father and brothers were riding toward unknown danger! And why? For what? Had she somehow brought all this on, or had it been simmering for the past twenty years and finally tonight the kettle was boiling over?

Mariah saw Josh and Dusty's horses, but no others. If the posse had been at the cabin, there was no sign of them now. She slowed her horse to a walk as the smoldering hull of the cabin came into view. Smoke thickened the air, burning her eyes and lungs, but still she edged nearer. The tiny cabin was now a gray skeleton of slow-burning logs. Most of the roof still stood, crackling against the low clouds as it continued to burn. Mariah squinted and made out the shadowy forms of two men standing within the flickering boundaries of the cabin. They were dragging something out into the clearing. Something that was smoking like a live coal and filling the air with the sickening smell of burning flesh. Mariah had helped her mother nurse burn victims and knew the smell the instant it reached her. The horrible odor of charred bodies.

Josh and Dusty dropped the huge bundle of black onto the wet grass as Mark, Luke and Mariah reached them. "Who . . . ?" Mariah couldn't bring herself to finish the question. She was suddenly thankful it was night. Mark raked a blanket over the wet grass, then covered the body with the damp wool.

"We found two bodies." Dusty pulled Mariah into his arms, both giving and needing strength. "Both were men but burned too bad to recognize. I think this is Cain. I remember his belt buckle being big and square. He was burned beyond telling much else."

"No!" Mariah screamed as she pulled away from Dusty. She dropped to her knees beside her brothers and cried softly. The words Cain had told her many times over the years drifted into her mind. "Mourning should be done when a person is born to this world, not when he leaves it for a better place." Mariah knew her cries were for her loss of Cain, for he was finally at that place he'd longed to go.

The incandescent flames of the cabin danced like ghostly shadows around Mariah. The roof creaked and began to crumble like a poorly built child's toy. Mariah turned and saw Josh running toward the fire. "Bethanie!" he shouted.

"No!" Dusty yelled and grabbed Josh, twisting him around just before he reached the steps. "Josh, she's not in there."

The roof crumbled, sending sparks and smoke flying everywhere. Josh jerked free of Dusty. "Where is she?" he shouted, his normally rational mind shattering into the edge of insanity. He was always in control, always a leader, but not now, not with his wife missing.

Dusty shouted above the arriving ranch hands. "Maybe whoever started the fire took her. Maybe she ran away." He yelled at his men. "Spread out and look for Mrs. Weston. If she's here, she couldn't have gone far on foot."

Josh nodded as he pulled himself together. He took a deep breath and drew on his years of wisdom. "Dusty's right, boys," he said to his sons. "I know your mother, and she would have found a way out if there was one." His mind was in full control now as he reasoned while he talked. "She couldn't have come out the front with the door blocked, so I'll check the back. Fire two shots in the air when you find her." There was no "if" in his order, for Josh knew he would keep looking until he found her.

* * *

Bethanie could hear someone calling her name from far away. She rolled her aching head back and forth in the wet grass. She opened her eyes but the world was just as black as with them closed. "Josh," she whispered. "Josh."

From nowhere Josh's arms were around her, holding her tightly to him. "Bethanie." He knelt on the muddy bank and pulled her close. "Are you all right?"

Bethanie held on to the man she had loved for so many years. There were no arms that would ever feel as welcoming as his. The familiar smell of him encircled her and drew her as it had all those years ago in the darkness of the cave. She could feel his strong hands moving along her body in a caring, searching action.

"I'm only bruised, Josh. I'm fine." Her words relaxed his body beside her as he pulled her even closer to him and buried his face in her tousled hair.

Josh cradled her head to his chest as he raised his gun and fired two shots into the air. Bethanie didn't have to ask why. She'd heard the code used many times with Josh and his sons when they were looking for something or someone.

Josh returned his Colt to its holster and held her so tightly she could hardly breathe.

After a long silence, he whispered into her hair. "Bethanie, I was so afraid I'd lost you." He covered her face with kisses. "Once I would have given anything to spend a year of my life at your side. Now, after all these years, I know not a year, not ten, not a lifetime will be enough. The day I die I'll curse the world for not having more time with you."

"I know, Josh. I feel the same way." Bethanie would never tire of this man and his love.

"What happened back at the cabin? I was so worried you might be inside."

"Josh, Cain's body is still inside. He died of a gunshot wound before the cabin was set on fire." Bethanie forced out the final words. "He's my father."

"I know, darling. He begged me once never to tell you."

A sudden anger flavored her words. "But I was his daughter!"

Josh's answer came slowly, as though he'd dreaded this time for years. "I gave my word. He never asked me for another thing more than to keep his secret. I had to honor his wish. You'll never know how often I wanted to tell you, but it was enough for him just to be near you. He loved you and Mariah so deeply he couldn't risk bringing up the past."

Bethanie brushed Josh's cheek in the darkness. She'd known him too many years to question his code of honor now. If he'd given his word to Cain, he had to keep it.

She closed her eyes, speaking her thoughts aloud. "When I think of all the years I hated him for leaving my mother and he was right beside me, always protecting, always caring."

"You and the children were a great pride to him. He wouldn't have wanted life any other way. We never talked of it, even when alone, but I could see the wealth you brought him in his eyes every time he looked at you or Mariah."

"Now he's dead." Bethanie fought back a sob. "Smith and Mayson killed him. They think they burned me in the fire."

"But why?"

"I know that Smith killed Elliot Mayson. He meant to kill Dusty, but shot the wrong man. Cain and I heard him confess to the murder."

"We'll get you back to the ranch and send for the

district marshal and any Rangers in the area. They'll straighten this mess out. By tomorrow we'll have this cleared up, and I'll see both Smith and Wes Mayson behind bars."

Josh pulled Bethanie to her feet and under his protective arm just as Mark and Luke came sliding down the incline. They almost knocked their parents over trying to keep from falling face first into the muddy gully.

Josh might grumble at them to be more careful, but Bethanie could only hug them both over and over as they moved back to the fire. They were her sons, her touch of immortality. Cain and Mary would live on forever as long as they had children and grandchildren.

Josh seemed to understand her need to wrap into her quiet world. He sent the boys back to the ranch and moved away to make sure the fire was under control. Bethanie went to where Mariah knelt beside Cain's body.

Mariah held her hand out to her mother. "I can't believe he's gone."

"I know," Bethanie answered as she lay a hand on top of Mariah's head. "Before he died, Cain told me he was my father." She looked away from the dark mass on the ground. "All these years and I never knew."

Mariah touched the blanket covering Cain's body. "He was my grandfather." Her voice broke at her final word.

"He had his reasons for never telling us," Bethanie whispered more to herself than Mariah.

"I could have loved him no more if I'd known." Mariah kissed her fingers, then spread them over the wool. "Good night, Grandfather. May you rest this night in peace."

Mariah stood and hugged her mother. "We all loved him so much. I've grown up feeling him near. I still feel him near."

Bethanie allowed tears to roll down her cheeks unchecked. "I do, too, darling. I do, too."

Mariah kissed her mother's damp cheek. "I'll go back with the boys and get everything ready. As soon as they get the casket made, I'll put it in the main room until dawn."

Bethanie nodded and warmed with pride at the way her daughter lifted responsibility from her own shoulders. She watched her children ride away. As they passed into the shadows, Bethanie found herself talking mentally to Cain. We did a good job on those kids, she thought. I couldn't have done it without you.

Bethanie had no idea how long she sat beside the blanketed body, but gradually she became aware of Josh standing behind her. The night had grown colder, and the fire was only a few crackling embers. When she turned, Josh whispered, "We must go. The men will be here soon with a wagon."

Bethanie nodded and stood. "I was just thinking of how lucky I've been. All my life I've felt sorry for myself for not having two parents. It turns out I've had one with me almost all the time.

"I'll miss him so much," Bethanie added. "But, like Mariah, I think it will be a long time before I quit looking around and expecting to see him behind me."

"He'll still be there in spirit."

"Maybe he will," Bethanie said with a smile.

Josh offered his arm to her, and they walked slowly toward the horses. They rode in silence back to the house. The ranch came into view just as the wind whipped predawn chill into the night air. All the windows were dark, but a lamp had been left burning by the barn door for their return.

Josh lifted his tired wife down from her saddle. Bethanie laughed as he groaned playfully in an effort to lighten her mood. "Better put me down, old man, you might hurt yourself."

"Old man, is it?" Josh chuckled. "When I get this mud off us both, I'll show you how old I am."

"You're not as young as you once were, and from the look I saw in Dusty and Mariah's eyes, it won't be a year before you're a grandfather."

Josh whispered, "And you'll be the most desirable grandmother in the West."

Bethanie laughed. "Aren't you surprised about Mariah finally finding a man to equal her spunk?"

"No." Josh nibbled at Bethanie's neck. "I'm only surprised you finally slipped. You said grandfather instead of great-uncle."

"But you said it didn't matter?"

"It doesn't really. I've always known she was mine."

Chapter Twenty-nine

They buried Cain in the Weston family lot just after dawn. The wind blew crisply out of the north as the family gathered around the grave. The sun was coming up warm, and within a few hours would rob the earth of its moisture. The mourners were all dressed in riding clothes, and all the men wore gunbelts strapped across their waists. Cain might never have worn a gun, but his murderers were still at large. Riders were stationed along the ridge to ensure the family's grief was uninterrupted.

A cross marker lay on the ground beside the open grave. The carving read simply, "Cain, beloved father and grandfather."

Josh stood at the foot of the grave with Bethanie at his side. Mariah cried softly, holding onto Dusty's arm as Josh read the final words from the Bible.

Bethanie stared dry-eyed at the coffin even after the others moved away.

Josh put his arm around her shoulder. "Are you all right?"

"I was just thinking that this is the way Cain would have wanted it. He could never have lived with himself if he'd had to bury Mariah or me. The only other choice was this. I'll miss him, but they're together now." Bethanie said.

"Who?" Josh asked.

"My parents."

Josh squeezed her fingers lightly in his hand. "Forever," he whispered.

Bethanie folded into her husband's arms. "It was their belief not to mourn the passing of this life, but I'll miss him so much. I wish I'd had the time to say how much he meant to me. It would have been nice if the children had known he was their grandfather."

Josh added, "They could have loved him no more if they'd known."

Bethanie's voice broke. "I wish I'd told him that I forgave him."

"He knew." Josh brushed her beautiful hair away from her cheek. "Cain must have told me a hundred times over the years how lucky he was to be seeing his grandchildren grow up. He was always crazy about Mariah, but he once said that young John was the most like him. Cain said John had religion in his blood." Josh smiled and kissed Bethanie's cheek lightly. "I guess Cain knew what he was talking about. Just before I left Colorado, we got a letter from John saying he wanted to go to the seminary this fall."

"But he's my baby, Josh. He's barely fourteen."

"He's old enough to know his own mind. Now don't worry, we'll go up and see him before he starts and make sure he's doing what he wants. All our children should be allowed to do what they want with their lives."

Bethanie nodded. "You're referring to Mariah. You think I'm wrong in not wanting her to go to medical school. I just can't bear the thought of her being laughed at and made fun of. She'd be one of the first women to ever go to medical school. Even when she's finished school, there will be many people who won't go to a female doctor."

"I haven't noticed people not coming to you when there's an illness. It'll be the same with Mariah."

"Maybe. I just remember what it was like to be different."

"I know, Bethanie, but you were a child and Mariah's a woman. Besides, it's her life."

"But now she's met Dusty?"

"I wouldn't bank on one week with Dusty offsetting a lifetime of stubbornness."

Bethanie smiled. "She must take after her father."

"Guess she must." Josh pulled her closer, and they walked back down toward the house.

Bethanie and Josh could hear the arguing even before they reached the porch. Mark and Luke were standing outside the house to avoid the storm within, as Mariah and Dusty's voices filtered through the cool morning air.

"What in the devil?" Josh would have entered the house, but Bethanie pulled gently on his arm. He looked to his young sons and waited for an answer.

"Sis and that cowboy are really going at it. Luke and me thought disappearing might be the best idea." Mark laughed, pushing Luke off the porch railing in fun.

"Yeah, Dusty doesn't know what he's in for if he's going to fight with Mariah." Luke climbed back on the railing and tried to knock Mark off. The two were mostly legs, feet, and appetite with too full a measure of energy blended in.

Luke suppressed a laugh when his mother raised an eyebrow in reproach, but couldn't keep from adding, "She'll have him for breakfast. He'll be a goner before the first bell."

Josh turned to Bethanie. "Shouldn't we put a stop to it?"

Bethanie shook her head as Mark piped in. "Dad, it'd take half the men on this ranch to calm Mariah down when she's as mad as I saw her."

Luke added, "Yeah, Dad, better to sacrifice one man than run the risk of us all getting hurt."

The brothers started laughing uncontrollably.

Josh shoved them off the porch. "Let's saddle some horses and all ride over to Mike and Allison's place. I need to talk to Mike about straightening out this mess with Elliot Mayson's murder."

"After what you told the marshal last night, I wouldn't think there would be any more trouble. Isn't it just a matter of finding Mayson?" Bethanie asked.

"That may not be easy. He knows this part of the country as well as any man. I told Dusty to stay out of sight today just in case he comes here."

Bethanie pulled on her hat. "I don't want to think about Mayson anymore. I just want to see Allison. Even though Wilbur was worthless, he was still her father and she buried him this morning, just as I buried mine. Let Mariah and Dusty work things out while we're gone. We should be back by dark."

Josh offered Bethanie his arm. "And give the loving couple a little quiet time?"

Mark and Luke disappeared into the barn, laughing as if their father had told a joke.

Bethanie, Josh, and their sons saddled up and were riding out of the barn when a shot rang out from inside the house.

Josh jumped from his horse and was halfway up the stairs when Ruth stepped out with a broom. "What's wrong?" he demanded as the old woman blocked his path as she swept the steps.

"Nothing." Ruth smiled calmly. "You might say the partners in this ranch are making a few adjustments."

"Is Mariah all right?"

"Mariah's the one who pulled the trigger. Neither one of those two are ever going to be happy until they're married or they kill each other."

Josh tried to pass Ruth. "I'm not standing by and allowing Mariah to get hurt."

"Josh." Bethanie's soft voice drew his full attention. "Mariah's a woman. Be it medical school or Dusty, she can take care of herself."

Luke whispered to Mark, "You ask me, someone should be protecting Dusty."

Mark laughed. "Think how mad she's gonna be when she splatters his brains all over her clothes."

"That's enough, boys." Bethanie couldn't keep from smiling. She'd seen Mariah take on all four of her brothers when angry and come out ahead. "If Mariah had meant to kill Dusty, she'd have needed only one shot."

Luke wouldn't stop. "Maybe the bullet went right through his head. He couldn't have many brains if he's thinking to tame Mariah."

Mark added, "Or maybe she only shot him in the leg when he was trying to get away without proposing. Our sister ain't any too young, you know."

Josh relaxed and climbed back on his horse. "Your mother's right, boys. That is enough. And she's right about me staying out of it. Come on, let's ride."

Mariah lifted the gun and pointed it at Dusty once more. "Are you going to listen to me now."

"You damn near blew my head off already. Give me that gun."

"If I'd wanted to hit you, you'd be bleeding right now. Put your hands in front of you."

Dusty's face was red with anger, but he tried to reason with the hellcat holding a gun only six feet from him. "All I assumed was that, now the trouble is over, you'd stay here with me."

"You assume too much," Mariah answered.

"You're as fickle as a cow with a belly full of loco

weed. You were willing to go anywhere with me last night, and today you say you're not staying."

Mariah raised the gun slightly as Dusty started to advance. "You don't listen to me, Dusty Barfield. You've never listened to me. You know nothing about women, and you don't seem to be willing to learn. But you're going to hear me out now." She moved a foot nearer. "I'm going to explain the way I feel, and you're going to listen if I have to add another hole above your ears to get the point over."

"I've had it with you." He would have left, but the gun slowed his movements. His golden eyes flickered with anger and a touch of uncertainty about how far she might go. "Trying to get along with you is harder than dancing in the eye of a dustdevil. I thought I was a sane man until you walked into my life a few days ago."

"Ruth!" Mariah yelled and was rewarded with the old woman appearing before the echo of her name died down.

"Yes." Ruth's answer was as calm as if nothing were amiss.

"Tie Dusty's hands."

Ruth lifted a cotton dish towel from the table and tied Dusty's hands as emotionlessly as if she were serving tea. Mariah expected him to protest the action, but his look puzzled her. The curve of his lip told her he thought she was playing a game, and the fire in his eyes seemed to warn her not to push him too far.

"Gag him," Mariah added, and smiled at the instant hostility exploded in his face.

As Dusty opened his mouth to protest, Ruth wrapped a napkin across his face, quieting the yell to a mumble.

Mariah pushed the gun barrel into his ribcage and pushed him toward the back door. "Ruth, we'll be in Dusty's cabin discussing a few things. If anyone asks, you haven't seen us."

Ruth nodded and turned to clear the breakfast dishes, as if kidnapping were becoming the morning activity in this house.

Mariah shoved Dusty between the trees and up the steps to his cabin. "Don't give me any trouble, or I'll put an end to this partnership right quick."

Dusty stumbled into the room that had been his refuge from the world for years. He jerked at his gag and had it almost off when Mariah, using all her strength, shoved him violently toward the bed. She tied a loose end of the dish towel to one huge trunk of the four-poster bed.

"Stand still or you'll be needing that gag to wipe up your blood."

Dusty gave up the protest and relaxed. She could see the playful anger in his gaze turning to passion and was thankful he was tied up, or she would have once again had trouble talking to him.

"If I remove the gag, will you promise to talk without yelling at me?"

Dusty nodded slowly.

Mariah pulled the gag from his mouth. "Now, you're going to stay here and talk to me or, so help me, I'll leave you tied until you starve."

"All right, Mariah, you've made your point. I'll hear you out." He twisted and sat down on the edge of the bed.

Mariah pulled up a cane chair and pointed the gun away from him for the first time. She stretched her boots out beside him and crossed her legs so that the side of her boot rested against his thigh. Mariah smiled at the reaction just her light touch had on the darkening of his eyes.

Mariah cleared her throat to sound very businesslike. "I've watched my mother work with sick and wounded people all my life. When I was no more than three, I remember wishing I could do what she did. I've learned the herbs and mixtures she learned from her mother, but I want to know more. I want, clear to my bones, to be a doctor. A few years ago, Boston opened its medical school to women and I'm going."

When Dusty didn't interrupt, Mariah continued. "I never wanted to sell the ranch to anyone but you. I would have sold it for a fraction of what it's worth if you'd offered me enough for two years of school."

"I don't need your charity," Dusty answered. "I could have offered you a fair price, but you already had another buyer."

"Stop it, Dusty. You're getting off the subject again. I looked at your books, and with the bad winter last year, you have little capital."

"I'd have enough. You're not selling your half to anyone . . . including me."

Mariah's cheeks reddened in anger. "There you go again, telling me what I can and can't do. Where is it written in Ben Weston's will that you have controlling interest?" She laid the gun on the floor and stood at eye level with him. Pushing her finger into his chest, she demanded. "Just because I'm in love with you doesn't mean I'm going to give up everything that's important to me and settle for being a ranch wife for the rest of my life."

"What did you say?" Dusty pulled at his bonds.

"I said, you thick-brained cowhand, that just because I love you doesn't mean I'm going to give up everything that's important to me."

Dusty yanked the towel away from his hands and pulled Mariah over onto the bed as she screamed in surprise. She twisted to face him and found he was smiling down at her.

"How did you . . . ?"

"Ruth never could tie a knot worth anything." Dusty

laughed. "Now, what was that you said about loving me?"

"We were talking about my selling the ranch."

"We were talking about you loving me," Dusty corrected.

Mariah tried to wriggle free of him. "That's another thing I hate about you; you always change the subject whenever it suits you."

"Mariah, did you or did you not say you loved me?"

"I've changed my mind. I would have to be insane to love someone who . . ."

Dusty stopped her words with his kiss. He spread his body over hers and kissed her with a passion that was born of anger and matured in slow understanding. He forced her lips to open to his desire. Mariah let out a soft cry as she wrapped her arms around him and pulled him closer to her. His kiss deepened as she returned his passion with her own. She moved her fingers into his hair as his hands encircled her waist.

Dusty showered her face with kisses then moved to her ear. "You love me, Mariah. Say it, again." As he whispered, his fingers slid under her blouse and touched her bare skin.

"I love you," Mariah whispered. "I do love you."

Dusty returned to her mouth with a feathery kiss that drove her mad as he brushed her breasts lightly with his fingers.

Mariah pulled at his shirt, for her need to touch him was a fire inside her. "Love me, Dusty. Please, love me."

Any control Dusty had left was lost when she pleaded. He had loved her all her life, and he couldn't stop to reason now. For the first time in his life he felt himself coming home, belonging to someone. She might yell and fight like a wildcat, but in his arms there was no mistaking her right to belong. No woman would ever feel so wonderful by his side. No woman would ever make him feel like Mariah did. Good or bad, yelling or loving, he was totally alive when she was near, and any life without her would be a walking death.

Dusty made love to Mariah with a fiery passion that molded them forever into one. He took and gave in a blending of harmony that created a melody of love for her to follow. A love that drew its roots from childhood grew into a passion that filled both their hearts with pleasure.

Mariah cried in pain and ecstasy as he entered her, for never would she be totally her own person again. A part of her would always belong to him, just as a part of him would always be hers. She loved him beyond and in spite of all that had gone between them. He was the only man who had ever broken the wall she'd built around herself for protection. He was the only man she'd ever wanted. She knew, even as he moved within her, that the need for him was building and would take a lifetime of loving to satisfy. She needed this man as she had needed no other, not just in bed, but in her life.

When their passion was spent, Mariah nestled into his arms and fell asleep. Her black hair spilled over his tanned shoulder as he pulled the covers over their nude bodies.

When she awoke, the shadows were long into afternoon and Dusty was not by her side. Mariah rolled over, feeling a sudden panic. She relaxed as she saw him kneeling by the fireplace.

Dusty turned to smile as he heard her sigh. "I thought I'd better build a fire to take the chill off the evening."

"I'm not cold." Mariah felt her body warm at just the sight of him standing before her with only his pants on. His chest was a network of strong muscles and light brown hair.

He moved the few steps to the bed as she pulled the covers just over her breasts. He leaned to kiss her lightly on the head. "Are you hungry? I could go up to the house and find something to eat."

Mariah ran her finger down the middle of his chest and circled the scar just above his waist. "You were hurt there during the Indian attack when I was two." Mariah stretched and touched his hair just above his ear. "I remember a bandage across your head also."

"You were too young to remember." Dusty laughed.

"No, I remember." Mariah's fingers brushed lightly just above his pants' waistband.

Mariah's fingers were warm, and Dusty felt suddenly out of breath. He tried to keep his breathing normal as he whispered, "I remember you slept at the foot of my bed, afraid to leave."

"If you were hurt again, I might do so once more." Dusty tugged at the blanket to reveal more of Mariah's creamy white breasts to his hungry eyes. "It would be worth being so near death, if I were sure to find you in my bed when I awoke."

Mariah laughed and slid under the covers. Dusty dove into the bundle of quilts and pulled her face free. "I love you, Mariah Weston. I love you more than I've ever loved anything or anyone in my life." He pushed her hair away from her face. "If I thought I could hold you by tying you to this bed, I'd give it a try."

Mariah pulled the covers down until her breasts were touching his bare chest. She moved her hands along his sides in a slow, arousing play.

Dusty stopped her action. "Tell me you love me, Mariah. I want to hear the words once more."

"I love you. Dear God, how I love you . . . but I haven't changed my mind about going to medical school." Mariah had to be honest even at the risk of spoiling the moment.

Dusty laughed, but there was little joy in his laughter. "I thought about it for an hour while I watched you sleep.

I know the only way I have a chance at ever holding you is to let you go." He kissed her tenderly on the mouth, and when she would have spoken, he silenced her with another kiss.

He stood and pulled his shirt on. "I'll go get something to eat and a pot of hot coffee. We've got a lot of talking to do before the others get back."

Mariah watched him leave in silence. She slowly climbed from the bed and pulled on her discarded clothes, not bothering to button her blouse. Without Dusty in the room, she grew suddenly cold. She pulled one of the blankets from the bed and curled up in the soft chair by the fireplace. Books lined two of the walls behind her in warm colors of browns. Everything around her smelled of Dusty and his life. She felt cocooned in his world and closed her eyes to simply enjoy the sensations for a moment.

Chapter Thirty

Dusty brought a tray of cold chicken and hot coffee back within what seemed like only minutes to Mariah. He spread the feast before her on the hearth and pulled another chair by the fire. The tiny room filled with the aroma of strong coffee. The crackling fire made Mariah feel like the rest of the world had vanished and only this one place in time and space remained.

"Anyone back yet from Mike and Allison's?" Mariah asked between bites of chicken.

"No. I heard a horse in the barn. Probably a cowhand coming in early. I didn't even stop to look, I was so anxious to get back to you." Dusty set his coffee cup down and stared at her as if memorizing every line of her face.

"What is it, Dusty?" Mariah felt nervous under such scrutiny.

"Do you have any idea how beautiful you are sitting there with the quilt tucked around you and your blouse open?" He leaned forward and pulled the quilt over her shoulder. "Now that we're talking, I've wanted to tell you for days that I love the way your hair curls around this shoulder and the funny way you look at me. There's a touch of the devil in every twinkle of your eyes." Dusty lightly brushed his fingertips along her arm. "Today I learned that sparks can also ignite passion."

Mariah looked away into the firelight. Her cheeks reddened from his compliments and the fire's warmth. He was right. She had spent the whole week here either fighting or loving him. Now it was time to understand him. "Tell me about all these books."

Dusty relaxed back in his chair enjoying the calmness of the moment. "Bethanie thought I should have schooling, so she hitched me up with a tutor back East. As the years went by, I enjoyed reading more and more. The tutor died, but his son continues to send all the best books. A few years ago when the open ranges started to be fenced in, I decided to study law. Before that, I enjoyed learning French. I used to go up to the settlement by Fort Worth and practice. I made some good friends among those people."

Dusty touched a row of books lightly. "Anyway, it's been first one thing then another, but law is fun because about the time you think you've got it down, it changes. I've never had a class, but I've read everything I can get my hands on."

Mariah was fascinated at this side of Dusty, though not surprised. "That's why Mike said he wants you in Austin with him."

Dusty nodded. "Mike helped get John Ireland elected governor in '83. The old guy has fought the building of railroads so long everyone calls him 'Oxcart John.' He took a liking to me, and Mike thinks I can influence him."

"To do what?" Mariah understood little about politics. Dusty chuckled. "Mostly to endorse Lawrence Ross to take his place."

"Ross?" Mariah interrupted. "Wasn't he in charge of the Rangers before the war? I think I've heard Uncle Josh talk about him.

"He's the same man."

"Would he make a good governor?"

"The best," Dusty stated without hesitation. "But if I

went to Austin, I'd be gone from the ranch quite a bit this next year."

"And you could never leave the ranch," Mariah finished.

"No, it's not that." Dusty stood and began pacing. "This ranch is like family to me. I never had anything of my own from the time I was six, except a watch my brother gave me before he died. That's why I could never let you sell part of it. It would be like selling off a sister or a brother."

"But do you want to stay here?"

Dusty raised his hands to one of the low ceiling beams. "Part of me wants to fight in Austin, but part of me will always be here." He turned his back to her and leaned his head against the mantel.

Mariah had seen this man fighting mad and so angry he couldn't speak, but never had she seen him in such agony. The muscles tightened across his back, stretching his cotton shirt tight in protest. His hands balled into fists as his face turned upward.

"Dusty?" Mariah whispered, not understanding his sudden mood change.

His words came to her in little more than a whisper, half a plea, half a command. "Don't leave me, Mariah. Don't go. It could be so perfect here with you."

"Do you know what you're asking of me?"

"I know . . . I know." Dusty straightened and pulled himself under tight control. "You'd hate yourself, and me, too, if you stayed, but I had to ask. I don't want to think of this ranch without you."

Part of Mariah wanted to reach up and hold this man until all the pain he felt vanished, while another part of her wanted to run as far as she could from him. She had always thought love would make everything simple and plain, not more confusing. "Dusty." Tears formed in her eyes. "We have to find an answer. I love you too much for there not to be a way."

Dusty stood behind her chair, his hands barely touching her shoulders. "Mike is pretty determined that I go to Austin this fall with him. There's a great deal of work to be done at the capital if ranchers are to get a fair shake. I've got enough work there to keep me busy for a year, maybe two."

Mariah brushed his hand with her fingertips. "Dustin Barfield, are you saying you'd wait two years for me."

"No." Dusty frowned. "I'm thinking we could get married now and spend what time we could together these next two years. I could come up to Boston when the House was not in session, and you could come to Austin in the summers."

Mariah liked the idea. "What about Christmas?"

"We'd spend Christmas here at the ranch."

Mariah tried to be practical. "There would be long train rides, and we'd have to sell off most of the cattle to afford my school and a house in Austin, and what if I got pregnant?"

"I wouldn't mind the train rides. Most of the cattle died last winter anyway, and Mike can buy the rest for a fair price . . . and what if you *are* pregnant?"

"Then I'd have the baby, strap it to my back, and go to medical school." Mariah laughed.

Dusty pulled her up and into his arms. "You would, too." He kissed her soundly. "Now, will you marry me, plan or no plan, or do I keep you locked in this cabin for life?"

"You're forgetting, I'm the one who kidnapped you."

Dusty lifted her off the floor to eye level with him. "Answer my question."

"I'll think it over." Mariah loved teasing him.

Dusty growled at her and swung her around the small room.

Neither heard the footsteps on the porch until an instant before the door flew open.

Chapter Thirty-one

Dusty's head jerked up as footsteps sounded on the porch. An instant later, the cabin door flew open. Dusty jumped for his gunbelt as a man in black bolted into the room. The blast of a round from the stranger's rifle froze Dusty's progress. He dropped to the floor with an oath of pain.

Mariah was at his side before the intruder could advance into the room. She watched in horror as blood dripped from a hole in Dusty's shoulder.

Dusty raised slowly to his knees and pushed her behind him, his gaze never leaving the man standing before them with his gun smoking.

"Mayson." Dusty whispered the intruder's name between clenched teeth like an oath. There was no pain in Dusty's eyes, only a hatred accumulated over twenty years.

"Well, well, what have we here, a little love nest?" Mayson's smile covered the width of his face, and his thin black mustache spread above his mouth like a charcoal-drawn upper border.

Dusty stood, drawing Mayson's full attention. Mayson yelled. "Make another move and I'll hit closer to your heart."

Dusty faced Mayson fearlessly. "What do you want?

You know I didn't kill your son, so don't think you can get away with murdering me."

Mayson seemed in no hurry to answer. He moved toward the fireplace as if he'd been asked to warm himself. "I've been out in the cold all day waiting for you to show yourself. I thought you were gone until I saw you walking back behind the main house a few minutes ago." He glared at Mariah. "I had no idea you were out here with your whore-partner."

Mariah opened her mouth to give Mayson a few choice words, but Dusty beat her to it.

"You just slither in to insult us, Mayson? If so, put down that gun and say the same thing."

Mayson laughed a high-pitched whiny cry that bore no hint of humor. "I'm not so young and foolish to battle with a man when age is not in my favor." He glanced at Mariah. "Or so dumb as my son to think I can sweet-talk a woman out of half a ranch. Though, if I'd know bedding was all she wanted, I might have come myself instead of sending a boy."

Mariah's fingers balled in anger, but Dusty stepped in front of her once more. "Leave her out of this, Mayson. This fight is between you and me."

"Wrong, kid. This fight's between me and the Weston Ranch. It's been going on for over twenty years, and I aim to end it tonight."

Mariah could see the light of insanity flickering in Mayson's eyes. She could think of no time in her life that she'd been scared speechless . . . before this moment. Mayson had nothing to lose. His son was dead, and the marshal would have a warrant out for his arrest by dawn.

"I thought I could have a pup like you killed." Mayson moved closer, blocking the path between Dusty and his gunbelt hanging on the far wall. "But, seems I'll have to do the job myself."

"You'll never get away with cold-blooded murder." Dusty's gaze was slowly darting around, looking for the gun that Mariah had carried into the cabin.

"I didn't get where I am in my life by not seizing every opportunity that came along. Everybody in town saw how hot-tempered your little filly is. I figure I can pump a few more bullets into that chest of yours, then put the gun to her head. It'll look like you two had a lover's quarrel and she shot you, then herself."

Mayson laughed. "This time I'll make sure all the Weston owners are dead, not like that fool Indian attack. I paid good money to have everyone killed, and then I hear you lived after five slugs were dug out of you. Well, don't plan on being that lucky this time."

"You *were* involved in those Indian raids." Dusty's voice held no hint of surprise. "Ben thought so, but Mike and I couldn't prove a thing at the time."

"And you never will," Mayson laughed. "You'll go to your grave with the knowledge that the next owner of the Weston Ranch will be me."

While Mayson laughed, Dusty cut his eyes from Mariah to the corner of the bed. She followed his gaze to see the butt of her gun on the floor. It was half covered by falling quilts, but the gun was within three steps of her.

Dusty moved away from Mariah toward the fireplace, and Mayson followed his slow path with his gun barrel. "Smith will never take all the blame for killing your son."

"Smith's dead." Mayson seemed proud of himself. "Fact of the matter is everyone who heard Smith's confession in that shack up on the north ridge is dead, except Bethanie Weston; and I've got a man who can slit her throat while she sleeps without even waking up her husband. 'Course if he does wake up, all the better."

Dusty leaned against the fireplace and cradled his

wounded shoulder. "Tell me one more thing, Mayson. Call it one last request before you shoot me. I knew it was your men killing off the cattle, but why? Why the Indian raids years ago, and why now, after all this time, the need to destroy Weston Ranch?"

"You don't understand, but I guess you got a right to see the whole picture before you die." Mayson leaned against the back of a chair, not noticing as Mariah took a step away from Dusty toward the bed.

Mayson's hard black eyes seemed to look far back in time. "A few years before the war my brothers and I came to Texas hoping to make some fast money. A day after we hit Fort Worth, we decided to save time and hold up the bank. The place wasn't much more than a general store with a safe in the back. We had the money and were in the alley when a cry rang out from the teller. I made it to my horse, but some kid walked into the bank and gunned down both my brothers before they could fire a shot . . . That boy was Ben Weston."

Mayson continued as Mariah moved another step closer to the foot of the bed. "I made it down the street, but knew my old nag could never outrun Ben's horse, and the gunshots were drawing people out of every store. I ducked into the shadows and waited for Ben to come." Mayson smiled in self-satisfaction. "I meant to shoot him, but I shot the horse. He went flying and landed on his back with the mount coming down hard on top of him. Everyone was so worried about Ben living, they forgot about hunting me. Ben never could point me out as the third robber, but I always felt like he knew. When I lucked into the Pair of Spades Ranch, the only cloud was the Weston Ranch being so close. Every time I had a good deal going Ben managed to spoil it."

Mayson was silent for a moment, and when he spoke his voice was blended with madness. "First my brothers, and now my son. I figure the Westons are going to pay once and for all."

Mariah could see the last thread of rational thinking breaking in Mayson's eyes. "You just got in the way, Barfield. I wanted to force you to sell the ranch so Mariah would come to Texas. I knew she would have to be killed. Would have done it years ago if that giant of a shadow, Cain, wasn't always at her side."

Mayson's hand shook slightly as he raised the barrel to Dusty's chest. "So long, Barfield." Mayson laughed.

In the fraction of a second it took Mayson to pull the hammer back on his rifle, Dusty and Mariah sprang into action. Dusty kicked the tray by the fire sending coffee and food flying across the room. Mariah dived for the gun on the floor. Mayson's shot sounded like thunder rumbling around the room as his bullet went wild.

Mariah lifted the gun and pointed it at Mayson as the man looked from her to Dusty, trying to decide which to shoot first. Suddenly he pointed his rifle at Dusty's gut. "Shoot me, girl, and I'll still have time to pull this trigger. You'll get to watch your lover die slowly of a gut wound."

Mariah lowered the gun. With all the fight in her, she could not bring herself to gamble with Dusty's life.

"That's a good girl." Mayson laughed. "Tell you what, I'll give you a choice." He backed to the cabin window. "Who do I shoot first, you or Barfield?"

Mariah looked up, not at Mayson, but at the man she loved. She knew she would rather die first than watch him die. He stood so strong and defiant against Mayson, yet she caught a glimpse of fear touch his golden eyes. Fear, not for himself, but for her. She knew that if he had to watch her death, it would be more painful than a bullet exploding in his own heart. She would silently prove her love by sparing him this last pain.

Mayson raised the gun to his cheek and took aim. "Choose, girl!" he yelled.

Mariah reached to grasp Dusty's outstretched hand. There were so many things she wanted to say, but all she could think of was how much she wanted to hold him before she died. As their fingers touched, a shot rang out and glass exploded into the cabin. The shot echoed around the room. Dusty pulled Mariah from the floor and into his arms.

The single shot kept resounding, but Mariah felt no pain and Dusty's arm never weakened around her. She heard a moan and turned to see Mayson's body hit the floor. Shattered pieces of glass from the window covered him like crystal snowflakes, and for a moment all the world seemed frozen except for the pounding of Dusty's heart near her ear.

Ruth's willowy frame appeared in the open doorway. The huge Walker-Colt was still smoking at her side. "I saw him sneaking behind the house. I knew it wouldn't take him long to find the cabin. Are you two all right?"

Dusty let out a long-held breath. "Never better, thanks to you and that old gun."

Mariah crossed the floor and hugged Ruth soundly. The old woman didn't return the hug fully, but Mariah could feel her still shaking. Mariah patted Ruth in a calming gesture. "Mother told me you were afraid of guns."

Ruth stood a little taller. "I don't like them much, but when I saw Mayson take aim, I had to shoot." She seemed self-conscious. "Better get Dusty into the house and practice some of that doctoring."

Mariah cuddled under Dusty's unharmed arm and guided him toward the house. As they reached the back door they were greeted by Bethanie, Josh, and the boys. Everyone started asking questions all at once. She felt like it was Christmas, the Fourth of July, and her birthday ll rolled into one moment. She knew Dusty felt the same, for even with her brothers watching he bent and kissed her.

As the stars filled the midnight sky, Bethanie watched her daughter and Dusty from her vantage point on the porch swing. She'd been watching as their silhouettes turned at the ranch gate and moved back toward the house. As they reached the porch steps, Josh emerged from inside.

Josh lowered himself beside Bethanie but spoke to Mariah. "We've been thinking, Mariah. If you still want to go to that school in Boston, we'll finance the two years."

"Wonderful," Mariah answered.

"No, thanks," Dusty interrupted. Not even the evening shadows could hide the fiery look Mariah shot him, but she didn't pull away from his arm.

Josh stopped the slow swing of the bench. "Now wait just a minute, Dusty . . ."

"Josh and Bethanie, I think I should say something right now. I don't think it's right for parents to pay for a wife's education."

Josh laughed as Bethanie silently hugged first her future son-in-law, then her daughter. "Well, this is good news," Josh announced. "But I can't say it's much of a surprise, the way you two have been acting all evening."

"Mariah will go to medical school, and I plan on spending some time in Austin. I figure I can restart the herd in two years."

Mariah added. "After being around Dusty a week, I think I might really need that medical degree."

Josh touched Dusty on his uninjured shoulder. "I'll make a deal with you. You talk Mariah into a small wed-

ing, and I'll start that herd of yours with a hundred o:
my best cows in two years."

"Sounds like a fair deal." Dusty nodded.

Josh grinned. "There's a hitch. You have to take Mark
and Luke under your wing for the next three summers
Colorado mining is too tame for their blood. They need
this open land."

Mariah shook her head. "That would be worth two
hundred head at least."

Josh laughed. "Agreed."

Mariah and Dusty moved into the house to say a private good night, and Josh joined Bethanie once more or
the porch swing. "You haven't said a word, my quie
wife."

"I was thinking about how my mother always said, to
everything there is a season. Mariah and Dusty's life wil
not be easy, being separated the next few years."

Josh pulled her under his arm. "Maybe it will help
them to appreciate the time they have together."

They rocked silently and watched the fireflies in the
distance. Josh's arm kept away the evening chill as
Bethanie thought of all the memories this ranch brough
back to her. Some good, some bad. But the bad were
no longer painful, and the good still held a warmth ir
her heart.

She turned and whispered into Josh's ear. "I love you."

"For forever," Josh answered.